WOMEN'S HUMOR IN THE AGE OF GENTILITY

Women's Humor
in the
Age of Gentility

The Life and Works of Frances Miriam Whitcher

Linda A. Morris

SYRACUSE UNIVERSITY PRESS

Copyright © 1992 by Syracuse University Press
Syracuse, New York 13244-5160

All Rights Reserved

First Edition 1992
92 93 94 95 96 97 98 99   6 5 4 3 2 1

This book is published with the assistance of a grant from the John Ben Snow
Foundation.

The paper used in this publication meets the minimum requirements of American
National Standard for Information Sciences—Permanence of Paper for Printed Library Materials, ANSI Z39.48–1984. ∞™

Library of Congress Cataloging-in-Publication Data
Morris, Linda.
    Women's humor in the age of gentility : the life and works of
Frances Miriam Whitcher / Linda A. Morris.
        p.   cm. — (New York State studies)
    Includes bibliographical references (p.   ) and index.
    ISBN 0-8156-2562-6
    1. Whitcher, Frances M., 1812–1852.   2. Women and literature—
United States—History—19th century.   3. Humorists, American—19th
century—Biography.   4. New York (State) in literature.   I. Title.
II. Series: New York State study.
PS3174.W45Z78   1992
813'.3—dc20
[B]   91-40053

Manufactured in the United States of America

This book is dedicated to my daughters,

ELIZABETH MORRIS MILLER

KATHERINE FINTON MORRIS

LINDA A. MORRIS is Senior Lecturer, SOE—English, and Director, Women's Resources and Research Center at the University of California, Davis. She is the author of *Women Vernacular Humorists in Nineteenth-Century America: Ann Stephens, Frances Whitcher, and Marietta Holley;* and coauthor, with Karl Zender, of *Persuasive Writing: A College Reader;* and, with Hans Ostrom and Linda Young, of *The Living Language: A Reader.*

Contents

❧

Illustrations

❧

Preface

y interest in American literary
humor began when I was a student of Henry Nash Smith, who
encouraged me to explore the holdings of the Koundakjian Collection of American Humor in the Bancroft Library. There I discovered,
much to my surprise and delight, a host of intelligent, appealing
women humorists who had at that time (mid-1970s) received almost
no critical attention. I wrote my dissertation on three of these writers,
Ann Stephens, Frances M. Whitcher, and Marietta Holley, under the
direction of Richard Bridgman and with the support of a Bancroft
Library Fellowship. A faculty research grant from the University of
California, Davis, later allowed me to conduct research in libraries
and archives in New York State, where I read for the first time the
letters of Miriam Whitcher. These remarkable personal, historical docu-
ments establish a clear, yet subtle, relationship between events in
Whitcher's life in Whitesboro and Elmira and the humorous sketches
she was publishing anonymously in Neal's *Saturday
Gazette* and *Godey's Lady's Book,* and inspired me to write this
biography.

I am indebted to many people for their interest in this project
and for their encouragement, including my parents, Gertrude and
Marvin Finton, and my daughters, Beth and Kate, to whom this
book is dedicated. Others, especially Catherine Gallagher and Virginia Palmer, offered encouragement from the beginning and
throughout the evolution of the project, and I wish to thank them
for their inestimable support. The finished manuscript has benefited
greatly by thorough and constructive readings of earlier versions by
Michael Hoffman, Howard Finton, Sandra Meyers, and Karen
Halttunen, and I gratefully acknowledge their contributions to this

work. I also thank Kate Winter, who encouraged me to publish this study, and Mary Bly, who shares my love of women's humor.

I also wish to acknowledge the capable research assistance of Patricia Tollefson, Sarah-Hope Parmeter, and Chris Janus. Finally, my appreciation to John Merchant of St. John's Episcopal Church in Whitesboro, and the staff of the Dunham Public Library, the Oneida County Historical Society, and the New-York Historical Society, and to Jenny Lawrence, who transcribed the Whitcher letters and gave me a copy of her typed transcriptions.

WOMEN'S HUMOR IN THE AGE OF GENTILITY

A Woman's Humor

The story of Frances Miriam Berry Whitcher is the story of a woman who became one of the most popular humorists in nineteenth-century America, yet whose identity as a humorist was known to few during her lifetime. Cloaked in anonymity, Miriam Whitcher wrote literary burlesques, parodic dramatic monologues, and ultimately brilliant social satires in the late 1840s. Taking as her setting villages that strongly resembled Whitesboro and Elmira, New York, Whitcher explored in her humor the society of women—exploding on the one hand the myth that women were somehow morally superior to men and satirizing on the other hand a society that encouraged women to vie with one another for social status and power.[1] Miriam Whitcher's life was not a long one—she died at thirty-nine—and her literary productivity was not extensive, especially by nineteenth-century standards, yet her fame and popularity as a humorist lasted almost to the end of the century. Her major works, when published posthumously in 1855 as *The Widow Bedott Papers,* enjoyed sales of over 100,000 copies by the 1880s. Her title character was eventually featured on the New York stage, with the part of the Widow Bedott played by female impersonator Neil Burgess.

Whitcher is most important to us now because of her early role in the emergence of a distinctive women's humor tradition in America, and because of the artfulness of her humor. By studying her life and the particular circumstances that gave rise to her humor, we can also understand the relationship between one woman's creative process, her social situation, and the economic and social changes taking place in communities across the Northeast in the mid-nineteenth century. In short, her life illuminates her work to a remarkable degree, while her work itself changed dramatically the course of her life. But her life is also interesting apart from the insights it gives us about her work. Growing up in the 1820s and 1830s in an era one historian has described as "tumultuous," Miriam Berry lived for thirty-five years in a popular inn run by her family in Whitesboro, Oneida County, New York.[2] All the major social reform movements of the day found their way to Whitesboro—Charles Finney's revival movement, early abolition foment, the advent of female reform societies—and all flourished on Miriam's doorstep. Many found their way, too, into her humor; meetings of church sewing societies, ladies' missionary societies, phrenology societies, and literary societies were all fair game in her humorous sketches.

The American Vernacular Humor Tradition

Miriam Whitcher's work belongs to the school of humor known as vernacular or dialect humor. Emerging in the 1830s in both the Northeast and old Southwest, vernacular humor is widely regarded as the first humor that was distinctively American in language, spirit, and subject.[3] This humor tended to feature a character who was relatively uneducated, who spoke in a distinct dialect or regional "earthy" idiom, and whose values were on the fringe of the dominant culture's.[4] The comic hero was sometimes a young onion farmer from Connecticut (Ann Stephens's Jonathan Slick), a con man from Alabama (J. J. Hooper's Simon Suggs), or an untutored schoolgirl from upstate New York, (Whitcher's first heroine, Permilly Ruggles). The authors were invariably better educated than their comic creations, who represented a different class altogether. Yet in some instances, the comic hero achieved a near-heroic stature and can clearly be understood to represent the author's own values. Mark Twain's Huckleberry Finn is without question the quintessential vernacular hero in this regard. More modestly, the vernacular hero or heroine could be seen as a horse-sense, or crackerbox, philosopher who might not be formally educated and might not speak standard English, but who could point out the follies of those who did.[5] Miriam Whitcher's Aunt Maguire, the primary persona in her satiric writing, was just such a heroine:

In Slabtown, every body knows jest what every body else says and does. It seemed raly wonderful to me how all that was said was trumpeted round. Private conversations was blazed all over town, that must a ben carried by the birds o' the air, or else ther must a ben a good many ears occurpied at a good many key-holes. I was wonderfully struck with this faculty in the Slabtown folks. They're a community remarkable for their *inquirin' minds.* If 't was applied to any useful purpose, ther's no calculatin' how much they might accomplish.[6]

At other times the vernacular hero was more fool than wise man. In these instances, he tended to be the butt of much of the humor. The most famous such character came from the humor of the old Southwest in the form of George W. Harris's Sut Lovingood, a self-proclaimed fool. As Sut explains in his extreme vernacular speech, his whole point ("pint") in life is to supersede his father as king of the fools:

George, every livin thing hes hits pint, a pint ove sum sort. Ole Bullen's pint is a durn'ed fust rate, three bladed, dubbil barril'd, warter-proof, hypockracy, an' a never-tirein appertite fur bal'-face [whiskey]. Sicily Burns's pint am tu drive men folks plum crazy, an' then bring em too agin. Gin em a rale Orleans fever in five minits, an' then in five minits more, gin them a Floridy ager. Durn her, she's down on her heels flat-footed now. Dad's pint is to be king ove all durn'd fools, ever since the day ove that feller what cribb'd up so much co'n down in Yegipt, long time ago, (he run outen his coat yu minds). The Bibil tells us hu [who] wer the stronges' man— hu wer the bes' man—hu wer the meekis' man, an' hu the wises' man, but leaves yu tu guess hu wer the bigges' fool. . . . I used tu think my pint an' dad's wer jis' the same, sulky, unmix'd king durn'd fool; but when he acted hoss, an' mistook hossflies fur ho'nets, I los' heart. Never mine, when I gits his 'sperence, I may be king fool, but yet great golly, he gets frum bad tu wus, monstrus fas'.[7]

Whitcher's Widow Bedott, the most popular and best known of her comic characters, was also clearly intended to be seen as a foolish comic heroine. Speaking in a relatively pure upstate New York vernacular language, generously sprinkled with malapropisms and comic mispronunciations, the Widow attempted to cultivate a public image of herself that she then unconsciously undercut. Between her comically absurd misuse of the language, her self-serving motivation, and her inflated ego, the Widow Bedott was an archetypal comic fool. For example, when the Widow hears that the recently widowed Elder Sniffles (whom she barely knows), has the flu, she tries to insinuate herself into his life:

> But I was a tellin' how overcome I was when I heerd o' your bein' attackted with influenzy. I felt as if I must go right over and take care of you. I wouldent desire no better intertainment than to nuss [nurse] you up, and if 't wa'n't for the speech o' peeple, I'd fly to your relefe instanter; but I know 't would make talk, and so I feel necessiated to stay away. But I felt so consarned about you, that I couldent help writin' these few lines to let you know how anxious I be on your account, and to beg o' you to take care o' yerself. O elder, do be careful—the influenzy's a dangerous epedemic if you let it run on without attendin' to it in season. Do be kerful—consider what a terrible thing 't would be for you to be took away in the haight of yer usefulness; and O, elder, nobody wouldent feel yer loss with more intensitude than what I should, though mebby I hadent ought to say so. (pp. 135–36).

Finally, some vernacular heroes and heroines were created by their authors primarily for burlesque purposes. Hooper's *Simon Suggs* was written to burlesque presidential campaign biographies, especially Andrew Jackson's. Hooper relied on both the form of the Suggs's tales and the character of Suggs himself to achieve his ends. With the essential character of Simon Suggs encapsulated in mottoes such as "Someone must pay," and "It's good to be shifty in a new country," Hooper comically indicted Andrew Jackson and his followers. The comic character created by Miriam Whitcher in the earliest of her comic writings burlesqued sentimental fiction. Whitcher's heroine, Permilly Ruggles, attempts to model her every act on the heroine of Regina Maria Roche's *Children of the Abbey*.[8] Relentlessly, Permilly is shown up as a fool for her attempts to imitate the actions of an English lady, and to speak in the elevated, artificial diction of English romances. Her efforts are made all the more comic by the inadequacy of her "natural" language and her vernacular perspective:

So I went into my chomber and was a wonderin' what Amandy
would a did in sich a dilamby—when all of a sudding I happened to
think how't when she had so much trouble with Lord Mortimer's
father she went off to Scotland and kept school, and thinks me, I'll
keep school tew. So I went into the kitching and sot down betooxt
uncle and aunt, and I says to 'em, says I, "Dear frinds—reduced as I
be to the dretful alternatyve of doing suthing for a livin' or beein'
shot up in a horrid dunjin, I've concluded what occerpation I'd
folly. "[9]

As the Whitcher material quoted above indicates, Whitcher's
three vernacular personae—Permilly Ruggles, the Widow Bedott,
and Aunt Maguire—represent a broad range of the comic possibilities inherent in the American vernacular prose tradition.
Whether viewed as a consummate artist in the native American humor tradition, or understood in the context of a tradition of
women's humor that began in the mid-1800s and carries forth into
our own times in humor as diverse as Lily Tomlin's and Erma
Bombeck's, Miriam Whitcher is a figure of special historical
significance.

By comparing her briefly to other humorists of her era, we can
begin to appreciate not only that she was one of the earliest vernacular prose humorists but also that she was highly innovative in her
contributions to the tradition as a whole. Only two northeastern
prose humorists preceded Whitcher—Seba Smith and Thomas
Haliburton—and only one of them, Seba Smith, created vernacular
humor per se.[10] Smith's popular fictional creation was a young Maine
farm lad named Jack Downing. Jack went to Portland to sell axe
handles, visited the state legislature when business was slow, and
wrote naïve letters describing all he saw to the folks back home in
Downingville. Before long, he made his way to Washington, D.C.,
where he became an unofficial advisor to President Jackson. Over
time, Jack grew somewhat less naïve and more calculating in his
personal ambitions, but he never lost his appeal to a wide readership
who enjoyed his political commentary.

The affinity between Smith and Whitcher resided primarily in
their pioneering development of first-person narrators. Many humorists of the nineteenth century wrote from a third-person point of
view, but first-person vernacular humor ultimately had the greatest

long-term appeal to generations of readers; it tended to be the best developed and most dramatic of all nineteenth-century forms of humor. No standard narrator stood between the reader and the vernacular character; no one else was present to interpret the action, or even to comment on it; instead, vernacular characters spoke in their own voices, they represented their own points of view, and they spoke directly to the reader. Their foolishness, their eccentricities, and their common sense all grew out of their characterizations.

The writer most often compared to Whitcher is Benjamin P. Shillaber, whose Mrs. Partington also remained in the public eye from the 1840s to the 1880s. Mrs. Partington was a widow renowned for her malapropisms and her inadvertently witty sayings. While the Widow Bedott and Widow Partington bear a superficial resemblance to each other, the differences between them are broad and significant. For one, Mrs. Partington speaks only within a conventional narrative frame that is dominated by a third-person male narrator. Although the narrator is clearly fond of Mrs. Partington, part of what he finds quaint and humorous about her appears to be inherent in her female condition; unlike the Widow Bedott, Mrs. Partington is funny not because of the choices she has made but because of her fundamental nature.

The first-person vernacular characters Miriam Whitcher created were thus among the first such characters in American literature, and she created not just one but three distinct personalities who carried the force of her humor. Of even greater significance for the purposes of this study, and for the place Whitcher occupies in literary history, is the fact that all three of her primary creations were women. Not until 1873 did another humorist, Marietta Holley, create a vernacular female protagonist who like Whitcher's Aunt Maguire was a strong, positive role model, a voice of reason and common sense.[11] For more than fifty years, Miriam Whitcher stood alone among women as the creator of vernacular humor that mocked not women, per se, but the way women behaved; not women as a sex apart, but women as morally responsible people who sometimes made poor (even comic) choices. Even when women were the targets of her biting satiric thrusts, always inherent in the humor was the possibility that they could change. When male writers created comic female personae, there seemed to be no such possibility.[12] Thus this study addresses Whitcher's pioneering role within a separate and parallel tradition of women's humor in America. This tradition, strong and unbroken to the present day, has not been especially well understood or appreciated. To understand Whitcher's place in a tradition of women's humor it is important to explore first the distinguishing features of women's humor in general and the relatively few but significant forays modern scholars have made into investigating the history of that humor.

Women's Humor Tradition in America

The greatest periods of activity in American humor have always occurred during times of social, political, and economic instability, so it was no coincidence that the native American humor tradition and the advent of a distinctive women's humor emerged in the 1830s. The presidency of Andrew Jackson ushered in what is sometimes called the "Age of the Common Man," a time when white men of all classes of society faced new social, political, economic, and geographic challenges. As opportunities opened for men, women's roles were often diminished. Once central to the family economy—as farmers, producers of essential commodities for the family, workers in home industry—by mid century many native-born women from both towns and cities no longer contributed directly to their family's economy.[13] Increasingly, they found themselves relegated to the private or domestic sphere, and cut off from the public world of their husbands, fathers, and brothers. In this era the "Cult of True Womanhood" emerged, with women granted only indirect power in the family through their influence over men. Women began to be regarded as the morally superior sex, which gave them in turn more responsibility for raising and educating their children, and for creating in their homes havens for their men when they returned from the dangerous world of commerce. Women became more active consumers, with their homes and their bodies becoming the showpieces for their families' financial success. Earlier values associated with domesticity came into direct conflict with the values of the rising middle class as women became increasingly idle and peripheral. Ironically, middle-class women especially faced a world of shrinking opportunities at the very time when political and economic doors opened wider for white males of all classes.

Women's most radical response to the social upheavals of the 1830s and 1840s was the birth of the woman's rights movement in upstate New York. The Seneca Falls convention of 1848, which concluded with the signing of the Declaration of Sentiments and Resolutions written by Elizabeth Cady Stanton and Lucretia Mott, marked the movement's symbolic beginning.[14] More than seventy years would pass before the women's rights movement would achieve its most modest goal—universal female suffrage. Whitcher's humor, which also responded to the rapid social changes of the era, was theoretically much less radical than the woman's rights movement, yet it generated reactions that were nearly as strong as those faced by the original signers of the declaration.[15] Like the feminists, Whitcher critiqued women's diminished role in society, especially the way women demeaned themselves and one another. But unlike the feminists, who offered political solutions to society's inequities, Whitcher exposed the hypocrisy that accompanied widespread scrambling for social status. Moreover, her humor eloquently reveals that the social and economic changes that characterized mid-Victorian urban society reached down to the very heart of village life: the Widow Bedott's kitchen table and Aunt Maguire's church sewing circle.

To say that a distinctive women's tradition of humor emerged in nineteenth-century America is not to say that all women humorists self-consciously viewed themselves as women writers, nor that they were necessarily aware that a women's tradition was in the making. This was especially true for the earliest humorists such as Caroline Kirkland, Ann Stephens, and Miriam Whitcher, yet each of these writers adopted a perspective unique to women's humor, and each pursued gender-based issues.[16] In a relatively short time, however, the humorist Kate Sanborn heralded the existence of a distinctive tradition of women's humor with the publication of an anthology of American women's humor entitled *The Wit of Women*.[17] She wrote the book in response to a challenge by Alice Rollins in *The Critic* for someone to demonstrate that "wit in women" was *not* a rare commodity.[18] As Kate Sanborn declared in her introduction, over the course of a summer she marshaled the strength of one hundred women to answer the challenge; her only problem as an editor, she said, was deciding which humorists to exclude. Given her initial emphasis on wit, Sanborn did not draw all her examples from literature, and while some of the writers she included, such as Louisa May Alcott and Harriet Beecher Stowe, are not now known primarily for their humor, many of the writers represented in her anthology were first and foremost humorists. The book was well received by the reading public and demonstrated admirably a wide range of wit and humor by women.

Many of the nineteenth-century writers Sanborn included in her collection figured centrally in a second anthology of American women's humor published fifty years later under the editorship of Martha Bruère and the noted historian Mary Beard.[19] *Laughing Their Way* acknowledged, as had *The Wit of Women,* that women's humor had been largely (and inappropriately) ignored in traditional treatments of the nation's literary humor, and Bruère and Beard took up the pleasant task of reintroducing the nation to its "diverse humors."[20] While they noted in passing that old myths die hard, they chose in the end not to answer the question they themselves had posed—why had women's humor failed to receive the attention it deserved?

Fifty more years passed between the publication of *Laughing Their Way* and the next historically based anthology of American women's humor—*Redressing the Balance,* edited by Nancy Walker and Zita Dresner.[21] Over fifty writers are represented, eleven of them from the nineteenth century, with the vast majority from the twentieth. Unlike *The Wit of Women, Redressing the Balance* includes longer selections, often several for each writer, and it also focuses exclusively on literary humorists. Also unlike the two historical anthologies that precede it, *Redressing the Balance* addresses squarely the issues of a women's humor tradition in America. The editors, both scholars of women's humor, outline the changing shape of women's humor over the centuries, including its frequent exclusion from the literary canon. They argue for the creativity of women's humor, for the distinctive way humorists have negotiated between their own experience as women and the social world in which they find themselves.

They argue, in short, for a separate tradition for women, and they support that proposition with an impressive collection of women's literary humor.

Serious literary criticism about women's humor has been nearly as scarce as historically based anthologies. Again, Nancy Walker is in the forefront with her book-length study entitled *A Very Serious Thing: Women's Humor and American Culture.* In much greater detail than in the introduction to her anthology, Walker explores the relationship between separate male and female traditions of literary humor. She notes from the outset that one of the central ironies of a tradition of women's humor dating back at least 150 years is the widespread belief that "women have been officially denied the possession of—hence the practice of—the sense of humor.[22] Women's humor, Walker points out, is filled with paradoxes: it seems to offer power to the powerless, it appears to reinforce stereotypes when in fact it undercuts them, and it represents an act of aggression on the part of those who are defined by cultural convention as passive. Women's humor, Walker goes on to demonstrate, grows out of—and reflects—the separateness of women's lives.[23] Further, she insists, when viewed within its cultural context, women's humor is by its nature highly subversive.

The tradition of women's humor in America owes its characteristics of theme, form, and language quite simply to the experience of the women who have created it. Just as the dominant humorous tradition springs from incongruities in America's political and business arenas, so the distinctive characteristics of women's humor are derived from the disparity between the "official" conduct of women's lives and their "unofficial" response to that conduct. Implicit in this humor is protest of a very specific sort, whether presented as direct satire or masked in irony; through apparent self-mockery and confrontation of the "other," women's humor seeks to correct a cultural imbalance.[24] Of greatest significance for this study, however, is the place Walker assigns to Miriam Whitcher in the whole tradition of American women humorists. Walker locates Whitcher at the very heart of her study. Whitcher is granted her rightful role as the first significant woman prose humorist of the nation, and she serves as a touchstone throughout the study. Walker cites her writing repeatedly to illustrate the complex interworkings of women's humor, whether of the nineteenth or the twentieth century.

Briefer explorations of women's humor have also been under-
taken in the past decade, but only by a small handful of women
scholars. One such scholar is Alice Sheppard, who brings together
literary history, feminist psychology, and social history to show that
the nineteenth-century doctrine of separate spheres for men and
women helps explain why male critics virtually ignored women's humor in the century following the publication of *The Wit of Women*.[25]
Another scholar, Judy Little, traces in her introduction to the comedy
of Virginia Woolf and Muriel Spark the relationship between transitional, or liminal, social events and the emergence of feminist comedy.[26] Traditionally, Little argues, when society celebrates "threshold"
occasions, a transitional period occurs when the world is turned up-
side down, when the jester can mock the king, literally and metaphorically. When the threshold passes, prevailing norms are
reestablished. In contrast, feminist comedy, according to Little, emerges
when transitional or liminal events are *not* resolved; the comedy "will
mock assumptions rather than ramifications; it will challenge a world
view."[27]

For example, Emily Toth argues in "A Laughter of Their Own:
Women's Humor in the United States" that many contemporary
anthologies of American humor continue to slight women's humor
because it "characteristically criticizes and subverts patriarchal norms"
and thus does not particularly amuse men. Toth's essay appears in a
recent collection of articles about the history of American humor
criticism, *Critical Essays in American Humor,* where, ironically, it is
the only contemporary article in the collection by a woman scholar
and the only article about women's humor.[28]

At its most radical, then, women's humor confronts the values of
the dominant culture and subverts them. For the woman reader, this
is a source of pleasure, but to the male reader/critic, it is often a
source of discomfort. As modern criticism about nineteenth-century
American humor has demonstrated, historical distance does not necessarily narrow the gap between men's and women's perceptions about
the efficacy of gender-based humor, and so women's humor is dismissed by male critics who do not find it funny or otherwise compelling.[29] There are, of course, notable exceptions, such as the late Thomas
F. O'Donnell, who fully appreciated the humor of Miriam Whitcher;
nonetheless, little has been written about the women humorists of

the nineteenth century, and almost all of it has been written by women critics.[30]

Another explanation of why women's humor in America has received disproportionately little critical attention compared to men's is that women's humor, especially in the nineteenth century, reflected women's own experience, as distinct from men's; it focused on issues that were pertinent primarily to women, and it served a different social purpose from men's humor. Sometimes, of course, the differences were in degree rather than kind, but often the subject matter of women's humor was dramatically different from men's. For example, in a 1981 article, Nancy Walker pointed out that one of the favorite targets of women's humor in the mid-1800s was sentimentality. "In their own work, the 'witty women'—'Fanny Fern,' Caroline Kirkland, Frances Whitcher, 'Gail Hamilton,' and Marietta Holley—consistently satirized the women who wrote pious, sentimental prose and poetry. Their efforts to demote this sentimental figure from the high status accorded her by genteel society were part of their rebellion against widely-held notions of woman's 'proper' role in American society."[31] To the extent that sentimentality symbolized women's powerlessness, Walker goes on to say, the humor of these women represented "an expression of confidence and power."[32]

As Walker suggests, sentimentality was closely associated with the notion of gentility, whose tenets were sweeping northern society as early as the 1830s. According to the cultural historian Karen Halttunen, with the emergence of a large, new middle-class culture in the 1830s and 1840s, sentimental values began to clash with genteel values. Halttunen defines sentimental values as "the cult of feelings that dominated middle-class literature and culture from 1830 to 1870," while genteel values consisted in large measure of conforming to an outward set of manners and behavior.[33] Halttunen further identifies what she calls "the genteel performance, a system of polite conduct that demanded a flawless self-discipline practiced within an apparently easy, natural, sincere manner."[34] For those newly aspiring to genteel status, however, there was nothing natural or sincere about their participation in a genteel performance. Anxious about how to conduct themselves as newly arrived members of the middle class, uncertain how to recognize whether someone else had the right to claim a comparable social status, Victorian Americans began increasingly to rely on advice manuals to tell them how to behave, and on magazines such as *Godey's Lady's Book* to tell them how to dress and how to furnish their houses. They became obsessed with the material goods that would identify them with their desired social position.

Indeed, the emergence of vernacular humor itself can be understood in opposition to the growing influence of gentility. Part of the appeal of the vernacular heroine was that she operated outside the restrictions of genteel society. All vernacular heroes were perceived as speaking with a freedom and candor not allowed those confined to proper society, but this was doubly true for women writers and women protagonists for whom the restrictions were greater than they were for men. Thus the constraints of genteel society, especially female genteel society, not only inspired much of the humor but also became a favorite target in women's humor. Whether she spoke as a farm wife or as a columnist for the *New York Ledger,* the nineteenth-century woman humorist attacked the assumptions of genteel society for as long as those assumptions prevailed; the tighter they pinched, the harder the humor hit them. Women's idleness, their presumed helplessness, their growing obsession with material goods and social status, their relegation to the private sphere, their economic dependence on men—all these tendencies became prime targets in women's humor from the 1830s to the 1870s, culminating in Marietta Holley's identification of gentility, per se, as the principal obstacle standing in women's way of achieving full political equality with men.

Part of the rich texture of women's humor in the nineteenth century and its ongoing interest for modern readers can be found in the values it upholds as well as the values it subverts. In this regard, one of the important distinguishing characteristics of women's humor is its ready affirmation of the details of domestic life. The humor abounds in these details, sometimes as the background for more central action, sometimes as the object of the humor itself. Even the most fiercely independent women of the nineteenth century lived their lives partly in a domestic world. The absence of domestic comfort is central to Caroline Kirkland's sometimes bitter indictment of the romanticized western frontier; the finery of the parlors of New York's most fashionable society excites the curiosity and mock admiration of Ann Stephens's Jonathan Slick; the creation of a church sewing society, complete with its projects, elaborate teas, and relentless gossip is the setting for Miriam Whitcher's finest social satire; while Josiah Allen's Wife's immersion in domestic farm labor ironically grants her the authority to advocate feminist reform. Male humorists, even when they adopt a female persona for comic effects (Shillaber's Mrs. Partington or the actor Neil Burgess's comic stage impersonations of the Widow Bedott and Samantha Allen), simply do not infuse domestic values into their humor as women do.[35]

This domestic strand directly links a nineteenth-century humorist such as Whitcher with modern writers such as Peg Bracken and Erma Bombeck. Marietta Holley's Samantha Allen carried the centrality of this theme forward from the 1870s through the turn of the century, where it was shortly thereafter picked up by a number of other women humorists—Betty McDonald, Mary Lasswell, and Shirley Jackson, to name but three. Lily Tomlin, by contrast, is linked to the pioneering humor of Miriam Whitcher not through an affirmation of domestic details but rather through the creation of multiple and diverse female characters. Although other modern comedians have developed a stable of offbeat characters, no one surpasses Tomlin in the delineation of distinctive vernacular characters. Seen in the historical context of the humor of Miriam Whitcher, Tomlin's characters only gain in significance.

Paradoxically, even when women's humor criticizes women's behavior or their obsessions, even when it challenges the limitations society has imposed upon women, the humor simultaneously affirms women's experiences. Nancy Walker and Zita Dresner state the issue in these terms:

> The use of self-deprecating humor by women could be a defensive reaction of those who feel themselves too weak or vulnerable to attack with impunity the forces that oppress them, but the seemingly defensive weapons of humor can also become offensive in the hands of women and other outgroups. For example, as psychologists have observed, laughing at one's shortcomings is not only a way of diminishing their importance and potentially overcoming them but is also a technique for cleansing them of pejorative connotations imposed by the dominant culture and, thereby, turning them into strengths. Similarly, the use of incongruity in humor by women as a means of targeting attributes and behaviors prescribed for them by the dominant culture is an act of rebellion. Finally, the use of

humor by women against women, when it is used to advance ideas that might conflict with those of the male establishment about women's roles and prerogatives, represents a step toward empowerment rather than capitulation.[36]

Nineteenth-century women's humor gave women readers permission to question their acceptance of themselves as passive, sentimental, and powerless beings. In doing so, it forged a bond between women. As Alice Sheppard has observed, "humor, an instrument of social correction and subversion, reinforced women's shared perceptions, strengthened social bonds, and in itself facilitated social change."[37] Even though women were often the immediate targets of the writers' wit, as they were for Miriam Whitcher, women's humor brought women together through their shared laughter and their shared pleasure. In the short run, Freud may have been right when he suggested that laughter safely discharges antisocial impulses that might otherwise be dangerous or hostile, but in much humor by women, the laughter instead subverts dominant cultural values and norms. As American women humorists of the nineteenth century so ably demonstrated, once cultural assumptions are exposed to the power of laughter, they can never again hold the same sway.

Major Themes in the Life of Miriam Whitcher

This chapter has addressed thus far the humor that made Whitcher famous, especially in the decades following her death and the subsequent publication of *The Widow Bedott Papers*, and her place in a distinctive American tradition of women's humor. But what of her life itself? What was its general shape, and what were its dominant patterns? What themes fashioned her creative imagination, and how did the particular nature of her humor develop? While the chapters that follow will explore these questions at length, it is possible to see in condensed form how seemingly paradoxical forces influenced her life and hence her works.

Born circa 1812 in Whitesboro, Oneida County, New York, Miriam Berry lived a life marked by complex and contradictory impulses.[38] She characterized herself as one in whom strains of melancholy and a heightened sense of the ridiculous ran side by side. By temperament she preferred an intensely private life away from public scrutiny and removed from traditional social interactions, yet when she was thirty-five she married an Episcopalian minister, the Reverend Benjamin William Whitcher, and was thrust into a public role filled with multiple social expectations. Uprooted shortly thereafter from her native village and close-knit family, she found herself a reluctant public figure in the rapidly growing village of Elmira, New York. There she had difficulty finding what she called suitable intellectual companionship, other than the company of her husband, and there she was the inevitable object of scrutiny and gossip. This painful alienation was the inspiration for much of the stinging and engaging humor she created while living in Elmira.

Politically and socially, Miriam lived a relatively traditional life, yet she fit none of the modes that have come to be associated with middle-class women in mid-nineteenth-century America. Thoroughly family oriented, she was nonetheless nearly a stranger to domesticity. When she married William, she had almost no experience with the rigors of housekeeping; she had little or no experience cooking, and none baking; she knew nothing, firsthand, about managing domestic help; and while she could sew, she did so only to furnish the necessities, certainly never to adorn herself. She forcefully rejected the genteel values emerging around her, especially as those values affected women's lives, and she also mocked in her humor women's recent excursions into the arena of social reform. A devout Episcopalian after the age of thirty-four she poked fun at all hints of religious sectarianism, pomposity, or sanctimony. While still a confirmed and apparently contented spinster, she created the celebrated Widow Bedott, whose chief aim in life was to rid herself of her dread single status; then, shortly after Miriam married the pastor of her own church—only a little more than a year after she had converted from the Presbyterian to the Episcopalian denomination—she puckishly set the Widow Bedott, an ardent Methodist, off in pursuit of the Reverend Shadrack Sniffles, a Baptist minister.

Miriam Whitcher was described by all who knew her as intensely shy and sensitive, yet from earliest childhood she entertained her family and friends by making fun of her neighbors and schoolmates. She held back from the public world in part because she feared rejection, and when the occasion demanded that she put herself forward, she did so with great hesitation; not surprisingly, her shyness and reserve were frequently mistaken for pride and haughtiness. Yet people were not in error to sense in her a ready ability to judge others harshly. She quietly defied social norms and expectations that she found objectionable, but there is no record that she ever spoke out in person against that which she rejected; instead her social demeanor was quiet, even reluctant, while her public criticisms found an outlet only in her anonymously published humor. By choice, then, she was often isolated, yet she observed society with a keenly critical eye and the gift of a finely tuned ear for what she called "peculiarities" of speech.

Miriam Whitcher was a deeply religious person who was interested not only in the state of her soul but also in the fine points of theology and church history; at the same time, she felt herself inadequate to the challenges of some of the most fundamental Christian doctrines. Most painfully for her, she believed that she was unable to fulfill the commandment to love others as she would be loved in turn; she believed she failed to do so in part because of her irrepressible lifelong impulse toward caricature—her keenly developed sense of the ridiculous. On more than one occasion, sometimes in near despair, she lamented that she could not be as good as she should, but she was unwilling and unable to set aside her sense of humor to achieve that end. Finally, the great strength of her mind and character was offset by the frailty of her body. From childhood on she had long bouts of illness, while as an adult she suffered from a congenital weakness of the respiratory system that ultimately led, at the age of thirty-nine, to the fatal onset of tuberculosis.

The life of Miriam Berry Whitcher was filled with both sadness and wit and humor. It is the story of an outwardly conventional and restrained woman whose satiric vision of village life in the 1840s was so firmly on target that readers across New York and New England thought their neighbors were the life models for Whitcher's characters. But before unfolding that story, it is important to go back to a time before Whitcher was born—to her earliest American ancestors—then to Whitesboro in the early 1800s, and to her large and close-knit family, the mainstay of her strength and security.

2

Whitesboro

The first member of the Berry family to settle in America fled the Puritan regime of Cromwell in the mid-1600s. He reportedly escaped from Sterling Castle, where he had been sentenced to death by the Cromwellian forces for fighting on behalf of the Stuarts.[1] He was thus fiercely anti-Puritan and proroyalist when he arrived in America, an attitude that filtered through the generations of Berrys down to the time of Lewis Berry, Miriam's father. Lewis Berry's own father was a King's Justice of the Peace in his native New Jersey, but with the outbreak of the Revolutionary War he sided with the colonialists. His son, Lewis, was born in New Jersey in 1767.

Lewis Berry moved from New Jersey to Washington County, New York, when he was in his early twenties—in approximately 1790. There he met and married Elizabeth Wells, and there they had nine children, five of whom survived infancy. In 1802, lured by the promise of new opportunities and driven, in part, by the economic pressures of his rapidly growing family, Lewis Berry packed his family into a wagon and headed for Oneida County, then on the western frontier of the state. The family settled first in the town of Westmoreland, where Lewis Berry set up a store on the Seneca Turnpike that kept the Berrys afloat economically for a few years. However, in 1806 his business failed and was sold by the sheriff to pay Berry's creditors. This failure brought Lewis Berry and his family to Whitesboro, where he was jailed as a debtor. Freed after only a brief stay in the small county jail on condition that he remain in the immediate area, he settled in the town of Whitesboro and took over an inn that had been operated for a short time by the White family. He soon regained the reputation he enjoyed before his financial trouble.

Berry's Inn was strategically located across the village green from the county jail and courthouse, and those who once sentenced Lewis Berry to jail now regularly crossed the green at noon to have dinner at his inn. While local lawyers and judges merely ate at the inn, court officials who came from distant towns when the court was in session rented rooms there as well.[2] The family inn eventually prospered, but it took Lewis Berry a while to overcome his earlier debts. According to stories later told by members of his household, one year when Berry was especially hard-pressed his neighbors brought him team-loads of wood to help get him through the winter. After the hardship years passed, his neighbors continued the custom of bringing him yearly donations of firewood; in return, he entertained his neighbors by inviting them to a meal that cost the family more than the value of the wood they had received in donation.[3] One of the humorous sketches that later helped establish Miriam Whitcher's fame as a writer concerned a fictitious donation party that forced a minister and his wife to resign from their parish rather than bear the expenses of hosting such a party again. After only a few years in the original White Inn, Lewis Berry moved his family down the street to another location on the corner of Main and Mohawk streets. He opened another inn, or boardinghouse, and there the family remained for the next forty years.

Arriving in Whitesboro with the second wave of settlers, Lewis Berry never gained the status of a "first" man of Whitesboro, but he gradually became a well-respected member of the community.[4] Politically a Whig, he was a staunch member of the Presbyterian church. He was also at one time a member of the board of trustees of the Oneida Institute, a liberal theological seminary located in Whitesboro. Later he broke with the institute when its second president, Beriah Green, combined the mission of the institute with the abolitionist cause, which many of the local Presbyterians regarded as too radical a position. Lewis Berry lived to be eighty-two years old, and he died in his sleep in the spring of 1849.[5]

Miriam's mother, Elizabeth Wells, also claimed an English ancestry.[6] The first Wells to arrive in America settled in Saybrook, Connecticut; her grandfather, Edward Wells, and six of his brothers all fought in the Revolutionary War. Settling first on the Atlantic seaboard, the Wells family eventually followed a familiar immigration pattern by moving up the Connecticut River valley and ultimately settling between the Hudson and Connecticut rivers in Washington County, New York. Elizabeth Wells was born in Cambridge, New York, in 1775; before she was eighteen years old, she had married Lewis Berry, eight years her elder, and given birth to at least one of their children. A strong, capable woman, for most of her adult life she managed not only her large family but also the Berry Inn. Her daughters helped her when they were older, but much of the work fell on her, including doing most of the cooking for large numbers of people. But the best proof of her physical strength and toughness was the fact that between the ages of seventeen and forty-five she gave birth to fifteen children, at least eight of whom she survived. Elizabeth Wells died in 1855 at the age of eighty.

Frances Miriam Berry was the thirteenth of the fifteen Berry children. One middle son and daughter bore their respective parent's name, and one granddaughter was named Elizabeth after her grandmother; however, the Berry family name ended with Miriam's generation, for none of the four male Berrys had sons. At a time in American history when families frequently separated because of westward migration or the pull of emerging urban industrial centers, only one of the Berry children moved more than a day's journey away from the family home. The lone exception was Miriam herself, and she did not move until her thirty-fifth year and stayed away only two-and-a-half years. Throughout Miriam's childhood and young adulthood, her family—especially her brothers and sisters—was her primary social group. Hers was a close-knit family, with the youngest children especially forming close bonds with one another. Even in later years never fewer than three adult children were living in their parents' home, and frequently there were as many as six. (The family was unusual even in its day for its size and its stability.) The Berry Inn was Miriam and William Whitcher's first residence when they married in 1846, and it was the place to which they returned when they left Elmira. Miriam Whitcher gave birth to her only living child at home in Whitesboro, and her older sisters helped raise that child when Miriam died only a few years later. The members of Miriam Berry's nuclear family are thus important to know.

The first surviving child of Lewis and Elizabeth was a son, Wendall, who was born in Cambridge in 1793.[7] Only a shadowy figure in

Miriam's life because he was gone from home before she was born, he was also one of two siblings to die while Miriam was still young. Wendall satisfied one of his father's fondest wishes by reading for the law and becoming a practicing attorney, but that practice took him away from Whitesboro and his family for most of his adult life. He died in 1828 at the age of thirty-five.

The second child who died during Miriam's lifetime was her sister Jane (b. Cambridge c. 1802), who died when she was sixteen and Miriam five. Unlike Wendall, Jane made a deep impression on her young sister, who remembered her with bittersweet melancholy. She remained fixed in Miriam's imagination as a singular figure of kindness and affection, as the following letter from Miriam to an unnamed friend reveals:

> I was quite alone all last evening, and my mind wandered to you. I cannot tell why it is, but your *idea* is always associated in my imagination with a dear sister of mine, who died at sixteen, when I was only five years old. I recollect her perfectly. They say she was a genius; and I remember that she was beautiful and joyous, and always good to me. I loved her better than any one else. She used to put me every night in my little crib, and sit and tell me stories till I went to sleep, and hear me say my prayers and little hymns. She had a thousand winning ways. There was one pretty mark of love that seems very pleasant to me now as I look back to it. She used often to reward me for being good, by putting some trifle under my pillow after I was asleep, and it made me so happy to wake in the morning and find it. How easy it is to please a child!
>
> This sweet sister took more pains with me than anybody else ever did. It was a great calamity that I lost her. Yet I have always felt that there was still a bond between us. When I was little, I used to dream of her almost every night, and, as I grew older, I thought about her a great deal. In my lonely rambles, I often fancied that she called me; even now I sometimes think I can hear her distinctly pronounce my name in the night.[8]

Given the lasting impression that Jane made on Miriam, it seems certain that her untimely death contributed to the strong sense of melancholy that Miriam associated with her childhood.

Four other children were born between Wendall and Jane—Wealthy, Mary, Morris, and Cornelia. The first of these, Wealthy, is the most shadowy figure of all in the Berry family. She was born in 1797 and lived until the age of fifty-six, but her name is never mentioned in any of the family records. The reason for this silence is clarified in the 1850 New York State Census, which affixed the official designation "idiotic" next to her name. Although the severity of Wealthy's disability is unknown, it is clear that she remained part of the Berry family household despite the presence of a thriving asylum on the outskirts of Whitesboro.

Mary (b. 1798) and Cornelia (b. 1802) were in adulthood an inseparable pair whom Miriam referred to fondly as "the girls." Neither ever married, and neither ever lived away from the family home. Both cared for Miriam during her final illness, and for a period after her death assumed major responsibility for raising Miriam's infant daughter, Alice. When William later remarried, both Mary and Cornelia moved into William's home and remained there, a part of his new family, until their own deaths: Mary's in 1856, and Cornelia's several years later.[9]

Morris Berry (b. 1799 in Cambridge), like his older brother, Wendall, attended Hamilton College and began his career as a lawyer outside Oneida County. He did not especially enjoy practicing law, however, and came home instead to Whitesboro where he served for a time as the postmaster; later he was a book tradesman in Saratoga, and still later, reportedly a librarian in Philadelphia. Morris married Eugenia Dorland of Poughkeepsie, New York, who later emerges in the family chronicles as a "difficult" person. They had no children who survived infancy.[10]

The next two Berry children were the two who were named after their parents, Elizabeth (b. 1806) and Lewis T. (b. 1808). In contrast to Miriam, who depicted herself as a lonely child, Elizabeth has been described as "the belle of society."[11] Elizabeth married O. L. Barbour, a lawyer from Rome, New York, who later became famous in law circles for his sixty-seven volume work, *Barbour's Supreme Court Reports*.[12] Elizabeth and Barbour, as he was called by the family, moved to Saratoga Springs sometime in the late 1830s or early 1840s, and Miriam often stayed with them there. She and William visited the

Barbours when they were first engaged, and again when they left Elmira and hoped to be appointed to a church in Saratoga. They became friends with Barbour's family, and they formed strong attachments to Elizabeth's children. Elizabeth died in 1856 at the age of fifty.

Lewis T. Berry, only two years older than Miriam, was close to her throughout their lifetimes. He encouraged her in her literary career, joined her in becoming a member of the Whitesboro Episcopal Church, and named one of his three daughters after her. By occupation a bookkeeper, Lewis was also one of the trustees of the village of Whitesboro from 1836–42, and he became one of the vestrymen of St. John's Episcopal Church when it was established in 1847. Married to a woman now known only by her first name, Emily, Lewis Berry died in Whitesboro in 1869.[13]

Katharine, or Kate, was the sister born immediately after Miriam (1817). As Miriam's extant letters make clear, Kate was her closest friend and confidante. It was to Kate that Miriam turned for emotional understanding and support, and to Kate that she most often revealed her sense of humor. Like Miriam, Kate was a writer, and while she was never as successful, she also published her work in *Godey's Lady's Book,* where it was apparently well received. Also like her more famous sister, she left the church of her childhood to become an Episcopalian. After Miriam's death, Kate wrote a two-part biographical sketch of her sister that was published in *Godey's;* this biography remains the only source of reliable information about Miriam's childhood and the final months of her life. Kate was married only after Miriam's death in her forty-second year to Hiram P. Potter of Whitesboro, the local coal merchant and a vestryman at St. John's. Childless, she died in November 1865.

The last Berry child was John, born in 1820. Like his sister Kate, he was an enthusiastic supporter of Miriam's literary career and had literary aspirations of his own; writing for the local newspaper seems to be as far as his hopes were realized, however. A machinist by trade,[14] John Berry never married; until the death of his father, he continued to live in the Berry Inn, and later was listed as living in his mother's household. Of all the children who survived to adulthood, John had the shortest life (thirty years); he followed his sister Miriam in death by less than a year, dying, like her, of tuberculosis.

Childhood Years

The sketchy records of Miriam's earliest childhood indicate that she showed a precocious interest in poetry, delighting the family when she was two by reciting verses they had read to her. This interest was clearly fostered and indulged by older members of the family, for her sister records that Miriam was dictating her own "poetic" compositions for others to write down before she was able to write. Even then, according to Kate, she was drawn to mock-serious themes, such as the death of a pet crow. She also was interested in drawing at an early age, and was apparently unable to resist drawing caricatures of anyone who struck her fancy; given the constant flow of visitors through the inn, she had an ever-fresh supply of subjects on whom to practice.

> Her first attempt to draw, when she was about five years old, was inspired by the strikingly ugly visage of a neighbor, a man of excessively polished exterior, a gentleman of the old school, whose efforts to win the confidence of the interesting child only served to terrify and repel her.
>
> Seeing him one day absorbed in a newspaper, she mounted a chair, at a high writing-desk, and "drew his likeness." In the midst of her artistic labors, he laid aside his paper, and, observing her occupation, walked to the desk, inquiring, with a profound bow, "What are you doing, my little dear? Writing a letter to your sweetheart?" Such a question completed her disgust and alarm; she caught up her unfinished production, and ran to another apartment.[15]

Miriam's own version of her early artistic projects supports her sister's, but adds poetry to her stock of resources for assaulting her neighbors:

> I received, at my birth, the undesirable gift of a remarkably strong sense of the ridiculous. I can scarcely remember the time when the neighbors were not afraid that I would "make fun of them." For indulging in this propensity, I was scolded at home, and wept over and prayed with, by certain well-meaning old maids in the neighborhood; but all to no purpose. The only reward of their labors was frequently their likenesses drawn in charcoal and pinned to the corners of their shawls, with, perhaps, a descriptive verse below.[16]

Miriam captured in this passage about her childhood a lifelong satiric tendency. Presumably her gift is undesirable because of the trouble it brought her, and because of its antisocial nature, yet a note of pride edges into her self-characterization. Her neighbors were always to some extent the objects of her humor, although in later years she seemed genuinely surprised when people recognized themselves as the objects of her satire. Her form of rebellion, too, remained remarkably consistent. When people's behavior offended her, she did not tell them so directly but instead "drew their likenesses" in her humor. There is no evidence that the neighbors in later years ever wept or prayed over her, but she often believed that she should have been a better person than she was; nonetheless, her "remarkably strong sense of the ridiculous" always prevailed. Even when it led to ostracism and isolation, Miriam was seldom able to resist exploiting the comic potential in social situations.

Closely associated in her mind with the impulse to ridicule was her feeling of melancholy that gave her a lifelong public air of diffidence and reserve. In the letter cited above, Miriam goes on to remark:

> Of course I had not many friends, even among my own playmates. And yet, at the bottom of all this deviltry, there was a warm, affectionate heart—if any were really kind to me, how I loved them!
>
> I think now that I was not properly trained. My errors should have been checked in a different way from that which was adopted. I ought to have received more tender treatment. I became a lonely child, almost without companionship; wandering alone, for hours, in the woods and fields, creating for myself an ideal world, and in that ideal world I lived for many years. At times I was melancholy almost to despair. My reserve and sadness were called haughtiness and pride.[17]

The loneliness that Miriam describes here and the criticism of the way she was trained are at odds with other pictures that emerge of her family. The lack of "tender treatment" must be laid at the feet of the adults in her family: many years later her daughter characterized Miriam's father as stern and harsh, as unfeeling. The loneliness, however, is a different matter. Surrounded by brothers and sisters who obviously doted on her, who in later life were close to her both emotionally and geographically and toward whom she expressed great affection, she still felt alone. Even a large and loving family could not offer a complete buffer against the larger social world. She was never fully at ease outside her family circle, which profoundly affected her personal life and her writing. Paradoxically, however, the very traits that brought her private pain enriched her humorous perspective. Her keen eye for incongruity and absurdity distanced her from her immediate social world. Hers was a laughter that was often born out of pain.

Miriam's formal schooling began inauspiciously when she was five: "Her first teacher was a sour-faced woman, who knocked the alphabet with her thimble into the heads of a little group of unruly children . . . with small love, and no just appreciation of the dawning minds under her care."[18] Within a few months, according to Kate Berry, Miriam transferred to the village academy where she was placed in a class with older children. Her family hoped that she would prosper in this environment, but in fact Miriam's situation only worsened:

> Woe worth the day to the little creature! The pedagogue was a stern, cruel, vindictive man, who literally whipped knowledge into his pupils' noodles, and in his hands the rod and ferrule were never idle. In this school, before she had completed her sixth year, Miriam passed some miserable months. To insure her good conduct, she was seated with a "big girl"—that is, one twelve years old—and this "big girl" proved to her defenseless companion a source of unmitigated suffering and terror. She belonged to a vulgar, uneducated family; and of the mutual forbearance and kindnesses that should be practised at home she was as ignorant as the swine which jostle each other from the same trough. Nor had her school influences any tendency to polish such a character, for in that unhappy community the master's tyranny and needless severity made deception, recrimination, and mutual distrust prevalent among the pupils.[19]

The cruelties that the "big girl" perpetrated upon Miriam and the punishments that she suffered at the hands of the schoolteacher ended with the school year, but the effects lingered—fear, unhappiness, and the memory of her sufferings. The twin events of the death of her older sister and the brutalizing first year of formal schooling fostered in Miriam Berry a large measure of the melancholy that remained so deep a part of her adult character.

Miriam's schooling after this first year became erratic. The offending schoolteacher was dismissed, and the next teacher, a classics master, left the younger children mostly to their own devices. Miriam continued to develop her love for literature, especially poetry, and she continued to draw caricatures of her companions. One hapless young man was especially ill-served by her ridicule:

> Sometimes a mischievous companion, possessing herself of one [of Miriam's drawings] would display it. If the unfortunate subject had the happy faculty of taking a joke, he passed it off with a laugh. But a matter-of-fact, shy, sensitive youth regarded Miriam afterwards with insuperable dread. We well remember one, who, finding himself graphically set forth with the quite imaginary addition of a parasol over his head, and bows, with floating ends, on his coat-skirts, left school in dismay, and did not again attend.[20]

In part because of ill health, Miriam as often spent the school year at home as at the academy. She had the option of going to a boarding school, but she was too shy and too unsure of herself to leave the family fold—to "trust herself among strangers," as Kate Berry expressed it. Nevertheless, Miriam Berry became a reasonably well-educated young woman. She read avidly through the local circulating library, absorbed history and light literature from her father's more limited library, and received brief instruction in art from an Englishman who lived nearby and loaned her art books. By the time she was sixteen, she had managed to secure for herself an education that her sister claimed would have compared favorably with the offerings of any of the female academies, save the addition of "those attainments usually styled accomplishments."[21] She added at least one accomplishment by studying French with a woman in Utica, becoming proficient both at reading and speaking the language. Although she had almost no opportunities to speak French in Whitesboro, she did teach it to young children when she stayed with her sister Elizabeth in Saratoga Springs. Her sister Kate praised her natural artistic talent, which she believed extended beyond Miriam's ability to draw caricatures, and regretted that she had not received proper formal training:

The itinerant professors of painting and kindred accomplishments who stopped, at times, in her native village, were incapable of improving such an endowment as hers. The *chef-d'ouvres* on velvet, their red and green birds, and extraordinary "flower pieces" done by theorems, their impossible Scripture scenes, gave her infinite amusement. She should have studied with a true artist, but no such opportunity presented itself—a subject of deep regret to her in after years, as therein she believed the proper development of her powers could have been found.[22]

Between this time, when Miriam was in her late teens, and 1846, when she joined the Episcopal Church of Whitesboro at the age of thirty-four, the record is nearly silent on Miriam's personal life. Kate Berry did, however, make a case for her Christian charity, which she said took Miriam out into the community to help the poor and the ill:

> Residing in a country village, where kindly offices in illness and affliction are reciprocally rendered, she was often called upon to attend the sick—a summons that she cheerfully obeyed, having the excellent qualification, of which no woman should be destitute, of being a gentle and skilful *[sic]* nurse. She did not hesitate to overtax her bodily powers, and frequent night-watching with her sick neighbors impaired her strength.[23]

It is probable, moreover, that she divided her time between Whitesboro and Saratoga Springs, where she lived with her sister Elizabeth; she also visited with her maternal relatives in Cambridge, New York, when she was in the eastern part of the state. Her time away from Whitesboro unquestionably enriched her life and broadened her outlook and experience. Nonetheless, Whitesboro and Oneida County in the two decades between 1820 and 1840 exerted a strong influence on Miriam's adult life; to know something of the richness of the story of Whitesboro in this era is to gain insight into the complexity of Miriam herself and her literary work. Miriam's humor was rooted in the social world of a series of fictional villages that bore remarkable resemblances to Whitesboro, and the values she upheld in her humor, as well as those she ridiculed, were all shared community values. Moreover, when she moved to Elmira in the late 1840s and wrote her satiric Aunt Maguire sketches for *Godey's Lady's Book,* the Whitesboro of Miriam's young adulthood was the standard against which she measured Elmira society; the disparity between the two inspired some of the finest humor of her career.

Whitesboro in the 1820s and 1830s

Situated on the banks of the Mohawk River, Whitesboro technically belonged to the western frontier until 1820, when the last parcel of available land was purchased. As the frontier moved further west and conflicts with Indian tribes subsided at the end of the War of 1812, New York State began work on a long-delayed project that profoundly affected the history of Whitesboro, Oneida County, and the state itself: the construction of the Erie Canal. The first shovelful of dirt was turned ceremonially in 1817 in Rome, New York, only a few miles west of Whitesboro; six years later, the canal was completed.[24]

Running 363 miles, from Lake Erie in the West to the Hudson River near Albany in the East, the Erie Canal opened up the markets of the West to the eastern seaboard. Before western farmers had a cheap and easy way to get their produce to the larger markets, they had no incentive to grow little more than they needed for their own families. Without cash crops, the farmers had no ability to buy the manufactured goods available to America's urban areas. The construction of the Erie Canal and its series of feeder canals brought significant change to the economies of all areas it touched. The cost of moving goods along the canal was fully 85 percent cheaper than any earlier form of transportation, so that once the canal opened in 1825, it was immediately used almost to capacity. Packet boats loaded with immigrants and their goods passed along the canal to the western frontier beyond the Great Lakes, and agricultural and forest products from the western part of the state easily found their way to the metropolitan coast. Traffic on the canal surpassed all expectations, with forty thousand immigrants heading west on the canal in the first year alone; tolls that year added up to three-quarters of a million dollars.[25] Existing towns up and down the canal changed dramatically, while many new ones sprang into being. A visitor to Utica in 1829 recorded the astounding changes that had taken place there since his last visit in 1820:

> Between five and six o'clock we entered Utica, which, nine years ago, the period of my last visit to it, ranked only as a flourishing village. It had now grown as if by magic, to the dimensions of a larger city; and it was with utter amazement that I beheld the long streets and rows of blocks of large beautiful country seats, stores and dwellings, through which our coach conveyed us in driving to the lodges I had selected. I had heard much of the march of improvement in Utica since the completion of the Grand Canal. But I had no idea of the reality. Rip Van Winkle himself, after his thirty year's repose in a glen of the Kaatsbergs, was not more amazed than I was at the present aspect and magnitude of this beautiful place. Bagg's Hotel, to which I directed my driver, was in the very heart of the village, and the center of business at the period of my last visit. Now, it was quite in the suburbs. The houses were then scattered, excepting in two or three principal streets, though some were spacious and elegant. But now they were closely built, lofty and spacious; and the length of some of the streets, like New York, began to look like a wilderness of bricks.[26]

The canal was completed in sections, starting with the relatively easy construction of the ninety-eight-mile stretch between the Mohawk and Seneca rivers. As soon as that section was completed, it was immediately put to good use, and Utica thus became the first jumping-off point on the canal in the East. As a result, in comparison to other canal villages such as Whitesboro, Utica grew rapidly: "Iron and brass foundries, plough factories, flour and cotton mills, potteries manufacturing stoneware, large tanneries, and several large breweries, one 'capable of turning out 200 barrels of ale weekly' were among the industries of Utica in the years immediately following the completion of the canal. . . . *The Utica Directory* [for 1832] boasted of forty-four dry goods stores, sixty-three groceries, twenty blacksmith shops, forty-three attorneys at law, thirty-two physicians, twenty-eight inns and five banks."[27] Though nearby Whitesboro retained its village character, its life and its citizens were inevitably influenced by all that the canal brought into their midst.

The canal era (1825–35) was a time of great religious fervor, of rapid economic expansion, and of unprecedented social reform along the Erie Canal, and the village of Whitesboro found itself repeatedly in the center of controversy and foment. In October 1825, during the first year the canal was open along its full length, a young preacher by the name of Charles Finney was invited by his former pastor, George W. Gale, to revitalize the local Presbyterians of the village of Western, near Utica. By January 1826 Finney's powerful evangelical preaching had resulted in 140 conversions in the small village. He was invited to conduct a similar series of almost nightly revivals in Rome, also in Oneida County; there his preaching brought in more than 500 new converts in only one month.[28] From Rome Finney went next to the First Presbyterian Church of Utica, where he added 500 new members by May. Before the summer was over, some 3,000 people were numbered among the converted in Oneida County and the surrounding area.[29]

A spirit of religious enthusiasm permeated the towns where Finney conducted his revivals, as he reported in his *Memoirs:*

> Indeed the town [of Rome] was full of prayer. Go where you would, you heard the voice of prayer. Pass along the street, and if two or three Christians happened to be together, they were praying. Wherever they met they prayed. Wherever there was a sinner unconverted, especially if he manifested any opposition, you would find some two or three brethren or sisters agreeing to make him a particular subject of prayer. . . .

> Indeed that larger hotel in the town [Utica] became a centre of spiritual influence, and many were converted there. The stages, as they passed through, stopped at the hotel; and so powerful was the impression in the community, that I heard of several cases of persons that just stopped for a meal, or to spend a night, being powerfully convicted and converted before they left the town. Indeed, both in this place and in Rome, it was a common remark that nobody could be in the town, or pass through it, without being aware of the presence of God; that a divine influence seemed to pervade the place, and the whole atmosphere to be instinct with a divine life.[30]

In this way, the Second Great Awakening, as it came to be called, grew out of the Finney revivals in Oneida County in 1826 and 1827

and spread along the northern-tier states. Fully a decade passed before the revival spirit subsided, and nowhere was that spirit more in
evidence than along the route of the Erie Canal and its network of
connecting canals, the region Finney himself named "The Burned-
Over District."[31] The town of Whitesboro was in the center of the
fervor. Finney's wife, Lydia Andrews, was a native of Whitesboro, and
Finney visited there frequently. Among his earliest and most devout
followers was John Frost, the pastor of the Whitesboro First Presbyterian Church, the Berry family church.

In March 1832, Miriam and one of her sisters were converted by
Finney at one of his revival services at the Whitesboro Presbyterian
Church, and their names were added to the roster of church members. Then twenty-one years old, Miriam joined a host of women
who overwhelmingly outnumbered men in their positive response to
the preaching of Charles Finney. The role of women in the revivals, in
fact, became one of the major controversies of Finney's movement.
The more conservative leaders in the Presbyterian/Congregational
coalition were outraged that Finney and his "Holy Band" encouraged
women to pray in public and in "promiscuous" gatherings, that is,
where men were present. The issue was hotly debated for nearly three
days at a New Lebanon gathering of the church leadership, with
traditional leaders such as Lyman Beecher adamantly opposed to
Finney's tactics "to get females to pray in school houses and circles
where men, and *ministers* especially, are present to *see* and *hear* them
pray for them[selves] and others."[32] Beecher and his associates ultimately lost the battle; women not only continued to pray in public in
mixed company, they also occupied increasingly important roles in
the myriad reform movements that grew out of the revival fever.

One of the central tenets of Finney's evangelical message was the
belief that people held it within their power to change their own
hearts, and from there to change the larger society.[33] As a consequence, moral reform societies of all descriptions sprang up in Oneida
County in the 1830s and 1840s. Societies with all-female member-
ships and all-female officers emerged to carry the evangelical spirit
into the world at large. One such society, the Female Moral Reform
Society of New York, announced in its first annual report that it had
forty women members in its Whitesboro chapter alone. Dedicated to
"the reformation of abandoned females," the society pledged also

"not to countenance the man who is licentious."[34] Mindful that as an all-female society they were reaching into a public sphere that had been dominated by men, and that the nature of their reform demanded that they address openly a subject many people felt they should not address as women, they conceded that their cause rightfully demanded the strength of men. Their first annual report went on to say, however, that since all but one man had "retired" from the cause, they were "duty-bound to help him." They then offered the following caveat:

> When the husbands and fathers and sons will come up to this work with the noble spirit they evince in other labors of Christian philanthropy, the wives and mothers and daughters will gladly retire from their present prominent station in the cause of Moral Reform, and become, as they were designed to be, the efficient helpers of the stronger sex. . . . [Meanwhile], why not marshal yourselves in bands and become a terror to evil doers?[35]

As Mary Ryan argues in *The Cradle of the Middle Class*, the energy and concern evinced by such reformers did not rest on their claims that widespread sexual license and prostitution existed in towns such as Whitesboro and Utica, but upon a dramatic change taking place in the family structure throughout this area of upstate New York. The newly developing economic opportunities offered by the factories and commercial ventures brought an influx of young, single men and women with no nuclear or extended family to watch over their moral development. Family households for these workers were replaced by boardinghouses, which made many women anxious about the fate of these young people.[36] Possibly with considerable bemusement, but more likely with pride that their inn was superior to the dens of iniquity in Utica, Miriam Berry and her family watched the Whitesboro reform society set out to counteract the social degeneration its members attributed to life in boardinghouses.

According to Ryan, participation in these societies not only assuaged some of the women's anxieties but also gave them a sense of power and satisfaction.[37] In examining the membership and officer lists of the Utica societies, Ryan discovered that certain key names appeared over and again, suggesting that the women were assuming roles of genuine power and authority.[38] Moral reform societies were only one of the many kinds of associations that blossomed during this period; along the canal, societies representing every conceivable interest emerged and thrived for at least a time—mesmerism, phrenology, temperance and Bible societies; Sunday school associations and pacifism societies; health fads such as water cures and Graham's diet; prison and educational reform—all flourished in the decades following Finney's working of the citizens of Oneida County.[39]

Whitesboro made its unique contribution to the reform movement of the 1830s and 1840s with the foundation of the Oneida Institute in February 1826. The institute was the inspiration of George Washington Gale, the pastor who had originally converted Charles Finney to the evangelical cause and who had invited Finney to conduct revivals in the village of Western. Based on the innovative concept of combining manual labor and education, the Oneida Institute prepared young men for the ministry.[40] For several years the institute continued quietly under the leadership of Gale and with the support of the Whitesboro Presbyterian Church and a board of trustees consisting of members of the Whitesboro community and leaders in the revival movement. But in 1833 Gale retired from the institute to take his principles of manual labor to new frontiers, and he recruited the Reverend Beriah Green of the Western Reserve College to take over as the new head of the institute.

In Beriah Green's inaugural address to the Oneida Institute in the fall of 1833, he immediately plunged the institute into a major controversy by calling for the "immediate, unconditional, and uncompensated emancipation" of all American slaves.[41] Thus the radical cause that called for the immediate abolition of slavery was brought to Whitesboro, with far-reaching effects. Green at one point characterized the institute as "an abolitionist training camp," proclaiming in 1835 that "here . . . we are all abolitionists to a man—trustees-faculty- & students."[42] Less than a year after his inauguration, one of Green's goals for the institute began to become a reality with the enrollment of the first black student, Samuel A. Jackson. Jackson was admitted not only to the Oneida Institute but also to membership in the Whitesboro Presbyterian Church. Within a short time at least a dozen other young black men became students at the institute, and, presumably, members of the Whitesboro Presbyterian Church.[43]

The Oneida Institute made a profound contribution to the growing antislavery controversy. Strong national leaders emerged from its student body: Joshua B. Grinnell, Henry B. Stanton, and Theodore Dwight Weld, to name only three.[44] In addition, Green and his followers helped organize both a state and a national abolitionist society, convening a meeting of the New York State Anti-Slavery Society in Utica in 1835. Twice the Anti-Slavery Society was forced to break up its meeting because of attacks by mobs of so-called "gentlemen of property and standing"; finally the society had to move its meeting to the farm of Gerrit Smith, who ironically was radicalized by the mob's actions into an active role in the leadership of the society.[45]

The more conservative members of the town and the board of trustees were outraged by Green's radical actions; almost nowhere else in the United States in the 1830s, for example, were blacks and whites educated together in the classroom or permitted to live side by side in the same dormitories. Green insisted, nonetheless, that it was useless to demand reform in the distant South unless one practiced full equality at home. Under the pastorate of the Reverend Ira Pettibone, Beriah Green and his radical ideas initially found support in the Whitesboro Presbyterian Church, but with the arrival in 1836 of a new minister, David Ogden, the overt hospitality ended. Ogden was as conservative on the issue of slavery as Green was radical; he was a "Colonizationist," who favored sending American slaves back to Africa, and he denounced as "fanatics" the Whitesboro abolitionists.[46] Green retaliated in a series of eight letters published in *The Friend of Man*. Members of the Presbyterian church became embroiled in a debate that ended only when seventy-one "communicant members, including most of the elders, joined in the exodus [from the church] and put themselves under the leadership of Beriah Green." They organized an independent Congregational church in 1838.[47]

Miriam's father, who had been a trustee of the institute, had no sympathy for Green and remained faithful to the Presbyterian church. According to the Reverend Mr. Ogden, Lewis Berry characterized the institute as a place that offered only "lectures on Nigerology."[48] The Berry family divided sharply over the issues of abolition and Beriah Green; while Lewis Berry remained adamantly opposed to Green and his radical views, Miriam's sister Cornelia became an ardent supporter of Green and the abolitionist cause. She left the Presbyterian church to become one of the founding members of Green's church. Although Miriam herself did not become a member of the newly formed Congregational church, she clearly appreciated much for which Green stood. As late as the 1840s she reported going to hear Beriah Green preach whenever she could because "one *hears something* there."[49] Still, Miriam did not participate actively in the abolitionist cause, nor for that matter in any other of the major reform movements of the day. Instead, she kept out of public controversy while nevertheless apparently thriving on its taking place around her. Later, when confronted with a town that lacked Whitesboro's history of reform activity and social consciousness, she poked fun at the townspeople for their devotion to purely secular matters.

In direct response to the flurry of reform activity and the emergence of societies dedicated to a wide range of good causes, a group of young Whitesboro men and women established a society of their own dedicated to Momus, the Greek god of satire. By its very existence, the society made an ironic comment on what its members perceived as the comic excess endemic to the proliferation of reform societies. Calling itself the Mæonian Circle, "the group met twice a month at one another's homes for reading, music, and conversation. At the instigation of brother Morris and sister Kate—both enthusiastic members—Miriam Berry joined the society and soon became one of its stars, regaling the circle with humorous poems and essays."[50] The Mæonian Circle appears to have been Miriam's only venture into the public arena. Her participation symbolically represented her lifelong relationship to the larger society around her: she stood apart from it, yet she was continually amused by its excesses; she was comfortable only in company of like-minded friends and family; and she regarded all social turmoil with the sharpest satiric eye, using wit as both a personal defense against an intruding social world and as a public attack against changes that threatened what she saw as the proper social order.

Finding in the Mæonian Circle an enthusiastic new audience for her wit, Miriam Berry began to take her own writing more seriously. Sometime around 1838, when she was twenty-five years old, she began to write an extended literary burlesque to read to the circle a chapter at a time. Between April and August 1839, her literary burlesque was published serially in the Rome *Gazette* under the title

"The Widow Spriggins," with the author identified only by the pen name "Frank." And so it was as Frank that Miriam Berry first went before the reading public.

The name Frank probably originated earlier in her family as a diminutive of Frances, a name she never used for herself; one of her brothers or sisters no doubt dubbed her with the nickname when she was very young. It was a name that stuck, too, in the most intimate circles, for her husband used it as a term of endearment when he wrote about his wife to family members or close friends. The name would have appealed to her sense of humor, representing as it does the notion of earnestness or frankness, each an ironic term to apply to someone writing literary burlesque. Further, using a pseudonym was common practice. Because few writers of the day wanted to be identified as *mere* humorists, many authors, male and female alike, used pen names or identified themselves by their literary personae. But unlike Miriam, nineteenth-century women humorists more commonly adopted female, alliterative pseudonyms: Fanny Fern, Fanny Forester, Grace Greenwood. Only one—Sherwood Bonner—adopted a male-sounding name, so Miriam's choice of a male pseudonym invites further speculation.

Presenting herself as a male writer might have made it easier for Miriam to get her first work published if the editor thought he was publishing a bit of humor in the Seba Smith, Thomas Haliburton vein. A male name might also have given her more authority with her readers for critiquing female foolishness. However, when she published her first Widow Bedott sketch, she made no attempt to use her male pen name to deceive Joseph Neal, the editor of the *Saturday Gazette*, about her gender. He knew from the beginning that she was female, and in fact he knew exactly who she was. He in turn went to considerable pains to make his readers understand that Frank was not a man but a woman. By the time Miriam published in *Godey's Lady's Book*, she dropped her use of Frank and was identified only as "the author of the Widow Bedott."

Frank, then, was Miriam's public identification when she was most distant from her central persona, as in the figure of the Widow Spriggins, an obviously ridiculous character. By the time she created her most compassionate persona, Aunt Maguire, Miriam had fully shed her male identity. Thus while it is tempting to speculate that her use of Frank reveals an innate antifemale bias, her critique of female behavior was most severe when she was writing entirely from a female perspective. "The Widow Spriggins," by contrast, is a relatively light-hearted piece of burlesque humor.

"The Widow Spriggins"

The eleven-chapter "Widow Spriggins" series was written as a burlesque of Regina Maria Roche's *Children of the Abbey,* a popular sentimental English romance featuring an aristocratic heroine named Amanda. Miriam's heroine is a rustic, young country woman who self-consciously models her every action on Amanda's, rejecting everything in her own humble life that does not conform to the plot of her favorite book, *Children of the Abbey.* The enormous disparity between Miriam's heroine, Permilly Ruggles, and Permilly's role model, Amanda—the circumstances of their lives, their education, their social standing—sets up the basic humor of the story. Permilly is an uneducated, rude, and extremely foolish young woman who is so taken by the world of romance that she attempts to live just as "Amandy" did, but under vastly different conditions. This instantly renders Permilly a ridiculous figure, a comic buffoon.

Whitcher's "The Widow Spriggins" had one important literary precedent, Charlotte Lennox's 1752 literary burlesque, *The Female Quixote.* Lennox's novel is an extended spoof on French romances and the foolish young ladies who took them seriously. Her heroine, Arabella, was raised in social isolation in the English countryside by her widowed father, a marquis. Cut off from "real" society, Arabella received all her ideas about courtship from French romances that her late mother had left in her father's library. From the romances, Arabella learned an impossibly high standard of expectations for any future suitor, plus an inflated language for expressing herself. The central action of the burlesque centers on a courtship theme, with Arabella expecting her suitor, Glanville, to overcome countless obstacles and to endure long years of absence from her to prove himself worthy of her love. On all other subjects Arabella is a charming and sane young woman, but on the topic of romance she seems literally deranged to those who do not understand her arcane points of reference or her quixotic tendency to confuse ordinary passersby with sinister figures, or common gardeners with disappointed noblemen. In addition, she is blessed with an uncanny memory for the details of the many romances she has read, and she continually cites them as her authorities.

Like Lennox, Miriam Berry created a heroine who took literally the story of her romance heroine, Amanda. Like Arabella, Miriam's Permilly Ruggles applies the artificial world of romance to her "real" world of Podunk, New York, and like Arabella, Permilly keeps her one true suitor at bay by imposing on him the expectations of a romance hero. Both heroines attract mock-suitors who understand the conventions of romance and exploit them for their own amusement. Unlike the true suitors, the mock-heroes speak the inflated language of the romances, which the heroines find irresistible.

On the subject of language itself Miriam Berry departs from Lennox's burlesque with a brilliant comic innovation: Lennox's Arabella is a rightful member of the aristocracy, but even for her the language of romance represents an artificially high style; Miriam's Amanda is an untutored country bumpkin whose natural language represents an exaggerated low style. Thus, Permilly's attempts to duplicate the language of romance are only more comic, more absurd. The result is a rich linguistic humor with striking scenes and passages in which Permilly's hopelessly mundane world clashes with the equally improbable world of romance: Sancho Panza tries to become Don Quixote.

The relatively uncomplicated plot of "The Widow Spriggins" focuses primarily on Permilly Ruggles's adventures out in the world, and in particular on her imagined betrothal to the false lover, Philander. At the story's beginning, Permilly leaves home because her father wants her to marry a local merchant who in no way measures up to her expectations for a romantic hero. After a series of misadventures in which Permilly persuades her younger sister to reject the suitor for her, their father threatens to whip Permilly into submission.[51] Instead, Permilly locks her father in a room, takes his purse, and leaves home to live with her aunt and uncle in Higgins Patent, New York—an inauspicious beginning for one who models her life on the fair Amanda.

Permilly Ruggles's arrival in Higgins Patent attracts the attention of a young man who calls himself Philander and who immediately courts her as though he, too, were a character out of *Children of the*

Abbey. In reality he is a student named Johnson who is home on vacation from Hamilton College and who sees an opportunity to amuse himself and his friends at Permilly's expense. After first professing his love, he tells her that he has to leave town. When she asks him for a picture of himself to ponder in his absence, he scribbles a childish drawing on a piece of paper, which she then puts in a tobacco tin and wears around her neck. To pass the time in Higgins Patent until Philander returns, and to earn some money, Permilly decides to open a school for young women, although she has absolutely no qualifications for doing so. Remarkably, even after they have a chance to interview her, many of the local families decide to send their daughters to her school. On the whole, the men understand that Permilly speaks gibberish, but their wives are impressed with what they see as the brilliance of her speech:

> [Deacon Peabody:] "Well, I never heerd sich a master sight of crooked words in my day. I rather guess my dorter han't no casion to lairn sich stuff. . . .
>
> [Mrs. Peabody:] "I ruther guess, mister Deacon Peabody, ittle be as I say. My Mirandy shall go to this ere young woman's school, for I never heerd nobody use eleganter language in my life, so you may shet yer head."[52]

Meanwhile, egged on by Johnson (Philander), three Hamilton College students repeatedly pay mock homage to Permilly, escorting her home from her school on an old nag, for example, and generally setting her up to be the butt of their jokes. Their attentions notwithstanding, she continues to remain faithful to Philander, telling imagined admirers that she cannot listen to their pleas for her hand. One such person, a local schoolteacher, genuinely admires her, but she discourages him.

Before long, attendance at her school drops, and Permilly learns that her mother is gravely ill back in Podunk. Although her father does not want her to come home and disturb the peace of the family, her mother repeatedly asks for her, and so her father sends for Permilly. Bidding a hasty farewell to Higgins Patent, Permilly sets off for Podunk by stage with a man who turns out to be Johnson/Philander's brother.

When he realizes what his brother has done, the man releases Permilly from her imagined betrothal by telling her that Philander has married another woman. While Permilly never catches on that Johnson and Philander are one and the same, she does come to understand that the three college students have been mocking her, and she soon has the opportunity to give them a thorough tongue-lashing. It is her only unaffected moment in the entire story.

Permilly arrives home to learn that her mother was buried the day before. The relationship between Permilly and her father is not much improved, so she is especially pleased when Jabez Spriggins, the school teacher from Higgins Patent, follows her to Podunk to propose marriage to her in the language of Lord Mortimer. She accepts his proposal, and they set off immediately for Utica, where they marry and spend their honeymoon in Oneida County.[53] There the story ends because *Children of the Abbey* ends when Amanda gets married, but Permilly adds a note to the effect that her marriage to Jabez Spriggins lasted fifteen years, until his death. At the time of the novel's historical present, she reports that she is about to marry Jabez's best friend, and so the story ends with not one, but two marriages for the heroine.

For an extended first work, "The Widow Spriggins" has much to recommend it, although it was never as popular as Miriam's more famous sketches featuring the Widow Bedott and Aunt Maguire. "The Widow Spriggins" nonetheless bears the unmistakable imprint of Miriam Berry Whitcher, who explores here some of the major themes and characteristics that she would later perfect. Foremost among these is her development of a first-person female narrator who speaks in a rustic, vernacular voice. Embedded within the comic first-person voice of Permilly Ruggles lies an energetic sense of play with language that transcends even Miriam's burlesque intention: the linguistic humor that is introduced in the first paragraph of this novel will remain central to her work right through her final Aunt Maguire story:

> I was born in Podunk, a charmin' and sequesterated villidge on the banks of the morantic and meanderin' Mohawk. My father's name was Nathan Ruggles; he was an emigranter from Vermount, and he married a Dutch young woman by the name of Vine Hogobome, a

natyve of Podunk. I was the oldest of ten children, five boys and five gearls. The boys was Nadab and Abihu, (twins), Cornelus, Bemas, and Gad. The gearls was Permilly, (that's me,) Mirtilly, Ketury, (that's a Dutch name,) Axy, and Vine. But I was the flower of the family. I've heern my mother tell that I was a wonderful cretur from the time I was knee high to a hop-toad. Afore I was 10 years old I knowd eny most all the primmer, and I could say them are vasses in't clean from "In Adam's fall," to "Zaccheus he did climb the tree," without missin' a word. And when I want but fourteen I knowd by heart, all that are gret long piece of poitry that John Rogers writ jest afore he was burnt to a stake. (p. 39)

As this paragraph demonstrates, hardly a sentence will pass from Permilly Ruggles Spriggins's lips that does not contain multiple misspellings, malapropisms, and strange constructions. Many of these are created because Permilly Ruggles tries so hard to imitate her heroine, Amanda, but others because they are the staple fare of vernacular humor: "My hair was of that lovely hue that folks calls red and novils calls auburn. Sometimes I suffered it to flow cerlessly over my alagaster sholders, and sometimes I confined it on the tip top of my head with a quill. My face was considered imminently honsome. My figger was oncommon greaceful, and I had a gret deal of dignitude" (p. 40). Elsewhere she speaks of being "manured" [immured] in a factory, of meeting someone "of Dutch distraction" [extraction] and of protecting a "shemale heart" (pp. 53, 114, 133).

Permilly Ruggles's abuse of English reaches its finest comic effect when she writes an advertisement announcing her intention to start a school for the girls of Higgins Patent:

Miss Ruggles, racently from Podunk, bein' obligated by unrecountable misfortins to lobsquander from the hum of her childhood, and desirin' to devairt her mawlancolly mind sumhow—would conform the inhabiters of Higgins Patent, and its civinity, that she has resolved to instruct a siminary of young wimmin, or shemales, from six years old along up. Miss R. would insure the public of her complete comptitude to undertake this undertakin', and hasn't no doubt she'll giv gineral satisfaction. Besides understandin' all the branches that's taught in any siminary she will larin 'em to paint on velvet, and to be perlite, and she don't want nobody to think she's a going to do it for money, for she dispises remoneyration, and only jest wants to teach to pervent herself from sinkin' in despair. She caliates to begin on Monday the 15th of June. (p. 57)

One of the central themes announced in "The Widow Spriggins" and carried over to the Widow Bedott sketches is the heroine's determination to write "occasional" poetry. Both widows are poets of comically poor quality who subject their neighbors, even casual acquaintances, to the products of their imaginations. Permilly Ruggles's favorite topic is her love for Philander. Here, for example, are a few lines she composed while sitting on a log and contemplating Philander's departure from her:

> 'Twas here I parted with Philander,
> Thro' the wide world he's gone to wander,
> Six times the mornin' sun has rizen
> Sen I beheld that face of hisn.
> . . . .
> The sorrers I indure; Good Landy!
> Are like the sorrers of Amandy.
> But whilst I'm blest with sich a beau,
> I'm willin' for to suffer woe.
>
> (p. 75)

The magnum opus of this work, however, is inspired by the death of Permilly's mother. Guided even here by how Amandy behaved at *her* mother's grave, Permilly produces the following poem "in about 15 minnits":

THE DISAPPINTED

> O! what a cat-a-strophy dire
>   In Podunk did befall,
> When she was called for to ixpire,
>   And leave us mournin' all.
>
> O! never was there greef afore
>   Like that of poor Permilly:
> That fair and interestin' flower:
>   That pale and droopin' lilly.

My heart is broke; my P.[hilander] estranged,
    My fond affections crushed,
My plans of futur' bliss derannged,
    And all my prospects squshed.

The world onfeelin', cruil, cold,
    Looks on with wonderin' eye,
My misery for to behold—
    I certingly shall die.

And when at last my heart-strings snap,
    And all my woes is dun,
O take the follerin' epitap
    And 'scribe it on my stun:

O! strannger, stop and wipe yer eyes,
    And spend a minnit weepin';
A broken-hearted sperrit lies
    Beneath this tombstun sleepin'.
                (pp.131–32)

Miriam Berry's mockery of romantic heroines and the growing army of women poets whose verse appeared in local newspapers (just as Permilly's poem above was printed in "the Mohawk Meteor and Marcy Republican") extended to members of the Mæonian Circle, herself included. Miriam's interest in writing verse did not end with childhood; her first published work (now lost) was a poem she wrote for the Mæonian Circle that another member, probably her brother, submitted to the local newspaper, and her first published work for Joseph Neal (Neal's *Saturday Gazette*) was a poem. Throughout her career she continued to write and publish serious verse, including several hymns she wrote for "The Gospel Messenger."[54]

In addition to her fascination with language, especially vernacular language as a vehicle for humor, three themes that emerge in nascent form in "The Widow Spriggins" become increasingly important to her later work. One of these is Permilly Ruggles's concern for the rituals of courtship, which are much more important to her than the character of the man who is courting. Permilly herself is not terribly concerned to find a husband (she repeatedly imagines "attachments" to herself where there are none), but her father raises several times the specter of her becoming an old maid—he would "bet a beef critter" on it:

> "Me an old maid?" says I, "Ile tell ye what, old feller, there's more young men than you could shake a stick at that would jump sky high to git me."
> "I gess they'de jump sky high *arter* they'de got ye," says he.
> I lookt at my hoggish payrent with a look of suverin' contemp, and riz up and went into my chomber. (p. 130)

The same tendency to imagine suitors where none exists also afflicts the Widow Bedott, but she has no concern whatsoever with courtship, only with an obsessive desire to find a husband. Widowhood sits heavily on her; she feels it not only as a profound loss of status in the community but also as a major financial liability. While Permilly Ruggles makes a fool of herself over her imagined suitor, Philander, the Widow Bedott makes a spectacle of herself trying to capture every widower who enters her sphere.

A second theme in "The Widow Spriggins" becomes by the end of Miriam's career an issue of the greatest significance: the code of gentility. Throughout her humorous works, women are targeted for ridicule directly in proportion to their aspirations to become genteel. At first a topic for goodnatured burlesque, gentility ultimately comes to represent for her a major human and social failure. The only direct reference to the theme in "The Widow Spriggins" occurs as part of a local joke: "The young man that set aside of me [on the stage] . . . was a rael slick lookin' feller—he telld me he lived in Utica; and like most of the residers of that extensyve and anncient city he was oncommon ginteel in his appearance, and refined in his monners" (p. 108). Indirectly, however, it is a key issue. The very language Amanda speaks and Permilly attempts to imitate represents a genteel departure from an implied norm, an idealized, romanticized version of "real" language.

Whether Permilly's aspirations to gentility assume a linguistic form or reside in her overt actions, her strongest, and most foolish statements about gentility concern her ideas about fashion. She always tries to make an impression with her appearance, and characteristically she accepts stares of disbelief for looks of envy and admiration.

> I reckoned twas time to habiliate myself for the company that was a comin' to see me, so I onlocked my chist, and took out a white dimity with a long short with a blue ribbin' round the botton on't, and put it on, and tied a red sash round my waist; then I took and tied a yaller ribbin round my head and stuck a number of mornin' glories in it; then I huv a pink silk long shawl round my neck, and my twilight was completed. So you see I didn't depart from the elegant simplicity always conspicious in my dress. (p. 60)

At this point in her career, Miriam had created only one character who embodied such a preoccupation with fashion and finery, but by the time she wrote her final sketches featuring Aunt Maguire, many of Permilly Ruggles's values had overtaken the larger female community. For Miriam, gentility came to represent not simply idiosyncratic bad taste inspired by romance novels, but a cancer eating away at more fundamental human values. In the decade that followed, burlesque ultimately gave way to biting social satire in the writing of Miriam Berry Whitcher.[55]

3
❧

Marriage and "The Widow Bedott"

The years 1846–47 proved to be two of the most eventful in Miriam's life: in 1846 she became a member of the newly founded St. John's Episcopal Church of Whitesboro; she became engaged to the church's pastor, Benjamin William Whitcher; and she published her first Widow Bedott sketch in Neal's *Saturday Gazette*. In the following year she married William, continued to write for the *Gazette,* where her work caught the attention of Louis Godey, with whom she subsequently published her first Aunt Maguire sketch; and before the year was out, she had moved to Elmira, New York, casting her fate, as she felt, with a village filled with strangers. Leaving her family and friends behind was traumatic for Miriam, but even with all her anxieties about how she would fare in Elmira as the new wife of the Episcopalian minister, life in Elmira fueled her comic imagination.

In 1806 a group of local women formed the Whitestown Female Charitable Society, amassing annual sums in the treasury as high as $125 to sponsor missionary activities; typically, they sent their money to the Hampshire Missionary Society.[1] In 1844 a society such as the one supported by the Whitesboro women appointed an Episcopalian missionary, the Reverend Benjamin William Whitcher, to serve several Oneida County villages. On August 1, 1844, William arrived in the area and began his missionary work; within three months, he was focusing all his attention on just two villages, Whitesboro and Oriskany.

William Whitcher was born in Rochester, Vermont, on December 8, 1811. He, too, came from an English family that had been in America for more than a century; its most illustrious member was William's first cousin, the poet John Greenleaf Whittier. William graduated from Geneva College in 1840 at the age of twenty-nine, then studied theology at the General Theological Seminary of the Protestant Episcopal Church in New York City. After being ordained by Bishop De Lancey in 1844, he received his first church assignment as the missionary to Oneida County.[2]

Under William's leadership, the Whitesboro Episcopal Church began to prosper, and on December 23, 1845, it was officially organized under the name of St. John's Parish.[3] Two wardens and six vestrymen were chosen; one of the latter was Miriam's brother, Lewis. The first celebration of Holy Communion took place on June 7, 1846, with thirteen communicants participating from the parish, and two from outside. Three months later, on August 2, 1846, Miriam Berry was confirmed as a member of the church. It was a very solemn occasion for her, as she explained to her sister Kate, who supported her in what Miriam described as her "defection" from her father's church:

> I missed you very much on Monday. It was a very solemn & impressive day to me & to every one. We were all delighted with the Bishop's manner of conducting the service. I say 'we'—but I scarcely know how I felt myself, I was so agitated. During the sermon, which precedes the confirmation, I tried very hard to fire my mind upon the speaker, but it kept wandering to myself, & the awful vow which I was about to take, & I had great difficulty to maintain my composure, & keep from bursting into tears, but I was enabled to get through with it better than I expected, for though I trembled violently when the holy hands were laid upon my head, no one but Mr. Whitcher noticed it—he stood very near. Well might I tremble at my unworthiness of so great a blessing.
>
> > "Forever on my soul be traced that blessing clear that dove-like hand—a sheltering rock in memory's waste—o'ershadowing all the weary land".
>
> You can hardly imagine what a relief it is to be able to express my feelings without restraint—to be settled, whatever the world may say, to feel that I have a home. The Bishop's sermon was very solemn & eloquent—sometimes almost awful—his subject was 'the Judgment' & after the confirmation he addressed the class confirmed in the most impressive manner.[4]

The letter, a long one, goes on to say that after the confirmation the Berry family had a "good many of the clergy to dinner," and that the bishop himself stayed at Berry's Inn, much to Mr. Berry's pleasure.

Leaving her father's church and taking vows in the Episcopal church was a matter of the utmost seriousness to Miriam, yet she was considerably amused by the way Mr. Long, the minister of the Whitesboro Presbyterian Church, went about transferring her membership. Rather than admit she was changing denominations, "he wrote a recommendation to 'the First Presbyterian Church at Utica, or any other church of Jesus Christ where in the providence of God I might go.' But he was very good & kind about it, & did not appear at all displeased at any going off, & I'm sure I do not wonder—for I never was an efficient member. I fancy they would not let you off so easy."[5] As will become clear later, the Reverend Mr. Long always proved to be a source of amusement to Miriam, even when he was associated with the solemn topic of death.

At the time Miriam was writing this letter to her sister, William Whitcher was not only her pastor but also her fiancé. No two events in her adult life affected her more profoundly than her conversion to Episcopalianism and her marriage to William, yet her ability to see the comic possibilities in such a convergence of events led her ironically to pattern the behavior of the foolish Widow Bedott on her own life's events. It was a source of great mirth in the Widow Bedott sketches that the Widow ultimately abandoned all her outspoken prejudices in favor of the Methodist denomination and against the Baptist to marry the Reverend Shadrack Sniffles, a Mr. Long–type figure. Especially given the disparity between Miriam herself and the character she created in the Widow Bedott, the parallels between the two characters reveal how fully Miriam was able to poke fun at herself and her own situation. Even as Miriam Berry was falling in love with William and preparing to make major changes in her life, she created an archetypically comic character preoccupied with finding a husband to relieve her of her long-endured widowhood.

Neither Miriam Berry nor William Whitcher was young when they met, by nineteenth-century standards, and Miriam especially was well past her prime marriageable years; theirs was clearly a marriage inspired by love and affection. In April 1846 they traveled together to

Saratoga, where they visited her sister, Elizabeth Barbour, and where no doubt Miriam introduced William to the maternal side of her family in nearby Cambridge, New York. Miriam's buoyancy and optimism at this point in her life are evident in a poem she published in Neal's *Saturday Gazette* (July 1845). The first half of the six-stanza poem entitled "Saratoga Sunset" describes her inability to express the depth of her joy at seeing a "gorgeous sunset glow," while the second half regrets that human sin has marred Earth's beauty. Even so, the poem insists, the beauty of the Saratoga sunset lies beyond the reach even of man's destructive powers. The touch of sadness that emerges in this poem is overridden by Miriam's private sense of hope ignited by her relationship with William: "O that my lips could speak / All that is kindling in my spirit now; / But words, alas! are weak."

The Widow Bedott's Table Talk

The fall of 1846 was an especially productive creative period for Miriam. Her first extant published poem appeared in Neal's *Saturday Gazette* on July 11, and the next issue contained a second, "Hope Ever." This poem urges the "pilgrim along time's weary track" to look toward the future instead of the past. The same July issue also contained a public acknowledgment by Neal that he had received a new story about a woman named "the Widow Bedott" that he would publish shortly. On August 1, the day before her confirmation at St. John's, Miriam's first sketch appeared on the first page of the *Gazette* under the title, "The Widow Bedott's Table Talk." The only authorial identification for this and all subsequent Widow Bedott sketches published in the *Gazette* was her pseudonym, "Frank."[6] Before the calendar year was over, Miriam Berry had published a succession of six Widow Bedott sketches in the *Gazette,* creating a readership that seemed never to get enough of her work. Only her insistence on anonymity prevented Miriam from establishing a significant public reputation as a humorist during this period, for according to Joseph Neal, from the moment of its first appearance, "The Widow Bedott's Table Talk" created "a sensation":

We are pleased to find—both for "Frank's" sake, and in confirmation of our own judgment—that "The Widow Bedott's Table Talk"—a second number of which is given to-day—is received with such general favor. The "Table Talk" makes a sensation; and among our numerous array of correspondents, there are few who do not ask something about the Widow Bedott, coupled with the highest praises of the manner in which she is presented to the public. A lady—herself distinguished in the walks of literature—declares that the first number of the "Table-Talk" aforesaid, is one of the best papers that has appeared in the present volume of "Neal"; and there are no differences of opinion relative to these capital delineations of unsophisticated nature, which almost induce us to believe that we, too, are listening to the garrulous relict of the respected Deacon. But we are not at liberty to answer questions here, further than to say that "Frank," so well acquainted with the Bedott family, is not Francis, but Frances—a lady, not a gentleman, as some suppose; and we may challenge the best of our humorous writers, to surpass the "Table Talk" in any of the qualities which constitute excellence in this species of composition.[7]

The first sketch that Neal referred to above is in fact vintage "Widow Bedott," a favorite not only of nineteenth-century readers but also of anthologists of our own day.[8] Although less pointed, less biting than some of her later sketches, it displays many of the characteristics that made the Widow Bedott stories famous. The sketch is written in the first-person vernacular voice of the Widow herself, who speaks directly to the reader as though he or she were sitting with her at her kitchen table. The sketch, supposedly focusing on a memorable statement that the late Deacon Bedott once said to his wife, ranges over a number of subjects connected only by the Widow's thought association and by her incessant need for self-justification. Miriam's use in these sketches of the first-person vernacular technique is analogous in its effects to a dramatic monologue: the narrator reveals far more about herself than she intends, with much of the humor residing in the discrepancy between what she says about herself and her neighbors, and what she inadvertently reveals. The voice of the Widow Bedott is one of the most entertaining to be found in the humor of the era; less extreme in her malapropisms than her predecessor, the

Widow Spriggins, the Widow Bedott nevertheless delights with her turns of speech, with her mistakes, with the authenticity of her country language. As one authority on New York literature observed, "Mrs. Whitcher's ear was as sharp as her eye, and so the dialect of her sketches is probably the most authentic representation in our literature of the speech of nineteenth century Yorker villages and farms."[9] Above all, the Widow Bedott's monologues entertain:

> He was a wonderful hand to moralize, husband was, 'specially after he begun to enjoy poor health. He made an observation once when he was in one of his poor turns that I never shall forget the longest day I live. He says to me one winter evenin' as we was a settin' by the fire, I was a knittin' (I was always a wonderful great knitter) and he was a smokin' (he was a master hand to smoke, though the doctor used to tell him he'd be better off to let tobacker alone; when he was well, used to take his pipe and smoke a spell after he'd got the chores done up, and when he wa'n't well, used to smoke the biggest part o' the time). Well, he took his pipe out of his mouth and turned toward me, and I knowed something was comin', for he had a pertikkeler way of lookin' round when he was gwine to say any thing oncommon. Well, he says to me, says he, "Silly," (my name was Prissilly naterally, but he ginerally called me "Silly," cause 'twas handier, you know.) Well, he says to me, says he, "Silly," and he looked pretty sollem, I tell you, he had a sollem countenance naterally—and after he got to be deacon 'twas more so, but since he'd lost his health he looked sollemer than ever, and certingly you wouldent wonder at it if you knowed how much he underwent. He was troubled with a wonderful pain in his chest. (pp. 21–22)

Before the sketch is finished, the Widow Bedott interrupts herself no fewer than half a dozen times; once she even contrasts herself favorably to Poll Bingham whom she accuses of being "the tejusest individooal to tell a story that ever I see in all my born days" because she never comes "to the pint" (p. 23). This story itself is pointless, of course, but the manner of its telling and the portrait it reveals of the Widow captivated not only that first generation of readers of Miriam's "Table Talk" but also generations of readers through the second half of the nineteenth century. By November 1846, Whitcher's sketch enjoyed a fate common to the best newspaper humor of the era—it was reprinted in other newspapers, without attribution and without compensation. Joseph Neal was greatly pleased, reprinting first for his readers a compliment paid to the unknown author of the sketch, then pleading for his contemporaries to give due credit to the *Gazette* and to the sex of the author:

> The first number of "the Widow Bedott's Table Talk" is floating about the newspapers, with no credit to afford evidence of its origin, but with the subjoined complimentary prefix, which seems to require a word from us:

> "Widow Bedott—We do not know the author of the following brief sketch of a long winded lady, but he is certainly entitled to a place in the same niche with Tom Hood and Major Jones."

> While agreeing fully in the commendation thus bestowed, allow us once for all to insist upon it that "Frank"—the author of the "Table Talk"—is not a gentleman, but a lady; and allow us also to state that the "Table Talks" have always appeared originally in the Gazette. "Frank" is a correspondent to be proud of, and we do wish that our contemporaries, in republishing her writings, would contrive to give the proper credit both to "Frank" and to the Gazette.[10]

Miriam was lucky to publish in Neal's *Saturday Gazette*. Joseph Neal, whose own reputation as a humorist was already well established with the 1838 publication of his satiric *Charcoal Sketches,* was quick to recognize talents in others. Popular writers who published in the *Gazette* during this era included Timothy Shay Arthur, Ann Stephens, Grace Greenwood, Ned Buntline, William T. Thompson, and on at least one occasion, Charles Dickens. Nonetheless, Miriam's work always received top billing and was prominently displayed on the front page. As with other publications of its day, the *Gazette* was eclectic in its purpose and scope. By its own proclamation, it was "devoted to domestic and foreign literature, news, agriculture, science, arts, amusement, and commercial and monetary affairs—independent of party or sect." Although this was ambitious coverage for a newspaper that was only four pages long, each page measured nearly two feet by three feet, with little space taken up by illustrations. The rare exceptions to this rule were Miriam's own occasional illustrations for "Table Talk" and the maps that frequently accompanied articles about the war in Mexico. The back page, called the "Ladies' Museum," also sometimes reproduced fashions from *Godey's* magazine, but never the full-page color prints that made the latter so famous. Published weekly, the *Gazette's* subscriptions sold for two dollars per year. Joseph Neal himself was more than just a publisher of Miriam Whitcher's work. He offered her words of encouragement at key points when her confidence lagged, he "introduced" her to Louis Godey at the latter's request, and he printed the Widow Bedott sketches as quickly as she could produce them.

Between mid-August and the end of 1846, Miriam Berry published five more Widow Bedott sketches in the *Saturday Gazette*. The scope of the humor in these sketches broadened as the Widow moved about in the community, but the Widow Bedott and the values she upheld remained the primary targets of the humor: she is a recognizable, if greatly exaggerated, village type—a gossip, a commentator on the social business of her neighbors, and above all else, a middle-aged widow with two grown children who is eager to be shed of her widowhood. In spite of her protestations to the contrary, she remained a widow only because she was unsuccessful in finding someone to replace her deceased husband, who left her nearly penniless in difficult circumstances. ("But now he's dead! the thought is killin' / My grief I can't control— / He never left a single shillin / His widder to console" [p. 30]). Any time she begins to arouse pity or sympathy, however, she immediately undercuts it by spreading some mean-spirited, self-serving gossip about her rivals or her would-be suitors.

According to Ann Douglas, the status of the widow in nineteenth-century America reveals a great deal about how the society viewed women in general:

> By the early nineteenth century...widows were conventionally viewed as pitiful charity cases. Numerous organizations formed to relieve "widows and orphans," stories turning on the pathos of the newly widowed bride or mother were popular. . . . In common nineteenth-century conception, the widow waited for a man—a brother, a son, a new lover—to help her; any show of self-reliance was valuable chiefly as evidence of her worthiness of such aid. She had no communal tasks deemed appropriate to her widowed state; she was obligated to undertake nothing but the heavily self-involved busi-

ness of mourning. The process of adjustment was seen as a private and psychological one. The widow had become a source of sentimentality; a woman without a man was an emblem of frailty and unproductivity.[11]

As would so often be the case in Miriam's humor, one of the chief targets of her wit was precisely the sentimentality Douglas identifies above. Nothing about the Widow Bedott could be said to be sentimental, either her character itself as it unfolds in the sketches or the attitudes she expresses. Nor, for that matter, was she in any degree frail; she was as hardy a vernacular character as is found in northeastern humor. In this regard, she overturns the common stereotype of the nineteenth-century widow, that is, Whitcher insisted on debunking the image of women as frail and sentimental. On the other hand, the Widow Bedott can be seen as reinforcing other parts of the stereotype: she believes her well-being depends upon finding a husband, and being excluded from any meaningful social position in the community, she fills her days with gossip.[12] Thus Whitcher, through the Widow Bedott, explodes the image of the fragile, dependent, sentimental widow while at the same time dramatizing the plight of women who have no meaningful role in the society unless they belong to a man. The Widow Bedott is desperate to find a husband, and in that desperation she is at once a comical character because of her excessive behavior and represents a serious indictment of the society that deprives her of social status in her own right.

In the third sketch, "Widow Jenkins' *[sic]* Animosity," the Widow Bedott learns that Timothy Crane, a man she has just described with contempt, is returning from the West because his wife has died. She immediately changes her tune about him: "He's an amazin' fine man. I said he dident know nothing? Kier Bedott, how you *dew* misunderstand. I meant that he was a wonderful unoffensive man, well-disposed toward every body" (p. 37). In her excitement over Mr. Crane's return, she almost forgets that she started out to tell why Poll Bingham Jinkins is her enemy; at the mention of Poll's name, she redoubles her attack on her character:

now I should n't wonder if she should set tew and try tew ketch Mr. Crane when he comes back, should you? I'll bet forty great apples she'll dew it, she's been ravin' distracted to git married ever since she was a widder, but I ruther guess Timothy Crane ain't a man to be took in by such a great fat, humbly, slanderin' old butter tub. She's as gray as a rat, tew, that are hair o' hern's false. . . . I think 't would be a good idear for some friendly person to warn Mr. Crane aginst Poll Jinkins as soon as he gits here, don't you? I *dew* feel for Mr. Crane. (p. 38)

The return of Widower Crane only stimulates her to step up her pursuit of widowers in general, and Timothy Crane in particular. Her behavior is shameless; the more she protests that she would never "change her condition" of widowhood, the more desperately she tries to change it. Her moves are bold. When Mr. Crane stops by to see her, as she has requested, she slanders Poll Bingham and plays on his emotions about his two "poor motherless daughters," boasting about how well her own children turned out. She then explains that she feels so upset about *his* "moloncolly sittywation I can't scarcely sleep o' nights. I've jest begun a piece o' poitry describin' you[r] feelins. . . ."

> Trypheny Crane! Trypheny Crane!
> And shan't we never meet no more?
> My buzzom heaves with turrible pain
> While I thy ontimely loss deplore.
> (pp. 44–45)

In the fifth sketch, "A Discourse on Pumpkins," the Widow Bedott hears that Crane is ill and forces her way past his housekeeper and into his parlor. Her ostensible purpose is to bring him the remaining forty-nine verses of the poem and to suggest cures for his ailment. Cornered, Crane is forced to listen to the Widow slander his help, Betsey, gossip about Poll Bingham, and generally sympathize with his situation from the perspective of one who has also lost her partner. The Widow Bedott insists that Mr. Crane try one of her husband's cures for chest pains—"skoke" berries soaked in rum. When he protests that he is a temperance man, she brushes aside his concerns: "You see the skoke berries counterects the alkyhall in the rum, and annyliates all its intosticatin' qualities. We jest put the rum on to make it keep." Her egotism knows no bounds; even her offers of sympathy are designed to insinuate herself into his good graces, certainly not to make him feel better: "You must feel yer loss oncommonly when you ain't well, Mr. Crane. If ever a departed companion's missed—seems to me it must be when the afflicted surviver's sick—'specially if its a *widiwer* that's lost his wife" (pp. 50–51).

In this sketch, something new happens: Whitcher introduces domestic details that take on particular significance for women's humor. For one, such details legitimate women's domestic arena by seeming to savor even the smallest items that make up women's daily lives. For another, they ground the humor that grows out of that arena in a distinctively female world, yet the humor is not *about* domesticity; Miriam never attempted to establish women's domestic world as in any way superior to the male public sphere, nor did she mock it. Even though the Widow Bedott brings domestic details into her conversation with the same self-congratulatory tone she adopts for all other topics, they begin to assume positive values of their own. Most of this sketch takes place, figuratively, in the Widow's kitchen. In running down Poll Bingham Jinkins, for example, she lists all the items Poll used to borrow from her—bread, tea, molasses, sugar, bake pans, washboards. Then she moves to her ostensible topic, which is the one time when the tables were turned and the Widow Bedott was forced to borrow from Poll. The item? One "miserable poor punkin" that the Widow borrowed when their own crop failed:

Well, next day Melissy and me we cut up the punkin—'twas dretful small and wonderful thin—and when I come to stew it—my gracious! how it *did* stew away! The fact is 'twas a miserable *poor* punkin—good punkins don't stew down to nothin' so. Milessy *[sic]* she lookt into the pot and says she to me, says she, "Granf'ther grievous! why mar I'm afeard this ere punkin's gwine to exasperate intirely, so ther won't be nun left on't." Well sure enough—arter 'twas sifted—as true as the world, Mr. Crane—ther want more'n a pint on't. "Why, mar," Milessy, says she—" 't wont make more'n *one* good sized pie." "Never you fear," says I—"I'll bet forty gret apples I'll git three pies out on't any way." Some folks, you know, puts eggs in punkin pies, but accordin' to my way o' thinkin, tain't no addition. When I have plenty o' punkin I never use 'em—but Miss Jinkinses punkin turned out so small, I see I shouldent have nun to speak on without I put in eggs; so I takes my punkin and I stirs in my molasses, and my milk, and my eggs, and my spices, and I fills three of my biggest pie-pans. "There," says I to Melissy, "did n't I say I'd make three pies, and, hain't I did it?" "Yes," says she, "but they're purty much all ingrejiences, and precious little punkin." (pp. 54–55)

According to the rest of the story, Poll waited until the pies were in the oven, then presented herself at the Widow's kitchen to sit a spell. She accepts the Widow's invitation to have a piece of pie when it is done, then helps herself to half the pie, leaving the other half for the Widow because she finds it too thin for her taste. Then, much to the Widow's surprise, Poll also picks up the two uncut pies and heads out the door for home.

> Arter she'd gone, I lookt at Melissy and Melissy lookt at me in a perfect state o' dumfounderment! we was so bethunderstruck, 't was as much as five minnits I guess afore ary one of us spoke a word. At last says Melissy says she, "Did you ever!" "No, never! never!" says I, and then we sot up such a tremendous laff that Kier heerd us (he was to work out doors), and he came in to see what was the matter, so I told him—and good gracious how he *did* roar! I tell you, he hain't never let me hear the last o' that punkin. (p. 57)

In the sketches Miriam Berry wrote in the fall of 1846, she began, too, to move the Widow Bedott out into the community where the author discovered the fullest canvas for her art. Although the Widow Spriggins had by no means been confined to the kitchen— in fact she was surprisingly mobile for an unmarried female heroine— Miriam's early series never focused on village activities; her focus remained fixed on Permilly Ruggles. The Widow Bedott's first tentative foray into the community concerns a quilting party the Widow had attended many years earlier. Because of her tendency to distract herself, she never gets beyond telling about the people who attended the quilting, and nothing concrete happens. Metaphorically, however, she establishes a direct association between quilting and gossiping. Miriam teases the reader into wanting to hear more—into becoming an eager listener to the Widow's gossip, and a participant in the gossip circle. As Patricia M. Spacks has recently demonstrated, gossip is nearly universally associated with women, frequently in derogatory terms.[13] When gossip is used negatively, as it almost always is in the hands of the Widow Bedott, it serves primarily to empower the one gossiping. But as Spacks points out, "inextricably mingled" with its negative quality is also "gossip's positive essence."[14] This is as true in the real world as in the world of fiction: "Fiction reveals more clearly what didactic texts only hint: that gossip, 'female talk,' provides a mode of power, of undermining public rigidities and asserting private integrity, of discovering means of agency for women, those private citizens deprived of public function. It provides also often the substance and the means of narration."[15]

In the Widow Bedott sketches, everything hinges on gossip in one form or another, from the original title of the sketches ("Table Talk") to the false rumors about courtship the Widow deliberately spreads about herself. She *wants* to be talked about, to have her name linked romantically with the widower of the hour. In the Widow Bedott sketches, gossip is both a narrative technique and a narrative subject. Firmly linked with women's domestic world, it becomes a paradoxical force that brings women together and empowers them, and it drives them apart. As Spacks contends, gossip is "morally dubious" and "indestructibl[y]" energetic.[16] The readers of the Widow Bedott sketches, both male and female, contemporary and nineteenth century, are invited to enjoy gossip's full paradoxical nature through the Widow Bedott, to shake their heads over the Widow's relentless chatter while enjoying it without reservation.

In the final sketch of 1846, "The Widow Loses Her Beau," the author steps fully into the community when she features an evening lecture by a touring phrenologist with the Dickensian name Vanderbump. The whole town converges on the lecture hall, including Mr. Crane, so of course Priscilla Bedott goes as well. The sketch is rich in humor, furthering on one hand the saga of the Widow's pursuit of Timothy Crane while exploring the humorous potential of a public gathering. A phrenology lecture, complete with its specialized vocabulary and its displays of plaster human heads representing famous and infamous people, offered an irresistible target of humor for a satirist. In exploiting this subject, Miriam firmly established her work in the social world of her era; the study of phrenology was but one of the fads that swept through Oneida County in the 1840s. Only a year before the publication of this sketch, on September 29, 1845, the Phrenological and Magnetic Society was formed in Utica,[17] and one man, George Combe, drew large crowds of people to his phrenology lectures.[18]

Miriam filtered the entire lecture through the Widow Bedott's report of it, adding the foolishness of her views to the inherent humor of the presentation itself:

> But that are head that sets aside o' the commentater—the one that's got such a danglin' under lip and flat forrid and runs out to such a pint behind—that's old mother O'Killem, the Irish woman that murdered so many folks—she was an awful critter. He said 't wa'n't to be disputed though, that she'd done a master sight o' good to menkind—he reckoned they ought to raise a moniment tew her— 'cause any body that lookt at her head couldent persume no longer to doubt the truth o' phreenyology. He told us to observe the shape on 't perticlerly. You see the forrid's dretful flat—well, that shows how 't the intellectible faculties is intirely wantin'. But he dident call it *forrid*. He called it the *hoss frontis*. I s'pose that's 'cause its shaped more like a hoss than a human critter—animal propensitudes intirely predominates, you know. That's what makes it stick out so on the back side—that's the *hoss hindis* I s'pose—*hoss frontis* and *hoss hindis*, you know. I felt oncomonly interested when he was a tellin' about her, 'cause I've read all about her in "Horrid Murders"—a book I've got—it's the interestinest book I've read in all my life. (pp. 64–65)

The Widow's momentary enthusiasm for the subject of phrenology is equaled by her ready dismissal of women's issues:

> What a curus consarn this phreenyology is, ain't it? What an age of improvement we live in! If any body'd a told us once how 't in a few year we'd be able to tell egzackly what folks *was* by the shape o' ther heads—we wouldent a bleeved a word on't—would we? . . . Ain't his wife a turrible humbly woman? Her head looks jist like a punkin', and hisen looks like a cheese, don't it? You gwine to hear her lectur to the ladies to-morrow? Guiss *I* shall—if it's as interestin' a lectur as hisen, it'll be worth hearin'—though I don't think much o' these here wimmin lecturers, no way—the best place for wimmun's to hum—a mindin' their own bizness, accordin' to my notions. You remember that one that come round a spell ago, a whalin' away

about human rights. I thought she'd ought to be hoss-whipt and shet up in jail, dident you? (pp. 66–67)

Given the ironic, even paradoxical, relationship between Miriam Berry and the Widow Bedott, the latter's condemnation of women's rights issues offers tantalizing evidence that Miriam might have sympathized with the cause. But it is not much to go on. In fact, to have been an active supporter of women's issues at this time would have located Miriam Berry on the radical edge of antebellum society; the Seneca Falls convention, which took place not far from Whitesboro and marked the symbolic beginning of the American woman's rights movement, was still two years away. Nonetheless, she responded to some of the same issues in her humor that her more outspoken counterparts did in their overt political statements.[19] The irony in the passage quoted above, of course, resides in the Widow's insistence that women's place is at home, "a mindin' their own bizness," which she was incapable of doing herself. Only at the end of this, her sixth sketch, do readers learn the meaning of the story's title, "The Widow Loses Her Beau." Having gone to the lecture because Mr. Crane did, having engineered it so that she sat next to him for part of the time, and having made sure to start rumors that he had been to her house to pay her a call, she tells her friend Miss Pendergrass that she "eny most" hopes he won't walk her home because that would only fuel the local gossip. Much to her distress, the Widow Jinkins (nee Poll Bingham) insinuates herself into his company at the end of the lecture, and the Widow Bedott looks on in dismay as her arch rival leaves the lecture hall on the arm of the Widower Crane. Nearly two months would pass before the readers of Neal's *Saturday Gazette* would learn whether Mr. Crane was able to resist either widow's advances.

Marriage

On January 5, 1847, Miriam Berry and William Whitcher were married; both were thirty-five years old. Theirs was not a marriage of convenience, a "last chance" attachment to avoid a bleak and lonely life; they seem to have been genuinely in love. In a letter to Alice Neal that Miriam wrote several years later, she recalled her lonely childhood, her reserve that was mistaken for pride, then added this candid revelation: "When the best part of my life, or rather what should have been the best part of it, was gone, I met my husband. He was the first who penetrated the icy veil about me, sympathized with me, and turned my feet into a better path than they had trodden before."[20] Looked at from one point of view, Miriam's marriage to William initially did not change her life as dramatically as it might have. Because the Berry family home was also an inn, it was large enough for the newlywed couple to live with her family and still retain some independence and privacy.[21] They called at least two rooms their own, one a bedroom and the other a study for William, and William was warmly welcomed into the family. This meant that Miriam eased into her new private role as a wife and public role as a minister's wife from the security of her family home and within the confines of a small community where she was known and respected.

Her adjustment to her new responsibilities as the wife of a minister went smoothly. Because the membership of St. John's Church was still small and local, Miriam already knew everyone; nor were her responsibilities great. She was expected to call upon the parishioners periodically, and especially to be on hand when anyone was ill or otherwise in need, but she already did these things as a matter of course. She visited the poor of the village, but again this merely extended habits already well established; it was not a new responsibility imposed on her by marriage. She was also expected to participate in the activities of the church—to attend services, which she did eagerly, and to join with the other women in their charitable activities. This duty, too, was easy for Miriam. By the spring of 1847, for example, she was actively involved in the church sewing circle, a group of friends and neighbors with whom she felt very much at home; she was proud when they were able to see tangible results for their labor.[22] The early months of her marriage were a time of adjustment and of contentment for Miriam, but the Whitchers' life together was soon to undergo dramatic change.

In April 1847, William received an unexpected call to become the minister of Trinity Episcopal Church in Elmira, New York, some one hundred miles south of Whitesboro. He left Whitesboro almost immediately to begin his duties as pastor in Elmira and to find a home for himself and his wife, while Miriam stayed behind with her family to begin the strenuous preparations for keeping house on her own. Separated so soon after their marriage, William and Miriam wrote each other often—two to three times a week—and Miriam's letters bear unmistakable witness to the depth of her affection and to her teasing humor; they reveal a side of her that appears nowhere else. (Unfortunately, none of William's letters from this period survives.) She invariably addressed him as "my dearest William," or "my own dear husband," and ended each letter with comparable words of affection: "Your loving wife," "Your ever faithful Miriam," and best of all, "Your own affectionate Frank."

None of her self-reported reserve comes through in these letters; instead, they reveal a tenderness not evident in her other writing:

> I did not attend the [sewing circle] meeting last Friday. It was the day after you left—& I felt too forlorn & desolate to go anywhere. I think I shall go tomorrow. I put the study to rights that day—arranged everything nicely—so as to have it ready for use in case it should be needed—but I did not touch the bed—thought I would leave that until the last minute—for there was the place where you lounged just as you left it—the pillows turned up endwise, with the little dent in them where your head rested. It looked more like you than anything else that you left behind (excepting the miniature) & I went in every day & kissed the little dent. But the other day sister Mary went & removed the cases to wash them—& the next time I visited the study & saw the alteration—(you'll call me a gumption perhaps) I sat down & cried.[23]

Only four days later she had to turn William's study over to a new boarder: "After he comes I cannot go in there & think of you & fancy you sitting there in your armchair as I do now. O! my dear husband, I have been very happy with you, more so than I can express."[24] At one point she suddenly realized that the letters passing between them were their first love letters: "Do you remember my once telling you to go off somewhere & stay long enough to write to me? Ah! what a foolish speech! I would rather have yourself than your letters—tho' they are the next best thing."[25]

The overt professions of love were matched by references to her loneliness in his absence, her longing for his return, and her occasional bouts of depression. The latter, which she called her "forlornness," or an attack of "Mr. Mullygrubs," she resisted as fully as she could, aided by William's advice to look on the more positive side of things. She was at least partially successful, and her discouragement and her melancholy were balanced by periods of playfulness and good-natured teasing. In one instance, William mentioned in a letter that he had bought a new hat but was keeping the old one for washing days; she responded by saying how surprised she was to learn that *he* intended to do all the washing: "I never thought before that you would be willing to do such work—in fact I did not suppose that you knew how."[26] A few lines later in the same letter, she assumed a voice reminiscent of one of her characters to tease William about forgetting to take a book, the "Clergyman's Companion," with him to Elmira: "Forgot me *hey*? Pretty business indeed! So you forgot me! Well, I'll give it up now! I did not expect the time would come when my pardner would forget *me*."[27] Several letters later, in the midst of expressing her genuine fear that she would be a miserable housekeeper, she bolstered herself by the reminder that she could learn whatever she needed to know—" 'where there's a will, there's a way' & surely nobody has a better will than I, for you dearest, are my *Will*, and with you & my own disposition to do right I think I shall in time find out a way to get along."[28]

The affection notwithstanding, a shadow hung over the Whitchers from the beginning of their marriage. An almost palpable sense of life's precariousness was exacerbated by Miriam's own poor health in the spring of 1847. Her letters of this period often reported serious illness and death among her neighbors and friends, yet her descriptions were not morbid. Instead, her matter-of-fact details bear quiet witness to the fierce virility of many diseases in the mid-1800s. People died suddenly and violently, and there was little the doctors or families could do to intercede. Miriam's letters reveal how much she integrated into her life an ongoing awareness of the possibility of imminent death. Phrases such as "if we live to see each other again" are sprinkled almost casually throughout her letters from this time, and they seem to be sincere expressions of doubt rather than conventional turns of phrase. More revealing, mention of those who are ill or recently dead is included without paragraph break or any other indicator to distinguish a change in topic or the introduction of an especially noteworthy subject. Miriam's treatment of death and illness in her letters was not in itself unusual for her time.[29] What was unique about her reports, however, was the way at times she infused them with wit and humor. A funeral conducted by the Reverend Mr. Long, pastor of the Whitesboro Presbyterian Church, offered one such irresistible opportunity:

> I attended the funeral on the day that you went away. I had been crying dreadfully you know. So I wore a veil to cover up my red eyes. But after a while, the room became very warm, owing to the great crowd & I was obliged to put aside my veil & expose my tearful & swollen visage. I suppose the good people thought I was wonderfully affected by the solemnity of the occasion, or by Mr. Long's pathetic eloquence.
> The occasion was a solemn one to be sure, but Mr. Long makes funerals most distressingly ludicrous!. . . . He twaddled on for a full hour in his usual strain, all about winding sheets, bones, death rattles, worms, grave yards—the *hollow silence* of the coffin &c &c— every few minutes stopping to inform the audience that "he did not intend to make any remarks on that occasion because, it was his purpose to improve the occasion on the ensuing Sabbath in an address to the young." Goodness! I thought he never would get through! But all things earthly have an end—& so did his performance. And then he most lovingly called upon brother Cole to pray. Brother C. accordingly addressed the audience over the Lord's shoulders (if I may so speak) for about half an hour & then the beautiful little Maria was carried to her grave. . . . The afternoon of Sunday Morris & Eugenia [Berry] went to meeting & heard the funeral discourse. . . . I asked Morris how Mr. Long made out—& his answer was that "he *sustained himself* admirably" that is he *out-Long'd Long*—All the congregation seemed to have a "great deal to think about"—even Eugenia spent a great part of the time in the *deepest meditation*.[30]

Spring came late to Whitesboro that year, and the cold and damp weather brought with it even more sickness than usual. At one point Miriam reported to William that the only *man* who seemed to take much interest in the affairs of St. John's Church was Dr. Thomas, but he had been too swamped with work to attend to the business of calling a pastor to replace William.[31] (Church records substantiate Miriam's insinuation about female domination of church functions. Of the communicants listed in the church record between the church's inception and 1854, forty are women and only six are men; all of the church officials, of course, were men. The pattern was not unique to St. John's.) There was an outbreak of fever at the York Mills, bordering on Whitesboro, and by mid-April, snow was still falling; Miriam had to cover her plants to protect them from frost: "It looks & feels just like winter."

Shortly after William left for Elmira, Miriam's own health deteriorated. What at first appeared to be merely a cold soon developed into what she characterized as "a lump on her jaw bone," presumably swollen glands in her neck. To a modern sensibility, her reports about the various cures and medicines available to her are both touching and alarming:

> The bump on my *jaw bone* has gone down. The day after you went it was very much swollen—& painful. We had lately heard that the marrow of hog's jaw is very good for such things. Mary was very desirous I should try it. So I did—& I think it helped it. There is a lump on the other side of my neck now. I am using the marrow every night & it is going down. I suspect it has come in consequence of coughing. I remember that the one I had last spring appeared just after I had a severe cough. We are expecting a boarder tomorrow or the next day, Mr. White, the new teacher.[32]

Two days later she confessed in a letter to her sister Kate (but not to William) that her condition was much worse—certainly too severe to underplay it by placing it side by side with news of a new boarder:

> I am not as sick as I was this morning. If I were I could not write a word. But I have been vomiting up some of the bile & am a little relieved. I have had for a week past a terrible cough that almost racked me to pieces. Dr. Thomas gave me some medicine that contained antimony—though I did not know it—& it made me so dreadfully sick that I didn't care whether I lived or died. I only took one dose of it—I never was so sick in my life. Yesterday John brought me over some drops from Dr. Smith, which I took, as I had got

nearly discouraged & was really afraid I should break a blood vessel coughing—John had great faith in the drops—so I took them last evening & this morning, & my cough is very much better. They are very pleasant tasting—I remember Liz used to have some from Dr. Peck that tasted like them. The stuff that Dr. Thomas gave me had made my stomach so sore vomiting that it nearly killed me to cough— therefore you can imagine what relief it is to stop coughing for several hours at a time—I think I shall soon be well again—I *have* been the sickest critter you ever *did* see—And so—having occupied a whole page in entertaining you with accounts of my health, I will proceed to other more interesting subjects.[33]

Four days later she told William she had *not* been sick, only that her stomach had been "out of order, rather bilious."[34] On April 28, however, she confessed that she had an "attack," but "the constant use of cold water agreeably to your directions has nearly restored me. I do not like to bore you with any ails & complaints, but I know that if you should find me out of order when you come, you would scold me for not telling you of it. I suppose this last attack was brought on by sitting too still in the house. I do not think of going out to take any exercise unless some one comes after me."[35]

Setting up Housekeeping

Preparing to set up housekeeping for the first time on her own proved to be a formidable task to Miriam. She had no furniture, no linens, no dishes, no rugs—nothing with which to establish a home for herself and William. And she had little advance warning: "If I had only known last winter that I should leave my father's house so soon, I should have been preparing & all ready now."[36] Even the simplest tasks, such as making bed sheets, seemed nearly overwhelming to her: she had to wait for both good weather and her own good health to walk to the mills on the outskirts of Whitesboro, where she picked out her cloth. Once there, she discovered she was not strong enough to carry the bolts of material home by herself, so she had to wait until someone in her family could go back with her. She also had to sew carpets and curtains, dresses and underclothing, pillows and pillow-cases, quilts and furniture covers. Fortunately, Miriam was surrounded by friends and family members to help her: "Miss Pease & Mrs Palmer are coming this afternoon to help me, & Helen is helping me all she can—but she has a terrible abcess *[sic]* under one arm which nearly disables her. Kate & I are just as busy as we can be—& Mary & Cornelia are hard at work for me. . . . I am hardly able to do anything today—having a terribly stiff neck. I know not whether it proceeds from the lump, or from a cold."[37]

In the interest of economy, the Whitchers considered buying secondhand furniture from a friend, but Miriam found it unsuitable: "It is old-fashioned & rusty—it would be cheaper to get new— excepting the mahogany chairs—they are nice & cheap—but we do not want them. We shall have nothing else to correspond with them."[38] She also had to buy or have built for her wooden packing crates for shipping all their belongings on a canal boat; her brother John took over this task in William's absence. All this had to be accomplished in less than two months' time.

The enormity of the task confronting Miriam Whitcher was increased by William's indecision over what kind of housing arrangement would be best for them, a boardinghouse or a rented house of their own. Surprisingly, when Miriam first broached the question to him a week after he left Whitesboro, it sounded as though they had scarcely discussed the matter. The context in which she raised the issue with William was in itself bizarre; she had just learned from him that the Reverend Mr. Van Zandt, the minister dismissed by Trinity Church in Elmira, remained in Elmira and was attempting to befriend William, even to persuade the Whitchers to room in his house: "For mercy's sake," she cautioned "shake him off!"

> Do get rid of him dear, at some rate or other. If you cannot do it without offending him, just offend him—better to quarrel with him than with your parishioners—much better. I cannot imagine what can be his motive in sticking to you so—board at his house goody gracious!! Tell him if you wish that your wife desires to go to house-keeping as soon as possible after she gets there. Tell me as soon as you can what you think about housekeeping, you will soon be able to tell what will be best for us. I am decidedly in favor of having a home of our own—even though it be a poor one. But if you see any reason for thinking otherwise, say so. I shall be governed entirely by your wishes in the matter. You will of course be the best able to

judge of the comparative expense & of other matters pertaining to it.[39]

Pursued on one side by Van Zandt, William was pressured on another by the Luce family, who wanted the Whitchers to board with them. The Luces were prominent members of the church who were putting William up while he looked for a more permanent place. For a brief time, the idea appealed to him. Having told William only the week before that she preferred they have a house of their own but that she would abide by his decision, Miriam then had to prepare herself mentally to live in the home of strangers:

> You say that the room [at the Luce's] is very large—larger than our parlor. I would much rather furnish a smaller room, as I do not like the idea of buying such an immensely big carpet as would be necessary for a room of that size. You know that whatever we purchase, will be used in our own house (if we ever have one) & should be got with a view to that. Now would we be likely ever to get into a house with a parlor large enough to require such a huge carpet as the room at Mr Luce's? I want to furnish our room, while we board, but I wish you to tell me just what to get. I hope there is a bedroom besides. It would be so inconvenient for you, if we were tucked up in one room. More so for a clergyman than for any one else. Tell me just exactly what to get the next time you write, for I shall have none too much time to prepare.[40]

For an entire month William remained indecisive, but time was running out. On about May 1, only ten days before he was due back in Whitesboro, William changed his mind again and proposed they take a house he had just seen. Miriam was perturbed:

> The thought of having a home of our own, a quiet home, where we can be unobserved & independent is very pleasant to me; but my dear William somehow I am so confused that I can hardly think or speak clearly on the subject. . . . I never was so puzzled in my life. How old a house is the one you propose taking? tell all about it when you write. I hope it is small. I cannot say half that I wish to. I am so bewildered that perhaps I have not made myself intelligible, & you will scarcely be able to know what are my wishes. So then to conclude, I will sum them up in few. I am entirely satisfied with the

description of the house—think the rent is reasonable—but that we ought to let out the surrounding land—as it will be impossible for you to cultivate it—however we must reserve a garden. And I will do my best to get ready as soon as possible—I shall look for you on the 11th.[41]

A full week later (only days before he was due back in Whitesboro) William still had not settled the house issue, but Miriam had become calmer, almost resigned, about the question: "Take any house you please dear, if you wish to secure one before I come. Yet, perhaps it would be better to wait till I get there on many accounts. We can board a little while."[42] So the easy transition Miriam experienced at the beginning of her marriage was more than offset by the difficult preparations for their move to Elmira. These difficulties were compounded by their separation from each other after only three months of marriage, by Miriam's poor health, and by William's indecision. William faced other challenges of his own in Elmira, where his first priority was to get off to a good start with his parishioners. Compared to Whitesboro, the Elmira congregation was large and well established, but it had suffered a series of upheavals under Van Zandt, who had essentially been turned out of the parish. Yet Van Zandt remained in Elmira, keeping the parish stirred up and dogging William. Money was extremely tight for the Whitchers. Miriam relied on humor to caution William to be careful how he charged for his services; she wrote her husband that she hoped the residents of nearby Corning remained in good health because the expenses William incurred at the last funeral he conducted there were greater than the fee he received. William literally did not have enough money to live on and urgently asked his wife to send him ten dollars, but because her letters sometimes got lost, she was afraid to entrust that much money to the mails. Meanwhile, no matter how they economized, moving to Elmira and setting up housekeeping was an expensive proposition.

Although William was as green as his wife when it came to domestic matters, he had to make several decisions before Miriam arrived. One of these was to engage a "girl" to help with the housework (she needed to be a good one, Miriam reminded him, since she herself knew so little about managing a household). He also was to pick the colors for the carpets (Miriam liked them "neither *very* light nor *very* dark—a happy medium. . . . A good deal of wood-color in them suits my taste"),[43] and he had eventually to decide where they would live. In the end, almost any other house would have been preferable to the one he chose.

Back in Whitesboro, Miriam experienced serious anxieties about how well she would be received in a community of strangers, and how she would fare in charge of her own household. As she reminded William, she had been only a "subfunctionary" in her mother's household. Even the most basic tasks were outside her experience: baking bread, doing the wash, cooking meals, managing a housekeeper—all were new to her. Her more serious concern, however, focused on how well she would be received in Elmira as a person in her own right and as the minister's wife. Here comparisons to the Van Zandts worked to her disadvantage; although *he* was, in Whitcher's words, "in very bad odor there," his wife was "beloved by every body."[44] As early as her first letter to William after he arrived in Elmira, she confessed her anxieties: "Your description of Elmira pleases me very much. I have no doubt I shall like it. My only fear is that *it* will not like *me*. I already feel interested in the persons you speak of especially Aunty Hill. I shall love every body that is kind to you—whether they love me or not."[45] In keeping with her resolve as expressed to William, she struggled to rise above what she perceived as her true nature, but she often felt unequal to the challenges facing her. Her social unease also had repercussions for her relationship with William. She regretted that she had not always made William as happy as he had made her, and she reminded him (with rare understatement) that she "often said things that have made you uneasy. If God in his mercy permits us ever to meet again, I hope & pray that He will enable me to be a better wife, but somehow it is so hard for me to do right. I think of your good counsels now in your absence & in all things try to do as I know you would advise me if you were here."[46] As events unfolded in Elmira, the very qualities that gave her personal pain— being outside, detached, wary—were precisely those that made her successful as a social satirist.

While Miriam quite naturally put her writing aside during the two months of hectic preparations for the move to Elmira, she had not been idle earlier in the year. Between January 1 and March 6, she published four more articles, three of them Widow Bedott stories for Neal's *Gazette,* and her first Aunt Maguire sketch for *Godey's Lady's Book.* In April she sent off a second Aunt Maguire sketch to Godey, but it was not published until summer, when it appeared almost simultaneously in both the *Gazette* and the *Lady's Book.* By this time, Miriam was comfortably established in Elmira and was beginning to write additional humorous stories.

The Widow Bedott's Courtship

The first of the three Widow Bedott stories mentioned above was almost certainly written in late November or early December, before Miriam's marriage to William. It takes up the theme of the courtship of the Widow Bedott and Timothy Crane just where it left off in November, with Crane's "walking out" with Poll Jinkins. The day after the phrenology lecture, the Widow and her two adult children, Kier and Melissy, are sitting down to tea when Timothy Crane pays a surprise visit. As might be expected, the Widow fusses excessively over the tea—apologizing for the quality of the butter, bragging about the quality of the pumpkin pie—all the while keeping up a steady stream of chatter. Once again, for a brief few moments, gossip itself becomes the focus of the sketch's attention as the Widow Bedott condemns seamstresses in general, and one in particular, for carrying gossip from one house to the next. The irony of her condemnation is not lost on her children, especially Kier, who cannot resist teasing his mother about her own loose tongue.

Undaunted, the Widow continues her obsession with the subject of widowhood by telling Timothy Crane the story of a Ganderfield farmer, Philander Bennet, who died when he fell off a haystack and broke his back, thus leaving Mrs. Bennet a widow:

> I s'pose 't wouldent a killed him if it hadent a ben for his comin' kersmash onto a jug that was a settin' on the ground aside o' the stack. The spine of his back went right onto the jug and broke it— broke his back, I mean—not the jug—*that* wa'n't even cracked— curus! wa'n't it? 'T was quite a comfort to Miss Bennet in her affliction—'t was a jug she vallyed—one 't was her mother's. His bein' killed so was a turrible blow to Miss Bennet, the circumstances

was so aggravatin'. I writ a piece o' poitry on the occasion and sent
it tew her; she said 't was quite consolin'. (p. 73)

For the first time in the Widow's fictive life—no doubt because of her
excitement over Crane's visit—she "disremembers" her own poetry
after only three stanzas. But three are sufficient:

> O Ganderfield!
> Where is thy shield
> To guard against grim Death?
> He aims his gun
> At old and young,
> And fires away their breath!
>
> One summer's day
> For to 'tend tew his hay,
> Mr. Bennet went to the medder—
> Fell down from the stack—
> Broke the spine of his back,
> And left a mournin' widder!
>
> 'T was occasioned by his landin'
> On a jug that was standin'
> Alongside o' the stack o' hay—
> Some folks say 't was *what was in it*
> Caused the *fall* of Mr. Bennet,
> But ther ain't a word of truth in what they say—
> (pp. 73–74)

After six pages of unrelieved Widow Bedotting, Timothy Crane
interrupts her abruptly to ask for a word with her in private, and the
sketch ends with the Widow in a genuine fluster: "Is it any thing
pertickeler, Mr. Crane! O, dear suz! how you *dew* flustrate me! not
that it's any thing oncommon for the gentlemen to ax to have privite
conversations with me you know—but then—but then—bein' you—
it's different—circumstances alters cases you know—what was you a
gwine to say, Mr. Crane?" (pp. 77–78).

The next sketch, published a month later, resumes with the Widow
assuring Crane that of course she does not believe it is wrong for him

to marry again only six months after his wife's death. It would be too soon for a woman, she adds, but not for a man. (The Widow Bedott has waited ten years for someone like "husband" to come along.) At the crucial moment Whitcher makes an uncharacteristic shift in the story's point of view, letting Crane speak in his own voice without any narrative comment:

> *Mr. Crane*—"Well widder, I was agoing to ask you whether—whether—"
>
> *Widow*—"Continner, Mr. Crane—dew—I know it's turrible embarrisin'. I remember when my dezeased husband made his suppositions to me, he stammered and stuttered, and was so awfully flustered it did seem as if he'd never git it out in the world, and I s'pose it's ginerally the case, at least it has been with all them that's made suppositions to me—you see they're ginerally oncerting about what kind of an anser they're agwine to git, and it kind o' makes 'em narvous. But when an individdiwal has reason to s'pose his attachment's reciperated, I don't see what need there is o' his bein' flustrated—tho' I must say it's quite embarrassin' to me—pray continner."
>
> *Mr. C.*—"Well then, I want to know if you're willing I should have Melissy?" (p. 81)

The Widow Bedott can only sputter for a moment in disbelief—nothing has prepared her (or the reader) for such a question. When she regains her control, she lets fly the full force of her rage and disappointment:

> Shet yer head, Tim Crane—nun o' yer sass to me. *There's* yer hat on that are table, and *here's* the door—and the sooner you put on *one* and march out o' t' other, the better it'll be for you. And I advise you afore you try to git married agin, to go out west and see 'f yer wife's cold—and arter ye're satisfied on that pint, jest put a little lampblack on yer hair—'t would add to yer appearance ondoubtedly and be of sarvice tew you when you want to flourish round among the gals—and when ye've got yer hair fixt, jest splinter the spine o' yer back—'t wouldent hurt yer looks a mite—you'd be interely unresistable if you was a *leetle* grain straiter. (pp. 82–83)

For one moment, the Widow Bedott has our sympathy; Crane's desire to marry the Widow's daughter, who is his own daughter's best friend, is completely unexpected and inappropriate. He also has to have been deaf and blind not to notice how the Widow has been throwing herself in his way; although her attempts to change her lot in life have been highly comic, this time she genuinely seems to be on the verge of success. Whatever sympathy she has gained she loses almost immediately, however, when Melissy returns home in the company of a man named Captain Canoot. First the Widow shifts much of her anger to her daughter, blaming her for leaving her at home alone in such disagreeable company, then she begins to create her own fiction:

> I should like to know what arthly reason you had to s'pose old Crane's was agreeable to me? I always dispised the critter—always thought he was turrible fool—and now I'm convinced on 't. I'm completely dizgusted with him—and I let him know it to-night. I gin him a piece o' my mind I guess he'll be apt to remember for a spell. I ruther think he went off with a flea in his ear. Why, cappen— did ye ever hear o such a piece of audacity in all yer born days? for *him—Tim Crane*—to durst to expire to my hand—the widder o' deacon Bedott! jest as if *I'd* condescen to look at *him*—the old numskull. (p. 84)

In the third and final sketch of this period, published in early March 1847, the Widow Bedott looks out the window and sees another widower, Old Uncle Dawson, walking down the street, and she literally "sets her cap" for him by having Melissy hurriedly spruce up a different bonnet for her to put on in case he comes by her house. When he walks the other way instead, she goes out, ostensibly to visit Miss Pendergrass and to catch up on the local gossip. The Widow Bedott who emerges in this sketch has changed to some degree. Excluded from a party the night before, she shows a bitter, vindictive side that now extends beyond those whom she sees as her rivals: "I tell you what, Melissy Bedott, I should like a chance to ride over the heads o' some o' these ere folks that feel so mighty grand, shouldent you? . . . For *my* part I'd like to be able to show Miss Coon 't I'm as good as she is and a leetle grain better, neverstandin' she dident invite me to her party, the miserable, low-lifed critter!"

(p. 87). Thwarted by Timothy Crane and informed that her arch rival, Poll Jinkins, is going to marry Old Dawson, she bursts out in a tirade of bitterness:

> The widder Jinkins a gwine to be married to old uncle Dawson! If that ain't the last thing I ever heerd on! What *is* this world a comin' tew? How redicklous! well, she's a mean, good-for-nothin', underhanded critter to go to work a settin' her traps for that poor old man, and conduce him to make such a flumbergasted fool o' himself in his old age! What a dog's life she'll lead him tew! Why she's the awfullest tempered critter 't ever was made. I've knowed Poll Bingham from a gal, and I don't bleve Bill Jinkins would a turned out such a misrable shack if he'd a had [a] decent woman for a wife. (p. 91)

On this note, Miriam Whitcher appeared to be drawing the Widow Bedott series to a close, for she has an unfamiliar, third-person narrator summarize for the readers a number of important changes that take place in the Widow's household after the close of this story. Over the Widow's objections, Kier Bedott became engaged to Timothy Crane's daughter, and Melissy to Jupiter Smith. The Widow herself, the narrator reports, became completely "dizgusted" with Wiggletown. At the end of the postscript, Joseph Neal announced to the readers of his *Saturday Gazette* that although he hoped they would hear from "Frank" again, this sketch marked the end of the "Table Talk" series.

Miriam had good reason to suppose she was finished with the Widow Bedott series, although as it happened she was not. She had carried the courtship theme about as far as she could—all the widowers in Wiggletown were taken—and the sketches ran the risk of becoming repetitious without a fresh approach. Miriam also associated the end of the series with the major changes that were taking place in her own life. At the same time, Miriam's relationship with Joseph Neal had begun to cool off considerably because she believed he was not giving her the recognition she deserved:

> I had almost forgotten to tell you that I received on Thursday a letter from Neal—He said that the call for me & my writings was so great that he would be glad to have me send more—& requested

me to write a series of sketches, à la Bedott, illustrative of local or natural peculiarities. He said he would pay a "reasonable compensation, say five dollars for articles the length of the Bedotts." The letter was as cool as a *cucumber* & sounded as if he wrote it because he could'nt help it—if he could'nt get me for nothing, he was willing to pay something. What do you advise me in the matter? I have no time nor opportunity to write anything at present—& doubt whether he would ever pay if I should. I have been half provoked at Neal, for taking so little notice of me when I have sent him so many things. But I must go fix for meeting.[47]

Finally, Neal was competing for Miriam's work with his friend and former associate, Louis Godey; the competition was formidable. *Godey's Lady's Book* was unquestionably the most prestigious popular American magazine of the day, enjoying a circulation in 1839, for example, that Godey claimed exceeded that "of any other three monthly publications" combined.[48] With Sarah Josepha Hale as its literary editor from the late 1830s on, the magazine flourished.[49] The full-color fashion plates still so highly regarded were becoming a regular feature of the publication (twenty such illustrations appeared in 1849, all individually hand-colored for each of the copies mailed to the thousands of subscribers). Overall, Miriam declared herself "greatly pleased" with the personal response she received from Godey. In addition to receiving ten dollars for her story, an amount she called "very generous," she liked the man:

> He expressed himself hugely delighted with my last article—Said that he should always be overpaying if he got such change as I sent, & requested me to write again when convenient. He said that the member of his family for whom his letter was in mourning, was a sweet little daughter five years old. He has three left. He says that he is very fat & fond of fun—& especially quiet kind of fun like Bedott & Magwire. In short his letter was a very pleasant & friendly one. I mean to write again when I get leisure which will not be in some time I fancy.[50]

What Miriam could not have anticipated was how perfectly suited her Aunt Maguire persona would be to her evolving satiric purposes. Although Aunt Maguire was the fictive sister of the Widow Bedott, she differed considerably from her predecessor. Her voice was more moderate, more muted. If at times her judgments of people were as harsh as her sister's, they were based more on principle: the Widow Bedott criticized everyone, especially those who thwarted her marriage schemes, while Aunt Maguire reserved her criticism for those who were pretentious, hypocritical, or otherwise set themselves above other people. She was not obsessive and self-absorbed as her sister was, and she was not given to excessive swings of mood and opinion. In addition, hers was also a voice of compassion. The thrust of the humor shifted, too, between the two series. Whereas the Widow Bedott was herself the butt of much of the humor in her sketches, Aunt Maguire was not; instead, the people and the society surrounding her were. The Widow Bedott was a fool, a recognizable village type whose excesses were exposed to public laughter; Aunt Maguire, in contrast, was a woman endowed with good common sense who served as a spokesperson for key public values. Her language, while a less extreme vernacular than her sister's, was still the language of an uneducated, country woman.

The first two Aunt Maguire sketches, written before Miriam's move to Elmira, establish Aunt Maguire as a reliable and entertaining narrative persona through whom the author would filter her own experience, observations, and imagination when confronted with a society that seemed so dramatically different from anything she had known in Whitesboro. In the first two sketches, Whitcher capitalized on the reputation she had already established by carefully linking Aunt Maguire with her well-known fictive sister, Priscilla Bedott. Aunt Maguire, too, speaks in the form of a dramatic monologue to an invisible guest (her niece Nancy), and in the first sketch she also digresses from her own announced topic several times before settling into her story, which harkens back to an experience with the Widow's late husband. On balance, however, the differences between the two sisters (and hence the two narrators) far outweigh the similarities.

Aunt Maguire

As with the first story, the second is cast in the distant past.[51] The butt of this story is the sanctimonious Deacon Whipple, who makes it his business to spy on other members of his church, then haul them up before the congregation for disciplinary action. "He had a stingy kind of walk—went along as if he begrudged the room he took up" (p. 347). The story concerns a night years earlier when Deacon Whipple brought two other reluctant deacons with him to the Bedotts to accuse Deacon Bedott of drunkenness. So pompous is Deacon Whipple that he is reluctant to tell Bedott what charges have been brought against him, declaring that Bedott's unwillingness to confess spontaneously is only further proof of his depravity. While the interrogation takes place in the Bedott's parlor, Aunt Maguire, Priscilla Bedott, and a young neighbor woman, Artemishy Pike, sneak into the buttery to eavesdrop through a crack in the door. Meanwhile, Joshaway Maguire and several of his friends are eavesdropping at the opposite end of the parlor through the keyhole in the front door. At the critical moment, Joshaway and his friends burst into the room and reveal that they have played a practical joke on Deacon Whipple by substituting cider for water in Deacon Bedott's shaving mug. That is how it came to be that Deacon Bedott was "half shaved with cider before breakfast."

With this revelation, the assembled group begins to laugh and "holler" until "ther was such a gineral roarin' and laffin' as I never heerd afore nor sence" (p. 357). Only Deacon Whipple is not amused. According to Aunt Maguire, the episode "cured Deacon Whipple of his *consarn* for the welfare o' Zion," and shortly after, he left town for good. This is a rare moment in Whitcher's humor when the curative power of laughter is the subject of the humor itself. Joshaway's very name as spelled by Aunt Maguire—to "josh" or joke "away"— reveals his character in this and in the sketches that follow. His son, likewise, is a tease who will go to some trouble to amuse himself. At the end of her second Aunt Maguire sketch, then, Miriam Whitcher expressed in the subject of her story what became the essence of her Elmira sketches: laughter's potential to cure society's ills. As would be true of her satires, this sketch also dramatizes that laughter has its own revenge. As we shall see, in "Parson Scrantum's Donation Party," which was her next sketch and also her first Elmira story, she made the final transition from the burlesque and parody perfected in "The Widow Spriggins" and "The Widow Bedott" sketches to full-fledged social satire.

On Friday, May 28, 1847, Miriam and William Whitcher set out for their home in Elmira, New York. Although only about one hundred air miles away, it was a long, tiring two-day journey. They first headed due west on the train from Whitesboro to Geneva: "I never was so weary in my life as then," Miriam wrote her sister. "The road is very rough & the cars jar & tip dreadfully. For the last two hours I could not hold up my head it ached so, but laid it on William's shoulder. He too was very tired. We stayed at the Franklin Hotel that night."[52] The following morning, Saturday, they boarded a boat and in three-and-a-half hours traveled the full length of Seneca Lake, some thirty miles. In contrast to the ride of the previous day, the lake crossing was smooth and serene, with Miriam enjoying the scenery along the shore—"a constant succession of hills—& sometimes ridges of rocks & little waterfalls."[53] They were met at the boat landing by Mr. Luce, who took them in his carriage to a nearby hotel where Mrs. Luce and dinner awaited them. Miriam reported that she liked the Luces immediately. After dinner they traveled by carriage the remaining distance to Elmira, approximately twenty miles, passing over a smooth road and through more scenery that Miriam admired. But riding in an open carriage took its toll, and she arrived at her new home tired and "dreadfully sunburnt. My face was swollen & as red as a blaze." It was still daylight when they arrived in Elmira, and they had time for a stroll through Mr. Luce's orchard, then "we went into the graveyard, which lies just behind the garden. We did not go to *our house*, but I saw it at a distance. It is a nice looking little box. Tomorrow morning early we shall go down & commence operations."[54]

Daguerreotype of Miriam Whitcher, probably taken to send to Louis Godey in January 1849. *Courtesy of the Dunham Public Library, Whitesboro, New York.*

Photo of William Whitcher, probably dating from the 1800s. *Courtesy of St. John's Parish, Whitesboro, New York.*

"Happy New Year to you all dear father & mother & sisters & brothers! We thought you would feel rather anxious to hear from us after my alarming letter. so after I got my chores done up & fixed myself for calls (if I should have any) I sat down to drop you a line to let you know that we got thro' the Sunday with whole skins. There was no demonstration on the part of the beligerents. The church was crowded all day. The Arnots were not there the old woman never comes, but the girls do occasionally they are a curse to the church. it will never prosper here till they leave it. The commotion caused by the article is as great as ever & every body insists upon applying Mrs Samson Savage to Mrs Arnot. She goes by the name every-where. & her admirers or echoes are called the "Stillman family." The young man of whom Capt. Husted I spoke in a letter some time ago as being the beau of Mrs T. (the woman who thought herself preached at) is called universally "Cappen Smalley" & they say it cuts him to death. A gentleman one of our friends. the Mr Chamberlain who went east with me once. says that he attended a very large party last week. where Mrs Arnot & the echoes were present. & for the first time, they behaved with propriety and did not "nopolise" all the conversation. But they are perfectly outrageous against me & William too. As yet we cannot tell what will be the result. I confess

The first page of a letter from Miriam to her family, January 1, 1849, in which Miriam tells about "the commotion" caused by her sewing society article and the immediate identification of Mrs. John Arnot with Miss Samson Savage. In this letter, Miriam tells how the Elmira townspeople helped keep the controversy alive by calling various residents by their "Sewing Society" names. *Courtesy of the New-York Historical Society, New York City.*

The Berry family cemetery plot in Grandview Cemetery. The Berry headstones include the five old-style markers to the left of the central marker (one partially hidden), the three modern and two old-style markers on the right, and the flat stone in the center that marks the grave of Miriam and her infant daughter, Mary.

Close-up of the marker brought from Elmira with the body of Mary, daughter of Miriam and William. The marker identifies Miriam's age at the time of her death as thirty-nine, but the date of her birth is obscured beyond recognition.

Illustration from *Godey's Lady's Book* entitled "Godey's Paris Fashions Americanized." This illustration appeared in the October 1849 issue of the *Lady's Book*.

Illustration for Timothy Shay Arthur's article entitled "The Daguerreotypist," which appeared in the May 1849 issue of the *Lady's Book*.

ELDER AND MRS. SNIFFLES SITTING FOR THEIR DAGUERREOTYPE.

Miriam Whitcher's own drawing for Neal's *Saturday Gazette* by then renamed *The Mammoth Saturday Gazette*, June 16, 1849. The story appears in *The Widow Bedott Papers* under the title, "The Rev. Mrs. Sniffles at Home." *Courtesy of the American Antiquarian Society.*

A portrait of Louis A. Godey, frontispiece for the January 1850 issue of *Godey's Lady's Book*.

Portrait of Alice B. Neal, illustrating an article about her in the December 1849 *Godey's Lady's Book*. Alice Neal would have been twenty-two years old in 1849.

4

Elmira

$\mathcal{M}$iriam's move to Elmira, New York, in 1847 put her in direct contact, for the first time, with a relatively fluid social order. In Elmira, as in villages all over the Northeast, townspeople who gained new wealth entered the middle class from the bottom and strove to make their way to the top. They reached for outward signs of success in arenas that would immediately highlight their ascendancy into a would-be genteel world: fashion and domestic architecture.[1] A certain degree of anxiety inevitably accompanied any such rapid mobility, for as easily as one could move up one could also move down; likewise, the neighbor who had formerly been on the edges of the lower class almost overnight could be sitting at the top of the social order, at least in terms of wealth and the social power that accompanied it. No one, of course, wanted to be left behind. By midcentury, a growing body of people aspired to achieve the outward trappings of gentility and to leave behind them the more traditional values the historian Karen Halttunen has characterized under the term "the cult of sincerity."[2] Women especially became interested in the outward signs of prosperity. They eschewed what Miriam regarded as traditional religious and domestic values and became more socially aggressive. They had more disposable income, more mobility, and as the Widow Bedott would soon demonstrate, less taste. If rapid social change gave rise to conflict and personal anxiety, it was also ready grist for a humorist such as Miriam Whitcher. During her stay in Elmira, and in direct reaction to watching Elmirans vying for social position, Miriam created her finest social satire.

Miriam was herself not free from social and personal anxieties as she entered Elmira society. Her friends and neighbors in Whitesboro

were thoroughly familiar with her and with her habits of social isolation, but she could not be sure how she would be received in Elmira
and in the parish of Trinity Episcopal Church. As a single woman in
Whitesboro, her desire not to go out in society or receive people in
her home did not matter much. Nor did her relatively high standard
for what she called "suitable intellectual companionship." But all of
this *did* matter when she entered Elmira society as the wife of the
Episcopal minister. Knowing herself well, she determined to try to
like people and to do her duty by William, but she feared for the
worst. On a more private level, she was concerned, too, how she
would fare domestically—how she would manage their household
and her housekeepers—and how she would handle her inevitable
loneliness, cut off as she was from her large and adoring family.
Socially, Miriam's values lay entirely with the more traditional, sentimental ideal characterized by personal and social sincerity, by simplic-
ity of dress and manners, by the eschewing of fads and fashions, and
especially in her case, by preferring a meritocracy based on intellectual
superiority rather than worldly possessions. While she may not have
had aspirations to wealth and gentility, she did have her pride, and
pride alone would have made her heartily disappointed by the house
William had rented.

The "nice little box" that Miriam Whitcher saw from a distance
her first evening in town turned out, on closer inspection, to be "the
most miserable, forlorn little caboose you ever saw."[3] Miriam had
good reason to complain: All the rooms were tiny, the kitchen was a
"mere shanty of rough boards stuck on behind . . . quite exposed to
the elements," and the house flooded in the rains and baked in the
sun:

> The whole house is very hot, there is not a particle of shade any-
> where about it. The parlor is very low & only whitewashed, &
> gracious! how light! It has three windows where the sun streams in
> with unmitigated fury. The man wo'nt put any blinds on. He is a
> right mean, red faced, boozy presbyterian deacon. The shades you
> know are very light & consequently no protection against the sun,
> so we have just got some dark calico & put inside. It looks awfully
> but it darkens the room 'to some extent.' But nothing can make it
> cool, or keep out the flies, the house is full of flies of every descrip-
> tion—& bugs too—but no bed bugs. As to a spare bed—there is

not a place in the house to put one, so I have been obliged to give up having any. The front room above, is a mere oven. For about two feet just thro' the middle I can stand erect, from thence the wall slopes down nearly to the floor, & the door is so low that I have to bend nearly double to go through it. There is no such thing as staying in it more than five minutes at a time in warm weather, it is so broiling hot—just like our garret at home. I mean *your* home, not mine any more. I use it for a place to hang up my dresses & stow every thing not in immediate use. I never go in it without hitting my head. . . . You cannot imagine how crowded we are & what dreadful times we have trying to wash. I leave my clothes in the parlor at night & go out there to dress in the morning—& William poor man! it's funny to see the trouble he has about washing. We have thought seriously of turning the parlor into a bedroom, but it is not practicable. The study is still smaller. It just holds William's books, chair & little table. I have got a carpet for my room, *four & a half* yards, but have not yet had time to make it.[4]

With no help forthcoming from the landlord, William tried to fix the kitchen roof, but the next storm proved his efforts to be in vain: "The rain poured through like a shower bath, completely soaking every thing. We ran for our lives, & contemplated the desolation at a distance. Martha [the hired girl] laughed ready to burst, declaring she never saw such a '*funny* old kitchen' before. I thought if Martha could laugh I ought not to cry, so I laughed too, & tried to turn the matter into a joke, but it was by no means a *dry* one."[5]

Publicly, at least, Miriam defended William's poor choice of a house, telling her sister Kate that he had taken the house without knowing anything about it, and at a time when he was tired and discouraged. And the rent, she maintained, was attractive—only seventy-five dollars a year. Her defense of William was also reinforced by a vow she had made her first day in Elmira: "I am *determined* to be contented and satisfied [emphasis added]." Privately, however, there were sure signs of strain. Even her vow reflects an underlying sense of dissatisfaction—a threatened absence of contentment—and living in a house so obviously inadequate and run-down could only have added to her anxieties about fitting into the Elmira community. It was one thing to eschew genteel values but quite another to live shabbily. In the end, the house added to her acute awareness of social distinctions in Elmira. Knowing that he had made a terrible mistake, William for his part worked so hard to make their house more comfortable that his wife feared for his health:

> William's cold is very bad this morning, he can scarcely speak. He made it worse by knocking about in the storm & trying to shut out the rain which drove in at a terrible rate round the dining room door, wetting the carpet half way into the room. . . . I think William has worked too hard since we came here. He has been just as busy as he could be ever since we came here. He has made shelves & a rough table for the kitchen, out of the big box, & also a safe for the cellar. He has had so much to do about the house that [when] night comes he is perfectly exhausted. And then having such an uncomfortable sleeping room he has but little chance to rest.[6]

In the end, the house was so miserable that the Whitchers planned to move as soon as possible. Mr. Luce had a tenant in one of his houses who wanted to trade for a smaller house, but the tenant was *not* willing to trade for the Whitcher's house. Even so, the prospect that they might be able to move into one of Mr. Luce's houses reassured Miriam in the heat of summer when she was eaten up by the flies that were attracted to their house by the hogs rooting nearby.

By the end of the summer, they had indeed arranged to move into a house owned by Mr. Luce, one that William had earlier considered but rejected. Initially, Miriam was delighted, telling her sister that Mr. Luce promised to fix up the house "with a view to my comfort," even planning to go so far as to paint the outside "a kind of stone color—to please my fancy,"[7] thus making it the first wooden house in Elmira to be painted any color but white, according to Miriam. But Mr. Luce was more prompt with his promises than with his actions. By late September, when the Whitchers were due to move in, he still had not made any repairs, and Miriam dreaded facing "the prospect of being in a hubbub there, all winter perhaps."[8] She grew impatient with Mr. Luce, and while visiting her family briefly in Whitesboro, she urged William to back out of the agreement.

> Do not say another word to Mr Luce about it, let him take his own way, do not ask him again to fix the kitchen, you have said enough

about that—and if it is not done immediately, tell him that you have concluded not to take it—he cannot find any fault I am sure if you choose to do so. I hope you will think this a good plan after you have considered it. Another very great objection to the place is having a yard in common with another family. It makes all our arrangements so public, & is always productive of a deal of trouble & annoyance. I noticed that those Jero's used the yard as much as Mr Fairchild's folks & that would be very troublesome. There ought to be a fence there & all communication cut off. I do not want to be unreasonable, but all these things appear so plain to me now, since I have had time to think of them, that I wonder we did not hesitate about taking the house.[9]

Miriam's concern for privacy as expressed here was a common issue in midcentury. Advice manuals, for instance, offered repeated warnings to their readers to respect their friends' and neighbors' privacy by not venturing past the parlor into private areas of the house. According to Halttunen, the very need for privacy in bourgeois American culture grew out of the need to participate in the "genteel performance."[10] Whereas she locates the parlor as the primary stage upon which the genteel performance took place, and the back regions the areas into which the family could retreat and relax in private, the area Miriam was trying to protect was the yard, where privacy was desired.

Despite the strength of Miriam's conviction that they ought not to take the house, she promised William she would "cheerfully concur" with whatever decision he reached. One month later, in October 1847, the Whitchers moved into Mr. Luce's house. Miriam was true to her word; she never again complained to her sister about the house, the Luces as landlords, or the communal backyard. (The one exception came when she discovered that Mr. Luce intended to charge them rent on the house from the first of August, which represented a significant financial hardship.) Five months after the Whitchers arrived in Elmira, they were settled at last in a house that met their standards for comfort. October 1847 began a period in Miriam's life of relative contentment and productivity, and in the end, she became quite attached to their house, where they remained for the rest of their stay in Elmira.

Housekeeping and Housekeepers

Miriam's attempts to take charge of her own household for the first time, and especially her uncomfortable relationship with a series of housekeepers, reveal her anxieties about her place in society. To do all her own domestic work proved from the outset to be impossible, even had she been more experienced, because the work was simply too difficult physically. This dilemma meant that from the beginning the Whitchers had to find suitable, dependable help in the form of a live-in housekeeper; it also meant that Miriam had to negotiate an appropriate, comfortable relationship to her help. As with so many middle-class women of her time, it was almost impossible to achieve the latter. Miriam was fascinated by the domestic detail that unfolded before her, often finding in it good-humored material for her private letters and public writings, but she was also uneasy about having to try to manage her help. Her housekeeper's egalitarian airs especially amused and distressed her, as comic sketches she later wrote for Godey reveal; this in turn suggests that she shared mid-Victorians' anxieties about their relative degree of respectability.

Miriam was not the first writer to address the issue of housekeepers in midcentury America. One of her most famous predecessors was Mrs. Trollope, who set off a lively debate in 1832 when she attributed her difficulty finding suitable help to misguided American notions about equality: "One of these [servants] was a pretty girl, whose natural disposition must have been gentle and kind; but her good feelings were soured, and her gentleness turned to morbid sensitiveness, by having heard a thousand and a thousand times that she was as good as any other lady, that all men were equal, and women too, and that it was a sin and a shame for a free-born American to be treated like a servant. When she found she was to dine in the kitchen, she turned up her pretty lip, and said, 'I guess that's 'cause you don't think I'm good enough to eat with you. You'll find that won't do here.' "[11]

Assisted by a full-time helper literally from her first day in Elmira, Miriam was surprised to discover that she enjoyed the relatively light chores she took upon herself, and William was pleased with how well she managed overall. Encouraged by her initial success, she wanted to take on more responsibility, even going so far as to "tease" William about letting her dismiss her help and doing all the work herself; William "said it was perfect nonsense to think of it."

> Still I kept at him about it, until Martha went away [for the week-end], & I really had all the work to do. I tell you I almost died—especially on Monday, when it was awfully hot. I did'nt wash of course, but I got dinner. I *briled my* fish & I *biled my* peas—& I roasted myself into the bargain. Our kitchen is a perfect furnace. It rained very hard in the afternoon & I was afraid Martha would'nt come back. "O William" said I "if Martha does'nt come home before noon tomorrow you must go over to Aunty Hill's & get dinner—for I cannot stand it to cook any more" (I was sick with a diarrhea all the afternoon) William laughed in his sleeve all the time but did'nt say anything till Martha got home & then he began to bore me, "ah—you're the woman that was going to do your own work all so fast—you're the woman that thought it was ridiculous for such poor folks as we to sleep a hired girl—how do you feel about it now." "William" said I "what *are* you talking about? I'm sure I do'nt know what you mean"—But I hav'nt said a word since about dismissing Martha.[12]

A bit later, when she had more confidence in her own abilities and when their strained financial situation prompted Miriam to dismiss her second housekeeper, she tried in earnest to do all the work herself. Many of the tasks were entirely new to her, and she found the hard physical labor overwhelming. The laborious tasks of washing pots and scouring knives were especially difficult and tedious. She did not even try to bake, nor to do either the washing or the ironing, all physically demanding and time-consuming jobs. Even so, the work exhausted her. Advice books of the period reveal why this might have been so. For example, in 1857 Sarah Josepha Hale, editor of *Godey's Lady's Book,* published what she called *Mrs. Hale's Receipts for the Million*—a "complete family directory . . . to awaken the attention of my own sex to these subjects, belonging, so unquestionably, to woman's department." The first eighty-eight pages of her seven-hundred-page tome concerned "Home and its Employments," and covered the following topics: "House cleaning—repairing furniture—cleaning stoves and grates—mending glass, china, &c.—coloring and polishing furniture, &c.—removing unpleasant odors—fires—water and cisterns—carriages and harness—washing—to remove stains—to clean silks, laces, &c.—paste, glue, and cement—dyeing—blacking for boots, shoes &c.—to destroy insects—the kitchen, &c."[13] To her own and William's satisfaction, Miriam did learn to do two new tasks—cook fish and cook meat—and she devised several labor-saving schemes to relieve some of her burden: she reused cooking pots several times before washing them, and she put "several uncongenial articles together upon one dish" to cut down on the number of dishes she had to wash. "But not withstanding all these labor saving plans, I had as much to do as I could possibly accomplish. The same routine every day—got breakfast—got dinner—got tea—& got tired to death."[14]

When she had the chance to hire a new housekeeper two weeks later, she eagerly did so. Still, two important lessons emerged from the grand experiment of being her own "functionary," as she called herself. She gained vitally needed self-confidence about her ability to manage her help—"I really feel much more competent to direct a girl than I did a fortnight ago"[15]—and having had the chance to test herself and to satisfy herself that she *could* do the work if necessary, she was able to lay to rest the idea of taking on housekeeping as her primary occupation. She was finally content to turn the work over to someone else.

Finding suitable help was in itself a task, however, and a string of housekeepers passed through the Whitchers' house before they finally found someone who satisfied them and who would agree to stay. In her letters home, Miriam's reports of her experiences with her hired help took on comic overtones; later, when she left Elmira for good, she used the material from her own letters, generously supplemented by her imagination, as the basis for her final story for *Godey's Lady's Book,* "Letters from Timberville, III."[16] The way she interwove a fictional style within her factual reports to her family, and factual details in her fictional account for the *Lady's Book,* exemplifies how even the smallest domestic detail was ready grist for her imagination. A comparison of the two written forms—her letters and her fiction— in the pages that follow shows not only how she exaggerated the facts of her situation for comic effect but also how the final bitter months in Elmira, as expressed in her fiction, colored her more sanguine initial personal experiences.

Martha, their first housekeeper, arrived in Elmira at the same time the Whitchers did and immediately set about trying to salvage their first house. Miriam seemed reasonably pleased with Martha, complaining only that she broke so many of their good cups that they had to buy common ones that were nearly indestructible. Martha stayed through most of that first hot summer, then apparently left by her own design. No one was immediately available to replace her, but Miriam soon left to visit her family in Whitesboro and William was attending a conference, so the matter was not critical. Little else is said about Martha in Whitcher's letters, but she looms large in "Letters from Timberville, III."

This sketch focuses primarily on how hard it was for the narrator, Mrs. Waters, to find good help in Timberville.[17] In this sketch, Martha is portrayed as Rowena Ruggles, "an overgrown, raw-boned girl." According to Mrs. Waters, "she could bake, and wash, and do plain cooking very well; but her notions of equality, and her utter ignorance of the proprieties of her situation, rendered it very difficult to get on with her" (pp. 328–29). As even with this brief passage reveals, the narrative voice in "Letters from Timberville" is unlike the vernacular voice of Miriam's other fictional characters. Instead, she adopted for these sketches the more common technique of American nineteenth-century humor in which a proper narrator sets up the story but occasionally lets the vernacular character speak in his or her own voice. Part of the humor of such stories can come from the stark contrast between the two voices, but "Letters from Timberville, III" works best when the more familiar vernacular voice dominates, as in the following passage when Rowena resigns from her job:

> "I'm a goin'," said she, "acause you've made an underlin' of me ever sence I come here. You hain't axed me to set down to the table and take a meal o' vittels with ye onct; and Miss Crandal's help allers eats at the table with 'em, and Miss Crandal's as good as you be, any day; and she says it's an impersition; and my sister Batsey lived a year and a half to Squire Huger's, to the Flatts, and she allers eat to the table with 'em; and they was respectabler'n you be, and lived in enough sight grander house. And then, to cap all, you told me I wa'n't wanted in t'other room last night, and I ain't a goin' to put up with it no longer; and *so*—and you may git yer work did the best way ye ken, for all I care." (p. 331)

The incident Rowena alludes to "in t'other room" took place when the narrator and her husband returned home to find Rowena entertaining three of their friends who had called on them while they were out. Her primary offense lay in claiming for her own her employer's parlor, for assuming the role of hostess in Mrs. Waters's own home. "We found Rowena in the parlor, seated in my rocking chair, with her feet on an ottoman, my Cologne bottle in her hand, and playing the hostess to Monsieur Laborde, Mr. Griffin, and Mr. Bunker. . . . The gentlemen had evidently been highly entertained with her easy manners and conversational powers. I was thoroughly vexed, and told her emphatically to leave the room" (p. 330). Not content merely to resign, Rowena has her "educated" brother write to Mr. and Mrs. Waters to accuse them of being conceited, which was one of the main charges leveled against Miriam by her Elmira parishioners:

> To mister fillip Wotters. sir
>   ef you Think that you and your Stuck up wife is a goin' to Sale to hevven in a grander bote than the one your help goes in, your Mistaken i gess. That interesting young Lady roweny ruggles That you Treted so shameful is kalkulated to Be a nornament to Sociaty and would Be ef it want for such Stick ups as you And miss wotters is. i rite to let you know what i And all rite minded gentle-men And ladis Thinks of such karacters as you Be. so no more From yours contemptably.
>
> Silas Brigham (p. 332)

In this instance, it is especially interesting how Miriam's literary humor stands in relationship to her private life. Clearly stung by the accusations that she acted superior to others in the community, Miriam here brings the same charge against her narrator. However, the accusation is made by one so obviously inferior that the comic effect is to exonerate Mrs. Waters, and by extension, Miriam Whitcher. The Mrs. Waters/Miriam Whitchers, so the story demonstrates, have every right to their claim of social superiority when compared to the Rowenas of the world.

When Martha left the Whitchers, they hired a young woman named Maria Ferris, but only two weeks after she began to work for them, Miriam decided to try to do all the household chores herself in the grand experiment described earlier:

> She is on the whole a very good girl, better than I expected to find here—dreadfully silly—but washes & irons nicely & makes good bread, & does common cooking very well. This morning I told her my determination [to do the work myself] & she felt very badly. Said she liked me better'n any woman she ever lived with, & she liked *him* tew, (She always calls William *he* & *him*) & she did wish how's I'd keep her. I told her I liked her very much, & if I kept any girl I would have her, & should I find myself unable to do the work alone, I would send for her if she had no other place. And I doubt whether she will get any place, she is so foolish about somethings.[18]

When Miriam let Maria go, she was immediately taken in by Mrs. Luce, in whose home she behaved miserably. "Her foolish yaw-hawing was such a bore. She is more disagreeable at Mrs L's than she was here—insists upon sitting at the table, where she is very disgusting. Mrs L will only keep her until she can get a better girl."[19]

Maria inspired Miriam's portrayal of Rowena and a second fictional character in "Letters from Timberville, III"—Polly Baily—who was faulted for her stupidity and her gross ineptitude. She puts salt in the coffee, turns the mutton chops to charcoal, and cannot remember how to greet guests or to perform the simplest tasks. But Mrs. Waters admires Polly's earnestness, and so works with her as best she can. Unfortunately, Polly tells the neighbors everything that goes on in the Waters's household, and she tells Mrs. Waters endless stories about how she was mistreated by other employers. Like her real-life counterpart, Maria, Polly is sorry to leave her employer after only two weeks. According to Mrs. Waters, "she liked me better than anybody she had ever lived with." Mrs. Waters does not, however, say anything about "him" (p. 339). The narrator soon jokes that she has become like the other people of Timberville who spend all their time talking about how hard it is to get good help. Not wanting to "bore her listeners with any more details," she writes no more than a sentence or two about her final two housekeepers. Even so, the picture of each is anything but flattering. One is described as a "thievish, intemperate Irish woman," and the other as "a lazy, saucy black girl." There were life models for these two characters, also, insofar as the Whitchers hired an Irish housekeeper named Ellen and a black woman named Jane, but here the resemblances end. What served Miriam's fictional purposes in fact distorted her reality in surprising ways.

After a fortnight without any help, the Whitchers were especially pleased when Ellen presented herself to them. She had several qualities to recommend her besides the Whitchers' realization that it was too difficult for Miriam to do all the work by herself. More critically, Ellen had been trained and recommended by Mrs. Van Zandt, who had an excellent reputation for managing domestic help. In contrast with Maria, who "yaw-hawed," Ellen apparently spoke only when it was necessary. Finally, "she has no ideas of equality, & does not seem to think of coming to the table with us."[20] Despite this promising beginning, Ellen also left the Whitchers after only two weeks when a young woman whom William had engaged the previous year suddenly showed up in Elmira, expecting to live "with us this winter, & we felt under obligation to take her."[21] Ellen was passed on to the ever-accommodating Mrs. Luce, the infamous Maria having left only a day earlier. "She takes my girls off my hands very kindly," Miriam reported to her family.

Jane turned out to be efficient, pleasant, and mature; twenty-five years old, she had the experience and strength to serve the Whitchers' domestic needs perfectly. For reasons that are not entirely clear, Miriam was also pleased that Jane was black. "It has been my ambition to get a good black girl," Miriam wrote her sister, but she did not elaborate.[22] Possibly she was hoping through Jane to live out one of Beriah Green's abolitionist tenets—that it was not enough to want emancipation for blacks if the races remained entirely separated from one another. By taking a black person into her home, albeit as a servant, she was clearly making a moral statement. Abolitionist sentiment was strong in Elmira; the town was active in the underground railroad, and it had a relatively large black population. But a black servant would also lay to rest vexing issues about social equality; by nineteenth-century standards, the relations between the mistress and her black housekeeper would be relatively more determined from the outset. On purely domestic grounds, Jane's arrival at the Whitcher household was entirely fortuitous. Miriam quickly became fond of her and respected her work. "Jane takes all household care from my mind. She is an excellent girl so far, & I hope I can keep her all winter. If I do I shall think she was providentially sent."[23] Evidently she was, for Jane stayed on with the Whitchers well into the next year, thus freeing Miriam for the first time to turn her attention to other activities. One of her priorities was learning to make her way in her new community, getting to know the parishioners and the town of Elmira.

Elmira in the 1840s

Located on the bank of the Chemung River, and nestled among gently rolling hills, Elmira in the 1840s was a lumber-producing village that made a very favorable first impression on Miriam Whitcher: "The village is full of roses & all other flowers. Climbing roses are very common. They are beautiful, white, like Helen's, & sometimes run up on the roof. Elmira is a very pretty village, some of the streets are quite handsome & neat; but the beautiful hills that surround us constitute the greatest attraction to me."[24] Although slightly smaller in population than Whitesboro, Elmira was experiencing the kind of growing pains that Utica had gone through two decades earlier. In just two years, 1845–46, Elmira's population increased by one thousand people.[25] In practical terms this growth meant that the society Miriam encountered in Elmira was far more fluid, much less stable, than she was accustomed to at home. The story of the meteoric rise of Elmira's most notable entrepreneur illustrates this point perfectly.

John Arnot, Sr., born in Scotland, arrived in Elmira in 1819 at the age of thirty; he came there, his biographer claims, "on a merchantile venture."[26] Understanding immediately the possibilities for personal gain, he remained in Elmira and married Harriet Tuttle, the daughter of Elmira's then most successful businessman. Within ten years, Arnot had surpassed his father-in-law and all other rivals in business, and that was only the beginning of his success. As late as 1892, a local historian claimed that the name John Arnot "is yet potent to conjure with in the county and in fact in all the counties."[27] Arnot took over Stephen Tuttle's mill, renaming it after himself; he was a founder and original stockholder of the Chemung Canal Bank, which he eventually owned outright; and he negotiated to bring the Erie Railroad through Elmira, and then won the contract to build the line. He took over ownership and operation of the company that furnished gas to the village, and he also was involved in bringing additional railway lines into the village, including one that opened up the Pennsylvania coalfields for his exploration. His children followed his example and exerted a powerful influence over Elmira for years to come; even today public buildings and parks bear the Arnot name. Miriam Whitcher might certainly have heard about similar but more modest success stories in nearby Utica in the decade following the opening of the Erie Canal, but she would have witnessed no such phenomenon in Whitesboro. The mood and tone of the two villages differed dramatically.

Elmira, for instance, was essentially bypassed by the Second Great Awakening that had such a profound effect on the people of Oneida County and on Miriam herself. As Whitney Cross has demonstrated, Finney's revivalism flourished where the agrarian economy had already reached nearly full maturity, as it had in Oneida County; "the portions of the southern tier which retained genuine frontier conditions had therefore little part in this history."[28] That frontier conditions continued to prevail in Elmira forcefully struck both William and Miriam Whitcher, as their letters to the Berry family attested. One of William's first letters back to Whitesboro in 1847 contained a description of the local doctors and what he called their strange tobacco habits; although the letter no longer survives, one of Miriam's letters to William tells him how much his descriptions amused her father, Lewis Berry, and became something of a family joke. When Miriam had to consult a doctor shortly after her arrival in Elmira, she hastened to reassure her family that he was "a good old gentleman & does not belong to the smokers & *chawers.*"[29] In much more graphic detail, Mrs. Trollope had explored this subject a decade earlier. She found the nearly universal male American habit of chewing tobacco and the incessant spitting that accompanied it a matter of the greatest personal disgust. Nor was the custom limited to the frontier, according to Mrs. Trollope, who found herself drawn back day after day to the Congress of the United States because of the "beauty of the chamber" itself: "It was, however, really mortifying to see this splendid hall, fitted up in so stately and sumptuous a manner, filled with men, sitting in the most unseemly attitudes, a large majority with their hats on, and nearly all, spitting to an excess that decency forbids me to describe."[30]

If the doctors of Elmira were faintly comic because of their addiction to tobacco, the local dentist seemed downright primitive compared to his Whitesboro counterparts; his office would have fit in better in a gold-mining camp than a prosperous village in New York State:

> William lost the filling from a tooth & went to Dr Potter—the best dentist we have—to get it refilled. He thinks he is a pretty good operator, but all his surroundings were so forlorn that William came home almost sick. He had a miserable dirty spitbox for his patients to spit in, & instead of a neat napkin gave him a piece of dirty cotton rag to stuff in his mouth, & to crown all, he never stopped to clean his instruments after using them for one patient, but stuck them right into another mouth. There is another dentist, a kind of methodist exhorter—an awful bungler. The set of teeth that he has for a sign would make Henry or Patten White dranged if they could but see them.[31]

There were, however, important similarities between the two villages, with one of the more striking being the pattern of abolitionist agitation. Whitesboro led the way by a decade, but in January 1846, only a year and a half before the Whitchers arrived in town, forty members split from the Presbyterian church to form an independent Congregational church they named Park Church. Like the Whitesboro Congregational Church, Park Church was founded almost exclusively by staunch abolitionists.[32] The memory of the split within the Presbyterian church was still fresh in the minds of the townspeople, and some people were routinely identified as abolitionists.[33] Also like Whitesboro, Elmira in the 1840s hosted a vast array of voluntary associations, which were always a source of amusement to Miriam, as the following excerpt from her first "Letter from Timberville" reveals:

> We have all sorts of societies, too. Missionary societies, bible societies, tract societies, sewing societies, maternal societies, mutual improvement societies, sons of temperance and daughters of temperance

societies, odd fellows' societies, and an odd ladies' society, composed chiefly of ancient maidens. We have freemasons' societies, literary societies, woman's rights societies, anti-everything societies, benevolent societies for all sorts of objects. . . . In short, we have every kind of society that you can possibly mention. (pp. 298–99)

As a growing, expanding village, Elmira embraced social and cultural values that amused Miriam, but none went more against the grain than what appeared to her to be a nearly universal preoccupation with money and all the trappings of upward mobility—with middle-class aspirations to gentility:

> As is the case in almost all new *enterprising* villages, the chief distinction among us is that of "rich and poor." So soon as a man is able to put up, or even to hire, a large house with two parlors and folding-doors, and furnish it showily, he takes his standing among the *first*. The one grand object of the Timbervillians is to get rich. They are all agog just now about California. Mr. Martin, and Mr. Crandall, and Mr. Wiggins, have almost made up their minds to abandon their respective occupations and set off for the gold country; and their wives are quite delighted with the idea; for Mrs. Martin wants a great many things which Mr. Martin, rich as he is, cannot afford now. And Mrs. Crandall is very desirous that Mr. Crandall should go, in order that he may come back able to build a grander house than Mr. Martin's, with larger columns and more green blinds. She knows she's as good as Mrs. Martin, any day, and she'd like to let other people know it. . . . "Gold! gold! gold!" is the cry from every mouth, old and young. Oh, we shall soon be a city.[34]
> (p. 299)

Again and again, variations on this theme are repeated in Miriam's letters and in her humor. The more she came to know the community, the more she objected to the social pretensions she felt governed people's lives. The dominant values of the community conflicted with her own, both personal and religious, stimulating her imagination more profoundly than anything else ever had. Nonetheless, it is important to keep in mind that while Miriam Whitcher found in Elmira the raw material for her social satires, the chords she struck, the nerves she exposed, transcended both time and place. She may have believed that Elmirans were unique in their pursuit of social status, but the readers of *Godey's Lady's Book,* and later *The Widow Bedott Papers,* knew otherwise. People all over the area thought that *their* village was the model for the anonymous sketches that appeared in the *Lady's Book.* Whether it was the Widow Bedott as she increasingly embraced the genteel values Miriam came to deplore, or Aunt Maguire exposing the hypocrisy of her fellow townspeople, the sketches that Miriam wrote during her Elmira period were unquestionably the most powerful and most compelling of her career. In them she captured the essence of an entire era.

The relationship between gentility and hypocrisy was a complex one in mid-Victorian America, and conduct manuals of the period identified hypocrisy as one of the major issues facing those aspiring to genteel status.[35] To dress in the latest fashions, to observe all the polite forms of etiquette, was in one sense to be false to more natural, sincere forms of self-expression. To betray these more traditional values made mid-Victorians anxious; to embrace social pretentions on the scale Miriam believed the inhabitants of Elmira did, was to engage in full-scale hypocrisy. Evidently the readers of *Godey's Lady's Book,* many of whom themselves could have been the targets of Miriam's humor, found her exposure of social hypocrisy endlessly satisfying. The forces of gentility Miriam Whitcher encountered in the 1840s were far too powerful to laugh out of existence, but not so powerful they could not be shown up as absurd.

"Cooking, Fixing, Scandal & Quilting"

The people of Elmira made at best a mixed impression on Miriam. Yet how Miriam responded to her new acquaintances became a matter of the utmost importance for her writing. However skillful her writing had been to this point, nothing in it anticipates the bitter sting of her final Aunt Maguire sketches. For this reason her first descriptions of Elmira's residents in her letters home take on special significance. The first time Miriam described the parishioners of Trinity Church, she identified the one quality that became key to her response to the people of Elmira—how they "rated" on "the intellectual scale." As the following excerpt from her letters suggests, because of the association of the Episcopal church with upward mobility, the Elmira parish consisted of numerous recent converts whom Miriam thought were more concerned with worldly issues than with church doctrine:

> They are—so far as I can tell very clever, well meaning people, but (with the exception of two or three families) are rather low in the intellectual scale. Of course I have not yet seen all the congregation—but those I have seen are a peculiar race of beings. There are none among them excepting Mr Luce's folks & a few others—who appear to know anything about the principles & doctrines of the church—This I attribute in a great measure to the fact that they have nearly all come in from various denominations around us. The men seem to be much better instructed than the women, a good many of whom have joined us because their husbands did. . . . I have noticed that the men are much greater readers than the women & consequently they are more agreeable companions. The women generally are pretty much occupied with cooking, fixing, scandal & quilting. The last named accomplishment is carried to an extent almost beyond belief. . . . There seems to be a perfect passion for quilting among the ladies—& a great strife to have the most elaborate patterns.[36]

Later in the same letter her writer's ear takes over, and she reports with considerable amusement how quaint she found the ladies' fondness for the word "so":

> They make great use of that word, & accent it very strongly. I can't make you understand without hearing them talk—*so*—I will introduce you to a bevy of ladies who are quilting for the parson's wife. Mrs A.B.C. & D—Mrs. B. has just taken her seat at the frame. Mrs A—"Mrs B: aint this a pretty quilt?" Mrs B. "It is *so*—something new these great squares"—Mrs C. "They are *so*—I always make my quilts in stripes when I have two colors—Do'nt you?" Mrs C. "I do *so*—but I think this looks very well—" Mrs B. "It does *so*—but seems to me you're putting very little work on it." Mrs A. "We are *so*—but Mrs Whitcher would'nt have any more on—" Mrs Whitcher "O! there's quite enough to suit me, as much as I've ever been accustomed to see on quilts—" Mrs B. "Why Mrs W! how you talk! why I never think of putting the lines more than the width of a pipe

stem apart on *my* quilts." Mrs D. "Mrs W. ought to see Mrs P's
quilt—why she had it on the frame a whole month & there was
some o' the neighbors in helping her almost every day too. O! it
was the beautifullest quilt I ever *did* see—you could'nt lay a six-
pence down anywhere on it, where t'want quilted—" Mrs C. "Yes,
that *was* an elegant quilt—" Mrs. A "but do'nt you think she missed
it putting that thimble work border on? to *my* mind double checks
make a prettier border." Mrs B. "They do *so*—but then you know
Mrs P's got such a curious taste—if every body else despised thimble-
work *she'd* have it all the sooner." Mrs A "Why, if you'll believe it
she told me a spell ago that she meant to make her next quilt
herrin-bone!—did you ever!!" Mrs Whitcher—"I think Mrs P's a
very pleasant lady" Mrs D "she is *so*—when she's a mind to be, but
she has her peculiarities as all of us have you know—" Mrs A "She
has *so*—but the world would'nt be made up without her."[37]

Immediately after writing this scene, Miriam cautioned her sister
not to repeat a word of what she said about Elmira folks to anyone in
Whitesboro: "I would'nt like to have it said anywhere that I make fun
of our parishioners—they are nice people, but they have their peculiarities—as they say about each other." Although there is no malice
in her description of Mrs. A, B, C, and D, only the old habit of
caricature coming to the fore, this passage does convey a sense of
Miriam's feelings of being an outsider. Note, too, that Miriam assumed the role of naïve troublemaker in the scene she described—
interjecting as she did the observation that Mrs. P is a "very pleasant
lady." On the face of it, such a remark would appear to discourage
the women's gossip about Mrs. P, but as Miriam well knew, it only
encouraged the women to continue.

It was one thing for Miriam to poke fun at the parishioners in
private, but quite another to believe the people of Elmira to be
generally inferior. Even before William first went to Elmira, the
Whitchers had heard that the people there were "not over refined.
For instance, the young ladies call the young men 'hosses' and their
parties 'opeeroes.' "[38] Predisposed by temperament to be a harsh
judge, and primed by what she had heard, Miriam was nonetheless
genuinely disappointed by the people of Elmira, whom she found not
only "unrefined" but also incurable socializers. Their apparent lack of
interest in intellectual matters was particularly upsetting, and their

dedication to going about in society troublesome; the first was a personal matter for Miriam, leaving her ultimately more isolated than she had expected, while the second was a matter of principle: "Brother John is right about it being a continual spree here. Of course we see nothing of it, but we hear enough. There are two or three parties every week. I do not believe there is another community so gay & thoughtless in the country."[39]

She especially disapproved of the amount of dancing that went on, and the drunkenness that sometimes accompanied it. Judging by the context in which she raised the issue in a letter to her sister, she took the matter very seriously indeed:

> What a terrible time you have had with the small pox at Whites-boro! They say there are several cases here, but I do not know whether it is so. It seems to create no panic. In fact, I do'nt think the people here would be seriously alarmed at any epidemic, unless it should be something that affected the *toes,* and interfered with *dancing.* I never heard of such a dancing community. There are two or three balls every week. There was one on *Saturday* night at the Eagle tavern. The first people of the village were there, & several gentlemen got so tipsey they had to be carried to bed. Thank heaven—they were none of our church members. But all denominations *go it.* Baptists, presbyterians, episcopalians & *nobodies*—all kick up their heels together in one promiscuous fandago.[40]

One of the first decisions the Whitchers made when they moved to Elmira was not to receive or return social calls, a decision Miriam said was understood and accepted by their congregation.[41] Such a decision suited her temperamentally and was entirely in keeping with the kind of life she was accustomed to in Whitesboro, but it was also a serious miscalculation on their part. Always vulnerable to the accusation that she was aloof, keeping herself apart socially from the community and congregation only reinforced that perception. She was inevitably compared unfavorably to her immediate predecessor, Mrs. Van Zandt, who had been very active socially and was well liked by the congregation. As one of Miriam's fictional characters said of the new minister's wife, "She doesn't go about in our set the way Mrs. Van Duzen did."

In describing for her family what she called "the New Year's fuss" when the men of the town went from one house to the next to be entertained by the women, Miriam prefaced her remarks by saying that she and William let it be known they did not plan to participate in the festivities. "The gentlemen *call* as if their lives depended upon it—& the ladies stuff them with '*coffee & oysters*' and all manner of knick *nacks*."⁴² Despite their protests, their friend and churchwoman Aunty Hill sent a wagon by to pick them up at dinner time, and rather than give offense, Miriam climbed aboard, dressed as she was in her "old duds," and William followed on foot through the mud and slush. In the end, Miriam was not sorry she went; the sight of the food alone, she declared, made it worth the outing. The found, much to their astonishment, two rooms filled with food for the callers— nuts, raisins, a turkey, pickled tongues, "oysters, raw & cooked in every way," plus cakes and candies. In addition, a back dining room was set up exclusively for the Whitchers and for Aunty Hill's family of grown boys.

> Aunty was perfectly happy. She came up to me & gave me a dig in the ribs, and said she "O Mrs Whitcher, it's a rale pleasant day we're a having and I hope we'll all meet and have just such another next New Year's—I say—I hope the Lord'll presarve us all & bring us together again, but he only knows—I say—the Lord only knows where we'll all be then, whether we'll be on God's arth or in etarnity—but I'm sure I hope wherever we be we'll be having a rale good time"—I thought I should capsize when she came to the climax, but I did'nt dare to laugh. We stayed to dinner & came home about two o'clock.⁴³

The Whitchers were fortunate to have friends such as the Hills who could rescue them, at times, from their own determination to remain apart from Elmira society. Such people, however, were few in number. As founding members of the Episcopal church, the Hills had been especially kind to William when he first arrived in Elmira, and so Miriam was determined to like Aunty Hill even before she met her. Yet initially Aunty Hill's "gabble" almost drove Miriam crazy, and when she first attempted to introduce her to her family via her letters, she was uncharacteristically at a loss for words, describing her only as "the queerest old woman I ever knew."[44] But slowly she warmed to Aunty Hill, finding her generosity, her good-natured affection for William, and her dedication to the church irresistible. A continual source of amusement to Miriam was Aunty Hill's way of talking under even the most solemn circumstances. Only two weeks after the New Year's Day celebration, Aunty Hill lay on her deathbed, suffering from coughing spells "that almost strangled her. When she got through [with one] she remarked, 'When I lie aisy the Lord is all sufficient, but when I cough so, deliver my soul, if I don't forget all about him.' I could hardly help smiling."[45] When Aunty Hill died in late January 1848, the Whitchers lost not only a good friend but also one of William's greatest admirers.

The Luces, meanwhile, despite some hard feelings over the house the Whitchers rented, continued to figure prominently in their lives. From the first, Miriam had liked Mrs. Luce; she was attracted by her kindness to William and her dedication to the affairs of the church, but she was also drawn to her obvious intelligence. The Luces, too, were founding members of Trinity Episcopal Church and were well versed in church theology. They extended many kindnesses to the Whitchers during their first year in Elmira. They took in overnight guests who could not stay with the Whitchers because of their small house; Mrs. Luce frequently furnished them with fresh fruit from her garden, and Mr. Luce with an abundance of fresh-cut flowers that Miriam loved, and they took them sleighing when snow covered the streets of Elmira. One of the tragedies of the Whitchers' stay in Elmira was that it ended with the Luces publicly turned against them, and it was Mr. Luce whom William ultimately blamed for stirring up the congregation against him. But especially in the early months, the Luces were true and valued friends.

Two other couples soon became the Whitchers' friends: Mr. and Mrs. Billington and Mr. and Mrs. Scribner, all relative newcomers to the town. In praising the Scribners to her family, Miriam also revealed her reservations about the people of Elmira in general: "If all our parishioners were like the Scribners, we might live & die here. They are really attached to the church—instructed & bro't up in it—Mrs. S. is a daughter of Dr Sheldon of Troy. She is a most estimable woman, vastly superior to the majority here."[46] Their contact with the Scribners, however, did not seem to be as regular as their visits to the Billingtons, whose log cabin in the country outside Elmira greatly appealed to Miriam. While no description of the Billingtons survives, Miriam did tell her family that their daughter seemed "superior" to the other young people the Whitchers had met in Elmira.

Just as Miriam decided not to go out in society, she also decided not to have any connection with the local literary society. Thinking it inappropriate for the wife of the minister to be a writer at all, let alone a humorist, she wanted to conceal her authorship from the congregation; even before the villagers figured prominently in her sketches, she was anxious that no one know she was the author of the Widow Bedott sketches. Nonetheless, she and William were both invited to join the local literary group shortly after they arrived in Elmira, and William anticipated attending the group at least a time or two. Miriam's initial decision not to participate in the literary society was reinforced by her encounters with one of the local luminaries:

> You would be amused at the attempts to be literary here. One lady, who is decidedly the most *pretentious* person in the village, in a literary point of view, actually told me the other day that she had been reading Dean Swift's John Gilpin!! She also said that she liked Dante's "vision of judgment" better than any of his other poems! She pretends to have read everything & has read nothing & could'nt understand if she should read. I have seen some of her writing—in fact I have a piece that I would like to keep to show to you—you never saw such spelling—"homage" is spelt "omage" and "issued" is "ishewed." And this lady is the editor of "The Weekly," a paper published in the society.[47]

In her first "Letters from Timberville," Miriam's narrator, Mrs. Waters, is invited to attend a literary "sawree" after the people of Timberville learn that she "*took the newspapers.*" Rather than include samples of the literature presented by the society members, Mrs. Waters focuses almost entirely on descriptions of the members and their claims to literary fame. The hostess, "that short, dumpy lady," resembles the editor of "The Weekly" described above, while her husband in the sketch is a horse trader who comes to the meeting fresh from the horse yard, which earns him his wife's glares. Two others, Mrs. Boors and Miss Quince, rarely speak, and then only in monosyllables; another is a belle who gets by with a certain "lawlessness" because of her beauty; another is a critic who never writes a word himself, and who admires nothing but Poe's "The Raven"; two old-maid sisters are described as having "too much fastidiousness," while another member is included in the society only because she has a large parlor, provides excellent refreshments, and admires indiscriminately everything the other members write (pp. 301–7).

The men of Elmira, much to Miriam's surprise, seemed more interested in literature and were more talented as writers than the women, a situation that greatly concerned her. For one, it nearly sealed her isolation. Although she was indeed reluctant to join in the public activity of the village, she was responsive to friendships, but such friendships would have been possible only among women. For another, she found it increasingly frustrating to be surrounded by women "who think of little else than dress & dancing."[48] From Miriam's point of view, the women of Elmira were not interested in intellectual matters, nor did they have the education or stimulation to become interested; instead, their attention was fixed upon social matters that she found wholly insignificant. For her these ranged from an innocuous preoccupation with how many stitches to put on a quilt to a morally reprehensible social pretentiousness and preoccupation with fashion and frivolity. Ultimately, these shortcomings were developed into the material of full-fledged social satire.

Trinity Episcopal Church

Trinity Episcopal Church to which William was called as pastor had a much longer history than its missionary counterpart in Whitesboro. Established in 1833 and officially organized in 1834, the church had its own building under construction as early as 1837, and had a large and active membership by the time William arrived there. It had, however, a troubled history with its pastors: in the fourteen years between 1833 and 1847 when William became pastor, six other ministers had come and gone. None stayed longer than three years, and one, the Reverend Kendrick Metcalf, remained only one. The tenure of William's immediate predecessor, the Reverend Washington Van Zandt, had been especially tumultuous. As one historian delicately observed, Van Zandt "was one of the most eloquent men in

the pulpit that ever took orders, but unfortunate in his social relations."⁴⁹ Van Zandt's troubles with the parish did not end with his
dismissal. At first Van Zandt's continuing presence in Elmira was
more of an embarrassment to William than a true cause for concern,
but soon it became clear that the former pastor was determined to
make trouble. Early in the Whitchers' tenure in Elmira, Van Zandt
was accused of posting on the church door what Miriam called a
"scurrilous handbill." Then he circulated copies of the handbill
throughout the community, "abusing the episcopal church—& some
of the ladies in the most indecent language. They were thrown into
yards, there was one in our yard."⁵⁰ One of the women singled out
for denigration was Aunty Hill, who came to the Whitchers "in a
terrible state of excitement about the handbill." During the same
period, according to Miriam, Van Zandt was "seen several times tipsy.
No doubt he will turn out a vagabond."⁵¹

Part of Van Zandt's vendetta against the church focused on the
fact that when he was dismissed the congregation still owed him two
hundred dollars, nearly half his annual salary. When the matter came
to William's attention, he collected the money from individual members of the congregation himself; he was motivated in part by a
strong desire to remove any excuse for Van Zandt to remain in the
area and, in part, by genuine sympathy for his financial plight. Collecting the debt was a difficult task, however, given Van Zandt's
disfavor among the congregation, as well as the difficulty ministers
had collecting their salaries even under the most favorable conditions.
Nor did William foresee how his efforts on behalf of Van Zandt
would contribute to his difficulty in collecting his own salary when it
was due, for the money he collected for Van Zandt's salary was
money that would otherwise have come to him.

Still, William's willingness to help Van Zandt endeared him to
some members of his new congregation. If Aunty Hill's deathbed
reaction was any indication, the debt had weighed heavily on the
minds of many conscientious church members, and William was blessed
for his efforts to put things right:

> "Sure I am" said she "that my Lord & Master is going to call me
> now, & I'm entirely ready to go, and I praise & bless his holy name
> that he did'nt call me a year ago when that miserable Van Zandt was

here, & when the church was in debt, & everybody was a quarrel-
ing. I say, I praise my Lord Master that he's let me live to hear my
dear good minister prache a few months, & to have him come &
see me & pray wid me when I'm sick, & give me the Holy Communion, & help me prepare to die, & to see him be the manes o'
payin that old church debt. I say I'm thankful that I've lived till this
time. I did'nt desarve such a mercy." She repeated this daily, &
hourly, & though she suffered dreadfully—never complained.[52]

Money would always be a problem for the Whitchers in Elmira
and after. The five-hundred-dollar salary pledged to William was essentially his to collect, a custom common in American churches as
early as the seventeenth century, and ministers were always behind in
their collections. To some extent, the Whitchers always depended
upon the generosity of their congregation and their friends for part
of their subsistence, and Miriam in her letters frequently comment-
ed upon the gifts they received from friends and parishioners:
the Billingtons sent them home loaded with bushels of apples, the
Luces brought them fresh meat, and Aunty Hill delivered all manner
of provisions to them. Given Miriam's pride, she might well
have resented such acts of charity, but she seemed always genuinely
appreciative.

The open goodwill with which William and Miriam were welcomed into the church community was amply demonstrated during
their first six months in Elmira. Besides receiving generous gifts from
individual people, and considerable help sewing carpets and setting
up house from the women of the parish, the Whitchers were given a
donation party by the church in November 1847. A fairly common
custom in many churches, a donation party offered the parishioners
and other interested people an opportunity to donate a large variety
of goods to the minister and his family as a means of supplementing
their meager wages. Usually planned for the fall of the year when
people's larders and cellars were full from the recent harvests, and
when provisions had been laid in for the winter, a donation party was
also an occasion for a large number of families to get together socially. When the Whitchers were first approached about the party,
Miriam wanted to decline, but knowing that a refusal would only
offend the congregation and the party's organizers, she agreed to let
the party take place in their house, as was the custom:

They tell me that all I have to do is to sit still & grin & bear it. A committee of ladies is appointed to attend to everything. They go round & ascertain *who will* provide *what,* so that there is no confusion, & no overplus of one thing & lack of another. They come to the house, bring everything necessary—for the entertainment. One lady is appointed to receive the donations. I except we shall have *rich* times. How I wish you could be here. I expect it will be a trying time to me. I do not feel like seeing so much company. But the congregation would be offended if we should decline. They calculate on a donation party every year.[53]

Much to Miriam's surprise, the party was an unqualified success, thanks in part to the organizational skills of the churchwomen. Mrs. Luce and Miriam had decided in advance that three servants would suffice, in contrast to the six Mrs. Van Zandt had used, and Miriam proudly reported to her family that Jane "did admirably & won golden opinions from every one." The afternoon of the event, William and Miriam were not allowed to lift a hand; while one team of women made and served tea to the Whitchers, others scrubbed a wash boiler and filled it with coffee; yet others set up banks of tables to receive the donations and the large quantities of food brought in for the evening.

They began to pour in about seven oclock & continued to come until nine, & I never saw such a crowd. William had taken down our bed in the morning & put it up stairs, & we were very glad afterwards, for without using that room we should have been dreadfully cramped. The house was as full as it could hold. Our own congregation & many others. The children were sent into the study which is a large room. One lady was appointed to receive the money & another for other donations. I was introduced to a multitude of new people. In fact I did little else all the evening but stand up & receive the company. And I have heard since to my great satisfaction, that I made myself quite popular. A number of persons— (particularly gentlemen) have said to William that they were agreeably disappointed in his wife—had thought until that evening that she was very distant & haughty. In fact I did my best to be agreeable— for I felt the necessity of it on that occasion. Every one seemed happy & contented. The children played up stairs, the young folks sung & flirted in the hall & middle room, & the old-folks *convarsed* in the parlor.[54]

Overall, the party was a complete success: the donations the Whitchers received were substantial in both quantity and quality, nothing was broken, a large amount of food was left over for the Whitchers, and above all, the party generated good feelings all around. Afterwards, William calculated the total value of the donated items as $102, the equivalent of one-fifth of his annual salary. Miriam, for her part, sent her sister an itemized list of the donations she and William received.

8 lbs beef—
1 turkey—
12 lbs sugar, very nice—
4 lbs white sugar—
3 1/2 doz eggs—
11 loaves of cake
    some nutcakes & cookies—
7 lbs butter—
3 lbs raisins—
8 lbs tea, 5 lbs candles—
24 lbs coffee—
8 lbs do-burnt—
10 lbs cheeze—
1 bottle prunes—
1 lb ginger—
1 bottle catsup—
1 bottle mustard—
1 Lounge—very nice, from the upholsterer—
1 piece sheeting from Mrs Arnot—
24 yrds shirting—in various shirt patterns—
1 black satin vest—very handsome—
materials for a comfortable, from a presbyterian lady—calico, cotton
    &c—
11 yds calico, very pretty latest style, black with red & blue *spriggs*
    in—
10 yds calico, dark brown with red spriggs
3 yds calico, awful, 3 yds very pretty, little

8 yrds cambrick, 2 pairs gloves, nice for me
3 linen handkfs—two fine, one coarse—
3 pairs stockings, two worsted, one cotton—
1 1/2 yd flannel (*yaller*, awful coarse)—
2 little flannel peticoats—
1 little blanket, very nice bound with broad white satin ribbon,
    5 yards diaper, very nice—
1 stone jar, very large, 1 large tin pail—
1 large solar lamp, very pretty from Mrs Luce
1 box of writing materials consisting of a pen, a pearl paper folder,
    & a paper weight something like the one the judge sent you—
    only having a butterfly for a handle—a beautiful thing from
    young Mr Bust to me.[55]

The largest and by far the most valuable gift was the parlor lounge, which so pleased Miriam that she drew a picture of it for her sister, describing it as "very low—just as I like them, & has an excellent cushion. It is on castors & covered with handsome dark calico."[56] Finally, Miriam listed cash gifts totaling $35—"this was quite unexpected & very acceptable." Her only complaint about the party, in the end, was that it fell on Thanksgiving Day, but that one reservation only underscored the party's success: "I was thinking of home all day—& thought if I could only have father's family with me my happiness would be doubled."[57]

Inevitably, Miriam often felt lonely in Elmira. She especially missed her sister Kate, her closest companion and a fellow writer who appreciated Miriam's sense of humor. Even as she crossed Lake Seneca her second day away from home, she pulled out Kate's portrait and wished they were together; time and distance did nothing to weaken their bond or lessen the pain of their separation. Her sense of melancholy surfaced frequently and only intensified her feelings of loneliness and isolation. On one occasion she described herself as "fretful," and confessed to an "infirmity of disposition" that concerned William,[58] and later she told her family that she made "constant, desperate efforts to be cheerful & William does all he can to keep me so."[59] She was disappointed in her inability to "love everybody," to fulfill the role of the model minister's wife who is charitable to all. With William's help, however, she battled against her feelings of depression, and for periods of time overcame them.

In spite of bravely describing herself as enjoying "excellent good health," problems continued to plague her. The swelling in her neck that had begun in the spring in Whitesboro flared up again in Elmira. She was treated by an Elmira physician, Dr. Brooks, and the "blistering"[60] he applied to her neck forced her "to lie by & quit work" for a while in early June. By early July, the symptom abated, and she never complained of that particular problem again. By mid-July, however, she was "troubled with my old complaint in the chest. It came on last week during the dreadful hot weather & for a few days I have hardly been able to breathe at all."[61] The symptoms of this complaint, whether as they appeared in July or later when she calls it "the croup," were essentially the same: a wracking cough, especially at night, and an abundance of phlegm. Unlike her earlier frightening reports made while she was still in Whitesboro, this time the problem remained under control. William's spontaneous cures proved to be as effective as anything the doctors had previously prescribed. When she feared she was choking to death on phlegm, "William got up & dosed me with the only thing in the house, i.e., some vinegar out of the pickle pot, which was a very good thing & soon relieved me."[62]

By August 1847, Miriam was exhibiting the first symptoms of pregnancy. At first she believed she was suffering from some form of mild stomach complaint,[63] but her true condition soon became apparent. Her bouts with morning sickness did not go away as the pregnancy progressed, and even in her sixth month she reported to her sister that "I am as fat as ever, though I continue to throw up almost everything—nothing tastes good & nothing sits good. My complexion is much clearer than usual, notwithstanding I eat a good many buckwheat cakes."[64] Carrying her first child at the age of thirty-six and troubled by vomiting through most of her pregnancy, Miriam nonetheless astonished the women of Elmira with her relatively robust health and her physical activity. On February 25, seven months pregnant, she reported to her sister that for the first time in her life she actively sought physical exercise, and she surprised her neighbors by taking a mile-long walk. The letter goes on to describe some of the local customs relating to pregnancy and childbearing, including a classic scene in which more experienced women try to frighten the novice half to death. Miriam's reaction reveals a good-natured appreciation for her situation and the neighbors' solicitude, plus a characteristic show of independence and pride:

It is the *custom of women here* to shut themselves up for about three or four months, & groan with back-ache & "*such* a pain in the side, & *such* distressed feelings in the head, it seems as if they *should die*." Hence they regarded me with perfect astonishment. But I have no back ache, no pain in the side, nor any where else, & I see no use in pretending to have any. Jane says that often when ladies come to call, they say to her at the door "Is Mrs Whitcher up? I do'nt want to disturb her if she's lying down." "Up?" says Jane "She's never anything else—you could'nt coax her to go to bed in the day time." One who has been lately confined called the other day, & gave me a long & interesting account of all she underwent before her confinement. She was just like Mrs. Bushnell at Saratoga, "had'nt *no* back" &c. &c. After she got through, I remarked that I had great reason to be thankful for my good health, & freedom from the sufferings that seemed to be the portion of most ladies *beforehand*. "O" said she "I've heard of such cases before, but they're always the *sickest* in the end—they seldom *live*." So that was all the consolation I got from her. Another one on the same day, said to me, "How wonderfully you keep up Mrs Whitcher—well—you're having your easy time now—you're just the *build* to be awful sick." She thought I ought to stop going to church. I told her that as long as God gave me strength to go to church I should show my gratitude by going. There might be a time when I should be unable to go at all—I have not stayed home yet.[65]

Behind this brave exterior, Miriam had her share of fears about her health and the health of her baby. Always one to be aware of life's precariousness, she made a special effort as her confinement drew near to put her house in order. She wanted first to complete all preparation for the baby, her "little sewing" as she called it, then to provide for William. "If I should die I want to leave him well supplied with shirts, drawers, &c. You cannot think how much this is on my mind. It would be a real comfort to me to be able to get everything in good order before I am sick. I also need new night gowns &c myself, but shall not attempt to make any—shall be glad if I can get everything else ready. I have not put out a stitch of sewing & do not intend to if I can help it."[66]

Her fears assumed a vivid form in a dream she had when she learned that her brother Morris's child had died:

> I was greatly distressed when I heard of the death of Morris's child. I had been thinking about it more than usual, & William & I had spoken of it often since I got Elizabeth's letter. A night or two before I heard of its death, I dreamed of seeing a dead infant that looked beautiful. I stood weeping over it, but had very confused ideas about it—could not tell whether it was my child or some one's else. The dream distressed me & I told William in the morning. I have a great many bad dreams & William reasons with me about being troubled at them. Elizabeth's description of the baby after it was dead is very much like the one I saw in my dream. We both feel very sorry for Morris & Eugenia. I have a great many sorrowful thoughts, some of them very selfish. We wrote to them the same day. How lonely they must be now![67]

Settled in her house and the new community, her housekeeping at last in order and in the able hands of Jane, Miriam was free to resume her writing even as she awaited the birth of her child. Had she been otherwise reluctant to continue her writing, financial hardship alone might have lured her back to publication, although the sums she was offered were not great.[68] With two editors eager for her material, a public clamoring for more stories by "Frank," and an imagination filled with new images and voices, Miriam Whitcher had two comic personae ready to carry her vision before the public. In the most productive period of her career, Miriam revitalized the stalled Widow Bedott series and realized the full satiric potential of Aunt Maguire's voice of reason and compassion.

5
❧

Aunt Maguire's Sewing Society

December 1847 to December 1848 was the most productive and controversial year of Miriam's life. She brought the Widow Bedott out of retirement and she developed the character of Aunt Maguire into the ideal persona for social satire. Whitcher's Aunt Maguire sketches electrified the readers of *Godey's*, who saw in her stories reflections of their own neighbors and communities. Miriam's Elmira neighbors also saw themselves and one another there, and they were highly displeased. Her sketches were always works of the imagination, not journalistic records of real life, but insofar as individual characters were modeled on people she met in Elmira, Miriam got herself into serious trouble with her husband's parishioners. She never abandoned her anonymity in her publications, but word got out that the author of the Widow Bedott sketches lived in Elmira, then that Miriam in particular was the responsible person, and the Whitchers found themselves in the middle of a raging controversy that haunted Miriam the rest of her life.

Before she wrote the most controversial of the Aunt Maguire sketches, Miriam, stimulated by the new social order in Elmira, revitalized her Widow Bedott series. If Miriam Whitcher could move to a new village, so could the Widow, where she could renew her pursuit of widowers; the relatively open society of Elmira/Scrabble Hill offered strangers such as the Widow an open stage upon which to create herself anew. No one there, but her sister, need know she was penniless. Whitcher took advantage of her break from the Bedott series to expand somewhat the narrative shape of the tales that followed. Rather than keeping strictly to the dramatic monologue form she had perfected with the earlier sketches, she invoked a more traditional narrative technique through which various voices could be heard. The effect was a lively series of sketches filled with new people, stepped up activity on the part of the Widow, and a renewed attack on genteel values as they were played out in village society.

The Widow Bedott Moves to Scrabble Hill

On December 4, 1847, Neal's *Saturday Gazette* published Miriam Whitcher's first Elmira Widow Bedott sketch, "The Widow Bedott Resolves to Leave Wiggletown," written in late October or early November of that same year. While it retains many of the hallmarks of the earlier Widow Bedott sketches, the story signals significant new directions for the series that follows. Fully half this first sketch, for example, is told through the language and point of view of the Widow's nephew, Jefferson Maguire, in a letter to his cousin Nancy. Jeff Maguire, who finds his aunt highly amusing, becomes intimately involved in the plot of the entire series when he contrives to interest his aunt in the Reverend Shadrack Sniffles, a recently widowed Baptist minister in Scrabble Hill. Introducing Jeff as a narrator/participant allowed Miriam to retain the energy and force of the Widow's vernacular language while moving the sketches beyond the limitations of the Widow's point of view. This first Elmira story, then, represents a transition for both the writer and her main character. In it, the Widow Bedott announces she is leaving Wiggletown because she is disgusted with all the gossip about her and Timothy Crane. "What a turrible place for talkin', Wiggletown is, though! a regular slander mill" (p. 99). No one is better qualified to offer that judgment than the Widow Bedott, who traces in this story the local gossip chain even as she spreads the very gossip she appears to oppose:

> Well thir *is* such a story all round Wiggletown—and I guess I know who started it, tew—and that was old Dawson's wife—she't was widder Jinkins—she's always a runnin' me down—and she feels oncommon ryled up against me now cause she knows the old man was arter me 'fore he took her. I know she started the story, cause Sam Pendegrasses wife told me on't—and she said she heerd it from Minervy Hawley—and Minervy Hawley heerd it from Major Coon's

wife—and Major Coon's wife and Miss Dawson is wonderful intimit—and I s'pose Miss Dawson told Miss Coon. But what she says ain't worth mindin'. (pp. 96–97)

Two options are open to the Widow Bedott in leaving Wiggle-town—she can visit her brother in Vermont or her sister, Aunt Maguire, in Scrabble Hill. She rejects the first option because the family is Baptist and she would have to "go to the Baptist meetin' and that would be a turrible cross tew me" (p. 100). Scrabble Hill actively appeals to her because "society is quite refined there," and so she sets off, uninvited, to spend the winter with Sister Maguire and to try her luck in a new town that closely resembled Elmira, New York. Before the sketch closes, she travels to Scrabble Hill and is escorted by Jeff Maguire to hear the Reverend Sniffles preach. In spite of her admission that she has "a sufferin' contempt for the Baptists . . . [because] they think nobody can't git to heaven without bein' dipped," and even though she remembers Reverend Sniffles from an earlier visit as "ruther a tall, scrawny man with eyes that looks like a couple o' peeled onions," she leaves church declaring she has never been "more edified" in her life. Elder Sniffles, she declares, is not "so bad *lookin'*" as she remembered, and she even wonders aloud if she had not been wrong "to be so prejudiced against other denominations. I should like to be introduced to Elder Sniffles, and hear him converse" (pp. 103, 105).

Initially, Miriam Whitcher and the Widow Bedott had little in common, but when the Widow quits Wiggletown and moves to Scrabble Hill, her life in many regards begins, ironically, to parallel Miriam's own: the Widow courts a minister from a different denomination, and she moves to a new community where people fuss over her in part because she is a newcomer. Paradoxically, however, as their life experiences draw closer, their value systems grow further apart. The Widow draws as much attention to herself as possible: going about in society, dressing conspicuously, publishing her poetry in the local newspaper. Everything Miriam distrusted or scorned privately, the Widow embraces publicly: local fashions, the literary society, a pompous and pietistic minister, and pretensions to gentility and wealth. In short, through the Widow Bedott Miriam exploited fully the comic potential inherent in her own life's choices and experiences, but she did so through a character who was otherwise utterly unlike herself, a character who was clearly a fool. The Widow Bedott, however, is no longer the only fool in the sketches; the society that lionizes her is equally foolish, as is the minister who lets himself be trapped by her advances and by the rumors that she is a woman of means. By the end of the Elmira Widow Bedott sketches, when the Widow would write in triumph to her daughter that she has shed her dread unmarried status, the townspeople become as foolish and as self-serving as the Widow herself.

In the fifteen months between December 4, 1847, and February 17, 1849, Miriam published nine Widow Bedott sketches in Neal's *Saturday Gazette,* making this the single most productive period of her life. Several factors combined to make such productivity possible, in addition to the rich stimulation offered by her exposure to Elmira society. One factor, mentioned earlier, was Jane's competence as a housekeeper and Miriam's subsequent surrender of her day-to-day domestic cares to her. Another came from unexpected quarters that could have spelled the end of the Widow Bedott stories altogether rather than a renewed commitment to the series. In July 1847, Joseph Neal died quite unexpectedly. The editorship of the *Gazette* passed into the hands of his young widow, Alice Neal, who soon formed a strong bond with Miriam through their correspondence. Miriam later said that because of her compassion and sympathy for Alice Neal, she felt an obligation to write more Widow Bedott stories. The friendship that developed between the two women, albeit entirely from afar, in part grew out of similar life experiences.

Born Emily Bradley (1827), Alice Neal, like Miriam Whitcher, was often ill as a child and young woman, but her illnesses were far more debilitating than Miriam's. For months at a time she suffered from severe eye problems that led to bouts of temporary blindness. When she was only nine her condition deteriorated to the point that her doctors treated her with an "application of leeches to her eyelids and face, day after day, for hours at a time."[1] The attacks of blindness came over her without warning, according to her sister, and culminated in a particularly violent attack when she was nineteen. Her illness was so grave that her brother-in-law asked his friend, Joseph Neal, to come to Emily's bedside. Emily had been writing for Neal's paper and had been corresponding with Neal, but they had never met; nonetheless, he clearly had fallen in love with his young contributor. According to Emily's sister's memoirs, Neal refused to leave her until she consented to marry him, and "from that time on her eyes were quite well." Her sister did note, however, that she began to suffer instead from "nervous headaches."[2]

Joseph Neal, who was then forty years old, brought his nineteen-year-old bride home to his widowed mother, with whom Neal had lived for years. The senior Mrs. Neal had known Emily Bradley only as "Alice G. Lee," the pen name she adopted for the *Gazette,* so "at the request of Mr. Neal, and his mother also, 'Alice' became the household name of the bride," and Alice she would remain until her death.[3] The three Neals apparently got along well together, but they did not have long to enjoy one another's company. Only a few months after Joseph and Alice were married, Joseph Neal suffered from a severe attack of what was called "brain fever." In the few months that remained of his life, he experienced only occasional periods of rationality. "My husband is, I fear, incurably insane, a fate more terrible than my imagination could have pictured," Alice Neal wrote in her journal.[4] Three months later, in July 1847, Joseph Neal died.

On her twentieth birthday, Alice Neal found herself a widow of two months and an editor of the *Gazette.* She won Miriam's heart from the beginning, inspiring a steady outpouring of Widow Bedott sketches that Alice featured, as her husband had, on the front pages of the *Gazette.* Although none of Alice's letters to Miriam survive, several of Miriam's to Alice do; one in particular reveals both her deep affection for her new friend and a side of her rarely seen elsewhere:

> I wish I could find words to express all that is in my heart, & tell you how much satisfaction your last [letter] gave me. I have often spoken of you in writing to my dear sister Kate at Whitesboro', & she has come to love you too. She wrote me the other day "I do love Mrs Neal for her kindness to you, & sometimes feel almost tempted to sit down & pour out my gratitude in a letter to her". Kate is the best girl in the world—a great deal more amiable than I am—in fact she is not at all like me, & moreover she has a much better mind. I wish I could have her with me, but she cannot be spared from home.

> I am very glad that you liked the verses I wrote you. They were
> not worthy of the theme, but they came from the heart. I thank
> God for blessing me with your friendship & affection. Friends (truly
> such) are rare. I have but few & I value them the more for the
> smallness of the number.[5]

Long after Miriam died, the parallels in their lives continued.
Like Miriam, Alice Neal converted to the Episcopal denomination
as an adult; like Miriam, too, she developed tuberculosis at a relatively young age and died of the disease in the prime of her life, aged
thirty-six.[6]

In Alice's first letter to Miriam she offered to continue the financial
arrangement proposed by her late husband, which was to pay five
dollars for each Widow Bedott sketch. Small though the sum seems
now, it served as a major incentive to keep Miriam writing; money
was scarce in the Whitcher household, and Miriam's earnings made a
crucial difference. Within two weeks of receiving twenty dollars from
Alice Neal for past work she had submitted to the *Gazette,* Miriam
sent her two more Widow Bedott sketches. Two weeks after that, she
received fifteen dollars from Louis Godey for her second Aunt Maguire
sketch, prompting her to report the following detail to her sister: "I
have now received forty-five dollars in all for writing, and begin to
think it has not been a waste of time after all. It has enabled us to pay
all our debts—tho' William insists upon my laying out the last remit-
tance from Godey for silver—a few more spoons. But I shall wait to
see whether I need them."[7]

Alice soon urged her new friend to think about publishing her
Widow Bedott sketches as a book. Encouraged, Miriam began to
collect her works in a scrapbook, which in turn inspired her to expand
the number and range of her Widow Bedott sketches. Ultimately, she
was thwarted in her attempts to find a publisher, and even the personal assistance of both Alice Neal and Louis Godey failed to persuade
anyone to take on the project in what Godey described as a depressed
book market. But Alice Neal never gave up on the idea, and it was she
who ultimately edited the collected Bedott and Maguire stories for the
posthumous publication of *The Widow Bedott Papers* in 1855.

However disdainful Miriam might have been about the people
and society of Elmira, she was fascinated by them, as her new Widow

Bedott sketches make clear. She explored in the stories the comic potential inherent in the new characters she encountered in Elmira, and the two fictive sisters residing in the same household were played off against each other even as they exposed some of the social customs Miriam found so amusing. The second Elmira Widow Bedott sketch ("The Widow Bedott and Aunt Maguire Discourse on Various Topics") was designed to explore the differences between the two personae and to let them gossip from their particular perspectives about the inhabitants of Scrabble Hill. They square off from the opening sentence:

> "I say, sister Magwire—this ere's a miserable mean kind of a world, for I've—"
>
> "I don't agree with you, Silly [Priscilla]. I think it's a very good sort of a world if a body looks at [it] in a right point o' view. Most o' folks in it used *me* well, and I guess they'll continner to dew so as long as I use *them* well. For my part I'm satisfied with the world ginerally speakin."
>
> "Well, s'pozen ye be, that's no sign 't every body else had ought to be satisfied with it. You was always a wonderful satisfied critter. You think every body's dretful nice and dretful clever."
>
> "Now sister Bedott you *know* that ain't so—you know ther's some folks 't I've got a turrible mean opinion of."
>
> "I know ther *is* a few 't ye don't like—but I mean as a gineral thing you seem to think the most o' folks is jest about right. For my part, I'd ruther see things as they actilly be. I shouldent want to be so *awful* contented."
>
> "I should think so—for you ain't never contented only when you've got some thing to be *discontented* about."
>
> "Well, if that's the case, I'd ought to be contented the heft o' the time, for my trouble is continniwal." (pp. 119–20)

Their conversation quickly drifts to townspeople who have paid particular attention to the Widow since her arrival in Scrabble Hill— Dr. Lippincott, "the science man" whom Aunt Maguire cannot understand because he "talks so big" and whom the Widow therefore admires; Miss Deacon Fustick who "seems to be intirely took up with the 'anti-tea-and-coffee society' "; the Widow Grimes, who is "a skew-jawed oncomfortable lookin' old critter" who is "tew stingy to *feel* comfortable" and who gets her "livin' by visitin' and borrerin," plus her ironically named daughter, Charity, who is not only miserly but haughty (pp. 121–25).[8] The sketch looks back, too, to a Wiggletown woman who was a Millerite.[9] She went from house to house to prepare her neighbors for the impending day of judgment to which the Millerites had fixed an exact date, October 23, 1844. At the end of the discussion the two sisters argue briefly over the Reverend Mr. Sniffles, whom Aunt Maguire dismisses as "a doughhead."

Their conversation changes with the arrival of Joshaway Maguire, who informs his sister-in-law that she has a rival for Elder Sniffles's affections—one Sally Hugle ("Hugeliner") who has published a poem in the local paper about the death of Mrs. Sniffles. Joshaway challenges the Widow Bedott to try "to beat 'Hugeliner' all holler" by writing her own poem on the subject and sending it to the same newspaper. When the Widow leaves the room to retrieve a poem she wrote about the Mexican War, Aunt Maguire takes her husband to task for instigating such a rivalry:

> "Now, Joshaway, ain't you ashamed o' yerself! You'd ought to know better 'n to go to puttin' Silly up to writin' poitry—first we know she'll be sendin' some of her stuff to the 'Luminary,' and it'll make *her* ridickilous, and us tew."
>
> "Don't fret your gizzard, Melissy. Nobody won't think nothing she does is ridickilous—for ye know its ginerally thought she's a rich widder, and every body'll be ready to swaller her poitry— I don't care if it's the tarnalest mess o stuff that ever was put together." (pp. 132–33)

The overt rivalry Joshaway inspires here suggests an underlying rivalry of Miriam's own with other literary women. Comic variations on this theme are repeated often enough to make it clear that Miriam was uneasy about her literary life; whereas her fictional literary ladies are brazenly public about their authorship, she felt an extreme need for privacy and anonymity. Aunt Maguire's fear that Priscilla's poetry will make the Maguires look ridiculous is the key to understanding Miriam's own anxieties here. By virtue of being a woman author, she was identified with a host of literary ladies whose "occasional" poetry filled the newspapers and magazines of the day; embarrassed to be identified with such poor quality literature, she distanced herself from the general mass of writers by making fun of them in her stories. In effect, Miriam Whitcher asserted her own sense of superiority by poking fun at the tasteless literature associated with the Hugeliners of her world. Thus a serious anxiety inspired a comic theme and a series of poetic parodies.

In introducing first Jefferson Maguire, then his father, as manipulators of the action and instigators of the Widow and the Elder's courtship, Whitcher created a character reminiscent of a staple character of the Southwest's humor tradition: the trickster.[10] In southwestern humor the trickster took on a variety of forms, including the half-horse, half-alligator riverboatman Mike Fink, Simon Suggs working a camp meeting, or, in the 1860s, the maliciously mischievous Sut Lovingood turning a mad bull and a nest of hornets loose at his former girlfriend's wedding. Even as they changed over time, these tricksters were all highly energetic, disruptive characters who got the last laugh no matter the cost. The Maguires—father and son—share energy, irreverence, and a love of mischief making with their more raucous counterparts, but as conceived by Whitcher, they are more civilized and domesticated; their pranks are not malicious and no one is hurt by their antics.

One other Widow Bedott story of this period, "The Widow Bedott Trades with a Peddler," firmly links Whitcher's work with a trickster tradition closer to home—the Yankee peddler who is a mainstay of early northeastern humor. According to Constance Rourke, the Yankee peddler was so relentlessly successful at driving a bargain to his own advantage that people fled their houses when they heard him coming, but to no avail.[11] No one could stand up to his tactics, and the Widow Bedott is no exception. The peddler introduced in this sketch is a man named Jabez Clark, who had swindled the Widow back in Wiggletown. When she recognizes him and accuses him of having cheated her, he readily admits that he had sold her inferior shoes back then. He goes further; he claims that he has gotten religion since then, and that his conscience has bothered him ever since for "taking" her so badly. He persuades her that the only way he can clear his conscience is to make restitution to her through more trade, and so he opens his boxes of merchandise and swindles the Widow once again. This is classic Yankee peddler fare, with the swindler using his confession of past wrongdoings to take in the victim one more time.[12]

The dominant story line in the Elmira Widow Bedott sketches is the Widow's successful pursuit of the Reverend Mr. Sniffles. Broadly stated, the story proceeds along these lines: after the Widow hears the Reverend Mr. Sniffles preach, the Elder is invited to Thanksgiving dinner at the Maguires, where he distinguishes himself by his pomposity. When the Elder falls ill shortly thereafter, the Widow uses his illness as an excuse to tell him in a letter how profoundly she has been moved by his preaching and to request further "instruction"; the Elder encourages her attentions and invites her to come to his home, which she does almost immediately. Frustrated that the Elder does not propose to her, and inflamed by Hugeliner's rivalry, the Widow boldly invades a grove behind his house and sings a song she has composed about her unrequited love for the Elder. He rises to the bait, and encouraged by the rumors of her wealth and the Widow's threats to leave Scrabble Hill, he consents to their engagement. In a moment of supreme triumph and relief, the Widow Bedott leans her head on the Elder's shoulder and declares, "We're engaged, and my tribulation is at an end" (p. 183).

The Elmira Widow Bedott series concludes with a letter from the Widow to her daughter, Melissa, boasting about her marriage and announcing that she will return to Wiggletown to show up all the people who formerly conspired against her. So incidental is Shadrack Sniffles as a person that the Widow forgets to mention his name in the letter until Jeff reads it and urges her to add a postscript identifying her new husband. Another postscript asks her daughter what she is going to name her baby, while a third consists of her "elegy" on her marriage to Shadrack:

> Priscilla the fair and Shadrack the wise,
> Have united their fortunes in the tenderest of ties;
> And, being mutually joined in the matrimonial connection,
> Have bid adoo to their previous affliction.

No more will they mourn their widdered sittiwation,
And continner to sythe without mitigation;
But pardners, for life to be parted no more,
Their sorrers is eended, their troubles is o'er.

O Shadrack, my Shadrack! Prissilla did speak,
While the rosy red blushes surmantled her cheek,
And the tears of affection bedoozled her eye,
O Shadrack, my Shadrack! I'm yourn till I die.

The heart that was scornful and cold as a stun,
Has surrendered at last to the fortinit one;
Farewell to the miseries and griefs I have had,
I'll never desert thee, O Shadrack, my Shad!

(p. 190)

For the Widow Bedott, marriage becomes not only an escape from her "affliction" but also an act of revenge against all those she imagines have wronged her in the past with their gossip, albeit gossip that perpetrated the truth rather than the fictions she tried to circulate. Her marriage is also revenge against all the other widows who succeeded when she had failed: "The widder Jinkins that was—she 't was Poll Bingham—and she's the very undentical person I want to keep it [the news] from till it busts upon her all of a sudding, like a thunder-clap. I guess I'll let her know 't I can hold my head as high as hern in futur, for who did she git but a decrippid old bung head that she wouldent a had if she could a got any body else" (pp. 184–85).

To the Widow it is ultimately irrelevant that the man she marries is a minister, but to the author it was everything. She obviously amused herself greatly developing the character of the Elder Sniffles and allowing the Widow to capitalize upon his profession in pursuing him. The two are worthy matches for each other, the Widow with her obsession and her self-absorption, and the Elder with his pomposity and barely submerged greed. One of the finest brief moments in the series occurs when the Widow flatters the Elder about his prowess as a preacher. "Sence the first time I heerd you preach, I've had had [*sic*] an undescriberble desire to hev some privit conversation with you, in regard to the state o' my mind—your discourse was so wonderful searchin' that I felt to mourn over my backslidden state o' stewpidity, and my consarn has increased every time I've sot under the droppin's o' your sanctuery. Last night when I heerd o' your sickness, I felt wonderful overcome." (p. 134). Accustomed as he was to receiving women's attention, of having women call on him for "instruction" as he invites the Widow to do, the Elder readily accedes to her flattery, revealing in the process his self-satisfaction couched in protestations of humility:

> Accept my most unqualified acknowledgments for the interest which you apparently take in my welfare—and for the articles which you so kindly transmitted by your nephew. Permit me, also, to assure you of my abundant gratification at the assurance that my unpretending discourses have been the feeble instrument of exerting a salutary influence upon your mind. I feel, most deeply do I feel, that I am but a poor unworthy worm of the dust; and it serves but to augment my humiliation to reflect that my labors in the field have been so signally blessed. (p. 139)

The Elder may have had good reason for accepting as a matter of course the attentions of the Widow: "It is from the clergy only that the women of America receive that sort of attention which is so dearly valued by every female heart throughout the world. . . . I never saw, or read, of any country where religion had so strong a hold upon the women, or a slighter hold upon the men."[13] If women received the attention they so badly wanted only from ministers, the reverse was also true, according to Ann Douglas: "The nineteenth-century minister moved in a world of women. He preached mainly to women; he administered what sacraments he performed largely for women; he worked not only for them but with them, in missionary and charity work of all kinds."[14]

Nowhere is the Reverend Mr. Sniffles's pomposity more in evidence, or more inappropriate, than at the Maguire's Thanksgiving dinner:

> "Elder Sniffles, let me give you another piece o' the turkey."
> "I'm obleeged to you, Mr. Maguire; you probably recollect that I remarked in my discourse this morning, that individuals were too prone to indulge in an excessive indulgence in creature com-

forts on thanksgiving occasions. In view of the lamentable fact that the sin of gormandizing is carried to a sinful excess on this day, I, as a preacher of the Gospel, deem it my duty to be unusually abstemious on such occasions: nevertheless, considering the peculiar circumstances under which I am placed this day, I think I will waive objections and take another small portion of the turkey." (p. 164)

The Elder insists upon discussing the virtues of every item of food offered him, and he appeals to Jeff, who is a medical student, to confirm his assessments; Jeff happily obliges the Elder, while mimicking his language for his own amusement. Meanwhile, the Elder affirms the boundlessness of his own foolishness:

> "Wife, fill the elder a glass o' cider."
> "Desist! Mrs. Maguire, desist, I entreat you! I invariably set my face like a flint against the use of all intoxicating liquors as a beverage."
> "Jimmeni! you don't mean to call new cider an intoxicatin' liquor, I hope. Why, man alive, it's jest made—hain't begun to work."
> "Nevertheless, I believe it be exceedingly insalubrious, and detrimental to the system. Is not that its nature, my young friend?"
> "Far from it, elder—far from it. Reflect a moment and you will readily perceive, that being the pure juice of the apple—wholly free from all alcoholic mixture—it possesses all the nutritive properties of the fruit, with the advantage of being in a more condensed form, which at once renders it much more agreeable, and facilitates assimilation."
> "Very reasonable—very reasonable, indeed. Mrs. Maguire you may fill my glass." (p. 169)

No single model inspired the characterization of the Elder, yet as often happened with Miriam's creations, her fiction so captured the truth about a particular character that a real-life model presented himself after the fact. Much to Miriam's amusement, she "met" the Reverend Mr. Sniffles in Elmira shortly after she had created him:

> The ministers of the village (of whom there are six or seven) have a meeting every Monday afternoon, to discuss the various moral & religious interests of the place. William goes sometimes, & has a

refreshing season. The methodist & baptist ministers are perfect noodles, & there is another old minister Mr Rosée, who always attends—a presbyterian—who lives in the village but preaches in the neighboring region—at *"Habtown"*, "Zion's Hollow", "Christian Kingdom" &c. He is a terrible bore—a perfect Sniffles. If I had seen him before I drew the elder's character I should certainly think I had taken him for the model. He talks so big & so precise. The first time I ever saw him he came in & took tea with us—the very day after I had written the Thanksgiving scene, & William & I were very much struck with the resemblance. He calls me "Mr Whitcher's *consort*". He always inquires about *"Sister Frost"* says he "regards her with a high degree of consideration" If he was a widower I should teaze Mrs Frost about him, but he has a *consort*.[15]

The wedding of the Widow and the Elder takes place offstage almost immediately after their engagement. After a wedding tour to Wiggletown, they are to return to Scrabble Hill and take up residence in the Elder's house, which the Widow plans to remodel "to make it look ruther more fashionable." Because she has felt so powerless as a widow, she relishes the prospects of making things jump when she becomes the Reverend Mrs. Sniffles (p. 189). In fact, her character will be transformed much for the worse, and she will become an overbearing, though highly amusing, termagant of a bride.

As a married woman and the wife of a minister, the former Widow Bedott comes to personify in the sketches that follow gentility itself, or at least all its worst qualities. She becomes obsessed with all the outward trappings of upward mobility and social acceptability: power in the community, fashionable clothing, a home that reflects her desired social standing. What matters to her is not her private conduct or her personal relationship to her new husband, but her public status. But all this is still in the future; when Whitcher married off the Widow to the Elder, she assumed for the second time that she had written her last Widow Bedott sketch for the Gazette.

"Parson Scrantum's Donation Party"

Nor long after she created Elder Sniffles, Miriam developed other characters who struck such a chord of truth that villagers throughout the region were convinced they could identify the very persons upon whom individual characters were modeled. Some of these characters appeared first in the Widow Bedott sketches, then were carried over to the Aunt Maguire stories where Miriam let loose the full force of her satire. The first story in which she perfected her social satire was "Parson Scrantum's Donation Party," which appeared in *Godey's Lady's Book* in March 1848. Given the enormous discrepancy between the Whitchers' own donation party and the fictionalized one she created through Aunt Maguire, however, it is critical to understand the publishing history of this sketch before examining its content and style in detail.

Though the sketch first appeared in *Godey's* fully five months after the Whitchers were feted at their own donation party, which would make it appear to have been based on their own experience, it had been written and submitted to Godey *before* the party took place. In November 1847, Miriam reported to her sister that a manuscript she submitted to Godey had been lost.[16] The following month, Godey wrote to give her a new address and to ask why she had not replied to "his repeated inquiries about me in the Lady's book."[17] Miriam resubmitted the manuscript in late December, and following the usual publishing pattern, it appeared in the *Lady's Book* in March.[18] The critical fact here is that her story was not a bitterly distorted fictionalized account of Whitcher's actual experience. Instead, it is an act of the imagination that reveals the depth of her anxiety about what lay in store for her in Elmira. Fearing that she could be humiliated, she struck the first blow. It exposes, too, with consummate humor, the vulnerability she felt as the relatively helpless benefactor of other people's charity. Most significant, the fictionalized account reveals the vividness of Miriam Whitcher's satiric imagination.

Aunt Maguire narrates the story of the donation party and also plays a key role as a participant and sympathetic supporter of the story's central figures, the Reverend Mr. and Mrs. Scrantum. Aunt Maguire's perspective on the behavior of the guests guides the satire, while her indignation informs the reader's response to the events. Whitcher structured the tale in an interesting way; before Aunt Maguire reveals details about the donation party itself, she describes what she says is the typical downward spiral in the relationship between ministers and their congregations. First, she tells us, the minister and his family are lionized and fussed over, then they are criticized because they spend too much time with one group and not enough time with another. Next, according to Aunt Maguire, the congregation finds it hard to raise the money to pay the minister's salary, and eventually they encourage the pastor to find a new parish where he can be "more effective." Aunt Maguire uses these prefatory remarks to explain why the town is making such a commotion about the new minister, the Reverend Mr. Tuttle, and his wife, who replaced the Scrantums:

> They hain't ben here but three months—and the foks are makin' a terrible fuss over 'em. You know it's the way they always dew when they git a new minister. They're ready to eat him up for a spell. And his wife—lawful sakes! ther's nothing equil tew her. They make an awful parade about her. Such treatment spiles the minister's wives. Afore long they begin to think themselves the most important characters in creation—and really expect the hull community to be a flyin' round all the time to attend tew 'em. (pp. 245–46)

At the outset of this sketch, then, Aunt Maguire acts not only as a narrator but also as an alter ego to the author, who is keenly aware of her position as the new minister's wife. At times in the sketch, and those that follow, Aunt Maguire will speak *for* Miriam Whitcher, voicing her perspective and defending her point of view, while at other key times she will serve as a voice of caution addressing herself, as it were, to the author. Immediately following Aunt Maguire's veiled warning to the new minister's wife to keep the congregation's flattery in perspective, she defends the outgoing minister's wife, Mrs. Scrantum, against those who criticized her for not being sufficiently involved in the affairs of the church:

> If any body was sick or sufferin', she was there to help 'em; but she seldom went out any other time. She was good to the poor, tew—and divided her mite with 'em. You'd a thought folks couldent find fault with *her*. But they did. Some grumbled because she w'n't more sociable—and some was mad because she wa'n't what they called an *active Christian*—that is—she wa'n't willin' to spend the heft o' her time a runnin' round on missionary bisness and distribitin' tracts, and so forth. (p. 247)

Only when she has said her full piece on the trials endured by ministers and their wives does Aunt Maguire proceed to relate the tale of Parson Scrantum's donation party. Wanting to give the Scrantums something they need and something of value, she buys Mrs. Scrantum an expensive new bonnet to replace her old, worn one; Jefferson Maguire, who eagerly agrees to accompany his mother to the party, buys the parson a ream of paper for writing his sermons. As it turns out, these are the only donations of value brought to the party.

In sharp contrast to the Whitchers' actual experience, the Scrantums have to furnish all the coffee, tea, sugar, and cream for the party, plus extra baked goods that Mrs. Scrantum sends for at the last minute when the food supply looks low and the crowd large. Aunt Maguire arrives at the party early only to discover Mrs. Scrantum struggling in the kitchen to make a wash boiler full of coffee—"ten pails full." Aunt Maguire takes over for her, and while Mrs. Scrantum dresses, some of the churchwomen boldly unwrap her new bonnet and pass it around among themselves, much to Aunt Maguire's disgust. Overall, the donations brought to the Scrantums are scandalously cheap. Aunt Maguire's litany of the contributions is interwoven with scathing delineations of the parishioners who bring them:

> You'd a thought from the number o' folks that was there, that ther'd been a wonderful sight o' donations brought—but as true as I'm a livin' critter—that table wa'n't half full. But then ther was a good many families that fetcht one article to answer for the hull. For instance, Deacon Skinner and his wife and four darters and tew sons was all there—and Miss Skinner fetcht a skein o' yarn to knit Parson Scrantum some socks. Miss Hopkins and her three darters and her son and his wife, that was a visitin' her, and *their* three children all come—and Miss Hopkins brought half a pound o' tea. And the Runyons with their four young ones—what do you think they brought? why, Miss Runyon fetcht a little fancy basket to stick on the center-table and put visitin' cards in. And the Miss Footes, three on 'em they brought Miss Scrantum a pair o' cuffs. And all the Binghams, they fetcht a neck ribbon for Susan. And Deacon Peabody and his tribe, ther's as much as a dozen on 'em, they brought a small cheese. I heerd afterward that half o' it was a donation and t' other half was to go for pew rent. And Cappen

Smalley and all his children was there. He fetch a box o' raisins out o' his store, ther was twelve pound in 't, and Susan told me afterward that ten pound was to go toward pew rent and the rest was a present. The Widder Grimes and Charity was there, of course. They dident go nigh the donation table for some time, and I was kind o' curus to know whether they'd brought any thing, and so I watch'd 'em, and bimebye, I observed Charity go up slily, when she thought nobody did n't see, and lay a little paper on the table. I had the curiosity to see what was in it, so as soon as I got a chance I took up the paper and peeped into 't, and lo and behold! there were two skeins o' thread! did you ever? Widder Grimes is well off, but she's tew stingy to be decent, and Charity's jest like her. Then there was ever so many belonging to other denominations, that dident bring nothin'; they come to show their good will, to let folks see that *they* wa'n't bigoted and prejudiced though they did differ in a religious pint o' view, and git their supper. And besides them, I noticed a great many that I never see before—nobody knows where they come from nor where they went tew. I guess they must a been raised up for the occasion. (pp. 255–57)

Jeff Maguire, always on the lookout for mischief, remains fairly well reined in by his mother until he has a chance to get back at Charity Grimes: "Stiff as a poker and prim as a pea-pod—you know what a starched up, affected old critter she is. Jeff went to school tew her when he was little and she snapped his ears and cuffed him round, so he's always hated her like pizen ever since" (p. 258). Finding her in the company of the recently widowed Cappen Smalley, Jeff embarrasses her by alluding to the fact that she was his teacher when he was young (thus revealing that she is older than she makes out), then teases her about the loss of the most recent object of her affection, Squire Fuller. According to Joshaway Maguire, the Squire was forced to get married in order to get Charity Grimes out of his hair. Just then supper is announced and the crowd pours into "the settin'-room" where "they pushed, and elbowed, and pulled, and hauled, and grabbed like crazy critters. 'T was amasin' to see 'em put down the vittals" (p. 261). "Afore long the table was purty well cleared, and Miss Scrantum had to go to the buttry and bring on all 't was left. I guess everything in the house that could be eat, without stoppin' to cook it, was made way with that night," including food

brought for pew rent and private provisions belonging to the Scrantums
(p.263).

Most reprehensible of all, however, is the behavior of the guests
after dinner. First they throw raisins at each other, then,

> when supper was about finished, Jane Elizy Fustick (she's always a
> tryin' to dew something cunnin'), she went into the store-room and
> got a chain o' sassages, that old Miss Crocker brought, and come
> along slily and throw'd it round Liph Peabody's shoulders. Liph, he
> was standin' by the tea-board a drinkin' a cup o' coffee. When he
> felt the sassages come floppin' round his neck, he was skairt, and
> whisked round suddenly and hit the tea-board, and knocked it off
> onto the floor, and smash went every thing on it! What made it
> more aggravatin' was, ther was a dozen chany cups and sarcers on it
> that Miss Scrantum had fetcht out after the folks come out to
> supper. They was some that she sot a great deal by; her mother giv
> 'em tew her, and her mother was dead. . . . and when the tea-board
> fell, they fell tew, and every one on 'em was broke or cracked. (pp.
> 263–64)

> While we was a pickin' up the crockery, all of a sudden ther was
> a terrible hullerballoo in the parlor—Jeff and me rushed in to see
> what was the matter, and gracious granfather! what do you s'pose it
> was? Why one o' them pesky seminary gals had throw'd a hunk o'
> cheese and hit Miss Scrantum's parlor lamp that was a settin' on the
> table, and knocked it over and broke it all to flinders. But that
> wa'n't the wost on 't—where it tumbled over it fell right onto that
> plum-colored sattin bunnit, and the ile run all over it in a minnit.
> Afore any body could ketch the bunnit, one side on 't, ribbon and
> all, was completely ruined. . . . All the ile that dident go onto the
> bunnit was soaked up in the paper that Jeff took, that was a lyin'
> right aside on 't, and the biggest part o' that was spiled tew.
> (p. 265)

Much to the surprise of the members who believe they have just
done the family a great favor, in the aftermath of the donation party
Parson Scrantum asks to be dismissed from the congregation. Rea-
soning that he could no longer support his family on the salary he
received, Parson Scrantum states his case as succinctly as possible:

Brethren, since I come among you, I've done my best to be a faithful pastor—if I've failed I hope to be forgiven. At first I had an idee that I should be able to rub along, on my small salary; and I don't know, but I might a done it, if it had n't a ben for *one thing.* Here he paused. "What was *that?*" says Deacon Peabody. Mr. Scrantum continued—"I've ben her tew years, and you've had the kindness to give me tew donation parties. I've stood it so fur, but I can't stand it no longer; brethren, I feel convinced that *one more donation party* would completely *break me down.* (p. 271)

Thus the Scrantums leave Scrabble Hill and the Tuttles arrive to take their place. Thomas F. O'Donnell calls this sketch "the longest, most indignant, the most excoriating sketch of nineteenth-century American manners Whitcher wrote. . . . a savage indictment of a parochial institution that American ministers and their wives had come to dread."[19] It brought to perfection, too, the satiric potential of the Aunt Maguire sketches. In the stories that followed, Miriam Whitcher invoked the sensibilities of Aunt Maguire in her satiric exposure of parishioners' hypocrisy as they vied with one another for social status. In the end, her own identity became divided between Aunt Maguire, who served her so well as a narrative voice, and the Reverend Mrs. Tuttle, the newly arrived minister's wife.

Childbirth

When "Parson Scrantum's Donation Party" appeared in the *Lady's Book* Miriam was anxiously awaiting the birth of her first child. As she explained to Alice Neal there were some miscalculations about the baby's due date:

I did not expect to keep about until this time. Owing to some peculiarities in my case I have not been able to "calculate" correctly, but still I had some reason to think that my troubles would be over several weeks ago. I try to be patient but I cannot help feeling nervous & uneasy. I thought I would not defer writing to you any longer for fear it might be a long time before I could do so again. Yet I think I will keep this on hand until the trial is over, & then William will add a line & tell you the result. O how happy I shall be

if I become the *living mother* of a *living & perfect* child! I hardly
dare to hope it. It seems too great a happiness for me to expect. It
surely is more than I deserve.[20]

As it happened, only disappointment awaited her; her earlier dream
about the dead child proved to be prophetic. The very day of the
birth, William described in moving detail the results of Miriam's
labors. His letter is repeated here in its entirety because of its elo-
quence under emotionally charged circumstances and because of its
rare glimpse into the character of William Whitcher.

Saturday April 1st 1848

Dear Alice

    The dreaded trial is at last over, and dreadful enough it was,
both in duration and severity, and I may add—its results. Her travail
continued from 7 o clock on Wednesday night to this P.M. [Satur-
day] at 1 o clock. Thus God gave her an other proof of His love in
that He thus made her to be conformed to the Image of His son by
suffering. And you would love her a thousand times more if you
had seen the fortitude, the gentleness, the patience the sweetness
the calmness the meekness and the self possession with which she
bore all her pains and subsequent disappointment and sorrow. For
alas God hath bro't our sin to remembrance and [ha]th slain our
child. The protracted labour was too much for its tender frame and
our dear little Mary (for that would have been her name) was born
dead. This was the crowning throe of suffering for poor Frank. Her
cup of bitterness was full. But with heavenly sweetness she said (and
meant what she said) "God's holy will be done". The physicians
give me great encouragement of her speedy recovery and more
firmly established health. But I cannot help fearing that sufferings
so intense, and continued (as was hers) for 76 hours, may produce
the most calamitous results. As we have no Sunday mail, I cannot
send this letter before Sunday evening, when I will add a P.S.
    Sunday 7 oclock P.M. Last evening about 9 oclock the nurse
came down and said "The dare 'oomun is tossin all abute, and
spakes so quarely". I ran up & you can only faintly imagine my
horror when I tell you that my own dear Frank did not know me,
nor anything which had happened. The ignorant old hussy of a
nurse had heated the room to 75 degrees, and placed the lamp

where it shone directly onto the bed. This was too much for the already excited nervous system of poor Frank, and it is no wonder that her brain whirled. I never found it more difficult to restrain my indignation at such brutal treatment. I dismissed the old woman from the room at once, with the determination to discharge her from our service in the morning. It required several hours before the excitement of poor Frank's brain could be allayed. But by God's blessing sweet sleep at last came to her relief, from which she awoke quite composed and looked on me and smiled. But she soon missed the nurse and wanted to know what had happened. I told her that I did not like her and had sent her to bed, and desired to dismiss her. I did not dare tell her all. "She is a poor woman" said Frank "and you must not dismiss her for it will spoil her reputation to send her away". So I shall let her remain, but only as a supernumerary. Poor Frank's life is far too precious to be hazarded to save the reputation of so shabby a functionary. Frank has had a very quiet time all this day, and by God's blessing (for which we desire your prayers) she will do well. Her symptoms are all improved, and she has slept about one hour to day. Sleep is what she needs. May the choisest blessings of heaven ever rest upon you dear Alice for your love of my dearest Frank. Let us hear from you soon.

Truly yours,
B.W. Whitcher

Miriam Whitcher's recovery from her "dreaded trial" took a full two months, partly in keeping with the medical practices of the time that confined newly delivered women to bed for protracted periods, and partly in response to the extraordinary trauma of this birth. Ten days after the delivery William reported to Kate Berry that Miriam was progressing well and seemed to be out of danger of contracting "milk fever," a condition thought to occur "when the milk leaves the breast and settles in the limbs."[21] He endorsed, too, the restorative powers of fresh air, which he let into his wife's bedroom daily, and he closed the letter with a long paragraph about his garden and the flower beds he hoped would be filled with bloom before Miriam left her room.[22] Then two months of silence ensued.

The next extant letter from Miriam Whitcher to her sister was dated June 8, 1848, and contained a report about a just-completed visit from the bishop and the challenges that visit held for her: "I

dreaded it for fear I should'nt be able to get through with it credit-
ably to myself. But I did very well."[23] In the process of writing about
the bishop's visit, she reported two details that reveal how protracted
her recovery had been. The first was that the previous Thursday
evening, when the congregation came to call on the bishop, was the
first time she "had *dressed* since I was sick. I put on my silk dress, &
was almost as much of a lion as the B[isho]p." The second followed
from the first: she had not yet left the house since her confinement
more than two months earlier.

"The Contemplated Sewing Society"

In the winter of 1848, the Whitchers' first winter in Elmira,
William organized a sewing society for the women of Trinity Episcopal Church, and Miriam Whitcher became an active member just as
she had been in Whitesboro.[24] The following spring, when Miriam
was recuperating from childbirth, she wrote an article for Louis Godey
entitled "The Contemplated Sewing Society," in which Aunt Maguire
helps a woman named Miss Birsley (a relative newcomer to town)
organize a benevolent sewing society for the Scrabble Hill Presbyterian Church.[25] The satiric thrust of the "Contemplated Sewing Society" is much gentler than the "Donation Party's." Here Miriam focused
on the foibles of the women of Scrabble Hill, and none of their
peculiarities threaten the social order of the town as they will later.
The story explores in a gently humorous way the complex fabric of
women's society. Aunt Maguire begins the story in a celebratory
tone:

> We're a gwine to have a Sewin' Society at Scrabble Hill. Miss Birsley,
> lawyer Birsley's wife, was the first one that proposed it. She hain't
> lived here but about a year, and she's always ben used to such
> societies where she come from, so she felt as if she'd like to have
> one here. Miss Birsley's jest the woman to take hold o' any such
> thing. She's a wonderful active little body, and a real good woman
> tew. But, above all, she's got a way o' sayin' jest what she pleases to
> every body without even givin' any offense. I've often wondered
> how it was that Miss Birsley could speak her mind so freely and
> never make no enemies by it. Why, if I should venter to talk half so

plain as she does I should be univarsally hated. But she comes right
out with every thing she thinks, and yet she's more popilar than any
other woman in the place. I guess it must be because folks has
found out that she never says no wuss about 'em to their backs than
she says to their faces. Well, she come into our house one day last
week (she and I's very good friends); she come in and axed me how
I'd like to jine a Sewin' Society for benevolent purposes? I told her
that not knowin' I couldent say, for I hadent never belonged to
none. So she went into an explanation; and after I understood the
natur of 'em I liked the idee, and said I'd go in for it. So she wanted
me to go round with her and talk it up to the folks; and as I dident
see no reason why I shouldent, I put on my things and off we
started. (pp. 273–74)

The story is thus structured on a domesticated picaresque pattern,
with the two central women prepared to go from house to house to
promote their idea, and incidentally, to reveal how the women of
Scrabble Hill spend their days.

Their first stop is at the minister's house to see what Miss Tuttle
thinks about the idea before they proceed; once they receive her
blessings, with the cautionary note that Scrabble Hill has no tradition
to guide the members in the "proper conduct" of the society, the two
women move out into the town. They stop at homes and shops, that
day and the next, until all the women they contact agree to attend
the first meeting at the home of Miss Birsley the following Wednesday afternoon. The foibles they encounter, the various resistances to
the new idea, and the means Miss Birsley employs to overcome all
obstacles form the core of their adventures and the emotional center
of the sketch. They visit the old-maid milliner, Liddy Ann Buill, not
because Aunt Maguire expects her to join but because "she never'd
forgive us if we dident call on her. She's a curus critter—consates that
some folks feels above her, and it makes her wonderful oncomfortable.
She's always on a look out for slights and insults, and o' course she
thinks she gits plenty on 'em" (p. 275). Liddy Ann greets them with
stiffness and "a real I'm-as-good-as-you-be look on her face," but
Miss Birsley wins her over to the idea of the society by a combination
of flattery and plain speaking. She confronts Liddy Ann with the fact
that she accuses her neighbors of having "tew much rastocratical
feelin," yet she holds herself aloof from them. When Liddy Ann

declares that Scrabble Hill is too divided to work for a single cause, Miss Birsley appeals to her to help unite it. By the time they leave Liddy Ann's shop, Miss Birsley has set her completely at ease (brought her nose down several levels, according to Aunt Maguire) and earned her full cooperation. Despite Miss Birsley's admirable ability to be both frank and honey-tongued, Aunt Maguire's more homely perspective prevails:

> Well I dew say for't, I never was more beat in all my born days than I was to see you git round that cross-grained old critter as you did! I dident know afore that you ever used any *soft soap,* but I'm sure you daubed it onto Liddy Ann right and left; 't was the best way after all though, for if you'd a took her to task about bein jealous and suspicious, she'd a ben tearin' mad, and like enough showed us the door, and then went round and jawed about us afterward. (pp. 279–80)

Charity and the Widow Grimes agree to come only when they are assured it will cost them nothing but their time, and Anny Mariar Lippincott, eighteen-year-old daughter of Dr. Lippincott, supports the idea only after Miss Birsley chastises her for being inappropriately proud that she does not know how to sew. Miss Birsley claims she will not let her nephew, Dick, continue to be interested in any young lady who is so poorly educated, and she promises to give Anny Mariar sewing lessons at the sewing society. At some houses, the ladies find their friends and neighbors gathered together for tea, and the interplay among the women becomes the focus for the humor. Miss Fustick and her daughter Jane Elizy are taking tea at Miss Peabody's, for example, which gives Aunt Maguire the opportunity to capture the dynamics among the four women, as well as the idiosyncracies of Miss Fustick in particular:

> Miss Peabody's entirely governed by Miss Fustick in everything, so she waited to see what Miss Fustick would say afore she expressed her opinion about the Sewin' Society; and Miss Fustick don't want to go into any thing without she can be head man, and as she was n't sure how she'd stand in the Sewin' Society, she hesitated a spell. At last she said she had her doubts about it—dident like to undertake a thing till she was convinced 't would promote the interest o'

religion—(Miss Fustick's awful pious accordin' to *her* idees o' piety.) Of course, Miss Peabody had *her* doubts tew, about jinin' the society. Miss Birsley and me, we both said tew 'em that we'd no doubt but what the Sewin' Society would be the means o' dewin' a great deal o' good if 't was properly conducted. Well, Miss Fustick said she was onsartin' about bein' able to attend—her time was pretty much took up—she was Superintendent o' the Maternal Society, President o' the Daughters o' Temperance, and Correspondin' Secretary to the Friends o' Humanity, and she was afeard she couldent consistently do much for the Sewin' Society; but she'd try to attend occasionally—at least she's make it a subject o' prayer, and try to find out what was *duty* in the case. Of course, Miss Peabody said she'd try to attend tew. (pp. 285–86)

In passages such as this one, Miriam Whitcher poked fun at women's self-satisfaction, with their certainty that they know what would "promote the interest of religion," with their smugness about being leaders of important-sounding societies, and with their confusion of social issues (and social status) with religion. Both Miss Fustick and Miss Peabody look foolish here, the one for her exaggerated sense of self and the other for taking all her cues from her friend—for having no mind of her own. The "true woman" of the 1840s also is gently mocked here insofar as Miss Fustick's range of activities corresponds to the popular image of woman as a morally superior person.

At two points in this story Whitcher departs from her depiction of the society of women to focus briefly on men who attempt to thwart Miss Birsley. The first such man is a shopkeeper, Cappen Smalley, to whom Miss Birsley appeals for a cash donation for the sewing society. Aunt Maguire warns her that Cappen Smalley is too tight to give away anything except talk, which Miss Birsley accepts as a direct challenge. True to his reputation, the captain readily approves of their plan for the sewing society and even presumes to tell the women that their charitable mission ought to be to make clothes for the poor. When he claims, predictably, that he cannot make a cash donation to the project he has just heartily endorsed, Miss Birsley picks up a bolt of shirting material and tells him that they will accept it as a donation in lieu of cash. The more he protests, the more she ensnares him. To prevent him from trying to get reimbursed for the material later, she coerces him into wrapping the thirty-two yards of cloth for them and writing on the package that it is his gift to the sewing society. As they leave the store in triumph, Miss Birsley sweetly tells Aunt Maguire that they must never tell anyone how they got the donation: " 'T ain't right to tell o' such things—we must let folks think he gin it of his own accord" (p. 284).

Through the character of Cappen Smalley, Miriam exposed the hypocrites who will happily talk about the value of a cause but will play no active part. An additional satiric overlay here is directed at the smooth-talking, self-satisfied man who thinks it is his right and duty to advise women how to conduct their business. This point is reinforced by a second, more problematical, digression featuring a man named Professor Stubbles, who totally dominates his wife while extolling the dignity of all labor, including women's labor. Unlike Cappen Smalley, Professor Stubbles acted on his beliefs, even when that action made him look ridiculous. When the women call on Mrs. Stubbles, the professor is in the kitchen, wearing his wife's check apron and churning butter; his son is likewise doing women's work—setting the table—while his daughter is outside chopping wood. Like the captain, he does not hesitate to give his opinions. But as Aunt Maguire says, "he has such a blind, twistical way o' talkin', that a body can't tell what he means half the time—husband says he don't know himself what he's a drivin' at":

"Ladies," says he, "it is high time that the dignity of labor was appreciated world-wide." (We see he was in for a speech, so we let him go on.) "It's high time that the purse-proud and vice-bloated aristocracy o' the land was compelled to toil like the hard-handed sons and daughters of honest poverty;—it's high time that the artificial arrangements of society was done away, and this sin-distracted, folly-bewildered, hag-ridden world was governed by such laws as the Great Heart of the universe originally intended. Ladies, the earth-mission of mundane souls is twofold; first, to discharge with self-interest-sacrificing zeal our duty toward down-trodden humanity; second, to perform with soul-earnest, wife-assisting, daughter-helping, labor-loving fidelity, such domestic services as shall be to be *[sic]* performed at home; and I pronounce that soul who refuses to acknowledge the dignity of household labor, a pride-besotted, contempt-deserving, heaven-provoking churl." (pp.289–91)

In creating the character of Professor Stubbles Whitcher trod on the toes of a man she greatly admired—Beriah Green of the Oneida Institute. Green was an outspoken proponent of the virtue of hard labor, and in addition to including physical labor as an integral part of the curriculum at the institute, Green chopped quantities of wood to keep himself fit and to reduce tension.[26] More significant in the context of the story, Green also helped his wife do the washing for their large family, much to the amusement of his neighbors in Whitesboro. When the story appeared in the *Lady's Book,* Green was offended by the characterization of the professor, assuming that it was meant to make fun of him, and indeed there were many similarities between the two professors. Miriam, however, was taken aback by the news that Green took offense at the characterization, declaring him "a goose" for thinking that he was the object of ridicule here. But she should not have been surprised. Enough people in Whitesboro knew she was the author of these sketches, and they knew of her lifelong tendency to caricature her neighbors. Green was such a prominent man in the village, and his views so well known, it would have been difficult *not* to see him as the model for Professor Stubbles. Despite her weak protestations to the contrary, what is especially important here is how boldly Miriam was beginning to use life models for her satiric portraits. When her sources of inspiration came from even closer to home—that is, Elmira—Miriam would no longer be able to shrug off the offense as she did with Green.

In the "Contemplated Sewing Society," Miss Birsley challenges the professor by insisting that he clean up the cream he splashes on her shawl and by telling him he would find more dignity in conducting the labor best suited to him as a man and leaving women's work to the women. She refuses to invite the professor to participate in the sewing society, even though she is sure he expects to be involved, and she persuades his wife and daughter to come. "The Professor looked real wrathy, but dident say nothing, and we left him a churnin' away for dear life" (p. 292). And so Miss Birsley easily gets the better of the two men in the story, one by cunning and the other by her outspoken confrontation and defiance. Miss Birsley is a powerful woman who will clearly brook no disappointment, but Aunt Maguire, not Miss Birsley, is Miriam's spokesperson in the sewing society sketches. Aunt Maguire's views are less extreme, less outspoken, and by and large more compassionate. Taken as a whole, the sketch is more moderate in its outlook than the scene with Professor Stubbles would suggest. Nonetheless, the progressive views of the professor are made to look ridiculous in this brief vignette, and Miss Birsley outwits this male opponent only by taking an antifeminist stand.

It is one thing to outwit and outtalk her male "opponents"; it remained to be seen whether Miss Birsley, for all her power, would be able to mobilize the sewing society into a single unit with the members able to agree upon a charitable purpose for their labor. The sketch closes with an air of expectation and a sense of satisfaction at the end of a good day's work. The readers of the *Lady's Book* did not have to wait long before being treated to the next installment—the first meeting of the society. In the interim, however, several important events took place in Miriam's life that set the stage for the uproar that broke in Elmira when the next sewing society sketch appeared in the *Lady's Book*.

After Miriam recovered sufficiently from childbirth, the Whitchers took a vacation trip to Saratoga. They stayed with her sister Elizabeth and her family of four children, and they also visited her brother Morris and his wife, Eugenia. William was not feeling particularly well when they arrived in Saratoga, and he looked forward to "taking the waters"; then they both got colds and were forced to extend their stay for several days. Elizabeth pleaded with them to stay even longer, and so they delayed their departure from Saratoga to Whitesboro until the second week in July. Once they finally arrived in Whitesboro, William was able to stay for only a brief visit. Miriam, on the other hand, remained nearly a month, returning to Elmira on August 14, 1848.

The few extant letters that Miriam wrote to William in this period show that she had lost none of the playful affection for him that appeared in her letters of the previous year. Predictably, she missed William when they were apart, and she looked forward to being with him again, but she surprised even herself by realizing she missed Elmira, which she now regarded as her home. Her letters are filled with domestic details. She wants William to exchange sheeting they had received from Mrs. Arnot at the donation party, and she illustrates with a diagram how wide Jane should make the hems on the sheets. She also wants Jane to begin the long process of sun-bleaching the sheets to get them to the right degree of whiteness. Finally, she expresses pleasure over William's report on the church fair, but displeasure over how the ladies decided to use the money they raised (to paint the church white with green blinds—"a piece of barbarism which I doubt whether any other enlightened congregation at the present time would perpetrate").[27]

In a letter dated July 27, 1848, she revealed how far along her plans had developed in preparing a volume of her stories for publication. She now referred to her book rather than to her scrapbook, and she told William that she thought she could get everything ready for the press if only they had "about three months entirely by ourselves."[28] Her original design assumed that she would write only a few more Widow Bedott stories, but it was never clear whether she intended to include any of the Aunt Maguire stories. She had even gone so far as to draw a few illustrations for the book, and Louis Godey was busily contacting Philadelphia publishers on her behalf. Had the project succeeded in her lifetime, it probably would have brought her considerable fame and financial gain, but it was not to be. As it was, Whitcher's reputation as a humorist increased with the publication of each of her stories, whether in Neal's *Saturday Gazette* or *Godey's Lady's Book*. Both Alice Neal and Louis Godey continued to heap praise on her for her work, and in November 1848 Miriam was surprised and gratified to receive a letter forwarded to her by Alice Neal from the popular writer Grace Greenwood (Mrs. Lippincott). "Among other things she said that herself & other good judges consider me the *first humorist in America!!* did you ever!"[29]

Miriam continued to be motivated by their financial woes as well as by her growing fame. On October 12, 1848, she wrote her sister that the only time William received any salary at all was when he

> goes a dunning & succeeds in drumming up a few dollars—his attempts are not always successful.
>
> I have been getting a new dress. I did not mean to get anything new this fall. But a merchant was owing us, & William wanted me to take it out in a dress. It is a sort of woorsted plaid stuff—looks very well—but quite plain. I shall have it fitted and make it myself. William took yesterday a lot of Post Office stamps from the P. M. [Postmaster] to go for pew rent. They are a good deal better than nothing.[30]

An even more distressing sign of poverty appeared when Jane decided in late October to leave Elmira. William had to go out borrowing to get the money to pay Jane the wages owed her.[31] In November, when the quarter's pay was due, William was able to collect so little that Miriam was prompted to sell for one dollar eight yards of dimity she had left over from the donation party. William, meanwhile, had once again "gone down town to try to raise some money."[32]

For all the trials of the year, Miriam was in remarkably good spirits in the fall and winter of 1848. Her letters frequently referred to people who called on them, and her complaints about Elmira and the parishioners greatly subsided; it seemed as though she had at last come to terms with the limitations that she found in Elmira society. To be sure she still could become outraged at ill-mannered people such as the audience at a harp concert whose chatter nearly drowned out the musicians, but she was clearly "at home" in Elmira.[33] There were fewer references in her letters to any health problems, and no further references to loneliness or bouts of depression. The names of new friends grace the letters of this period, but mostly she speaks of her own domestic happiness and contentment. When Jane left, the Whitchers decided once again to do without a housekeeper, and this time the decision stuck. Miriam took on most of the chores, with a woman coming in once a week to do the washing and to help with the heaviest work. The first benefit from this arrangement was in saving Jane's salary and considerable expense in food. Best of all, Miriam and William had the house entirely to themselves: "William is snoozing on the lounge. He says he has been happier for the last fortnight than at any time before since we kept house. I could not get along so well if he were not so good & easily pleased."[34]

This period of calm and contentment was short-lived, however, because Miriam was no longer sure that her anonymity as an author was secure in Elmira. The previous spring a young Elmira man visited Miriam's family in Whitesboro, where he learned that she "was" the Widow Bedott:

> We had young Howel to spend last evening with us. It was very pleasant to see one who had just seen you. He seemed highly pleased with his visit at Whitesboro', but especially delighted at finding out the authorship of the Bedotts, having always taken that paper, &

become quite interested in the "widder." . . . Howel is very much respected here. I was rather sorry that he learned about my writings. I did not care to have it known here, & of course he'll blaze it.[35]

In May, the Elmira *Gazette* reprinted "Parson Scrantum's Donation Party," two months after it had appeared in the *Lady's Book,* and by November, when the "Contemplated Sewing Society" sketch came out in the *Lady's Book,* Elmirans had begun to suspect that their village was supplying the models for some of Miriam's characters. But nothing was as yet confirmed.

Amidst such an atmosphere of suspicion, William Whitcher got into trouble of his own with some of his parishioners over a case of mistaken identity about a supposedly hypothetical character in one of his sermons. On Advent Sunday, in early December, William preached what his wife called "a powerful" sermon about "the certainty & awfulness of the Judgement, & the terrors of the dreadful day when the secrets of all hearts shall be revealed. I never heard him preach so powerfully. He dwelt at some length upon the horror of meeting the partners in guilt on that day."[36] The effect on the congregation was greater than William had bargained for:

The house was crowded. It seemed as if the Lord sent all the hard cases in town to church that afternoon—some who had not been there in years, infidels & all sorts of people. And it was as still as death, excepting the loud sobs of one poor lady who sat near me—a presbyterian whose husband is a miserable wretch. It was a sermon calculated to make people thoughtful, but there was one man who was *peculiarly* affected by it. He has a pretty wife, whose character unfortunately needs a great deal of *defending.* He has always before been friendly to William. But on Monday morning he came up here in a furious passion—to *whip* William for preaching about *his wife.* William of course was thunderstruck, but with christian calmness he endeavored to convince the man of his error. He assured him that he did not mean his wife, when he spoke of adulterers &c, (for the woman is not criminal, but so very gay & thoughtless that she has for some time been the subject of scandal)—and not long before William had been to see her & warned her of her danger, as a pastor ought to do, for she is a communicant. She received the warning & advice kindly, nor did her husband, who was present seem to be offended at the time, tho' he said that *he* did'nt care for what jealous people said about his wife. She might ride & visit with *"the Captain"* (who by the way is a ridiculous fop—he was at church too.) So the next morning he came up boiling with rage to *flog the parson*. He left the house somewhat cooled down—at least enough so to *defer* the flogging, but still declaring that he'd whip *somebody* before he let it drop.[37]

With a forthrightness that prefigured William's role in the "Sewing Society" scandal that was soon to break in Elmira, William confronted the offended couple several days later in their own home:

> On Friday evening William went without my knowledge to their house—it is not far from here—to make a final effort at bringing them to reason. He found them at home also the Captain and another gentleman, a friend of ours whom they had hauled up & accused of stuffing Whitcher's ears. The lady was calm & very anxious that peace sho'd be restored, but the three men were as mad as pipers. I will not go into detail—suffice it to say that William after a while succeeded in exculpating Col. S.[cribner] (our friend) & restoring good feeling among them, & towards himself, & they parted good friends.[38]

Miriam's final summary of the affair reveals a naïveté, possibly even a disingenuousness, not often evident in her character. The following Sunday evening she reported, "Mrs. T. (the aggrieved lady) & her champions have been to church, & unusually attentive today. I feel very much relieved that the affair has terminated so amicably. I was so fearful it would result in mischief to William, but was'nt the man a goose to take the sermon in that way?"[39] For the second time in only a few months Miriam used the term "goose" to describe a man who thought he was being publicly criticized by one of the Whitchers, which suggests that she may have been engaged in self-denial, that she was unwilling to admit even to herself how closely she modeled her characters on people she knew. If so, she had ample warning that fellow townspeople could easily become offended by her characterizations; on the other hand, she might finally have understood that people were quick to see themselves even in the most negative lights. Once warned, however, Miriam pressed on with renewed determination, and rather than hide her intentions better she made even less

effort to disguise her models when she felt that her material justified it.

While the sermon incident clearly took William and Miriam by
surprise, they recognized that Miriam's "Sewing Society" sketch due
to be published at the end of the month might indeed cause trouble
in Elmira; William was more cautious than his wife. "The first article
[draft] that I wrote, William would'nt let me send—he thought the
characters would certainly be recognized and make trouble. The last
one too, he thought too personal, and would not consent to my
sending it for some time. I tried a third time, but I was discouraged
& gave it up in despair. So after suggesting some slight alterations he
permitted me to send the second."[40]

"The Sewing Society" and Miss Samson Savage

The "Sewing Society" sketch is a brilliant piece of social satire in
its own right, but when read in the context of Miriam's life in Elmira,
the sketch contains irony upon irony. Firmly based on Elmira society,
but *never* limited to it in implication, the story in turn influenced
what happened in Elmira in the aftermath of its publication; "art"
and "life" imitated each other in Elmira in the winter of 1849. Nor
did the complexities end with the single sketch and its immediate
effects on Elmira society; the complex interplay between fiction and
fact itself became the theme for a third sewing society story that
Miriam wrote several months after the story in question appeared in
Godey's Lady's Book.

The sketch starts out innocently enough, with Aunt Maguire
emphasizing how much the women talked at the sewing society meeting, and how little they accomplished:

> I wish to gracious you could attend one of our Sewin' Society
> meetin's. You never see nothin' to beat 'em, I'll be bound for 't.
> We've had tew now. At the first one, at Squire Birsley's, ther was
> twenty-five present. Miss Birsley had got some shirts cut out o'
> Cappen Smalley's cloth, and as fast as they come in she sot 'em to
> work—at least she gin 'em some work, but ther was so much talkin'
> to dew ther was precious little sewin' done. Ther tongues went a
> good deal faster 'n ther fingers did, and the worst on 't was, they

was all a runnin' at once. There was an everlastin' sight o' talking',
but it did seem as if they wouldent never come to no decision in
creation. . . . Some was for meetin' once a week, and some thought
't was altogether too often. Some was for stayin' to tea, and some
was opposed to 't. Some thought 't would be a good plan to stay
and work evenin's, and some was of opinion 't would n't pay, bein'
as we'd have to burn so many candles and lamps. Ther wa'n't
nothing said about what object we'd work for at the first meetin'—
thought we'd leave that till next time. (pp. 293–94)

The women do manage to elect officers and to decide to meet
every other week, after which Miss Birsley serves a modest tea that
she hopes in vain will set an example for the meetings to follow. At
the second meeting, the disagreements are more substantive, focusing
on what to do with the money they raise; suggested projects range
from missionary societies to the Sons o' Temperance, and only Aunt
Maguire's suggestion that they use their money to fix up the church
wins nearly universal approval:

For my part [said Miss Birsley], I think we couldent dew better: the
meetin'-house is in a miserable condition; the plasterin's a comin'
off in ever so many places, and the pulpit's a forlorn old thing, away
up in the air; it's enough to break a body's neck to look at the
minister, and shakes like an old egg shell. Mr. Tuttle says he's
a'most afeard to go into it. Don't you think 't would be a good
plan to tear it down and build another? Now don't all speak at
once. We never shall dew nothing in creation if we don't have some
sort o' order. (p. 297)

When the proposition is put to a vote (after much discussion and
considerable digression in which the Widder Pettibone is hauled over
the coals), only two women fail to support the idea, Miss Ben Stillman
and her daughter, Polly Mariar. Initially, they are a bit coy about
giving their reasons for not supporting the plan, but Polly Mariar
finally says what is on her mind.

"The fact is," says Polly Mariar, stretchin' her great mouth
from ear to ear and displayin' all her big teeth—(Jeff says her mouth
looks like an open sepulcher full o' dead men's bones)—"the fact

is," says she, "mar and me's of opinion that we hadent ought to vote till Miss Samson Savage is consulted."

"Miss Samson Savage ain't a member o' the Society," says Miss Birsley, "and she don't go to meetin' once in six months. I don't know what we should want to consult her for, I'm sure."

"But you know," says Miss Stillman, "her means is such that she's able to contribbit a great deal to any object she approves of."

"And we'd ought to be careful about offendin' her," says Polly Mariar, "for, you know, she withdraw'd herself from the Baptists because their Sewin' Society dident dew as she wanted to have 'em."

"Did the Baptists break down after it?" says Miss Birsley. (p. 301)

The discussion is suddenly interrupted by the entrance of Miss Samson Savage herself, "a great, tall, raw-boned woman" (pp. 305–6), who "marches" into the meeting and promptly dominates it. Whereas the humor to this point has been relatively gentle, exposing only the utter impossibility of viewing women's society with any overlay of sentimentality, and dispelling any notion of women's natural moral superiority, the satiric thrust here becomes sharp and deadly. Miss Samson Savage sets herself above everyone else and prides herself on her gentility; she is in fact arrogant, pretentious, and domineering, for which she bears the brunt of Whitcher's full disapproval. Aunt Maguire's initial description of Miss Samson Savage is the longest, most comprehensive, and most critical characterization in Miriam Whitcher's stories. Aunt Maguire holds nothing back:

She's one o' the *big bugs* here—that is, she's got more money than a'most any body else in town. She was a tailoress when she was a gal, and they say she used to make a dretful sight o' mischief among the folks where she sewed. But that was when she lived in Varmount. When Mr. Savage married her, he was one o' these ere specilators. Wonderful fellers to make money, them Varmounters. Husband says they come over the Green Mountains with a spellin'-book in one hand and a halter in t' other, and if they can't git a school to teach, they can steal a hoss. When they first come to our place, he was a follerin' the tin-peddlin' bisness; he used to go rumblin' round in his cart from house to house, and the rich folks ruther turned up their noses at him, or he consated they did, and it made him awful wrathy; so he determined he'd be richer 'n any on 'em, and pay 'em off in their own coin. Old Smith says he's heerd him time and agin make his boast that he'd ride over all their heads some day—dident seem to have no higher eend in view than to be the richest man in Scrabble Hill. He sot his heart and soul and body on 't, and knowin' how to turn every cent to the best advantage, and bein' wonderful sharp at a bargain, he succeeded; every thing he took hold of prospered, and without actilly bein' what you could call dishonest, afore many years every body allowed he was the richest man in the place. So he built a great big stun house and furnished it wonderful grand, his wife wouldent have a bit o' furnitewer made here—nothin' would dew but she must send away to Philadelphy for 't. . . . So she sot up for a lady. She was always a coarse, boisterous, high-tempered critter, and when her husband grow'd rich, she grow'd pompous and overbearin'. She made up her mind she'd rule the roast, no matter what it cost—she'd be the *first* in Scrabble Hill. She know'd she wa'n't a lady by natur nor by eddication, but she thought mabby other folks would be fools enough to think she was if she made a great parade. So she begun by dressin' more, and givin' bigger parties than any body else. Of course, them that thinks money's the main thing (and ther's plenty such here and every where), is ready to flatter her and make a fuss over her, and approve of all her dewin's. If ther's any body that *won't* knuckle tew her, I tell ye they have to take it *about east*. She abuses 'em to their faces and slanders 'em to their backs. Such conduct wouldent be put up with in a poor woman; but them that would be for drummin *me* out o' town if I should act so, is ready to uphold Miss Samson Savage, and call it *independence* and *frankness* in her. She's got so she prides herself on it. She says *she* ain't afeard to tell folks what she think of 'em—if *she* don't like any body, they *know* it purty soon. Husband says she wouldent think it no harm to set her neighbor's house a fire if she done it in the *day-time*. (pp.301–4)

Even after such a thorough indictment, Aunt Maguire finds it in her heart to show some brief pity for Miss Savage:

But it's plain to be seen with all her pretensions she feels oneasy and oncomfortable the hull time. I've noticed that yer *codfish gentility* always dew. She knows she ain't the *ginniwine article,* and so she tries to make up for 't in brass and bluster. If any thing goes on without her bein' head man, she always tries to put it down. She was gone a journey when the Sewin' Society was started, and I s'pose she was awful mad to think we darst to git up such a thing without consultin' her. (p. 305)

Miss Samson Savage is determined to disrupt the sewing society, and the members offer her a ready opportunity by asking her opinion of their plan to repair the church. She cares nothing for the meeting-house, but more to the point, she despises the minister and his wife. Once she starts criticizing them, other women join, and the whole discussion becomes vicious:

"I'd look purty wouldent I a workin' to fix up that meetin'-house for Tuttle to preach in!" "So you don't like Mr. Tuttle, hey?" says Miss Birsley. "Like him?" says she; "not I. He don't know nothin'— can't preach no more'n *that stove-pipe*"—(she hates Parson Tuttle 'cause he hain't never paid no more attention to her than he has to the rest o' the congregation)—"he's as green as grass and as flat as a pancake." "That's jest what mar and me thinks," says Polly Mariar Stillman. Miss Savage went on: "He don't know B from a broomstick, nor bran when the bag's open." "That's jest what I think," says Miss Stillman. "I says to Mr. Stillman last Sabbath, as we was a comin' from meetin', 'Mr. Stillman' says I"—But what 't was she said to Mr. Stillman, dear knows, for Miss Savage dident let her go on. "I say," says she, "I'd look beautiful a comin' to Sewin' Society and workin' the eends o' my fingers off to build a pulpit for Tuttle to be poked up in Sabbath after Sabbath, and preach off jest what he's a mind tew. No—ye don't ketch me a takin' a stich for such an object. I despise Tuttle, and I'll tell him so tew his face when I git a chance. Ye don't ketch me a slanderin' folks behind ther backs and then soft-soapin' 'em to their faces, as some folks dew"—(here she lookt at Miss Stillman and Polly Mariar.) "And where's his wife, I'd like to know? Why ain't *she* here to work to-day? A purty piece o' bisness, I must say, for you all to be here a diggin' away to fix up Tuttle's meetin' house when *she's* to hum a playin' *lady*." "Miss Tuttle ain't very well," says I. "That's a likely story," says Miss Savage; and from that she went on and blazed away about Miss Tuttle at a terrible rate. Miss Stillman and Polly Mariar, and a number more o' the wimmin, sot tew and helped her whenever they could git a word in edgeways; and such a haulin' over as Miss Tuttle and the parson got, I never heerd afore in all the days o' my life. (pp. 307–09)

Only the serving of an elaborate tea ("biscuit and butter, and crackers and cheese, and cold meat and pickles, and custard and whipt cream, and three kinds o' presarves, and four kinds o' cake, and what not!" [p. 309]) interrupts the gossip, and the conversation turns instead to compliments about the superior quality of each item served at the tea, which is countered by the hostess's apology for what she calls the poor quality of everything. "A person that dident know how wimmin always go on at such a place, would a thought that Miss Gipson had tried to have every thing the miserablest she possibly could, and that the rest on 'em had never had any thing to hum but what was miserabler yet" (p. 311). As Aunt Maguire observes, "every thing arthly comes to an eend, and so did that tea after a spell, and purty soon after we went hum." She had only one comment to make at the end, when she discovered that the little sewing they had accomplished had to be ripped out and done over because of the poor quality of the work: "For my part, I feel eny most discouraged about the Sewin' Society" (pp. 311–12).

Within days of the January issue of *Godey's* reaching the public (in late December 1848), the "Sewing Society" was reprinted on the front page of the Elmira *Gazette*. The story set the town of Elmira on end, and Miriam Whitcher's anonymity was destroyed once and for all:

> I cannot give you any idea of the terrible muss which "Mrs Samson Savage" has created here. About a week ago the town began to be ablaze with it. We do not know who first noticed the article, but it spread like fire, & for some days has been the theme of conversation in all places. High & low, rich & poor are all agog about it. There are two bookstores here at each of which the Lady's Book is taken. At one of them the demand for the book was such that the bookseller ordered & sold immediately forty extra copies, & the other one said he could have sold fifty in two hours. I suppose there never was as much reading done in Elmira before as there has been the past week.[41]

What so ignited Elmira's imagination was just what William had feared: people recognized themselves and each other in the story. Depending upon who they were, they were either delighted or furious. Most intriguing of all was the immediate and universal recognition of the town's most prominent woman, Mrs. John Arnot, Sr. (nee Tuttle), as the unmistakable model for Miss Samson Savage:

> Mrs Arnot was recognized at once, to her infinite rage & that of her friends & *toad-eaters.* As she is almost universally disliked of course there is a deal of crowing & triumphing at seeing her taken off. William's enemies are making a handle of it to injure him, & some of his friends are so much afraid of the miserable woman, & such worshippers of money, that they are dreadfully alarmed. There are some who are bold enough to stand by their minister & tell him to fear nothing, but let the "galled jade wince". It is not very pleasant for me, who have hitherto been so retired & unnoticed here, to be thus hauled into notoriety, & subjected to all sorts of mean insults from Mrs Arnot & her clique, as I shall be. The woman who thought herself preached at a few weeks ago, is one of them, & has already grossly insulted us. I will not give the particulars. I do not care for such people, but I fear that William will have trouble.[42]

John Arnot, Sr., a director of the bank and an entrepreneur involved in almost every major business venture in Elmira since the 1830s, could not have been very happy over his characterization, either; the Arnot character comes perilously close to being called outright dishonest. The Arnots must have been further insulted when Miriam Whitcher mischievously named the pastor and his wife "Tuttle" after Mrs. Arnot's father and Mr. Arnot's former business partner.

At first, many friends and church members faithfully stood by the Whitchers, countering in part Miriam's fears that William would have trouble over the affair. As the passage above indicates, some supporters of the Whitchers were especially pleased that the story put Mrs. Arnot in her place, according to their light, which must have enraged her all the more: "We have a great many friends, & the way that I am clapped & applauded by most of the townsfolk for 'showing up' Mrs *Savage*, is very amusing. I am not at all sorry for writing the piece, but I am astonished at the muss."[43] At this point in the controversy, however, Miriam felt she could no longer count on the Luces, who had been the Whitchers' friends and allies from the first day William arrived in Elmira. Whereas one week before Miriam had stayed with the Luces while William preached in another parish, she now believed she was no longer welcome in their home: "I shall hardly dare to show my face there again, they are so alarmed about the 'article.' They are good people, but very timid & act like fools." Later, the cause of part of the Luces' "alarm" became known to Miriam: "There is a Mrs Hatch & her daughter who are very much like 'Mis[s] Stillman & Polly Mariar', and every one thinks so. In fact they know it themselves, but they have succeeded in making Mrs Luce & Mrs Post believe that those characters are meant for them, & that is the principal cause of the L's enmity to us, & Mrs Hatch congratulates herself on having made them our enemies, thus strengthening her party materially."[44]

Miriam's sense of humor did not desert her even in the midst of the worst turmoil: "I am mad to think that I got 'out of cog' here [that is, became known as the author of the articles]. If I had'nt I could enjoy the fun."[45] But nothing could stop her from enjoying how fully the humor hit home not only in Elmira but also in neighboring villages:

> I received a letter from Godey the other day, containing $20. He "calls for more" articles. I wrote him yesterday & gave him an account of the fuss here, & begged him to notice in the Dollar that several villages were contending for the honor of being the birth place of "Mrs Samson Savage", which is an amusing fact. A man from a village in Seneca county, came into one of our bookstores the other day to get some Lady's Books, saying that they were all alive about it in his place, because they had a Mrs Samson Savage there. And we have heard from Havana—a village twenty miles from here—they have fitted the coat to a woman there.[46]

Still later, an irate husband from another village threatened William with a lawsuit for exposing *his* wife's character, and William had to retain a Utica lawyer to protect himself against yet another "wronged" husband. Evidently, women who bore striking resemblances to Miss Samson Savage tyrannized villagers throughout the region. Everywhere local people sought a role for themselves in Whitcher's stories, no matter how insignificant. According to local lore, the wife of a Presbyterian minister in Utica, Mrs. Fowler, "claimed to be the original of 'the Rev. Mrs. Togo of Albany,' quoted by the famous peddler, Jabez *[sic]* Clark, as having purchased the first pattern of the famous grody flowery brocade silk he was trying to sell to the Widow Bedott."[47]

Elmira sources claim that William himself let it be known that his wife was the author of the Aunt Maguire sketches, and he was otherwise directly implicated in the scandal. William organized the sewing society in the first place, he approved the draft of the article that Miriam ultimately sent to Louis Godey, and he took considerable pleasure in the "muss" that ensued. At the end of Miriam's December 28 letter to Kate, William added a note of his own that clearly indicated his special interest in the affair:

> Frank has just read to me that part of her letter relating to the "savage" commotion; but it does not convey any adequate idea of the stir and noise which is going on. Bar-rooms,—stores—shops—streets wherever men women or children meet are the scenes of the tragico-comedy. Some rage, some laugh some swear,—some look grave and shake the head. The senior warden in the ch[urch], a good, but very timid man, came to me trembling,—literally shaking from head to foot and thot I had better resign at once. The great godess Diana, has been hit and the Ephesians are in an uproar & the greater part know not wherefore. After the smoke clears away I shall go round to see the extent of the damage & will report. In the mean time I shall strive to keep cool—say but little—*work hard not to put out the fire, but to make it burn only the stuble.* [emphasis added][48]

Unlike his sermon on the adulterous woman, William could not smooth over the commotion caused by the sewing society article. The fury of the Arnots and their friends would not be dampened and in fact was only fanned by the delight other townspeople took in calling their neighbors by names ascribed to various characters in the sketches: "Every body insists upon applying Mrs Samson Savage to Mrs Arnot. She goes by the name every-where, & her admirers or echoes, are called the 'Stillman family'. The young man Capt. Hasted of whom I spoke in a letter some time ago as being the beau of Mrs. T. (the woman who thought herself preached at) is called universally 'Cappen Smalley', & they say it cuts him to death."[49]

Nor was the fire fully extinguished for years to come. A resident of Elmira who was interviewed over half a century after the sketch was written had no intention of ever forgiving Miriam Whitcher; she was upset not because her friends were targeted for ridicule or she herself was caricatured in the sketch but because she was slighted:

"Know her? Yes I did! She was an awful woman. She slandered everybody. It was awful. She put me and my sister in the book. We were the Peabodys." But, [the interviewer] says, "She didn't say so much about the Peabodys did she?" "Of course she didn't! You'd a thought our family didn't amount to anything. But we were just as prominent as anybody and I guess we were thought as much of."[50]

In large measure, however, the controversy remained alive because the humor struck at the heart of the social anxieties of the emerging middle class, the very people who read *Godey's Lady's Book.* The sketch satirized upward social mobility, the "codfish gentility" whose wealth, not character, gave them social standing. It exposed the hypocrisy of those whose vulgarity and whose desire for power overshadowed all other characteristics. The readers of the *Lady's Book* heartily enjoyed seeing the "savages" exposed for their false claims to genteel social standing, while at the same time many of those delighting in the satire were themselves no doubt on the rise socially.[51] Louis Godey could not keep up with the demands for back orders of the January 1848 *Lady's Book,* and subscriptions to his magazine jumped to forty thousand copies a month by June of the same year, an unprecedented high.[52] Miriam admitted it was "imprudent" for her to have written the piece, but, she added, in a halfhearted effort to defend herself, "I could not help it. I thought it a good subject for ridicule, & I was provoked beyond measure at seeing William abused & insulted as he was here all last summer."[53]

Unwilling to leave while the controversy still raged because it would appear that the Arnots had forced him and Miriam out, William nonetheless began actively looking for another parish. Stillwater, New Berlin, Oxford, Waterloo, Mechanicsville, and Duanesburgh were at one time all mentioned as possibilities, and William pursued any option that he thought might work. Stillwater, located near Saratoga, was Miriam's first choice. Her brother-in-law Barbour and her brother Morris both actively campaigned there on William's behalf. Miriam, for her part, believed that whatever problems might await them in Stillwater, "it could [not] be as bad as this place."[54]

In February, the Elmira *Gazette* refocused attention on the controversy by reprinting two Widow Bedott sketches and announcing that "the author of [these sketches] resides among us."[55] Ironically, the sewing society that inspired Whitcher's series kept alive the gossip about the minister and his wife, while members of the vestry, according to Miriam, "act[ed] in a most contemptible manner against William."[56] On the evening of February 12, 1849, William called a meeting of the vestry and prepared a statement to read to the members: "He gives a minute account of all that has transpired since he came here—What the people have done, & what he has done, & all that he has had to endure. It is very calm & dignified, but very plain."[57] With this act, William played out in reality the role created for the fictional Reverend Scrantum at the end of the "Donation Party" sketch written the year before; even Miriam's use of the word "endure" echoes the language of Parson Scrantum recounting for his churchmen all the trials his family had endured in the Scrabble Hill parish.

After the meeting, which took place in the Whitchers' home, William added to his wife's letter to Kate an extended description of the meeting. He revealed, too, that the townspeople were not alone in calling key Elmirans by their "Sewing Society" names:

> Miriam wants me to give you an account of the meeting of the vestry last night, a thing somewhat difficult as the affair was so desultory, random shots on all sides, and some which were not at random,—home thrusts that told their own story without any explanation. But to be more particular, those of the vestry who were unfriendly to me came first, and for a time I feared a quorum would be made up of these before my friends came, in such case I was determined to adjourn the meeting, but after a while all were assembled, not a man wanting, after prayer, I called upon the senior warden to state the object of the meeting; (he had requested the meeting to be called) but he could not tell any object; but that it [seemed] best to meet & talk over the state of the Parish. I then read to them my statement of its affairs which made two of them bite their lips, i.e., Mr Luce & Mr Hatch. Mr Hatch had appropri-

ated $140, of the churches money to his own use, my allusion to this sealed his mouth effectually when he began his complaints. Mr Luce next began to complain of my unpopularity, and I convinced the rest of the vestry if not himself, that he had been the main cause of it, which shut him up for the rest of the evening. My friends now began to talk, and it was soon seen that a strong cement was setting in my favour. The conversation then became more general, and the merits of "Aunt McGuires" *[sic]* Article were fully discussed, both as to its local and literary merits, Mr Hatch thot it was silly, (an opinion in which I suppose all the Stillman family will agree) others thought it to the life, whether considered as local or general, and the grand result in regard to it was that it was a very small affair for ten grave men to talk seriously of allowing it to disturb the harmony of a Parish. I then asked them man by man the clerk and all, whether they intended to support me if I remained, and even, Luce, Hatch and old Strouse, (the unfriendly ones) said they would do so, and all the others of course said they would. A general good feeling thus pervading the meeting, I told them that it was my intention so soon as I could without loss to myself to leave them, and that my object had been to show them that I would never be driven away on mere grounds of feeling. All went home apparently well satisfied. I have no room for the great amount of my love.[58]

The Whitchers had yet one more indignity to endure. Two days later, on Valentine's Day, their postmaster warned them not to read the Valentines they found in their mail box, "as he doubted not that they were abusive." A young woman who was visiting the Whitchers read two: "One was quite good but the other was a most scurrillous & abominable thing—perfect outpouring of envy & malice, from some quarter, such valentines are very common here."[59]

In the midst of the turmoil, Miriam appreciated more than ever the kindnesses extended to them by some in the parish. Many members earnestly wished William to stay with the church, fearing that if he left it would fail completely. But the most touching tribute of all came from the children of the church. Realizing that the adults had no intention of giving the pastor and his wife a donation party, the children asked permission from the Whitchers to do so themselves, and a date was set. At first it seemed to Miriam and William as though the adults thwarted the children's plan, for no children showed up on the day when they were expected. The following Saturday, however, they *did* appear, and Miriam reported to her sister the full, happy details of the day:

> I was not expecting them, & had eaten up all the cracked nuts & tarts. Moreover I was not well, & on that account had declined accompanying William to call on a bride over the river. He had started, & on his way met half a dozen little girls coming, so he turned round & came back with them. There was about a dozen came. One of them brought a little basket of cookies, another, a paper of raisins, and with these, and some cake that I had on hand, I set the supper table for them. Butler was here sawing wood, & I got him to crack some nuts, so we had plenty of refreshments. The donations were as follows. Beside the cookies & raisins, one girl brought a half-dollar, another a little pail of cream, another—little Eleanor Riker, a godchild of mine—brought a very mysterious looking bookmark. Another, a pretty pencil-drawing of her own. She was a beautiful child. I never saw her before—her parents are presbyterians—but she goes to our Sunday School. Another one brought a funny little paper heart, & another a piece of muslin—about enough for a chemise. Dr Bush's children & one or two more, did'nt bring anything. They came at two o'clock, & stayed till after six, & such fun as they had was never enjoyed before. They played all sorts of plays, & would have stayed all the evening if we had permitted them. They said they never had so much fun in all their lives before. But such a time as I had cleaning up after them I hope I may not have soon again.[60]

No matter how much support the Whitchers had in Elmira, William's effectiveness as a pastor was clearly at an end. The church, not for the first time, was deeply divided, with factional interests set above the interests of the church as a whole. With Miriam "out of cog," her ability to remain in Elmira and continue to be productive was at best problematic. She wished for nothing more than to leave the Elmira parish. Nonetheless, her desire to cut short her time there was fulfilled in an unexpected way: in mid-March, her father became dangerously ill, and she had to leave immediately for Whitesboro.

Although William had not yet found another position, both he and Miriam intended that when she left Elmira for Whitesboro her leave-taking would be permanent, and so they packed up all her personal belongings to prepare for a journey to Whitesboro. William expected to be away from Elmira two or three weeks; "he will then return, & (if he has another parish) box his things, preach his farewell sermon & quit."[61] These were Miriam Whitcher's last words from Elmira, but they were by no means her last words on the subject of Scrabble Hill. At Louis Godey's request, she planned to write a follow-up story about the sewing society from the security of her Whitesboro home. One can only imagine what her feelings must have been when she took her final look at the village that had so fired her imagination and had brought her such fame and notoriety.

6

❧

Return to Whitesboro

On March 25, 1849, shortly after Miriam and William returned to Whitesboro, Miriam's father died. The cause of death was listed in the 1850 New York Census as "old age"; he was eighty-four years old and died peacefully in his sleep. Remarkably, Lewis Berry was the first one of his large family to die since the death of his daughter Jane circa 1816. Yet within three years three more Berrys would die in succession: Miriam, John, and their mother, Elizabeth. Just as Miriam and William had planned, Miriam stayed with her family while William returned to Elmira to finish his business there and resign from his pastorate. William's absence, however, only increased Miriam's sense of loss in the death of her father. "We all miss father more than ever since you went. I keep connecting you together in my thoughts, and it seems sometimes as if you had gone with him."[1] They had no way of knowing then that in the next two years they would be apart from each other as much as they would be together. They would never again have a house of their own or a settled, secure life together.

Home for Miriam now consisted of an all-female household, headed by her seventy-four-year-old mother, Elizabeth Wells Berry. The family continued to take in roomers and provide meals for Whitesboro residents who contracted only for board. For example, the Reverend Mr. Long took all his meals with the Berrys while his wife was away visiting her family and the Berrys were thus treated to daily dinner-table conversations that rivaled Elder Sniffles's Thanksgiving dinner talk.[2] The management and major work of the inn fell to the three unmarried sisters—Kate, Mary, and Cornelia—whom Miriam referred to as "the girls." John Berry, the younger bachelor brother, no longer lived at home, so when William was in Whitesboro, he became the male head of the household, and the one to whom the Berry women turned for advice in the months to come.

"A Little Heap of Corruption"

In her first few months at home, Miriam often thought about death. When Lewis Berry died, the family bought a large burial plot in Grandview Cemetery; it was a choice lot situated at the front edge of the cemetery's hill, overlooking the town of Whitesboro, the Mohawk River valley, and, in the mid-1800s, the Erie Canal. At the same time, the Berry family also decided to exhume the body of Jane, buried over thirty years earlier elsewhere in the cemetery, and to move her next to Lewis. The decision was common enough, given that their intention was to establish a family plot where eleven members of the Berry family ultimately could be buried, but what followed is by modern standards an extraordinary event. Brothers John and Lewis were not only in charge of moving Jane's body to the new plot but also of actually digging up and inspecting the remains. Miriam reported to William with great interest and wonder the details of the exhumation and the family's subsequent careful examination of Jane's body:

> Lewis & John came up & brought three men from the factory, & they were all the afternoon busy in the grave yard. Did not get through till 8 o'clock in the evening. Kate went up & stayed till Jane was taken up & buried again. It is thirty years since she died, but still we were in hope that the coffin would be entire, though we had no reason to think so, as there was no outer box. But it was all decayed excepting a few pieces of the board. They dug very carefully, & found the shape of the place perfect. All the marks where the shovel went in the first time were still there & served as a guide to the diggers. It was so long before they found anything that they became fearful that the body had been taken away, & Lewis got so distressed & agitated that he left the spot for some time. But Kate stayed by & watched every movement. At last, after going to the depth of eight feet, one of the men announced that he struck something, & after cautiously removing all the dirt with their hands,

the mouldered & blackened coffin appeared. The sides were decayed, & the top & bottom had fallen together & crumbled almost
to dust. They took off the top, which fell all to pieces, & there were
the bones of our beautiful & beloved sister all entire—the hands
crossed just as they were laid at first. The bones all came apart at the
joints, but they were all there. The clothes were all gone excepting a
piece of what appeared to have been white twilled silk. It laid over
the face, & was double—about half a yard long. Mother thinks it is
a piece that was fastened at the head of the coffin to turn over the
face. They use muslin now instead. Kate brought away a piece of it.
The twill is still perfect, & we ravelled some of it & found out that
it was silk, though it is nearly black now. The bones too were very
dark. All the teeth remained & in the head firmly excepting one,
which was a little decayed & loose. Mary remembers perfectly that
it was in that condition when she died. They laid the bones in the
box provided & re-buried them, never to be disturbed again till
God calls for them.[3]

In the same letter, Miriam described for her husband the stone
marker the family erected at the Berry family grave site. The work-
manship she describes was so careful that the marker survives to this
day, perfectly upright, a silent testimony to Miriam's claim that "it is
the prettiest & best proportioned one there":

> On the same afternoon they prepared the foundation for the
> monument, & laid the base marble. They did it very firmly, putting
> in a great deal of stone & water-lime. The next day the monument
> was erected. It is done very handsomely, & much to our
> satisfaction. . . . It can be seen from a great distance—even mother's
> dim eyes can discern it distinctly. The inscription is as follows on
> one side

Lewis Berry
born May 29 1767
fell asleep in Jesus March 25th 1849

On another side, Wendell & Jane are recorded. The Cross is beauti-
fully cut in an oval panel. I think you will like it all. "Fell asleep in
Jesus" was my suggestion. I do not like "died" nor "departed this
life." And besides it is so expressive of the manner in which our dear
father left us, & it certainly is scriptural, do you not think so?[4]

Miriam found considerable comfort in knowing that her father and sister lay next to each other at the top of the hill, visible from their house, but she still could not be satisfied until her still-born infant daughter, Mary, also was laid to rest in the Whitesboro cemetery:

> I hope you can bring up the baby when you come. My heart is set on having it buried here. I dreamed last night that you came up with it, that we opened the coffin & found the dear little thing alive, & I took it out & nursed it. I thought there was a great many people present, & they tried to get it from me & bury it again, but I clung to it & would not let it go. I think I should be happier if it were lying where my dear father & sister sleep, & where my own name will probably be recorded.[5]

Miriam's matter-of-fact tone describing this terrible nightmare barely hides her underlying sense of despair and loss, as well as a premonition of her own early death. There was no question but that her wishes regarding the infant Mary would be honored. And so, one of William's last chores before leaving Elmira was to arrange having the baby shipped to Whitesboro; he ordered, too, a stone marker to lie flat on the ground over the body of Mary. It was to read, simply, "Mary, April 1, 1848."

Both the body and the marker were shipped to Whitesboro with the boxes containing the Whitchers' household furnishings and personal belongings. Because of the urgent need to rebury the child, John arranged with the warehouseman to notify him as soon as the Whitchers' belongings arrived off the canal boat. As with Jane, they intended to examine the body before burying it, and planned carefully for the event. John was to bring the coffin to the Berry house and open it. If the remains were in good condition, Miriam would be allowed to see her infant daughter for the first and only time; if they were not, she would be spared the sight. Because she never saw her baby at its birth—the length of her labor and the trauma of the birth had made that impossible—seeing the baby now represented her only chance to let go of the infant she clung to so tenaciously in her dream. Miriam waited anxiously. When the day came, stormy and rainy, John proceeded according to their plans. As he opened the coffin, his sisters gathered round while Miriam remained inside and out of sight:

> But they were so long that I became impatient & went to the door. They were discussing the propriety of calling me, & thought on the whole that I had better not look at it. There was quite a strong smell when it was opened & John had laid the lid back, but not fastened it. I begged to see it, so he removed it & I looked at it a moment. Then I laid a snow-drop on its little breast & came away, for they did not wish me to stay long. It laid exactly as it was placed at first, with a cotton pillow under the head & the little hands crossed, & the gown smoothed down & drawn over the feet. It did not appear to have fallen away at all. We thought at first that there was a cloth laid over the face, but John took hold of it softly to raise it up & found that it was a thin coat of white mould. We could see all the little features distinctly through it. We were all perfectly astonished at its size. Mary said it was as large as most children at three or four months old. We were all surprised that it was so well preserved. We had expected only to see a little heap of corruption with no form to it. The dress & the cotton under the head looked as white as they did when it was first buried. There was no change excepting the mould on the face. I cannot describe to you my feelings as I looked at it. I could not make it appear as if it was my child—my impressions of its birth are so dreamlike & strange. Do you remember that I fancied myself in the back stoop at father's when it was born? It was a strange coincidence that it should be brought there for me to look at. I am glad that I have seen it. I never should have felt satisfied without.[6]

That same day, in keeping with Miriam's wishes, Lewis and a friend buried the infant Mary in the Grandview Cemetery next to Jane Berry. "I always imagined them together in Paradise & I wish their bodies to lie side by side."[7] Miriam put aside writing her letter to William in order to watch the whole proceedings from the front window of the Berrys' home. Saddened and depressed, she felt as though "the foreboding of some heavy calamity" had fallen over her.[8] On that rainy day in May 1849, as Miriam watched her firstborn laid to rest in the family burial plot, she was three months pregnant with a second child. In addition to her grief over Mary, she was haunted by the fear that she would soon "suffer another such affliction."

As long as William remained in Elmira, the town and the parishioners were still very much in Miriam's thoughts. In contrast to the bitterness expressed in her final letters from Elmira, Miriam's Whitesboro letters spoke kindly of a large number of Elmira friends. She had gained some emotional distance from the controversy surrounding her departure, and she had begun to distinguish between what she called "a certain class of people," and the majority of the Elmira congregation. She especially appreciated those who had been "constant friends"—those who had supported the Whitchers through their entire stay in Elmira: the Tallents, Noes, Hopkinses, Hallidays, Daniels, Briggs, Baldwins, and the Staggs; Mrs. Cooley, Mrs. Smith, Mr. Richardson, Mrs. Scribner; the McCanns, Towners, Brooks, and Bushes.

Still, disagreeable Elmira business remained. Before Miriam left Elmira, the Reverend Mr. Hull of New Berlin had proposed to William that the two men permanently exchange parishes. If such a plan were to come about, each man would have to do a great deal of work on the other's behalf in his current parish. Although the Whitchers had some reservations about taking on the church in New Berlin, it was an option they could not lightly discard. And so William began campaigning in Elmira on behalf of the Reverend Mr. Hull. After long negotiations, he in fact secured an offer for him from Elmira's Trinity Episcopal Church. Much to the Whitchers' dismay, Mr. Hull exerted no such effort on William's behalf in New Berlin, even though he had suggested the exchange in the first place, and so no comparable offer was forthcoming. Miriam was angered by the situation, and her letters to William in this period almost all express feelings of outrage toward the Hulls, which in turn stirred up feelings of ambivalence toward the Elmira parish. She knew her first such outburst would earn her a scolding from William, but she had her say nonetheless. She hoped, she said bitterly, that Trinity Church would in fact call the Reverend Mr. Hull, "for I would like them to know by experience the difference between an active clergyman & a lazy one, between a quiet minister's wife, & a mischief-making gossip as Mrs. H. is." Once said, her better nature asserted itself, and she admitted that she would prefer that Elmira got "a good pastor: there are a good many excellent people in Elmira, some whom I love very much."[9]

A week later she was incredulous to learn that Trinity Church had agreed to Hull's terms; her anger was divided between the Hulls, for what she called their lack of honor, and the Elmira parish, for their shabby treatment of William:

> I was rather surprised at the haste with which the Elmira vestry had acceded [*sic*] to Mr H's terms. They are a good deal *greener* than I thought them. If H. has one spark of honor in him, he will decline the call unless you go to New Berlin. In fact I do not see how he can do otherwise after the mutual arrangement between you. But perhaps you think differently. I am *unanimously* of the opinion that he cares for no one but himself. If he can get a good pond to fish in, plenty of cigars to smoke, and enough listeners (not to his sermons but) to his stories, he cares for nothing else, not even his amiable *consort's* perpetual scolding. But after all he is a clever sort of man, & I hope he'll go to Elmira, for with all his laziness he knows how to take care of himself and will not stand abuse & the starving system.[10]

By an ironic twist of fate, according to one report, the Reverend Mr. Hull turned out to be one of the most effective pastors in Trinity Church's early history.[11]

As the letter above implies, the Hulls were no strangers to the Whitchers. Mrs. Hull and Miriam had at one point been friends in Whitesboro, where Mrs. Hull's family lived. Miriam thus felt doubly betrayed when Hull failed to fulfill his end of the bargain with William, and in large measure she blamed his wife for New Berlin's lack of interest in the Whitchers:

> I entirely approve of your letter to Mr Hull, it was called for by his to you. I think it was exceedingly *cool* in him to write to you in the way he did, making those remarks about me & then requesting you to get him a house. I hope you will not trouble yourself to do it. I am quite confident that she will go there & talk against me to my friends, & perhaps injure me in their estimation. I should regret it, & I wish you would give them a hint about her lying propensities. She has concluded not to spend the summer here because none of her friends, or relations, will keep her so long. I have no idea that she will write to me, & I do'nt see what she could say if she should. I wish no farther intercourse with her. But one thing could induce me ever to renew the friendship—that is a full confession from her that she *has said those things,* and is sorry for it. And this I do not

expect from her. I think also that Mr H. has treated you shabbily. He went to Elmira & urged you to exchange parishes, giving you a *promise* that you would receive a call to N.B. You labored hard & secured him a call to Elmira, which he coolly accepts, & as coolly tells you that there is no prospect of your being called to New Berlin on account of a prejudice against your wife. A prejudice which he cannot but know was created by *his* wife. It is very mean & very selfish indeed.[12]

"A prejudice against your wife"—this phrase represents one of the rare acknowledgments by Miriam about her responsibility for her husband's fate as an Episcopal minister. She was of course fully aware that her exposé of the Elmira parish in the pages of *Godey's* made it impossible for William to remain effective in Elmira; that knowledge was always mixed, however, with her strong sense of the shortcomings of the parish itself and the community at large. Even at her worst moments she could explain their removal from Elmira as a choice they had made themselves, one that was justified and welcome. But when her reputation cost William potential positions as it did in New Berlin, she had no such consolation. Miriam's offense against the Elmira parish, however justified and appreciated by the readers of *Godey's Lady's Book,* made it literally impossible for William to find another permanent position. The readers of the Aunt Maguire stories were delighted to see the "Savages" of their communities taken to task in the pages of the *Lady's Book,* but they were not ready to welcome an author with such a satiric vision into their own parish. As a consequence, Miriam became increasingly disillusioned with her own writing and conscious of the damage it had done to William. In December 1850 she compared herself to another minister's wife who was a "slouch of a woman—quite a drawback to her husband. Perhaps you will say you know *another minister's wife* of whom the same might be said."[13]

The Return of Aunt Maguire

Before she could put aside Aunt Maguire forever, Miriam Whitcher wanted to write one more story for the readers of the *Lady's Book.* Responding to an urgent request from Louis Godey to make the "fuss" over the sewing society sketch the subject of another story, Miriam took one last, long look at the whole affair in Elmira in its fictionalized form. Her final sketch, entitled "Aunt Maguire's Visit to Slabtown," demonstrates Miriam's understanding of the cause *behind* the social malaise she found in Elmira. From the safer perspective of Whitesboro, Miriam was able to gain some distance from what she had seen in Elmira; this distance, combined with the reception her stories received throughout the Northeast, helped her to understand that an entire value system lay behind the social disruption epitomized by Miss Samson Savage. As people such as Miss Samson Savage and her followers aspired to become more genteel, the very word *genteel* became almost an obsession for Miriam Whitcher.

Capitalizing on the fact that villagers throughout New York and New England believed that *their* local sewing society had been satirized in the *Lady's Book*, Whitcher set her final story in a village called Slabtown, where Aunt Maguire goes to visit her husband's relatives, Sam and Eunice Bentley. The women of Slabtown, Cousin Eunice included, are obsessed with outward signs of social status: "Eunice has got her idees raised a good deal, and had some wonderful curus notions about *gintility*. The house was furnished mighty grand, and she dident dew her own work as she used to at the Holler, but kept a great slatterin', imperdent hired gal, that done jest as she was a mind tew about every thing" (p. 314). Pressed by Aunt Maguire to explain why she keeps Marthy when she has to bribe her to get her to do her job, Eunice responds that it would be unthinkable for her to do her own work—"none o' the *first* here don't dew their own work, taint considered *ginteel*. . . . And besides, it's very necessary to have a gal to go to the door when I have a call. 'T wouldn't be ginteel to dew it myself. None o' the first don't."[14] Abandoning the argument about hired help, Aunt Maguire switches instead to the concept of gentility: "I never got so sick of anything in all my born days, as I did o' the word *ginteel* . . . Eunice used it every third breath she draw'd . . . it sartinly is the silliest word in the Inglish language" (LB, p. 425). While Aunt Maguire criticizes the use of the word *genteel*, Whitcher's humor also critiques those who would describe *themselves* as genteel. Paradoxically, if one called herself genteel, by definition she was not; Whitcher's readers would have understood this paradox even if the humor had not called it to their attention.

Overall, Aunt Maguire disapproves of how her cousin's family has changed since they moved to Slabtown. The two children especially earn her scorn:

> Lucy, tew, she was a growin' up ginteel. She's got to be the proudest little thing that ever I see, peart and bold, and right up in every body's face and eyes, stickin' in her gab all the time, and nippin' round with a couple of awful long pigtails with bows on the eends, a danglin' down her back.
>
> Henry, he's about as hateful a young one as ever went unflogged. I used to dread his comin' hum from school; for he went yellin' and hollerin' round the house, kickin' and spittin', and sassin' every body that spoke to him. I actilly heerd him swear a number o' times. (p. 314)

The husband, Sam, has stopped disciplining his children and has let his religion lapse both at church and at home, but it is Eunice who has changed most of all; her public treatment of Aunt Maguire is boorish:

> Eunice dident seem to be very proud o' me, I'm such a plain, homemade body. She never introduced me to none of her ginteel acquaintances when they called; so, as I dident have nothing to say, I used to have the benefit of all the conversation, and sartinly 't was quite entertain'. They ginerally begun with the fashions. Next, they took up the subject o' hired gals, and when they'd wore that out, the neighborhood in gineral had to undergo a haulin' over. (p. 315)

Nothing about the genteel life appeals to Aunt Maguire, and her descriptions of the most fashionable people make anyone's aspirations to gentility seem foolish indeed:

> One afternoon, there was a youngish married woman by the name o' Miss Teeters called. She and Eunice are quite intimit; though, after all, Eunice don't seem to think much of her, but she considers her wonderful ginteel. Her gintility seemed to consist in her wearin' more colors than I ever see on to once afore in all my born days. She had on a yaller bunnit, with a great pink artificial on it; a red shawl, and a green silk frock, and blue ribbin round her neck, and I

forget what all; but t' was enough to make a body's eyes ache to look at her. (pp. 315–16)

Aside from the direction the plot of this story will take regarding the infamous Scrabble Hill sewing society, one of the minor ironies of this story resides in its relentless comic exposure of the failings of gentility being played out on the pages of a magazine that was synonymous with the very word *genteel*. The *Lady's Book* was the most famous and prestigious fashion magazine of the 1840s; full-color plates of the latest fashions in women's dresses contributed greatly to the magazine's popularity. Other magazines followed the *Lady's Book's* lead, but none of them offered significant competition until well into the 1860s.[15] By then, the editors of *Godey's* had overcome their earlier reservations about fashion's ability to overpower women's modesty and natural reticence. Miriam, however, had not; her final story reveals that she was squarely on the side of the sentimental lady whose plain style reflects her inner sincerity.[16]

The issue in which Miriam's final sewing society story appeared (December 1849) contains two woodblock plates showing "Fashions for December," directions for "netting" one's own opera cape, the floor plans and an exterior view of a "model cottage in the Gothic style," three illustrations of fashionable "morning caps" suitable for "the young matron," three illustrations of lace capes, and of course one of the famous hand-colored, full page fashion plates, this one featuring two women wearing the latest "Paris fashions Americanized."[17] Devotion to the genteel ideology in the *Lady's Book* went well beyond the visual content of the magazine. The monthly fashion column in the December 1849 issue typifies how the magazine instilled in its readers a genuine taste for elegance. It is devoted to a detailed description of the L. J. Levy Company of Philadelphia—a store that employed eighty-four people to help each customer find just what she wanted in its elaborate specialized departments. One item brought to the readers' attention was a piece of antique lace for sale for five hundred dollars, the equivalent of William's annual salary in Elmira, had he been able to collect it.

The overall plot for Miriam's story is ingenious, full of curious twists and turns that are played out against the backdrop of a would-be genteel family in a would-be genteel society. While Aunt Maguire is visiting in Slabtown, the latest issue of the *Lady's Book* arrives. It contains a story about a church sewing society that becomes the talk of the town. The residents of Slabtown are convinced that the story is based on *their* sewing society and written by *their* minister's wife:

> "O dear me," says Miss Hawkins, a blowin' herself with her handkercher as hard as ever she could. "O dear me, ther's the awfulest piece that you ever see, come out in the 'Ladies Book,' and it's all about our Sewin' Society, takin' us off to an ioty, and tellin' all how we go on; and, of course, 't was writ in this village."
>
> "You don't?" says Miss Teeters, says she.
>
> "It's a fact," says Miss Hawkins. "And what's worse yet, our minister's wife writ it."
>
> "How you talk!" says Miss Teeters.
>
> "Well, I shouldent wonder," says Eunice, says she, "for I've heerd that your minister's wife writes for the papers. But, pray, what does it say?"
>
> "Oh," says Miss Haekins, "as true as I'm a live woman, it's got every one of our members in, and shows us all up shamefully, only jest me and Sary Ann. I can't see as ther's any body in it that resembles us a mite. But you're drawed out, Miss Teeters; and Cappen Sapley, he's down large as life; and the Bomans are in for 't; and so's Bill Sweezen's wife, and Samanthy Cooper, and Tom Baily's wife, and Miss Ben Curtis; and there's a Miss Stillman and her daughter, that's meant for the Longs. They're all fictitious names, to be sure, but it's easy enough to tell who's who. But the squire's wife ketches it the worst of all. I tell ye, it takes her off to fits. Nobody can mistake it." (pp. 317–18)

The "wrong" minister's wife who is blamed for writing the story is maligned by the townspeople in much the same terms as Miriam Whitcher was in Elmira. She is even compared unfavorably at one point to the previous minister's wife, Miss Van Duzen (Mrs. Van Zandt), while the chief sin laid at her feet is her indifference to "society" and fashion:

> "I say," says Miss Teeters, says she, "it's high time we got rid o' the minister; he ain't the man for us. A ginteel and intellectible congregation like our'n had ought to have a man o' great eloquential

powers. And as for his wife, I never could bear her, with her old stripid dress that she wears every Sunday, rain or shine. I don't believe she was ever accustomed to ginteel society."

"Nor I neither," says Miss Hawkins. "I took a dislike tew her when they first come here. I don't like yer mum characters that never say nothin' about nobody. It seems she's ben savin' on 't up to let off in the newspapers. Bethiar Nobles says she told her she thought our congregation drest tew much; and I shouldent wonder if she did, for she stuck to that old straw bunnit and everlastin' stripid dress all winter, and I s'pose it's to set an example o' plain-ness afore us, jest as if we'd foller *her* lead. For my part, I think she might better spend more time a dressin', and less a writin' for the newspapers. And they say he incourages her in it, and likes to have her write. I wish they was both furder off." (pp. 319–20)

After all Cousin Eunice's friends have left her house and she is alone with Aunt Maguire, she explains that the congregation in ques-tion, not her own, is notorious for mistreating its ministers:

I've always heerd that that Sewin' Society was a reg'lar slander-mill, where the principal busines is to brew mischief against the minister; and I'm glad they've got showed up at last. The minister's a good man, and a smart man tew; but the biggest part o' the congregation is such a set of ignoramuses, that they don't know a smart man from a fool. They always make a great fuss over their minister when he first comes; but if he don't preach smooth things tew 'em all the time, they soon contrive to starve him out or quarrel him off. When they gin this one a call, they agreed to give him five hundred dollars a year, and pay it quarterly. And it is a solemn fact, that half on't hain't ben paid yet. Betsey Hall, a girl that used to wash for 'em sometimes, told me so. She said she'd often listened to the door, and heerd the minister and his wife a talkin' over their troubles; and she says that ther ain't more'n half a dozen in the congregation that pay their dues reglarly; and if 't wa'n't for what the minister's wife gits for writin' for the newspapers, they wouldent be able to pay their house-rent and keep out o' debt, no way. (pp. 320–21)

This story is filled with Miriam's ambivalence about her Elmira experience. Clearly she took great delight in exposing once more the hypocrisy she encountered in Trinity Episcopal Church, but at the same time, she partially diffuses the harshness of her criticism by attributing the conditions in Elmira to a new fictitious village. While simultaneously confirming how badly the parish had treated the Whitchers, this story also partially exonerates Elmira by showing that similar conditions prevail elsewhere. It raises new issues, too, such as Miriam's suspicion that the girls who worked for her were key links in the gossip chain about the Whitchers' personal life. Yet the hapless Betsey Hall quoted above sympathizes with the minister and his wife, offering on Miriam's behalf the familiar apology used by other nineteenth-century women writers: financial necessity.

In this story, Miriam also dramatizes one of her greatest disappointments in the whole Elmira scandal: the way Mr. and Mrs. Luce ultimately turned against the Whitchers. In the real world of Elmira, the Luces were persuaded to believe that the Stillmans in the "Sewing Society" sketch were meant to portray them, which Miriam claimed was not so; according to Miriam's account to her sister, Mrs. Hatch, a friend of the Arnots, deliberately engineered this deception to turn the Luces against the Whitchers. In the fictional world of Slabtown, Miss Hawkins similarly misleads Mrs. Long into believing she was the model for Miss Stillman, with the same devastating outcome for the minister's family:

> Miss Hawkins, she kept the ball a rollin'; devoted her hull time to runnin' round the neighborhood and blazin' away about it. She was what folks call "toady" to the squire's wife, and every body said that the "Miss Stillman" in the piece, that was makin' such a muss, meant her, and she tho't so tew. But she tho't that if she could make folks believe 't was intended for Miss Long, she could accomplish tew ends: she'd git rid o' havin' the names o' Miss Stillman and Polly Mariar tucked onto her and her daughter, and, what was purty important, turn the Longs against the minister and his wife. Now the Longs was very stiddy, go-to-meetin' sort o' folks, and had always been very friendly to the minister's family. So Miss Hawkins went puffin' and blowin', round town, makin' a terrible fuss about the "piece," and dwellin' partic'larly on the awful shame it was to take off the Longs so. (pp. 326–27)

As Miss Hawkins explains to the Squire's wife (Miss Samson Savage), "if we can once git the Longs set against the minister's folks, they'll have to quit in short order" (p. 327). Mr. Long is represented as a "stiddy old poke, for he hain't no more mind of his own than that pair o' tongs" (p. 328), while Mrs. Long is shown to be a coward; when she becomes convinced that the characterization of Mrs. Stillman was meant for her, she fails to confront the minister's wife in person, "like a Christian ought to," and instead declares her unfit to be a minister's wife. Miss Hawkins's tactics work perfectly in the end, for Mr. Long supports the petition drive to have the minister removed. Again, authorial ambivalence abounds in these scenes. Miriam Whitcher paints an entirely unflattering, demeaning picture of the Longs while simultaneously granting that they are "steady" support-ers of the church and important friends of the minister and his wife. Although they are manipulated by others into believing a false-hood, the failure is finally their own for being too weak to resist the misrepresentation.

Miriam Whitcher also gets her moment of revenge against those she called two-faced, that is, those who pretended to support the Whitchers while working against them behind their backs. The real-life issue was more complicated than Miriam's representation of it in this sketch, but it makes an effective fictional point:

> But the tew-sided party was the most numerous. They circulated round from the minister's friends to his enemies, and pretended to belong to jest the side they happened to be with. To the minister's friends they said, "that was a first-rate article in the Lady's Book; 't was capital—'t was true to nater—it took off them that deserved it richly; and they hoped that the author'd write more, and give 'em another dig." When they got among the opposite party, they said " 't was a slanderous thing—'t was shameful—'t wa'n't to be put up with;" and then they carried back and forth all they heerd on both sides, and made a sight o' mischief. Mr. Sweezer was one o' this kind. He had about as much as he could attend to for a spell, runnin' from one side t' other carryin' the news. (p. 332)

Near the end of the story when the minister and his wife have been damaged beyond the point of return, the plot takes a curious and improbable turn, with Miriam shifting responsibility for the sew-ing society sketch away from herself as author and onto the shoulders of her own creation, Aunt Maguire; eventually she even blames Louis

Godey. Because the *Lady's Book* has been in such demand in Slabtown, the Bentley family and Aunt Maguire had not actually seen the article for themselves. Suddenly it dawns on Aunt Maguire that by "The Lady's Book" the people of Slabtown must mean *Godey's Lady's Book,* which in turn means that she herself might be responsible for all the trouble brewing in Slabtown. Although she had not written the article in question, she remembers having *told* her friend Mr. Godey all about her own sewing society back in Scrabble Hill. She quickly surmises that Mr. Godey wrote up her story and published it in his magazine. Insofar as there is a responsible author, it appears to be Louis Godey. As soon as she realizes what has happened, Aunt Maguire tells cousins Eunice and Sam that the people of Slabtown have been making a terrible mistake believing that the article was about *their* sewing society. Most pointedly, she realizes that the Slabtown minister's wife is thereby *falsely* accused of having written the story and is innocent of any wrongdoing. Aunt Maguire urges Sam to "go right off down street" and tell everyone the truth, but he flatly refuses to do so. No one would believe him, he argues, and besides, he is having too much fun watching the townpeople's reactions. Eunice, too, refuses to cooperate: "If they're a mind to take it tew themselves, let 'em; they deserve a usin' up, and I'd be the last one to tell 'em they hadent got it" (pp. 339–40).

Powerless as an outsider to persuade the townsfolk of their mistake, Aunt Maguire is deeply chagrined that she has unintentionally caused the innocent minister's wife so much harm. Against the advice of both Sam and Eunice, she decides to apologize directly to the minister's wife for all the trouble she has caused her. What ensues is a remarkable scene in which one purported author, Aunt Maguire, tries to accept the blame for all the trouble she has caused another purported author, the innocent minister's wife, while the real author stands silent in the shadows. For her part, the minister's wife absolves Aunt Maguire of all blame in the matter, arguing in the best satiric tradition that Aunt Maguire had merely told the truth about human nature. Everyone, except Mr. Godey, is exonerated in this the final scene of the final sketch in the series, and the innocent minister's wife, far from being angry with Aunt Maguire, is instead a model of Christian understanding and forgiveness:

"I hope you'll pardon a stranger for intrudin' on you?" "No intrusion at all," says she; "every body's welcome to the minister's house." So then, I felt relieved, and says I: "I come from Scrabble Hill to visit a relation o' mine that lives here; and I've happened to come just in the midst o' the muss they've kicked up about that piece they're a layin' to you. I know all the folks that it tells about."

"You do?" says she. "And do you know Aunt Magwire?" *[sic]*

I riz up, and makin' as good a curchy as I know'd how, says I: "I'm that individdiwal, at yer service."

"Indeed," says she, comin' up to me and shakin' hands with me; "well, I'm very glad to see you though you *have* got me into a muss."

"O dear me," says I, "I hope you don't think I know'd that story was a gwine to travel to Slabtown, when I told it to Mr. Godey?"

"Law, no," says she; "don't give yourself the least trouble about it; you ain't a bit to blame."

"Well, I'm glad you feel so," says I; "but ain't it curus that the Slabtown folks should take it all to themselves as they dew?"

"Not at all," says she; "human natur's the same every where."

"I guess so," says I. "Any how, your Sewin' Society must be wonderfully like our'n, or they wouldent be so detarmined it means them; but what hurts my feelin's is, that you should have to suffer for 't. I was so distrest when I heerd they was a layin' on't to you, and usin' on 't to injure yer husband, that I felt as if I must come right over and see you, though you was a stranger. If any body's to blame, I'm willin' to bear it."

"O fie," says she, "don't you fret yourself a bit about it. If people chooses to fit your coats to their own backs, 't ain't your fault; and if they fit nice and snug, perhaps they'll do as good service as if they were made expressly for 'em."

"Jest so," says I. "But it does seem tew bad that you should suffer for 't. Ain't ther no way o' puttin a stop tew it?"

"Never you mind," says she; "we minister's folks must have our trials, of one sort or another, where-ever we go. If we hadent this perhaps we should have somethin' still worse."

"But," says I, "what if they should drive you away from here?"

She smiled, and dident say nothin'.

"Well," says I, "to judge from what I've seen o' Slabtown since I come here, I'm bold to say that, if they do drive you away, they can't possibly drive you to a worse place."

"Hush, Aunt Magwire," says she, "human natur's the same every where; we must expect trouble wherever we go. I feel prepared for almost any thing."

"Yes," says I, "I s'pose you feel a good deal as that fox in the story did, when them miserable insects was a bitin' him. 'Let 'em alone,' says he; 'for if you drive 'em away ther'll come a hungrier swarm.'"

Well, that was the amount of our conversation. The minister's wife was very polite to me, and I invited her to call on me if ever she come through Scrabble Hill. She said she would, and hoped we should git better acquainted.

I come away a few days after that, and I ruther guess it'll be a good while afore I go a visitin' to Slabtown agin'. The place is tew awful *ginteel* to suit my taste. (pp. 341–44)

With this, Miriam Whitcher ends "Aunt Maguire's Visit to Slabtown" and the entire Aunt Maguire series. The sketch comes full circle in the end, reminding the readers of *Godey's* that the underlying cause of all the trouble was gentility, but articulating in the process a cogent theory of social satire that invites people to fit the coat to their own backs, whether it was intended for them or not.

"Aunt Maguire's Visit to Slabtown" was completed within two months of Miriam Whitcher's return to Whitesboro, but as with her previous "Sewing Society" sketch, William initially would not permit his wife to forward the story to Louis Godey. At the time, William was still living in Elmira and trying to restore peace to the Trinity parish; he had enough trouble on his hands without rekindling the fire that had finally begun to subside. Ultimately William relented, but not until he too had left Elmira for good. The article appeared in the December 1849 issue of the *Lady's Book,* eleven months after the publication of the offending "Sewing Society" sketch. All the turmoil and disruption notwithstanding, Miriam Whitcher had the last word on the "muss" that her writing created. If the Whitchers were driven away from Trinity Episcopal Church, so too were the Arnots and their immediate friends. From Miriam's perspective, it was at worst a draw. No one, except the two purported authors—Aunt Maguire and the innocent minister's wife—escaped the thrust of her satiric weapon.

The Return of the Reverend Mrs. Sniffles

As she closed the final chapter on the Aunt Maguire stories, Miriam appeared to back away from writing social satire. Elmira still figured in her literary work, but now as Timberville. Written in standard English rather than the vernacular, the Timberville sketches featuring Mrs. Waters lacked the satiric bite of Miriam's Aunt Maguire sketches. Burned by her experience in Elmira, Miriam nonetheless found her irrepressible sense of humor once more on the rise. Just as she could not resist her satiric impulse as a child, even if it resulted in her being prayed over by the neighbors, as an adult with her cloak of anonymity stripped from her, she took up a new attack on social pretentiousness by embedding her critique of genteel values in the character of the Reverend Mrs. Sniffles, formerly the Widow Bedott. She had more personal and artistic distance from the Widow than she had from Aunt Maguire, and because the Widow herself was a fool, the object of humor who represented the stereotypic seeker after gentility, Miriam was able to keep the spotlight on what she perceived as dangerously false social values *and* to retain her keen sense of the absurd.

In the late spring of 1849, with William still without prospects for a permanent parish and the Whitchers' personal finances more precarious than ever, Miriam turned once again to the Widow Bedott and Neal's *Saturday Gazette*. In addition to the four stories she published for the *Lady's Book* between May 1849 and March 1850 (the final Aunt Maguire story plus the three "Letters from Timberville"), she wrote four Widow Bedott stories for the *Gazette*. No longer a widow on the edge of society, Priscilla Bedott Sniffles threw herself headlong into the pursuit of a fashionable life and into the pursuit of personal power. Already self-preoccupied and socially aggressive, the Reverend Mrs. Sniffles became the living comic embodiment of the genteel values Aunt Maguire found so objectionable in Scrabble Hill and Slabtown.

Any thought that marriage would improve Priscilla Sniffles's disposition is quickly put to rest in the first story, "'The Rev. Mrs. Sniffles at Home," written in May 1849 and published in the June 16 issue of the *Gazette*. The story opens with Priscilla Sniffles soundly

abusing her "girl," Sal Blake. First she rudely orders her to go up-
stairs to fetch a daguerreotype, chides her for not moving fast enough,
calls her a "huzzy" for looking at the daguerreotype over Aunt
Maguire's shoulder, then orders her to the kitchen to peel apples and
scour pans. Treated as though she is the most delinquent of servants,
Sal Blake had in fact been raised by the late Mrs. Sniffles as though
she were her daughter. Aunt Maguire is quick to point this out to her
sister, and to urge kinder treatment for the bewildered Sal, but Priscilla
Sniffles rejects the suggestion outright: "I rather guess I'll larn that
critter to know her place, afore I've ben here much longer. She hain't
never had no instruction about what belongs to her sittiwation, at
all. . . . I mean to show her the difference betwixt genteel folks and
them that's born to be underlin's" (pp. 205–6).

Sal is not the only one to bear the brunt of Priscilla Sniffles's rude
and domineering ways. In telling her sister about her wedding tour,
Mrs. Sniffles boasts of having deliberately abused one of her host-
esses. To save the cost of staying at an inn, the Sniffleses present
themselves, uninvited and unannounced, at the home of the Pidgin
Pint Baptist minister, where they make it clear that they expect to be
fed and housed for a full week. Priscilla immediately recognizes Mrs.
Cumstork, the minister's wife, as someone she knew only casually
many years earlier in Wiggletown; she disliked her then because the
good woman would not gossip with her, and she dislikes her now
because Mrs. Cumstork does not immediately recognize her. Determined to get even with her for these imagined slights, Priscilla Sniffles
shows contempt for her hostess's every act of kindness and hospitality. Even though the Cumstorks have finished supper when the
Sniffleses arrives, Mrs. Cumstork fixes them a meal; first Priscilla refuses the mutton offered her, turns down the cold meats offered in
place of the mutton, then refuses the same meats warmed up, and in
each instance she does so with a rude comment. She finally eats
dessert, rice pudding, but only after insulting her hostess once more:

> I eat some tew, for, to tell the truth, I was awful hungry, but did n't
> want 'em to think I eat it because 't was good, so, I says, says I,
> "rice puddin' 's terrible plain; but it's better 'n nothin', and I s'pose
> I shall be sick if I don't eat somethin'." When we was alone the
> elder undertook to take me to do *[sic]* about findin' fault with the

vittals, but I told him he need n't be consarned, for I meant to let the Cumstork's see 't I know'd what was what though I had n't been a schoolmarm. And I made it a pint to turn up my nose at every thing in the house all the time I was there; and I tell ye, I could n't help laughin' in my sleeve to see how oncomfortable it made 'em feel. (p. 213)

The patient Mrs. Cumstork says nothing; she is the model of the long-suffering minister's wife, and as such she seems more an ideal type than an individual character. The representation of Priscilla Sniffles, however, is inspired by Miriam's own experience; the Reverend Mrs. Hull, it would appear, earned a place for herself in Miriam's portrait gallery. This supposition is supported by Priscilla Sniffles's next indiscretion; during her week's stay she tries to turn members of the congregation against Mrs. Cumstork. The parishioners genuinely admire their minister's wife, which of course galls Priscilla, so she tells them that the people of Wiggletown (herself included) held Mrs. Cumstork in no such esteem. Priscilla Sniffles puts aside even the most elementary rules of human conduct in her determination to make her presence felt in Pidgin Pint. When the appalled Aunt Maguire asks if she believes such behavior was "Christianlike," Priscilla responds that the only thing she cares about is to show people that she "know'd what was what." And, she adds, because she was once married to a deacon and is now married to a minister, she has no need for her sister's advice. When her husband comes home, he receives the same high-handed treatment. She assaults him verbally for tracking invisible mud into the house, and then insults his first wife by suggesting that she had not kept a clean house. At the end of the story, she turns against Sal once again, boxes her ears, locks up the cupboard where the food is kept, and gives her only cold pork and potatoes for supper. In short, in an attempt to assert herself and her new marital status, the "genteel" Priscilla Sniffles shows herself to be mean, domineering, demanding, and rude.

Between these outbursts of bad temper that frame "The Rev. Mrs. Sniffles at Home," the author inserts a lighthearted story based on another experience she had late in her stay in Elmira. In January 1849, Louis Godey asked Miriam for a picture of herself, and so she sat for a daguerreotype. Godey in turn sent her his picture.[18] Miriam was pleased with the result of her sitting, and as this sketch reveals, she was fascinated by the entire daguerreotype process. In the story, Priscilla and Shadrack have a "daggertype" made at the urging of Priscilla's daughter, and Priscilla explains the mysterious process to Aunt Maguire:

> "Ther's a pole stuck up in the middle o' the floor, with a machine atop on 't—kind of an uplong shaped consarn—looks for all the world like the old cannon they haul out on Independence and training days about *so* wide and *so* long. In the little eend on 't ther's a hole, and into that hole the daggerotyper slips the steel plate that the picter's to be made on, and kivers it up. Then ye have to set down in a cheer about as fur from the machine as from here to that stove, on an average. Then he fastens yer head in an iron consarn to keep it still—for ye've got to set as onmovable as a waxwork, and as stiff as stillyards, or the picter 'll be spiled. Then ye must look strait at the machine that stans there a pintin' right at yer face—"
>
> "Grammany! I should think 't would be an awful sittiwation. I should be frightend out o' my wits."
>
> "Lawful sakes! I wa'n't a bit skairt. Well, ther's a winder right aside o' ye, and a white sheet fastened up all round ye, and when ye've got fixt, he takes the kivver off o' the machine, and the light reflects into the winder and onto yer face, and from yer face it refragerates onto the steel plate, and executes the picter in a minit."
> (pp. 214–15)

The same month that Miriam wrote the story and submitted it to Alice Neal, the popular writer Timothy Shay Arthur published his own sketch about the daguerreotype process in a story in the *Lady's Book*. Included in a series called "American Characteristics," Arthur's sketch also emphasized what it was like to sit for a daguerreotype: "In taking their places in the chair, [people] get so nervous that they tremble like aspens; and others, in a vain attempt to keep their features composed, distort them so much that they are frightened at their own image when it is placed in their hands."[19] An illustration for Arthur's article shows the daguerreotypist's assistant about to fasten the subject's head into a metal clamp; a look of apprehension, if not outright terror, is fixed on the subject's face, and even a nearby pet dog shrinks back from the scene. Miriam was so fascinated by her subject matter that she contributed one of her own, rare, illustrations to accompany the text of her story in the *Gazette*. It is one of the most whimsical of all her Widow Bedott illustrations, and one of her last.

Through a long coincidence, the daguerreotypist turns out to be the infamous Yankee trader, Jabe Clark, operating under a different name. In his previous appearance in the Widow Bedott stories, he had twice gotten the better of Priscilla Bedott in their trading, and she happens to be carrying with her a "gold" pin that Jabe had tricked Shadrack Sniffles into buying; the pin has long since turned green. Jabe Clark does not recognize Priscilla, but she does him, despite his disguised appearance; for once in her life she holds her tongue. When the first daguerreotype does not turn out well—"the Elder he hysted his eyebrows—it's a trick o' hisen—and so his pictur had as much as a dozen pair of eyes"—they have a second taken. Then a third, then a fourth. When it comes time to settle the bill, Priscilla pulls out the green pin and offers to trade it for the daguerreotypes. Faced with the prospects of public exposure and the loss of a thriving business, Jabe Clark settles for the pin and Priscilla's silence. She is a shrewd, formidable opponent, as unscrupulous as the Yankee peddler himself.

Miriam's next Widow Bedott sketch was published October 13, 1849, and was entitled "The Rev. Mrs. Sniffles Attends the Meeting of the 'Scrabble Hill Female Universal Diffusion of General Elevation and Amelioration Society.'" The story was omitted from both the *Widow Bedott Papers* and *Widow Spriggins, Mary Elmer and Other Sketches,* and is thus virtually unknown to modern readers; it is reprinted in the Appendix. The story features Priscilla Sniffles as the president of a local reform society referred to by its members as the "F.U.D.G.E. and A. Society." She holds her presidency by virtue of her status as the minister's wife, and it is in this latter role that she first appears in the story. Before leaving home for the society meeting, she instructs her husband how to "manage" Sal in her absence. First she accuses him of being too kind to Sal, then she berates him for smoking a pipe. Although he does not defend himself about Sal, he reminds her that before their marriage she claimed she enjoyed his smoking. She slams out of the house with this admonition: "O, mighty! I spose you think you've *said* it now. For my part I think a minister might be in better bisness than to be a throwin out insinniwations against his wife. Puff away—smoke yer eyes out for all I care, you hurt yerself more'n ye dew anybody else."[20]

The scene then moves to the meeting of the F.U.D.G.E. & A. Society. In an understated comic manner, Miriam Whitcher satirizes both the meeting itself and the "good works" of the members. As one might expect with Priscilla presiding, the discussions descend again and again to outright gossip, which is interrupted only when the persons under discussion arrive. Between gossip sessions, Hugle (Hugelina, the poet) reads the minutes of the previous meeting, adding one of her own poetic compositions on the joys of "diffusing high Elevation." The sketch mocks the society's efforts to "elevate and ameliorate" its members' neighbors. The members have "visited and labored with fifty-three families, have distributed sixty-seven copies of the tract entitled 'Mental culture and Intellectual Development'—twenty-five copies were bestowed upon the colored population at the Corners" (p. 8), even though none of the latter group can read or write. The women are discouraged, though, by what they consider rude treatment they receive when they visit an Irish washerwoman. At first she welcomes them, thinking that their tract is a pamphlet about labor-saving methods of washing clothes, but when she discovers the tract's true nature, she loses all interest in what the women have to offer. What most offends the ladies, however, is that she fails to observe the rules of genteel behavior regarding hospitality; instead of receiving them as honored and welcome guests, she keeps right on scrubbing clothes. Sister Twitchell prays aloud: "Oh! that the eyes of her benighted soul may be opened to a sense of her deplorable condition!" (p. 9). Crass insensitivity is thus added to Miriam's growing list of genteel characteristics.

Whitcher would have had no dearth of models upon which to base the Scrabble Hill F.U.D.G.E. and A. Society, with female reform societies abounding in Oneida County between the 1830s and the 1850s.[21] For example, the Female Moral Reform Society, active in Whitesboro as early as 1806, and in Utica by 1837, was dedicated to fighting "licentiousness" wherever it surfaced, and in whatever form. According to Mary Ryan, the Utica society formed a "visiting committee" in 1841 that "ventured out into the streets of Utica," at first tentatively, but soon boldly and militantly. There they collected signatures on a petition to stop prostitution, they attacked what they called lewdness on the streets of Utica, and they "accosted licentious men in the streets and entered taverns to interrogate bartenders."[22]

In targeting a female reform society in this sketch, Whitcher specifically poked fun at activities such as distributing tracts to those who could not read, invading the privacy of people's homes, and worrying only about someone's manners while ignoring abject poverty and backbreaking labor. Behind her criticism, too, was the more fundamental issue of hypocrisy: Christian charity à la Priscilla Bedott Sniffles certainly did not begin at home, and the backbiting that took place at the society meeting suggested that the women's own manners might not stand up to public scrutiny. She called into question, as well, the way such reform societies invaded territory that had belonged to the family or the church by becoming self-appointed guardians of people's private behavior.[23]

The rest of this sketch focuses on Miriam Whitcher's hallmark as a humorist—the intricate relationships among women. For instance, the rivalry between the two poets, Hugelina and Priscilla, heats up in this sketch. The group wants to start a newsletter, and they all agree that it would be enriched by original poetic compositions; Priscilla Sniffles not so subtly invites praise and support for her poetry, while the group clearly favors Hugelina's. When Priscilla senses that the tide is turning in Hugelina's favor, she abruptly declares she is going home so Elder Sniffles will not get lonely. Graciously the hostess sends for Shadrack to join them for tea, and the discussion ends. Determined as ever to put herself in the best possible light (and conveniently forgetting how she treated her husband when she left for the meeting), Priscilla puts on a great show of concern and affection for the Elder. She rushes forward to kiss him when he arrives, worries how he has been in her absence, and inquires solicitously after Sal. She even chides him gently for making Sal work so hard when he reports that she was carrying out all of Priscilla's orders.

True to the genteel values she espouses, Priscilla Sniffles is never satisfied with what she has. The main object of her dissatisfaction in the next story, appropriately enough, is the parsonage itself. In "The Rev. Mrs. Sniffles Expresses her Sentiments in Regard to the Parsonage" (December 29,1849), Miriam Whitcher mocks the current fash-

ions in furniture, art, and architecture. Unlike her author, Priscilla
Sniffles aspires to keep up with the "better set" in her husband's
parish, and she believes that the shabbiness of the parsonage stands in
her way. Priscilla's description of the parsonage that opens the sketch
is one of the finest single passages in the *Widow Bedott Papers:*

> I say I'm disgusted with this old house; 't ain't fit for ginteel folks
> to live in; looks as if 't was built in Noah's time, with its consarned
> old gamble ruff and leetle bits o' winders a pokin' out like bird
> cages all round. Painted yaller, too, and such a humbly yaller; for all
> the world jest the color o' calomel and jollup! . . .
>
> I say 't ain't fit to live in. I'm ashamed on 't. I feel awful
> mortified about it whenever I look at Miss Myerses and Miss
> Loderses, and the rest o' the hansome sittiwations in the neighbor-
> hood, with their wings and their piazzers and foldin' doors, and all
> so dazzlin' white. It's ridicilous that we should have to live in such a
> distressid lookin' old consarn, when we're every bit and grain as
> good as they be, if not ruther better. (p. 222)

In contradicting her husband's protests that the house is comfortable
as it is, Priscilla Sniffles replies, "Comfortable! who cares for comfort
when gintility's consarned! *I* don't." (pp. 222–23)

Nothing is too good for Mrs. Sniffles. She wants walls torn out,
rooms added, a "piazzer" built in front, new furniture, and new art in
the latest New York style. In one passage describing Priscilla's fondness for particular pieces of art, Miriam Whitcher anticipates Huckleberry Finn's admiration for the furnishings of the Grangerford's parlor:

> I seen one on 'em [New York pictures] t' other day in to Mr.
> Bungle's shop, when I went in with Sister Tibbins to look at her
> portrait that he's a paintin'. I see one o' Miss Billinses picters there.
> 'T was a splendid one, as big as the top o' that are table, and
> represented an elegant lady a lyin' asleep by a river, and ther was a
> little angel a hoverin' in the air over her head, jest a gwine to shoot
> at her with a bow and arrer. I axed Mr. Bungle what 't was sent to
> his shop for, and he said how't Miss Billins wa'n't quite satisfied
> with it on account o' the angel's legs bein' bare, and she wanted to
> have him paint some pantaletts on 'em, and he was a gwine to dew
> it as soon as he got time. (pp. 223–24)

The fad for scriptural pictures is gently mocked, too, especially when biblical figures are depicted in Victorian fashions:

> Them Scripter pieces that Sister Myers has got hangin' in her front parlor—them she painted afore she was married, strikes me as wonderful interestin', especially the one that represents Pharoh's daughter a findin' Moses in the bulrushes. Her parasol and the artificials in her bunnit is jest as natral as life. And Moses, he looks so cunnin' a lyin' there asleep, with his little coral necklace and bracelets on. O it's a sweet picter. And I like that other one, tew, that represents Pharoh a drivin' full tilt into the Red Sea after the Isrelites. How natral his coat-tails flies out. I think some Scripter piece would be very approbriate for a minister's house. (p. 224)

The tone in these passages contrasts nicely with the sharpness we find elsewhere in Miriam's sketches. While the whole genteel code was Miriam's satiric target, she distinguished among its many facets. Those parts that genuinely harmed other people, that diminished people because of their social position, that overthrew traditional Christian and humane values, that put the self above others, that substituted wealth and fashion for personal character and integrity— all these received the full force of Miriam Whitcher's satiric thrusts. Those parts, in contrast, that were merely swept along in the rush for social position, that represented matters of taste rather than moral fiber—those received Miriam's gentle, witty touch. Both forms existed side by side in these sketches of Miriam's mature period.

Priscilla's attitude changes abruptly when her husband reminds her that the church owns their house and that they live there rent-free (a luxury the Whitchers never enjoyed); further, the Elder reminds his wife he does not have the means to make the kinds of changes she wants, but he encourages her to pay for the remodeling and refurnishing from her own funds. He adds that he has been wanting to know ever since their wedding the full value of her property, and he has been disappointed that she has told him nothing. Priscilla immediately and bluntly insists that she has no property whatsoever, which is a far cry from her response to similar questions before they were married; the Elder then reminds her that he had been led to believe that she was a woman of means:

> "A-hem—I mean to say that you did not deny it when I delicately alluded to the subject. On the contrary you led me to infer that such was the fact, and under that impression I was induced to accede to your proposal"
>
> "My proposal? What do you mean to insinniwate?"
>
> "I should have said your—your—evident inclination for a—a—matrimonial engagement. I deeply regret, Mrs Sniffles, that you should have allowed your self to practice upon me what I can not consider in any other light than that of a heinous and unmitigated deception. I regard it as an act quite incompatible with your religious professions." (pp. 227–28)

The Elder seems fully justified in his anger, and for one fleeting moment, Priscilla Sniffles has been put in her place. True to form, however, she has the last word on the subject by showing the Elder up for being as hypocritical as she herself is, and the argument ends in a draw. " 'I tell ye agin, I couldent help what you *inferred,* and s'pozen I could, which was the most to blame, me for lettin' you think I was rich, or you for marryin' me *because* you thought I was rich? For my part, I think *that* was ruther incompatible with *your* professions. *Ministers* had ought to have their affections sot above transiterry riches' " (p. 228).

The sketch closes with excerpts from Mrs. Sniffles's diary; they are filled with self-deceptive self-congratulations, including a lament about her trials as president of the F.U.D.G.E. and A. Society, plus the extraordinary news that the vestry has agreed to repair the parsonage to her specifications. This scene, which was inspired by the Whitchers' own experience in Elmira, no doubt owes a debt as well to Trinity Church's ready accession to the Reverend Mr. Hull's demands. What is remarkable about the whole situation, given Miriam's experience, is its relative freedom from rancor and bitterness. Instead, her readers are invited to enjoy Priscilla's self-deception about the remodeling plans as revealed in her final diary entry:

> My beloved Shadrach *[sic]* has jist informed me that the parsonage is to be repaired and made comfortable. My dear pardner has requested it to be done intirely to please me, and quite unbeknown to me. It's true it needs it bad enough, but then I never should a thought o' complainin' about it. I feel that I'm a pilgrim and a sojourneyer

here, and hadent ought to be partickler, and so I told the elder when he proposed havin' the house repaired. But he insisted on 't and I consented more for his sake than my own. O that I may be truly thankful for the blessins I injoy especially for such a pardner!

> Blessed be the day o' sacred mirth
> That gave my dear companion birth,
> Let men rejoice while Silly sings
> The bliss her precious Shadrack brings
> (pp. 230–31)

Whitcher wrote one more Widow Bedott sketch, "The Rev. Mrs. Sniffles Abroad." In retrospect, it is reminiscent of Whitcher's original stories about the Widow Spriggins. It is full of good-natured humor, an unconscious harkening back to her earliest themes, and a self-conscious concern for the fate of writers like herself. For one last time Priscilla Bedott Sniffles acts as Miriam Whitcher's ironic alter ego. The story opens with Priscilla on the road to visit her husband's cousin in Libertyville, where she intends to stay (uninvited and unannounced) until the remodeling of the parsonage is finished.[24] As did the Widow Spriggins, Priscilla recites her love poetry to two strange gentlemen she meets in a stagecoach, and as in the earliest stories, the men are imposters who feign admiration for her poetry to amuse themselves at the poet's expense. More inventive than their earlier counterparts, they convince Priscilla to sing aloud with them to the tune of "Haddam" her poem "To My Own One." When they leave the stage at Punkin Hook, they exit with a copy of the poem, supposedly so they can publish it in the local newspaper that one of the men claims to edit. Miriam returned here, also, to another of her earlier themes—the literary society. Welcomed with open arms by "husband's" relatives, Priscilla Sniffles accepts an invitation to attend the local literary "swearee." The sketch concludes with a relatively long description of the local literary luminaries, most of them women with alliterative pseudonyms. "Nell Nox," according to Priscilla, presented the "most extinguished article":

She's a very fleshy woman, with a wonderful small head. I took particular notice of her 'cause she's so notorious in a literary point o' view. She had a singlar lookin' head dress stuck atop of her head.

> Her nose is awful long, and turns up at the eend; very handy, saves
> her the trouble o' turnin' on 't up every time she reads a poor piece
> o' poetry, and she don't seem to read no other exceptin' Cousin
> Briggses. She was drest in a sky blue muslin dress with flounces
> almost up to her waist, that made her look shorter and fleshyer than
> she actilly was. She had a dretful severe critisism on the American
> poits, espeshially a certing long-feller, as she called him, some tall
> indiwidiwal I s'pose. She cut him all to pieces, declaring that he had
> never writ a line that could be call poitry in all his born days. She
> said that his Eve Angeline was a perfectly nonsensical humbug.
> (pp. 197–98)

After "Nell Nox" read her piece, the editor of the paper read an
article on "the prospects of the literary horizon," then "Fenella
Fitzallen" read a poem on the death of a deacon's daughter. Finally
came "Kate Kenype," the most memorable of all those attending the
swearee.

> The last indiwidiwal that read was an olderly young woman,
> named Samanthy Hocum, a wonderful tall, slabsided, coarse lookin'
> critter. Her hair looked singular, 't was all raked back off her forrard,
> and made her phizmahogany look amazin' broad and brazen. She
> certainly was oncommon odd and ornary lookin.' Had on a red
> calico dress, and a queer kind of a bobtailed little thing, made o'
> green silk, with brass buttons down it. Take her altogether, she was
> about as singular a critter in her appearance as I've seen in some
> time. But she's oncommon smart. She had an article on the subject
> o' "Woman's Rights." 'T was a powerful perduction. She hild that
> the men hadent no bizness to monopolize every thing, and trammil
> the female sect. I thought to myself they hadent showed no great
> disposition to *trammil* her so far. She writes for the "Pidgin Pint
> Record of Genius," and signs Kate Kenype. (pp. 199–200)

Never one to be outdone, Priscilla Sniffles waits until everyone is
enjoying refreshments, then reads aloud her new poem about Shadrack.
When she finishes, the editor asks permission to publish the poem in
his paper, which Priscilla gladly gives. Only later does she remember
that she had also given one of the men on the stage permission to
publish it in *his* paper, and she immediately imagines herself in the
middle of a fight between the two papers over who has the right to

her poetry. Her greatest fear, she claims, is that she will be "drawn into public notice in a manner very imbarrasin' to my retirin' disposition" (p. 201). With the greatest of irony, Miriam Whitcher has Priscilla Sniffles pronounce this benediction on the fate of writers: "We literary characters must expect to be subjected to a great many more onpleasant things than falls to the lot o' privit indiwidiwals—it's the fate o' genius" (p. 201).[25]

Alice Whitcher

In her first weeks back in Whitesboro—the period of the death of her father and the reburial of both Jane and Mary—Miriam alluded to fears that her second pregnancy would end as her first. This time her fears were needless; on November 6, 1849, Miriam gave birth to a healthy baby girl. Named Alice after Alice Neal, the baby soon became the one bright light in Miriam's otherwise increasingly dark life. Beyond the predictable motherly doting over the antics of a first-born, it soon became clear that by any standard Alice Whitcher was a precocious child and a source of great joy to her mother. At eight months, "Ally" as she was often called by her mother, said her first words, and Miriam reported this fact to her sister with unabashed pride and pleasure:

> The first she said was "Hatty." I was sitting by the window with her, and Dr. McAllister's little girl was in the street. Said I "There's Hatty" & she repeated it after me. "Hatty" I said it again, & she said it again & repeated it after me a dozen times or more, and quite as distinctly as I said it. I was very much surprised, & sorry that I was alone with her, & nobody to hear her. When William came in I told him of it, & tried to make her say it again. But the little huzzy would not all that evening, & her father could'nt believe that she had spoken—he thought it was my imagination. However, the next morning when she first waked, I laid her over by William & said I, "now tell father about Hatty." So she drew up her little head & said "Hatty" three or four times very plainly, & he was convinced. Since then she has learnt a good many words, but she only sticks to one a day or two—sometimes only says it once & does not try it again. She says "Boss" to the cows, & "Kate", & "tee" for

tree. She watches the trees a great deal as they wave in the wind, holds up her little hands in wonder & whispers "tee-tee." I play "hide & coop" some times with her. She tucks her head down in my lap & I say "Where's Alice!" two or three times, then she bobs up & says, "he he" for "here." She has two sharp teeth, the last one came before we knew anything about it. In short, though I say it myself, she is the dearest, sweetest child I ever knew—just as good & happy as she can be all the time.[26]

At nine months Alice abruptly stopped talking and instead, according to Miriam, devoted all her "lung-power" to whistling.[27] This latter activity, like her talking, was deliberate, repeated, and a source of obvious pleasure to her mother:

Ally has waked up, & is standing by the lounge, slapping it & singing & whistling, occasionally tumbling over, but she does'nt mind falling at all. She picks herself up again & whistles & slaps with renewed energy. I presume William will go to Whitesboro next month, but I don't know. He has just come in, laid down on the floor & Ally has clambered up on him. She is always delighted when he comes in & greets him with an unusual whistle. He sends love to all of you, & so do I.[28]

Best of all, from Miriam's point of view, Alice seemed to have a sense of humor all her own. At one time she described her simply as "the funniest little trot you ever saw,"[29] while elsewhere she builds more slowly for a particular effect, as when Alice was fifteen months old and recovering from an illness:

The Dr has just been in, & says that Alice is doing very well. The fever has left her & she begins to have a little appetite. John brought a good supply of soda crackers on Saturday, which she seems to relish. She is very weak yet, & wants to be constantly in my arms, when she is awake. She is sleeping now on the lounge. You will be pleased to know that she has not omitted saying grace every time she has been at the table since you left. She was not at the table with us at dinner on Saturday, but at tea-time she was. As soon as she was fixed in her chair, she put down her head & buzzed away for some time. Mother was perfectly astonished.[30]

Alice's precociousness can be in part attributed to the quality of the attention she received from the women in the family: her mother, her grandmother, and three devoted aunts all found her to be a fresh and delightful presence in their household. As it turned out, her aunts were shortly to play a critical role in her life, for as Alice grew stronger, her mother grew weaker. And for the immediate present, no matter how devoted her father was to Alice, he was frequently absent from home.

One of the greatest trials Miriam had to endure in the final two years of her life was months of separation from William. After he left Elmira in the late spring of 1849, he was home in Whitesboro only intermittently. By the following March, when Alice was only four months old, he had accepted a temporary position in Saratoga Springs, and Miriam and Alice remained in Whitesboro until Miriam recovered from her confinement. By mid-May, however, she was well enough to travel to the Springs. There the three Whitchers boarded with a couple by the name of Rogers. The arrangements suited Miriam well; she was pleased with their rooms, she found Mrs. Rogers to be an agreeable landlady, and the Rogers's two young daughters vied for the privilege of looking after Alice.

> Mrs Rogers is very attentive to us, & appears anxious to make us as comfortable as possible. We have a good table, and eat by ourselves—I pouring the tea & coffee, excepting on Sundays, when we eat with the family, that is, Mr & Mrs Rogers, & a scared greeny apprentice who boards here. I told Mrs R. that I wished to take care of my rooms myself, so she furnished me a broom & dustpan. There is also a pail kept filled with water in a little room adjoining ours, a slop-pail also, & our wood is piled in the garret—on the same floor with us. I do not have to go down for anything.[31]

With the Barbour family and Morris and Eugenia nearby, Miriam felt at home at the Springs. By July Miriam dreamed of establishing their own home, one closer to downtown where William went every day, but it was to remain only a dream. However promising the prospects might once have looked, by August it was clear that there was no hope for William's obtaining a permanent position in Saratoga. Miriam blamed one person that she described as "an interloper" for turning the vestry against William and crushing all hopes of their staying on:

> As for our prospects, they are dark. We shall stay here through this month, & probably no longer. Morris has told you of the performances, & I need not recapitulate. It does seem strange that a set of vestrymen should sit still & let one interloper put such an insult upon the clergyman. William does not know what he shall do, or where he shall go. He has been invited to a parish in Maryland, & sometimes thinks he'll go there. I feel discouraged. I cannot bear the thought of his being laid aside again without employment or means of support. But we will trust in Divine Providence, & hope for the best.[32]

Shortly thereafter, William finished up his duties in Saratoga Springs and Miriam was living back in Whitesboro.

Meanwhile, life had changed dramatically in Whitesboro for the Berry family. In May 1850 the Berry women moved out of the inn they had called home for nearly thirty-five years. Elizabeth Berry, now seventy-five years old, was not well. Among other problems, she suffered from a serious cough.[33] The Berrys continued to take in boarders, but by the following November they decided to move once more. Their rented house was alive with mice that "run around the parlor every evening as if they had a perfect right there. And so they have, the whole house is just fit for rats & mice."[34] With each move, the Berry women became more isolated and sad. By November, William had left the Springs and gone to Oswego on another temporary assignment, and Thanksgiving Day found the women entirely alone, with even their boarders absent for the day. They made every effort to be cheerful, but it was a struggle:

> We had a very quiet Thanksgiving all by ourselves. The gentlemen were invited out, & we took a family dinner with mother down in her room. She says it was the first time in more than thirty years that the family had been alone on such an occasion. There were many things on our minds to make us all feel sadly, but we tried to be cheerful & merry, & laughed heartily at each other's wit, or attempts at wit. If we had'nt, I believe we should every one of us have cried. I know I should.[35]

Christmas was even sadder for Miriam because William could not come home. By mid-December she worried that he would be gone so long Alice would not recognize him. Often in her letters to her husband she had said how much she missed him and how glad she would be when they were together again, but the letters of December 1850 marked an all-time low in her feelings; her halting syntax reinforced the sense of her flagging spirits: "It has been a long & lonesome day to me. We have had no service here, Mr. Matson not having returned. I grow more impatient for your coming as the time draws near. It seems to me I never wanted to see you so much. I certainly never felt so lonely & desolate as I do this winter, tho' Alice affords me constant occupation."[36] As she tried to rally her spirits and wish her husband a "Happy New Year," Alice "drew her finger over that word happy just after I wrote it. I told her I hoped she would not thus mar our happiness in after years."[37] At year's end, William could find no church that wanted him as its full-time pastor, and Miriam's health slowly began to deteriorate.

"Mission to Muffletegawny" and "Potato Pudding"

For a short while longer Miriam continued to write. Although she focused most of her attention on a longer, "serious" work of fiction that remained unfinished at her death, she wrote two short pieces in a comic vein during this period. Neither piece is on a par with her best work, but both warrant brief examination here. In a letter of July 14, 1850, Miriam made an enigmatic reference to an article she had sent to Godey that she asked to have returned to her, unpublished. Godey, for his part, insisted that he had a right to publish it, and a struggle between the two ensued: "Godey will not return my piece as I requested—says he wants to publish it as soon as he dares. But I shall not let him do it if I can prevent it. He politely discharged me from his debt & wants to begin even again, but I have done with magazines."[38] In the end, Miriam won the battle, but the article was not lost entirely. It was published posthumously in *Widow Spriggins, Mary Elmer and Other Sketches* under the title "Aunt Maguire's Account of the Mission to Muffletegawny."

It is easy to see why Louis Godey would have wanted to publish the piece. It features Aunt Maguire and includes a cameo appearance by the infamous Miss Samson Savage, as well as an ad hoc meeting of the church sewing society. The story's plot centers on a young woman named Ann Eliza Fustick, an old classmate of Jefferson Maguire's, who is giving up her spirited life to marry a missionary and move with him to Muffletegawny. The neighbor ladies agree to help her with her extensive sewing preparations, and Aunt Maguire reluctantly goes along with their plans. Although readers of the *Lady's Book* would have taken up the story eagerly, expecting more social satire and more top quality entertainment, Miriam recognized that it lacked focus and purpose. She was also apprehensive about reintroducing the character of Miss Samson Savage, whose earlier appearances had already done so much harm. The story satirizes in passing two different missionaries who return to the states to distribute their many children among willing families, thus freeing them to devote *full* attention to the "heathens." More centrally, it satirizes the missionaries and their supporters for their devotion to material goods, but Miriam draws no connection between the different satiric points. Aunt Maguire even briefly calls into question the value of the whole foreign missionary enterprise, suggesting that the missionaries' energies would be better spent just down the road "to Puddenbag Lane," but this perspective is not developed or sustained. The final satiric point of the piece strikes at the notion of genteel values being transported to "heathen" lands, with Jeff Maguire expressing in a sardonic passage the full absurdity of the situation that unfolds in the story. Looking over Ann Eliza's wedding gifts, he professes to feel sorry for the natives because of their obvious social deprivation: "Why, they never saw nor heard of *napkin-rings, butter-knives, silver forks, and so forth!* and I don't s'pose they know a smokin'-cap from a stage-driver's jockey!" (p. 361).

Miriam also included a passage about the minister who replaced Parson Tuttle in Scrabble Hill. Unlike the real-life Mr. Hull who replaced William in Elmira, Parson Pulsifer is single, which means that the church can pay him even less money; it also means that all the unmarried women in the church are smitten with the pastor. According to Aunt Maguire, he basically makes no sense. Clearly intended to represent a transcendentalist, he comes from a town "near Boston," writes poetry, and talks all the time about the "great All-soul of Creation" (p. 357). His poetry, according to Aunt Maguire, is "full of wrong-endforemost words, and goes hitchity-hitch along. Sounds to me like sawin' through a board full of rusty nails" (p. 358). In short, the sketch is full of false starts and shows a measurable deterioration in Miriam's mastery over her comic form and material.

Miriam and Louis Godey eventually reestablished a cordial relationship, and in February 1851 she forwarded another humorous story to him that he declared "the *funniest* thing he ever saw in all his life";[39] modern readers are unlikely to agree with Godey's judgment, but the piece is not without merit. Entitled "Potato Pudding" and written in standard English, it concerns a wealthy man who decides to endear himself to the "lower sort" to enhance his political career. He invites several of his poor neighbors to dinner and has his cook make potato pudding. One guest likes the pudding so much he insists his wife get the recipe from the politician's wife, but when she tries, she is treated rudely by both the man's wife and his cook. She accidentally overhears a private conversation between the two and learns how much even the servant holds people of her class in contempt. In the end, the politician loses the election, as he deserves to, and the cook loses her job, as she deserves to—all over a recipe for potato pudding. The plot seems implausible and contrived, while the class-oriented humor has lost much of its sting with the passage of time.

"Mary Elmer"

In the spring of 1851, Miriam slowly began work on a serious, sustained work of fiction entitled "Mary Elmer." It was this project that held her attention to the end. In March she sent the first chapter to Godey, and before the year ended, she sent him three more chapters, but Godey never published the story. It remained unfinished at her death and hence was of no use to him. Miriam's final intentions for the story are unclear because the original manuscript did not survive, but a form of the story was published in the 1860s. It was finished by another writer, the second Mrs. Benjamin William Whitcher. Nonetheless, the work is of interest because it was the last piece Miriam wrote, and it occupied much of her final productive time.

Miriam's story resembles traditional sentimental stories that appeared in the pages of the *Lady's Book*. The Mary Elmer of the title is a young girl who, through a series of family setbacks, is sent to live as a servant in another household. A bright, near-angelic child, she is badly mistreated by a familiar type in Whitcher's work—an uneducated, crude woman whose husband has recently acquired wealth and who is trying to make a place for herself in genteel society. The real hero of the piece is a wealthy widow named Mrs. Lee who befriends the Elmer family, takes a special interest in young Mary because of her resemblance to her own recently deceased daughter, and becomes a benefactor to the family when the father throws over a prospering business to seek his fortune in California. There he reportedly dies, leaving his wife and children destitute. Through a series of crossed messages and unhappy accidents, the family fails to receive money that Mrs. Lee sends them. As a result, little Mary is fated to become a serving girl in the home of the Smith family, while her family as a whole suffers an agonizing series of losses.

Many familiar sentimental trappings abound in this novella, from the unstable husband/father, to the child whose "natural" goodness gives her the patience to endure even the harshest treatment. Like Little Eva in *Uncle Tom's Cabin*, little Mary can soften even the most hardened heart with her piety. She teaches a fellow-servant, Jerusha, how to pray, and in gratitude he steals morsels of food for her out of the Smith's kitchen. Up to the midpoint of the novel, the story is more or less of a piece; the tone is relatively unified in its solemnity, and the plot line consistent. Then marked shifts in tone and plotting suggest that the story is no longer the work of Miriam Whitcher. In the end, the supposedly dead Mr. Elmer returns from California where he had been suffering from amnesia and where he was recalled to his senses by hearing someone sing a few lines of his daughter's favorite hymn. With his return, Mary is rescued from her servitude, the family is reunited, and they all move back into their own little cottage.

Inappropriate references to earlier Whitcher themes also begin to intrude upon the story. A woman named Mrs. Squire is introduced as a ruling luminary in a local benefit society, and a local "Aid Society" meeting takes place, with the ladies squabbling over whether to help the heathens abroad or an impoverished family at home. In short, the second Mrs. Whitcher interjected into the story what she took to be the hallmarks of Miriam's art, but her handling of the material is so clumsy that the novel had little to recommend it when she finished. Miriam's deathbed wishes were never realized: " 'I wish,' said she, 'to leave something that shall be useful for my child to read, when she reaches an age capable of understanding it.' "[40]

The Decline

As early as fifteen months before her death, Miriam's family suspected that she was slowly dying from tuberculosis.[41] Typically, Miriam enjoyed "bright" periods when her symptoms eased, but everyone knew the inevitable course the disease would run. The family could do nothing but watch the slow degeneration. In the spring and early summer of 1850, Miriam's cough became much worse and a pain in her side and chest became so great that she had difficulty breathing.[42] She knew that she was seriously ill, yet she faced the prospect of her own death calmly and matter-of-factly: "I am very thankful that she [Alice] keeps so perfectly well, while I am so forlorn. My cough was better for a while, but it is very bad again, and I have a pain in my side & chest all the time, with great difficulty of breathing. I think I shall wean the baby in the fall if I live. She does not like any food but milk, which I feed her occasionally."[43] By October 1850 she coughed so much that she shunned all social gatherings and resorted to homeopathy for medical treatment, faithfully swallowing spiders' eggs to relieve her condition. Comically, the prescriber of this treatment, the Whitesboro Episcopal minister, Mr. Matson, could not remember how many eggs she should take at a time, "whether it must be six three times a day, or six a day two at a time. I therefore take as many as my judgement dictates—sometimes two, sometimes six." As for the efficacy of the treatment—"I think I am some better too, my appetite has improved, & I cough much less at night."[44]

The ties between Miriam and her sister, Kate Berry, grew even stronger in the final months of Miriam's life. Encouraged by Miriam at home, and introduced by her to her Philadelphia editors, Kate Berry began to contribute regularly to the *Lady's Book* just as Miriam's work began to disappear from that publication. Unlike her sister, Kate always wrote under her own name. Her work included poetry, short stories, articles, and sketches that can best be described as childhood nostalgia pieces.[45] Never as talented as Miriam, Kate nonetheless had the satisfaction of publishing her work in the same distinguished publication and sharing with her sister for a few brief months a common outlet for her creative talent. It was Kate Berry in the end who wrote the only extant biography of her sister and published it in *Godey's Lady's Book* barely four years after Miriam's own work had electrified the readers of that magazine.[46]

William Whitcher returned to Whitesboro in time to celebrate his and Miriam's fourth wedding anniversary on January 5, 1851, but in less than two weeks he had to return to Oswego without his wife and daughter. Shortly afterward, Miriam announced to her husband that she and her sisters were going to try to get along without taking in any boarders. When they put their plan into effect, it was the first time since Lewis Berry's release from debtor's prison in 1806 that the family home had not served also as an inn or boardinghouse; the sisters were excited by the prospect of not taking in boarders, but saddened that a long personal era was at an end.

Their "experiment," as they called it, was threatened almost immediately when Mary and Kate Berry were summoned to appear in court to answer for a bad debt their brother John had incurred. In the end, however, John extricated himself from his financial tangle without his sisters' help. At William's insistence, Miriam contributed some money for her own board, but money continued to be a major concern in the household. Miriam's letters from this period almost all contained mention of at least one unresolved financial problem. She had to sell off some of their household goods, an item at a time, and she worried that people were taking advantage of them financially in William's absence. Even so, life became immeasurably easier for the sisters when they no longer had to cook special meals, do extra laundry, or otherwise take care of their boarders.

Without boarders, however, Miriam became much more lonely and isolated than she had been. In early February 1851, she wrote to her husband that she felt so lonely that she believed "the whole world" had forgotten her. "We are completely shut up here. We do'nt see anybody, and nobody calls once a month. I do not care a great deal for society you know, but I really feel the want of it now."[47] However alienated she had felt in Elmira, her years there were rich and stimulating in contrast. Although she never said so, she had to some extent learned to appreciate being near the center of activity, and now she was alone.

In March 1851 her letters to Willlam stopped abruptly; Kate explained in "Passages" that she was confined to bed from early March until early May. When she was well again, paradoxically, it became clear that her illness was terminal: "And now, a harassing cough, a wasting frame, the attenuated hands and eyes so strangely brilliant, spoke no uncertain language."[48] By midsummer a new symptom of her illness had appeared—a pain in her side that was so violent it took "blistering" to alleviate it. When she had sufficiently recovered from that treatment, her doctor advised her to join William in Oswego for a brief time. She had to leave Alice behind with her mother and sisters; she found being separated from her child nearly intolerable, but she followed her doctor's advice. Even though she was essentially an invalid, for one last time she enjoyed receiving the attentions due a clergyman's wife. She was openly grateful for the many small kindnesses the Oswego parishioners extended to her, and she enjoyed being involved at least peripherally in the affairs of the parish. By the time she understood that she was a more public person than she had ever imagined, she was too weak to play any active role in the congregation or the community. Taking even thirty steps, she reported to her family, exhausted her. Nonetheless, she improved slightly while in Oswego, and by the end of the month she was able to travel with William on to Lake Ontario and from there to Niagara Falls. "Travelling by the most easy and luxurious conveyances, watched over with assiduous care, she accomplished the journey with less fatigue than was anticipated, enjoying every incident and view with keen relish."[49]

At the end of August, Miriam was back in Whitesboro and healthy enough to take brief walks outdoors and to enjoy what she called some "comfortable days," that is, days "marked by a respite from pain."[50] But winter came early to Whitesboro in 1851, and the rain and snow put an abrupt end to autumn. According to Kate, some "thoughtless" person said in Miriam's presence that "consumptive persons often died 'when the last leaf fell.'" When November blasts and frost had swept the elms and maples bare, some peach shrubs in the garden still retained their leaves. She sat looking out one day on the wintry prospect, and remarked, 'I am watching those peach-trees every day; the last leaf has not fallen yet.' "[51]

Miriam's strength waned. Soon she was no longer able to sit up for more than a few hours a day, and not long after that she was too weak even to hold Alice in her arms:

> But "good days" were still at times granted her, which she occupied in writing and walking from room to room. One morning, about six weeks before the last, she arose after a night of unwonted ease, and pronounced herself as feeling better than for many months before. And throughout the day she had no paroxysms of pain. In the evening, when preparing for rest, she remarked, with a look of quiet resignation, "I have been so comfortable all day that I cannot help thinking that this will be my last good day."
> And so it proved.[52]

As Christmas approached, Miriam used what little strength remained to her to make small gifts for her family and friends, and generally to prepare for her favorite holiday. Christmas Eve was at once a sad and joyful time:

> On Christmas eve, she left her own rooms for the last time; it would seem as if she rallied expressly that there might be no drawback to the enjoyment of that little gathering. It was an evening not soon to be forgotten by any of us. The tree was so prettily furnished, the children were so happy, and Miriam sat leaning back on her cushions quietly enjoying the whole. There were two of that small company on whom Death had already set his mark: Miriam and a brother, a few years younger than herself, whose wildly brilliant eye and hollow cough already betokened the months of suffering like her own, which, in a half year afterwards, consigned his wasted frame also to the grave.
> On Christmas day, for the sake of some friends who dined with her, she made a strong effort to restrain all outward indication of suffering; but exhausted nature gave way so rapidly, that only three days subsequently she was unable to rise and dress as usual.[53]

Her only wish at this point seemed to be that her suffering not endure, and in this one wish she was fortunate. On New Year's Eve,

1851, William administered holy communion to his dying wife. She was only able to whisper her responses to the rite, but she was alert and conscious.

> The next day, she said to those around her, "Pray for me; pray all the time; I cannot pray for myself now;" and expressed her sorrow that extreme pain and weakness hindered the fixing her thoughts on heavenly things. We have no triumphant expressions to record, no ecstasies, as marking Miriam's deathbed. Self-abasement and patient waiting for her Saviour alone distinguished it—that gracious and powerful Saviour, in whom she had trusted while in health, and who now, while bodily and mental powers were failing as nature's dissolution approached, was her only and all-sufficient hope and stay. On Friday, she suffered a great paroxysm of pain, a struggling respiration, terrible to witness. She thought herself at the immediate entrance of the dark valley, and the terrors of death made her afraid. But she revived, stayed another day with us, and on Sunday morning early, "while it was yet dark," the "Lord's kind angel" came, when she fell asleep very gently, like an infant in the arms of its mother.[54]

On the fifth anniversary of her wedding to William, Miriam Whitcher died. She was thirty-nine years old. Miriam was buried in Grandview Cemetary next to her father, her sister Jane, and her infant daughter, Mary. As she wished, the only stone marking her grave and her passing was the one already laid for Mary. The stone now reads:

Mary
April 1, 1848
and her
Mother
Frances Miriam
Whitcher
Aged 39 Years
January 7, 181[2]

As the remaining members of the Berry family were one by one laid to rest, Miriam was surrounded on all sides by her large and supportive family. Remarkably, in addition to the immediate Berry family, two others are buried next to Miriam; her daughter Alice W. Wood, who died in 1934 in Muskegan, Michigan, and her husband, William, who died in 1889. Thirty-seven years after the death of his wife, and with a new family of his own buried elsewhere in Grandview Cemetary, William nonetheless chose to be buried next to the woman who was his wife only five years and who, by all accounts, was the undoing of his career as an Episcopal minister. Their graves bear silent witness to the strength and depth of the love they shared.

❧

Epilogue

*F*our years after Miriam Whitcher
died, her dream of publishing the collected Widow Bedott stories
finally became a reality, thanks to the persistence of her friend Alice
Neal.[1] *The Widow Bedott Papers* was published in 1855 by one of
America's foremost publishers, James Derby, and included both the
Widow Bedott stories and the Aunt Maguire stories, with an appreciative introduction by Alice Neal. The book's success would have
stunned Miriam: In the nine years between 1855 and 1864, it went
through twenty-three editions and sold over 100,000 copies; then
after a period of relative quiet, it was reissued again in 1883 and
continued to sell well until the end of the century.[2] *The Widow Bedott
Papers* enjoyed a remarkably long life for humor whose roots were so
firmly planted in the era of its creation. In the wake of the success of
this first book, Miriam's remaining writings were published in 1867
under the title *Widow Spriggins, Mary Elmer, and Other Sketches*. This
collection appealed to a more limited audience and was reissued only
once, but the fact of its publication alone indicated that Whitcher's
humor was considered a good risk in post–Civil War America. In
addition, the circumstance of its publication offers interesting insight
into how fully Miriam's presence played a significant role in her
family's life even after her death.

Approximately a year and a half after his wife died, William married a young woman by the name of Martha Ward, a native of Jefferson County, New York. A woman with literary aspirations of her
own, Martha Whitcher nonetheless lived in the shadow of her predecessor. She apparently felt the need to try to compete with Miriam,
both privately and publicly, and the only way she could do so success-

fully was to immerse herself in Miriam's career and her writing. She collected the minor writings of Miriam Whitcher into a single volume (including a few miscellaneous pieces that had been omitted from the *Papers*), wrote a biographical introduction to the volume, and placed her name on the title page nearly as prominently as the author's own.[3] More significantly, as we have seen, she "finished" the text of "Mary Elmer." Although she claimed in the introduction that she finished the work herself only after trying in vain to find someone else to do it, she essentially put herself before the public as a coauthor with Miriam Whitcher.

One of the main curiosities about the book, and one that reveals how much Martha Whitcher stood in the shadow of Miriam, appears in her introduction. Martha Whitcher never identified her relationship to Miriam, or to the Berry and Whitcher families, nor did she reveal that all the information she included about Miriam came to her secondhand.[4] Although many of the details about Miriam's life that Martha Whitcher related in the introduction presumably were told to her by members of the Berry family or by William, some of the conclusions she drew were decidedly her own, and a number of them were grudging and self-serving. For example, even as she acknowledged Miriam's "genius" as a writer, she emphasized her social and personal limitations. The introduction contains no unqualified praise for one who had achieved and sustained the status of a best-selling author of national fame. Instead, it stresses details about Miriam's life that are trivial even if true; for instance, we are told that Miriam Berry was "far from being a favorite" of her paternal grandfather. Most conspicuously, Martha Whitcher stressed that Miriam had not been a suitable minister's wife: "Her peculiar traits of character were not particularly adapted to her new sphere in life; her retiring and reserved disposition illy qualified her for a position which makes so great demands upon the demonstrative sympathies."[5]

In the 1870s, a decade after the publication of *The Widow Spriggins,* public interest in Whitcher's work was rekindled in a wholly unexpected way: David R. Locke, the creator of the Civil War comic anti-hero, "Petroleum V. Nasby," adapted selections from *The Widow Bedott Papers* for the stage. No copy survives of Locke's original drama, "The Widow Bedott," but by all accounts the play incorporated significant selections from the Widow's monologues, and in all ways but one was faithful to the spirit of Whitcher's original prose version. The one all-important exception is that the role of the Widow Bedott was played by a man, Neil Burgess.[6] "The Widow Bedott" opened at Harverly's Theatre of Brooklyn in the winter of 1879 and enjoyed a modest success for several years throughout the East.[7] Then, sensing that he could capitalize even more on the comic potential inherent in having the husband-hunting Widow played by a male actor, Burgess rewrote Locke's play as a farce. He renamed the play "The Widow and the Elder," and continued to play the lead role and to collect all royalties for himself. The linguistic subtleties of the Widow's dramatic monologues disappeared in Burgess's rendition, while the farcical elements were made even more pronounced.[8]

Burgess's play focuses on two courtship attempts, one featuring Timothy Crane that remains relatively faithful to Whitcher's original conception, and the second featuring the Elder Sniffles, which represents a considerable distortion of the original. The Elder, for example, learns on the day he first meets the Widow that she has received an inheritance of fifty thousand dollars. Before the day is over, he marries her. Most of the action takes place on Thanksgiving Day at the home of the Maguires; Jeff Maguire is renamed Fred, the Widow's daughter retains the name Melissa but is depicted as rude and impudent, and Elder Sniffles acquires a daughter named Dotty whom Fred courts. All three couples are married or engaged at the end of the play, and the Elder has already agreed to remodel his parsonage.

Burgess's version of the play was a resounding success on the East coast for nearly a decade. By the time it reached the end of its run, Burgess had relinquished the lead role to another cross-dresser named Joseph Palmer.[9] There is, in fact, no record of the role ever being played by a woman. Clearly part of the humor for the post–Civil War audience resided in having a man play a woman's role, especially a courtship role. By one contemporary account, however, part of the appeal resided in Burgess's skill as a cross-dresser: "I still see him," George Odell wrote, "as Widow Bedott in the kitchen, making pies, straightening out the affairs of the neighborhood, and personifying, in spite of his sex, the attributes of a managing woman. He was not the least bit effeminate, not at all like the usual female impersonator of minstrelsy or of variety, and yet he was Widow Bedott to the life, and with little suggestion of burlesque."[10] In this light Neil Burgess helped keep the Widow Bedott in the public eye for nearly a decade.

Miriam Whitcher's humor was also memorialized in another way in the 1880s, but this time without a word of it being spoken or printed. In 1885, when the humorist Kate Sanborn published *The Wit of Women*, the first anthology of humor by American women, her pattern was to make a few introductory remarks about each author, then to include a brief selection of her writing. The entry for Miriam Whitcher consisted only of introductory material with no main entry; instead, Sanborn observed: "I shall not quote from them *[The Widow Bedott Papers]*, as every one who enjoys that style of humor *knows them by heart*. It would be as useless as copying "Now I lay me down to sleep,' or 'Mary Had a Little Lamb' for a child's collection of verses!"[11] It is only in the twentieth century that Miriam Whitcher's works have faded from public view, and only then after more than a half century of popularity. Some historical anthologies of American humor continue to include the Widow Bedott stories to this day, but the Aunt Maguire sketches, so electrifying to the readers of Whitcher's day, have never received in our times the attention they deserve.

The aftermath of the "fuss" in Elmira continued for William even after Miriam's death. Repeatedly frustrated by his failure to reestablish himself as a permanent pastor of a church, William ultimately left the ministry. In an even more dramatic move, he also left the Episcopal church and converted to Roman Catholicism, becoming a member of St. John's Catholic Church in Utica, New York. Although William's dissatisfaction with Episcopalian theology went back to his seminary days, according to his story, it is difficult to imagine his converting to Catholicism in Miriam's lifetime; at the very least, it is impossible to imagine her following his lead. However devoted she was to William, she seemed at home, theologically, in the Episcopal church. Given, too, that she was first brought into the Presbyterian denomination through Charles Finney's revival efforts, it is difficult to image her moving ultimately to Catholicism. She would have disliked intensely a religiously divided home, but finally it is easier to imagine her supporting William in his move than moving herself.

To explain the extraordinary change in his religion, William wrote a sermon for his former parishioners that he expanded into a monograph and published under the title *The Story of a Convert*.[12] The monograph proper spoke primarily to issues of church doctrine, to William's long fascination with Catholicism, and to his doubts about points of Episcopalian theology. In the introduction, however, he mentions in passing how ministers were frequently mistreated by their parishioners, and how the parishioners' dislike of a minister's wife could affect his career. On the subject of the Elmira controversy, per se, and Miriam's reputation as a writer, however, he remained silent.

Far from severing his ties with the Berry family, or gradually drifting apart from them as he established a new family and fathered three more children, William continued to be an integral part of the Berry family, and they a part of his. Having abandoned his profession as a minister, William became simply a farmer and took up residence within the town of Whitesboro.[13] In 1855, three years after the death of Miriam, his household consisted of his new wife, the five-year-old Alice, an infant daughter, Mary, and Miriam's two maiden sisters, Cornelia and Mary. Their mother, Elizabeth Berry, and their brother John had both died, and Kate Berry, at the age of thirty-five, had married a local merchant and fellow Episcopalian, Hiram Potter. While the two sisters Cornelia and Mary lived in William's house, Kate lived across the street on the eastern end of Main Street.

Aunt Mary and Aunt Cornelia dominated the memories of Alice Whitcher Wood in her later years when she wrote about her famous mother and her own childhood in Whitesboro. She all but ignored her stepmother. The mother Alice was too young to remember occupied an important part of her imagination when she was a child, and even when she became an adult:

> [T]here never was a child who mourned an unknown mother more than I did. I was a baby when she died, and before I was four years old my father brought home a step-mother. I well remember slipping away from the house night after night, climbing the long hill that led to the old "burying ground" threading my way without a thought of fear among the deserted graves till I reached the sidehill where rested a little stone bearing the simple legend, "Mary and her Mother." There I would seat myself on mother's grave and reason thus: "If I have faith even as a grain of mustard seed I might say to these hills: 'Be thou cast into the sea,' and they would drop right into the Mohawk river. So if I have faith and shut my eyes for a long

time, when I open them I shall see my dear mother." So I would close my eyes tightly, only to open them with the same barren result. I always laid my lack of success in this my dearest wish to my not having the requisite amount of faith. And even now, when I go into the home of a friend, I envy her not her imported rugs and costly pictures, but when I see my friend's mother sitting by the fireplace, holding, it may be the youngest grandchild on her knee, then indeed do I feel that I have been defrauded by fate of that greatest blessing life can know, a mother's tender love.[14]

As with her father before her, when it came time for Alice Whitcher Wood to be buried, in spite of the fact that she lived in Michigan and had a family of her own, she had her body returned to "that old burying ground" in Whitesboro. There she lay next to her mother and infant sister, across from her father, and close by her aunts Cornelia and Mary.

Miriam Whitcher's influence lived on, too, through her work. As one of the nation's first women humorists, she passed on a significant legacy to scores of other women writers in the nineteenth century: Rose Terry Cook, Mary Mapes Dodge, Mary Abigail Dodge (Gail Hamilton), Marietta Holley (Josiah Allen's Wife), Katherine MacDowell (Sherwood Bonner), Mary Noailles Murfree (Charles Egbert Craddock), Sara Willis Parton (Fanny Fern), Ellen Rollins (E. H. Arr), Kate Sanborn, Metta Victoria Victor, and Constance Fenimore Woolson. Of these writers, only two ever rivaled Miriam Whitcher for popularity—Sara Willis Parton and Marietta Holley—and their successes were legendary. Sara Parton's work represented one of the options characteristic of nineteenth-century American humor, the development of a genteel narrator who represented the mainstream of urban society, while Marietta Holley pursued the second option of speaking from a rustic, vernacular point of view representative of more traditional, rural values. Thus Whitcher's connection to Holley is more apparent and more direct, but her relationship even to Parton should not be underestimated.

Sara Willis Parton began writing brief humorous pieces for the Boston press in 1851, but unlike Whitcher she was able to publish her early collected writing at the beginning of her career and watch that book, *Fern Leaves*, become a bestseller.[15] In 1855 she became a regular columnist for Robert Bonner's New York *Ledger,* and for the next decade and a half entertained her readers every week with her observations about genteel society. Like Whitcher, she wrote about issues that were close to home for her, but unlike her predecessor, she directed her sharp barbs as freely at men as at women. Ultimately, she gained a reputation as an outspoken feminist and critic of women's restricted social and economic opportunities. If Whitcher was the humorist of the 1840s, Parton was the humorist of the 1850s and 1860s. With the death of Parton in 1872, that distinction passed to Marietta Holley from Jefferson County, New York.

It was Holley who most directly inherited, and extended, Whitcher's specific humor legacy. Going before the public as "Josiah Allen's Wife" (and later simply as "Samantha Allen"), Holley owed a clear and direct debt to Whitcher. Holley's feminist protagonist shares the same first name as the only woman's rights advocate in Whitcher's work, Samantha Hockum; Samantha's stepson is named Jefferson, as is Aunt Maguire's son; and Holley's strongest apologist for women's subordinate position in society is a husband-seeking spinster named Betsey Bobbet (Bedott). Not incidentally, Betsey Bobbet writes poetry that rivals the Widow Bedott's in its comic effect. Holley used the vernacular language Whitcher perfected to full advantage in the creation of her protagonist, Samantha Allen, adding to Aunt Maguire's common sense and compassion the crucial ingredient of acute political awareness. Samantha Allen was an outspoken feminist who helped popularize the woman's rights movement, and she was a staunch supporter of the temperance movement. Filtering her sometimes radical views through the language and perspective of a commonsensical farm wife, Holley was able to bring her causes before the public in a nonthreatening way; her sense of humor, just as Whitcher's, exposed the absurdity of the genteel ideology even as her audience laughed with pleasure.[16]

Appendix

Notes

Works Cited

Index

❀

Appendix

Widow Bedott/Mrs. Sniffles Story*

The Rev. Mrs. Sniffles
Attends the Meeting of the "Scrabble Hill Female Universal
Diffusion of General Elevation and Amelioration Society."

"There! it's two o'clock—time I was off to society meetin half an hour ago; now I'm President I'd ought to be punctable; but it takes me the hull time to look after Sal; can't pretend to dew nothing else. I'd ax you to keep an eye on her while I'm gone if I thought you'd dew it. She'll be up to all sorts o' tricks if she aint watched. I've gin her directions what I want done, but that aint no sign she'll mind me, aggravatin critter. I told her when she gits done moppin the kitchen, to take up that are entry carpet and hang it out on the line, and whip it till all the dust's out on't; and after that to go to weedin out them sass beds. We shant have a mite o' garden sass fit to eat all summer if them beds aint wed out once in a while. Will you see 't she does it?"

"I will most assuredly Mrs. Sniffles, I will."

"Well, I know you wont as well as I want to know it, for you always let her cut up jest as she's a mind tew when I'm away. There! can't as much as wait till I'm out o' the house afore ye begin to haul out yer pipe and tabacker. I wish to gracious that everlastin old pipe was in Ballyback—"

"Mrs. Sniffles—"

*Reprinted from Neal's *Saturday Gazette*, Oct. 13, 1849. Courtesy of the American Antiquarian Society.

"I say of all things, a *smokin minister's* the wost—its ridicilous; its settin an awful example afore yer congregation—"

"Mrs. Sniffles, allow me to remark that—"

"I say its perfectly disgustin. You've hild that old pipe handle in yer mouth so much, that yer lips has got all drawd up to a continniwal pucker."

"Mrs. Sniffles, permit me to remind you that previous to our union, you affirmed that tobacco was by no means offensive to you; on the contrary—"

"O, mighty! I spose you think you've *said* it now. For my part, I think a minister might be in better bisness than to be a throwin out insinniwations against his wife. Puff away—smoke yer eyes out for all I care, you hurt yerself more'n ye dew anybody else." (She departs, and the Elder proceeds to the kitchen.)

"Sally, you will remember to elevate the entry carpet according to Mrs. Sniffles's directions."

"Yes, sir."

"Your next operation will be to suspend it from the line; after which you will proceed to chastise it thoroughly. Having accomplished the eradication of the dust, you may proceed to amuse yourself in such a manner as shall be most congenial to your taste, until five o'clock, at which time you will commence to weed the garden in further pursuance of Mrs. Sniffles's directions. Remember, Sally, it is my desire that Mrs. S. should find you thus occupied on her return. It may contribute essentially to the repose of the establishment."

"Yes, sir, I'll do just exactly as you say. After I've whipped the carpet, I guess I'll go over and see Betsey Wilson; I haint been there in ever so long, and Betsey's afraid to come here lately—but the minute it's five o'clock I'll cut home like split, and go to weeding."

"Good afternoon, ladies! I spose I'm a leetle behind the time; but the Elder and me got very much engaged in conversation, and the time slipped away afore I was aware on 't—he's *so* interestin in conversation. I could set and listen to him all day. O, Sister Rawley, I'm glad to see you able to git out agin; you've had a tejus time on 't, haint you?"

"Yes, I've enjoyed miserable health for quite a spell. 'Twas a great deprivation not to be able to attend the meetings."

"It must a ben. It's a tryin thing to be an invalidinarian, especially when a body feels anxious to be a laborin for the good o' menkind. See, I bleve twas a speshie of malicious irrysepelas you had, wa'nt it?"

"Yes, it's a very distressing complaint. It really seemed—"

"Yes, I know it. My first husband, Deacon Bedott, was more or less troubled with it for a number o' years afore he died. He was a great sufferer that man was! O, it *is* such a comfort to me that my precious Shadrack enjoys such gineral health! But I spose it's time for us to come to order, thought the members dont seem to be all assembled yet. Sister Johnson, aint the rest on em a comin? Where's Sister Myers and Sister Simmons, and Sister Hugle and Sally?"

"Well, I expect Sister Hugle and Sally in every minute; but Sister Simmons has got company from the Pint, and Sister Myers has gone over to the corners a visitin."

"And Sister Bedunderhue, she'd ought to be here, bein as she's on the visitin' committee. Sally Hugle, too, she's a purty secretary, I must say, to stay away so late. But I spose she haint got drest yet to suit herself. I wish she didnt think so much o' such things, dont you, Sister Coville?"

"I do *so*. I was telling Augusty Ann the other day that I didnt see how anybody that enjoyed religion could be so took up with dress. But them I presume she wants to make the best of herself. She aint as young as she once was, is she, Sister Odle?"

"O, my, no! She was flourishing long enough before I was married, and that's—let me see—how long *have* I been married? Mandy Sophia, how old are you?"

"I'm eighteen, ma."

"Well, I've been married almost twenty years. Sally Hugle's full forty-five, every minute of it. The older she grows the more she dresses. Mandy, what was it Eunice Smith said about her when she was sewing to our house the other day?"

"Why, she said she'd often known her to be three hours a fixing to go out to make calls."

"You dont! three hours! well, I should think twould take as long as that to git them stringlets in reglar rotation."

"But that wasn't all Eunice said. She told how she makes poetry; she says she's lookt through the keyhole and seen her many a time. She sits down before her looking glass, and always has a piece of paper lying ready on the table; and there she sits hours together, combing and brushing, and curling and powdering; and writing poetry between whiles."

"Well, that's quite an idee—kill tew birds with one stone. They say—"

"Hush, Sister Sniffles, she's a coming!"—(Hugelina enters.)

"You're ruther late, Miss Hugle."

"Yes, Sister Sniffles. I regret exceedingly that my arrival has been somewhat retarded by unforeseen circumstances."

"Well, for my part, I think we hadn't ought to let nothing interfere with punctability, especially when the interests of our feller critters is consarned."

"Unquestionably, Sister Sniffles; but I—"

"I was a leetle belated myself. The Elder and me was convarsing on a

very interestin tropic—and when I'm a listenin to him I forgit almost everything else. But I spose we'd ought to begin if we expect to rassack [*sic*]
much bisness today. Miss Hugle, you may read the proceedins of last meetin."

"Ahem!—em! The 'Scrabble Hill F.U.D.G.E. and A. Society' met on
the fourth of May, at the habitation of Mrs. Benjamin Ingols, Mrs. Sniffles in
the chair—"

"That aint right—I sot on the sofy."

"Ahem!—Mrs. Sniffles on the sofa. A majority of the members were
present. A delightful degree of harmony pervaded the meeting, the interest
of which was greatly augmented by the reading of a highly interesting communication from our sister society at Punkin Hook. The reports of the
Visiting Committee, Sisters Buck, Cady and Tibbins, were deeply interesting,
and exhibited a pleasing manifestation of the progrees of Elevation and
Amelioration in our midst. After much interesting and edifying conversation,
the society adjourned to meet at the habitation of Mrs. Jerusha Johnson—
having previously appointed Sears, Twitchell and Bedunderhue to constitute
the Visiting Committee for the subsequent month.

> O, 'tis a glorious work of love
>   To diffuse high Elevation
> 'Mongst ignorant individuals
>   In every situation.
>
> O soul of mine! promulge my powers!
>   Expand thy loftiest wing—
> And o'er earth's sublunary spere
>   Wide Elevation fling!
>
> Thus let the wondrous work advance
>   Till all this vast creation
> 'Neath General Elevation smiles,
>   And enjoys Amelioration.
>   Sarah P. Hugle, Secretary."

"Has the report of the Visitin Committee ben handed in?"

"It has so, I now hold it in my hand, it was prepared by Sister
Bedunderhue, who transmitted it to me this morning, accompanied by the
intelligence that she would be unable to attend the meeting to-day, in consequence of having been sent for to visit Mrs. Ferris, who is quite sick."

"It's amusin that Sister Bedunderhue always calls it *visitin* when she
goes out a nussin the sick—curus pride some folks has—spose she feels above
being called a nuss. What ails Miss Ferris?"

"I believe she is suffering from a severe attact of Nuralgia."

"Noraligy! I wish folks would larn to call things by their right names. It's rhumatis that the Widder Ferris has, and everybody knows it; wonder if she 'magines it'll make folks think she's any younger 'n she is to deny havin the rhumatis? She's a curus old critter—Sister Sears, you said you meant to ax her to jine the Society—did ye?"

"O law yes—and she said she'd rather be excused. I told her it wasn't to be confined to our seck—we wanted all denominations to come up to the work. But she said she didn't approve of such mixed up concerns, they aways ended in difficulty. We all know well enough that *that* aint the reason though. She's afraid she'll have to give something if she joins us, and she's *so* tight— Sister Loder, you remember that trick she served Sister Myers?"

"Law, yes, I guess I do. I've heard Eunice Smith tell it all over. She was sewing at Mrs. Ferris's at the time it happened. Sister Sniffles did you ever hear it?"

"I don't bleve I ever did, what was it, pray tell?"

"Well, you see Sister Myers had let Mrs. Ferris have a firkin of butter— first rate, beautiful butter, you know—now I've had butter of Sister Myers myself, and I must confess that as a general thing her butter aint the best I ever eat—still I have reason to think that the firkin she put down for Mrs. Ferris was the best quality of butter—Eunice Smith says 't was, and Eunice is a good judge, you know. Well, Mrs. Ferris used up the—"

"Stop! Sister Loder—you can tell Sister Sniffles about it some other time—Caroline Perry's a coming in—'t wont do to say anything before her—she'll go straight and tell Mrs. Ferris every word—you know they're quite intimate—folks say she's trying to catch John Ferris, but if she succeeds, John Ferris is a bigger fool than—"

"Good afternoon, Miss Perry! very glad you've got to the meetin to-day. Miss Hugle is jest a gwine to read the Visitin Committee's Report."

(Hugelina reads)

"The Visiting Committee of the 'Scrabble Hill F.U.D.G.E. and A. Society' have cause for devout thankfulness that their humble exertions in the great work of General Elevation and Amelioration have been so signally blest during the past month. Wednesdays and Saturdays of each week have been faithfully devoted to the business of seeking out suitable objects for Elevation and Amelioration. Your Committee have visited and labored with fifty-three families, have distributed sixty-seven copies of the tract entitled 'Mental Culture and Intellectual Development'—twenty-five copies were bestowed upon the colored population at The Corners. We were deeply pained to find this interesting class of our fellow creatures plunged in a state of the most deplorable ignorance, not an individual among them being able to read or write. Your Committee are compelled to acknowledge that appearances at the Corners are at present unpromising. Some circumstances connected with our labors in this degraded portion of our field are somewhat discouraging. For instance, we are credibly informed that *Big Pete,* as he is called, has pawned for a quart of whiskey all the tracts which we distributed in his numerous family. O, 'tis melancholy to reflect that an immortal being should be so debased as to barter away that which might develop his darkened understanding for liquid fire! Several other circumstances have transpired which might have had an attendency to dampen the zeal of your Committee had they trusted in their own strength. Molly McMakin, the Irish washerwoman, who is a degraded and benighted catholic, treated us with great rudeness. Soon after our entrance into her miserable abode, we presented her with the tract, remarking that it would prove highly beneficial to her. She received it with apparent pleasure, and said that she had been trying to get hold of it for some time—there was a man along with it to sell a few days before, but he charged a dollar for it and she couldn't afford to buy it. She was very much obliged to us for giving it to her for nothing. She'd get her man to read it to her, for she couldn't read herself and he could.

We perceived that she was laboring under some mistake, we therefore explained to her the nature of the tract, whereupon she returned it to us, saying in her Irish way, 'she thought for sure it was the resate for *washing made aisy* she'd heard so much about, and she thought it would larn her to wash without rubbing the skin all off her hands, and killing herself entirely every week. We might give it to somebody that could understand it, but she didn't want it at all at all!'

Previous to our departure, sister Twitchell addressed the throne of grace in her behalf, and we were deeply shocked to perceive that while sister T. was thus engaged, the wretched creature continued rubbing away over her wash tub. Oh! that the eyes of her benighted soul may be opened to a sense of her deplorable condition! These are specimens of many of the trials which we have been called to undergo during our recent visitations. Yet in the midst of much that looked dark and umpromising, your committee have cheerfully labored on in the confident assurance that the good seed which they were sowing, would in the course of time bring forth an abundant harvest.

Philinda Bedunderhue"

"See—we was to consider the subject o' startin a newspaper in the society this afternoon, wa'nt we, Miss Hugle?"

"We were so, and I think it must be manifest to all that the increasing importance of the 'F.U.D.G.E. and A. Society,' demands an organ. Our correspondence with the Parent Society, as well as with our sister societies at Pigeon Point and Punkin Hook, and also the highly interesting reports of our visiting committees, to say nothing of the Secretary's record of the proceedings at our meetings, would undoubtedly exert a vast influence if promulgated to the community at large. I am firmly persuaded that our society requires only the aid and assistance of the press to render it an engine of immense moral power. What are your sentiments, Sister Sniffles?"

"Well, I think twould have a favorable attendance for us to git up a paper, and I don't know as I'd have any objections to furnishin the poetry myself."

"Ahem! I should be happified to receive occasional assistance from you in that department, which I presume I shall be expected to fill."

"Shall hey! Well, I didn't offer to dew it jest for the sake o' paradin my writins afore the world as *some folks* dew. It's despisable to write poetry an stick it in the papers week after week without no object, only jest to show off. I'd never be guilty on't. But I thought I'd as lieve as not write poetry in a good cause where there's a prospect of exartin a favorable influence by it. Our talents wa'nt gin to us for nothing; don't you think so, Sister Johnson?"

"Yes I do, and I think that such a decided talent as sister Hugle has, ought to be employed in the services of the Society, ain't that your opinion, sister Kittles?"

"Certingly. We can't keep up our paper no how without sister Hugleses assistance—and than her poetry would contribbit to extend the circulation all over the country, for it's universally admired. It's ben copied into the 'Pidgin Pint Record of Genius,' and a number of other papers, you know, Sister Sniffles."

"Well, fix it out any way you're a mind tew. I must go home, sister Johnson."

"Why no, sister Sniffles, you mustn't go before tea. I'm going to get it now. I insist on your staying."

"But I promised Mr. Sniffles I'd be back as soon as I could, he can't bear to have me stay away long, and then it's so awful lonesome for him to drink his tea alone, ye know."

"Oh well, I'll send over for him to come and drink tea with us, so don't you think of going."

"Good afternoon, elder. I'm very glad you've come, sister Sniffles has been in a terrible taking to get home to you, but we persuaded her to stay to tea, and have you come over here."

"Well, no wonder I've felt uneasy," she rushes forward and receives him with a tender kiss, "the time seems so awful long when I'm away from you. I keep a thinkin o' what the poet says

> 'Each day I spend with my dear friend
> Seems like a half a minute,
> Each hour's a day, when he's away,
> There ain't no comfort in it.'

Come here and set down by the winder, Shadrack, it's cool and pleasant here. And what have you ben a dewing to pass away the time, while I was gone, darlin!"

"Well, I have been very agreeably engaged in—"

"And what did you leave Sally about, Shacky dear?"

"She is at the present time occupied in weeding in the garden, in accordance with your commands."

"Weedin! dear me! why didn't you tell her to stop? I'm afeard she'll work tew hard and make herself sick."

"You recollect, Mrs. Sniffles, that your orders were—"

"Shadrack! did you ever notice sister Johnson's hoss chesnut tree? ain't it a hansome one?"

Notes

1. A Woman's Humor

1. Nancy A. Walker, *A Very Serious Thing: Women's Humor and American Culture* (Minneapolis: Univ. of Minnesota Press, 1988), p. 21.

2. For an extended discussion of the social history of Oneida County, New York, in the mid-1800s, see Mary P. Ryan, *Cradle of the Middle Class: The Family in Oneida County, New York, 1790–1865* (Cambridge: Cambridge Univ. Press, 1981).

3. Walter Blair, *Native American Humor* (San Francisco: Chandler, 1960), pp. 3–37.

4. Henry Nash Smith, *Mark Twain: The Development of a Writer* (Cambridge, Mass: Harvard Univ. Press, 1961), pp. 125–29.

5. These terms were popularized by Walter Blair, *Horse Sense in American Humor, from Benjamin Franklin to Ogden Nash* (New York: Russell and Russell, 1962); and Jennette Tandy, *Crackerbox Philosophers in American Humor and Satire* (Port Washington, N.Y.: Kennikat, 1964).

6. F. M. Whitcher, *The Widow Bedott Papers* (New York: Mason, 1880), pp. 322–23. All further references to the Widow Bedott stories will be cited in the text.

7. Blair, *Native American Humor*, p. 375.

8. *Children of the Abbey* was a popular sentimental novel of the period.

9. F. M. Whitcher, *Widow Spriggins, Mary Elmer, and Other Sketches,* Mrs. M. L. Ward Whitcher, ed. (New York: Carleton, 1867), p. 53. All further references to this work will be cited in the text.

10. Haliburton's comic hero, Sam Slick, Yankee peddler and clock maker, was an archetypal Yankee figure. He shared a number of characteristics with traditional vernacular heroes, but the humor is presented from a standard narrative perspective.

11. For varied perspectives on Holley's humor, see Linda A. Morris, *Women Vernacular Humorists in Nineteenth-Century America: Ann Stephens, Frances Whitcher, and Marietta Holley* (New York: Garland, 1988); Kate H. Winter, *Marietta Holley: Life with "Josiah Allen's Wife"* (Syracuse: Syracuse Univ. Press, 1984); Jane Curry, ed., *Samantha Rastles the Woman Question* (Urbana: Univ. of Illinois Press, 1983).

12. See Jane Curry, "Women as Subjects and Writers of Nineteenth Century American Humor," (Ph.D. diss., Univ. of Michigan, 1975); Linda A. Morris, "Wolves in Sheep's Clothing," in *Women Vernacular Humorists,* pp. 226–76.

13. The change in women's conditions has been well documented. Among the most interesting studies are the following: Nancy F. Cott, *The Bonds of Womanhood: "Woman's Sphere" in New England, 1790–1835* (New Haven: Yale Univ. Press, 1977), esp. pp. 63–100; Judith Fetterley, ed., *Provisions: A Reader from Nineteenth-Century American Women* (Bloomington: Indiana Univ. Press, 1985), pp. 1–40; Barbara J. Harris, "The Cult of Domesticity," in *Beyond Her Sphere: Women and the Professions in American History* (Westport: Greenwood Press, 1978); Glenna Matthews, *"Just a Housewife": The Rise and Fall of Domesticity in America* (New York: Oxford Univ. Press, 1987), pp. 3–34; Mary P. Ryan, "Creating Woman's Sphere," in *Womanhood in America: From Colonial Times to the Present,* 2d ed. (New York: Watts, 1979); Kathryn Kish Sklar, *Catharine Beecher: A Study in American Domesticity* (New Haven: Yale Univ. Press, 1973); Carroll Smith-Rosenberg, *Disorderly Conduct: Visions of Gender in Victorian America* (New York: Oxford Univ. Press, 1985); and Barbara Welter, "The Cult of True Womanhood: 1820–1860," *American Quarterly* 18 (1966): 151–74.

14. Mari Jo Buhle and Paul Buhle, eds., *The Concise History of Woman Suffrage: Selections from the Classic Work of Stanton, Anthony, Gage, and Harper* (Urbana: Univ. of Illinois Press, 1978), p. 97.

15. See Linda A. Morris, "Frances Miriam Whitcher: Social Satire in the Age of Gentility," in *Last Laughs: Perspectives on Women and Comedy,* ed. Regina Barreca (New York: Gordon and Breach, 1988), pp. 99–116.

16. Caroline Kirkland's first work was *A New Home—Who'll Follow? or Glimpses of Western Life,* 1839; Ann Stephens's one work in the humorous tradition was *High Life in New York by Jonathan Slick, Esq.* 1843.

17. Kate Sanborn, *The Wit of Women* (New York: Funk and Wagnalls, 1886).

18. Cited in Sanborn, *The Wit of Women,* p. 13.

19. Martha Bruère and Mary Beard, eds., *Laughing Their Way: Women's Humor in America* (New York: Macmillan, 1934).

20. Ibid., p. vi.

21. Nancy Walker and Zita Dresner, eds., *Redressing the Balance: American Women's Literary Humor from Colonial Times to the 1980s* (Jackson: Univ. of Mississippi Press, 1988).

22. Walker, *A Very Serious Thing,* p. 8.

23. Ibid., p. 29.

24. Ibid., p. 70.

25. Alice Sheppard, "From Kate Sanborn to Feminist Psychology: The Social Context of Women's Humor, 1885–1985," *Psychology of Women Quarterly* 10 (1986): 155–70.

26. Judy Little, *Comedy and the Woman Writer: Woolf, Spark, and Feminism* (Lincoln: Univ. of Nebraska Press, 1983).

27. Ibid., pp. 178–79.

28. Emily Toth, "A Laughter of Their Own: Women's Humor in the United States," in *Critical Essays in American Humor,* William B. Clark and W. Craig Turner eds. (Boston: G. K. Hall, 1984), pp. 199–215.

29. See, for example, Alfred Habegger, "Nineteenth-Century Humor: Easygoing Males, Anxious Ladies, and Penelope Lapham," *PMLA* 91 (Oct. 1976): 884–99.

30. Thomas F. O'Donnell, "The Return of the Widow Bedott: Mrs. F. M. Whitcher of Whitesboro and Elmira," *New York History* 55 (1974): 5–34.

31. Nancy A. Walker, "Wit, Sentimentality, and the Image of Women in the Nineteenth Century," *American Studies* 22.2 (1981): 5–22.

32. Ibid., p. 6.

33. Karen Halttunen, *Confidence Men and Painted Women: A Study of Middle-Class Culture in America, 1830–1870.* (New Haven: Yale Univ. Press, 1982), p. xiv.

34. Ibid., p. 93.

35. See Morris, "Wolves in Sheep's Clothing."

36. Walker and Dresner, *Redressing the Balance,* p. xxiii.

37. Sheppard, "From Kate Sanborn to Feminist Psychology," p. 167.

38. There is some controversy over the date of Miriam's birth. I accept 1812 as most probable, but the date cannot be established definitively.

2. Whitesboro

1. Daniel E. Wager, "Whitesboro's Golden Age," in *Transactions of the Oneida County Historical Society of Utica, 1881–1884* (Utica: Oneida County Historical Society, 1885), p. 127. Other useful biographical sources on the Berry family include Pomroy Jones, *Annals and Recollections of Oneida County* (Rome, N.Y.: [author], 1851); D. Gordon Rohman, *Here's Whitesboro: An Informal History* (New York: Stratford House, 1949); and Daniel E. Wager, *Our County and Its People: A Descriptive Work on Oneida County, New York* (Boston: Boston Historical Society, 1896).

2. Miriam was one of two children born in the original Berry Inn in Whitesboro. Built in 1784, the inn was a double log cabin with a porch running the full length across the front. According to family records, "a door at the eastern end opened into the bar room, while one at the opposite end opened into a large room which served as a dining room and a sitting room. A frame lean-to at the back contained the kitchen, the store room and the back stoop," while the oven itself was located outside. Martha L. Whitcher, "Berry's House in the Whitestown County," Manuscript in the Dunham Public Library, Whitesboro, N.Y.

3. Wagner, "Golden Age," pp. 128–29.

4. The first settler was Hugh White, who came to what is now known as Whitesboro in 1784.

5. The New York Census for 1850 lists the cause of his death as "old age." Today, a large oil painting of Lewis Berry hangs in Whitesboro's Dunham Public Library, which is located near the site of the original Berry Inn.

6. Wager, "Golden Age," p. xxx.

7. Local historians do not agree about the birth dates for a number of the Berry children, and the chronology I am offering here in some instances matches no one else's. Cemetery records are sketchy, and the dates carved on some of the Berry markers are too eroded to read; nevertheless, census records help round out the picture that has been available to this time, while evidence offered in the Whitcher letters corroborates much of the information found in the pages that follow.

8. Kate Berry, "Passages in the Life of the Author of Aunt Maguire's Letters, Bedott Papers, Etc.," *Godey's Lady's Book* 47 (July 1853): 52.

9. Wager, "Golden Age," lists Cornelia's date of birth as 1812, but the New York Census of 1850 lists her place of birth as Cambridge, New York, which would put the date back at least a decade.

10. Wager, "Golden Age," p. 129.

11. Ibid., p. 131.

12. Ibid., p. 130; *Dictionary of American Biography,* vol. 1 (New York: Scribners, 1928), pp. 593–94.

13. Date of death established by tombstone.

14. According to the New York Census of 1850.

15. Berry, "Passages," pp. 49–50.

16. Letter from Frances Miriam Berry Whitcher to Alice Neal. Quoted in Berry, "Passages," p. 50.

17. Berry, "Passages," p. 50.

18. Ibid.

19. Ibid., p. 51.

20. Ibid., p. 53

21. Ibid.

22. Ibid.

23. Ibid., p. 54.

24. Promoters of the "Grand Canal," such as Judge Jonas Platt, who lived next door to the Berry family, made extravagant claims for the canal, but even hyperbole such as the following ultimately understated its effects: "Co-operation and aid in making a canal navigation between the great lakes and Hudson's river, which, in the opinion of the Legislature of New York, will encourage agriculture, promote commerce and manufacture, ficilitate *[sic]* a free and general intercourse between different parts of the United States, tend to the aggrandizement and prosperity of the country, and consolidate and strengthen the Union." Quoted in Archer Hulbert, *The Great American Canals: Vol. II, The Erie Canal,* vol. 14 of *Historic Highways of America* (Cleveland: Arthur H. Clark, 1904), pp. 56–57.

25. Walter D. Edmonds, "The Erie Canal," in *40' × 28' × 4': The Erie Canal— 150 Years,* ed. Lionel D. Wyld (Rome, N.Y.: Oneida County Erie Canal Commemoration Commission, 1967), p. 12. Surveying the swamp and forest lands, carving out a 40' × 28' × 4' ditch, constructing a series of more than fifty locks to connect Lake Erie with the Hudson River, 564 feet lower than the lake, constituted a major feat of engineering. The speed with which the canal was completed was matched in kind only by the speed with which it allowed people to travel from Buffalo to New York City— instead of six weeks, the journey could now be made in eleven days. According to Edmonds, in the first year alone, "19,000 boats and rafts passed through Troy; often 40 boats pulled west from Albany in a single day; and more than 40,000 immigrants went west over the canal. Tolls in 1826 amounted to three quarters of a million dollars; in 1830 they passed the million mark; and in 1831 the Erie alone brought in over a million. In the first eight years of full operation the canals earned more than their initial cost, plus maintenance" (p. 12).

26. Col. William Leete Stone, "Col. Stone's Tour in 1829, from New York to Niagara. Journal of a Tour, in Part by the Erie Canal, in the Year 1829," in *The Holland Land Company,* vol. 14, (Buffalo: Buffalo Historical Society, 1910), p. 219.

27. Virginia B. Kelly, "Utica and the Impact of the Canal," in Wyld, *40' × 28' × 4',* p. 35.

28. Howard A. Morrison, "The Finney Takeover of the Second Great Awakening during the Oneida Revivals of 1825–1827," *New York History* 59, no. 1 (Jan. 1978): 27–53.

29. Morrison, "Finney Takeover," p. 32.

30. Charles G. Finney, *Memoirs of Rev. Charles G. Finney* (New York: Fleming H. Revell, 1876), pp. 171, 177.

31. The single most useful discussion of the Finney revivals is by Whitney R. Cross, *The Burned-Over District: The Social and Intellectual History of Enthusiastic Religion in Western New York, 1800–1850* (Ithaca: Cornell Univ. Press, 1950).

32. Quoted in Morrison, "Finney Takeover," p. 47.

33. Richard L. Manzelmann, Revival and Reform," in *The History of Oneida County* (Oneida Co.: n.p., 1977), p. 55.

34. "First Annual Report of the Female Moral Reform Society of the City of New York" (New York: W. Newell, 1835), Papers in the Oneida County Historical Society, Utica, N.Y., p. 6.

35. "First Annual Report," p. 13.

36. Ryan, *Cradle,* p. 122.

37. See also Carroll Smith-Rosenberg, "Beauty, the Beast, and the Militant Woman," in *Disorderly Conduct: Visions of Gender in Victorian America* (New York: Oxford, 1985), pp. 109–28.

38. Ryan, *Cradle,* p. 123.

39. Cross, *Burned-Over District,* p. 235f.

40. Manzelmann, "Revival," p. 57.

41. Milton C. Sernett, *Abolition's Axe: Beriah Green, Oneida Institute, and the Black Freedom Struggle* (Syracuse: Syracuse Univ. Press, 1986), p. 37.

42. Quoted in Sernett, *Abolition's Axe,* p. 44.

43. Ibid., p. 52f.

44. Joshua B. Grinnell became a prominent politician in Iowa, a missionary, and the founder of Grinnell College; Henry B. Stanton was one of the leading early New York abolitionists and the husband of Elizabeth Cady Stanton; Theodore Dwight Weld became one of the best known of the early abolitionists.

45. Manzelmann, "Revival," p. 58.

46. Sernett, *Abolition's Axe,* p. 83.

47. Ibid. pp. 87–88.

48. Quoted in Sernett, *Abolition's Axe,* p. 85.

49. Whitcher Letters, Manuscript Collection, New-York Historical Society, New York City. I am especially indebted to Ms. Jenny Lawrence, who transcribed the letters, for making a copy of her transcription available to me. All references to the letters will be to the typed transcription, which has page numbers. Apr. 11, 1847, p. 1.

50. O'Donnell, "Return of the Widow Bedott," pp. 16–17.

51. Jane Spenser, in *The Rise of the Woman Novelist: From Aphra Behn to Jane Austen* (Oxford: Blackwell, 1986), observes that Lennox's Arabella actually gains more power through acting out her illusions than she would if she had obeyed her father and married Glanville from the outset. The same may be said of Permilly Ruggles. Her father's choice of an unappealing butcher, and his threats to beat her into submission when she disobeys him, make her decision to plunge into the world more than a convenient plot device.

52. F. M. Whitcher, *Widow Spriggins,* p. 62. All further references to this work will be cited in the text.

53. Miriam's use of local place names such a Oneida County, Utica, Baggs Tavern in Utica, and Hamilton College reveals, I believe, how much she set out to entertain her first audience, the Mæonian Circle of Whitesboro.

54. Miriam Whitcher would not be the last "serious" poet to make fun of women poets—Marietta Holley (Josiah Allen's Wife) included a significant number of seriocomic verses in her early feminist novels (1870s), all written by the sentimental figure Betsey Bobbet; even more than Miriam, Holley felt her true talent lay not in her popular vernacular humor but in her poetry. Yet both humorists took great pleasure in mocking the verse that poured forth from the pens of their sentimental contemporaries, verse that to a modern sensibility was not unlike their own.

55. One recent critic, Clyde G. Wade, seriously misunderstands the importance of an issue such as fashion for Miriam Whitcher's larger female audience: "Because Permilly was herself the object of Whitcher's satire, the scenes in which the woman's perspective is important tend to deal with *matters of little consequence* [emphasis added]. For example, when Permilly dresses up for a party, the point of view is obviously feminine, but it serves little purpose except to create an instance of broad humor" [pun presumable not intended]. *Dictionary of Literary Biography,* vol. 11, pt. 2 (Detroit: Gale, 1982), p. 562.

3. Marriage and "The Widow Bedott"

1. "Whitestown Female Charitable Society," Pamphlet in the Oneida Historical Society, Utica, N.Y., 1806.

2. Wager, "Our County," p. 309–10.

3. "Record of the Organization of St. John's Parish, Whitesboro, from Papers and from the Diocesan Report," St. John's Episcopal Church, Whitesboro, N.Y.

4. Whitcher Letters, Aug. 9, 1846, pp. 1–2.

5. Ibid., p. 3 The "Certificate of Transfer" is included in the Whitcher Letters in the New-York Historical Society.

6. All of the Widow Bedott sketches in the *Gazette* were published under the title "The Widow Bedott's Table Talk"; the titles used throughout this study are those given to the sketches in *The Widow Bedott Papers,* edited by Alice Neal after Miriam Whitcher's death.

7. Neal's *Saturday Gazette* 3, no. 97 (Aug. 15, 1846): 2.

8. See, for example, Walter Blair and Raven I. McDavid, Jr. eds. *The Mirth of a Nation: America's Great Dialect Humor* (Minneapolis: Univ. of Minnesota Press, 1983), pp. 27–30.

9. O'Donnell, "Return of the Widow Bedott," p. 7.

10. Neal's *Saturday Gazette* 3, no. 110 (Nov. 14, 1846): 2.

11. Ann Douglas, *The Feminization of American Culture* (New York: Knopf, 1977), pp. 51–52.

12. Walker, *A Very Serious Thing,* pp. 62–63.

13. Patricia M. Spacks, *Gossip* (Chicago: Univ. of Chicago Press, 1986), especially chapt. 1.

14. Ibid., pp. 45–46.

15. Ibid., p. 170.

16. Ibid., p. 45.

17. "Record of the Phrenological and Magnetic Society," Paper in the Oneida County Historical Society, Utica, N.Y., 1845.

18. O'Donnell, "Return of the Widow Bedott," p. 21.

19. Morris, "Social Satire," pp. 99–101.

20. Quoted in Berry's "Passages," p. 50.

21. Whitcher Letters, Apr. 14, 1847, p. 3.

22. At one meeting, a man identified only as Mr. Palmer dropped by to pay the sewing circle six dollars he owed them for work the women did for him; this sum represented one-half a month's salary for William when he was still a missionary. Whitcher Letters, Apr. 24, 1847, p. 6

23. Ibid., Apr. 14, 1847, p. 3.

24. Ibid., Apr. 18, 1847, p. 4.

25. Ibid., Apr. 24, 1847, p. 1.

26. Ibid., Apr. 18, 1847, p. 3.

27. Ibid., p. 3.

28. Ibid., May 1, 1847, p. 1.

29. See, for example, Thomas Dublin, ed., *Farm to Factory: Women's Letters, 1830–1860* (New York: Columbia Univ. Press, 1981).

30. Whitcher Letters, Apr. 14, 1847, pp. 1–2. For an extended discussion of mourning customs in this era, see Halttunen, chap. 5, "Mourning the Dead: A Study in Sentimental Ritual," *Confidence Men,* pp. 124–52. In Halttunen's terms, the Reverend Mr. Long is an example of one putting on a genteel performance.

31. Whitcher Letters, Apr. 24, 1847, p. 2.

32. Ibid., Apr. 18, 1847, p. 3. According to Rene and Jean Dubos, *The White Plague: Tuberculosis, Man and Society* (Boston: Little, Brown, 1952), p. 4, "Involvement of certain lymphatic nodes is one of the constant manifestations of tuberculosis. The expressions 'scrofulous' and 'strumous glands' were frequently used in the past to describe these tuberculous nodes, particularly those of the neck. The adjective 'scrofulous' suggests resemblance to a sow, and 'strumous' means 'something built up.' " Given how the medical mind of the nineteenth century worked, it is thus not surprising that one of the treatments for Miriam's "scrofulous" condition was the application of the marrow of hog jaw to the afflicted area. It was analogous to treating fire with fire.

33. Whitcher Letters, Apr. 20, 1847, p. 1.

34. Ibid., Apr. 24, 1847, p. 1.

35. Ibid., Apr. 28, 1847, p. 2.

36. Ibid., May 6, 1847, p. 1.

37. Ibid., May 11, 1847, p. 2. The Helen mentioned here is Helen Wetmore, who was undoubtedly Miriam's closest friend outside the family. Miriam mentions her a dozen times in her letters over the years, yet I have been frustrated in all attempts to find out more about her. A William Wetmore was one of the original wardens of St. John's Church, and he in turn was probably a son of Amos Wetmore, one of the early prominent citizens of Whitesboro; yet the name William is not identified by Wager as one of the surviving sons of Amos. I would speculate that Helen was the daughter, not the wife, of William, but even that cannot be asserted with certainty.

38. Ibid., May 11, 1847, p. 2.

39. Ibid., Apr. 18, 1847, pp. 1–2.

40. Ibid., Apr. 24, 1847, pp. 1–2.

41. Ibid., May 1, 1847, pp. 2–3.

42. Ibid., May 6, 1847, p. 1.

43. Ibid., May 11, 1847, p. 1.

44. Ibid., Apr. 20, 1847, p. 1.

45. Ibid., Apr. 14, 1847, p. 4.

46. Ibid., Apr. 18, 1847, p. 4.

47. Ibid., Jan. 2, 1848, p. 6.

48. Frank Luther Mott, *The History of American Magazines,* vol. 1 (Cambridge, Mass.: Harvard Univ. Press, 1939), p. 581.

49. Ibid., p. 584.

50. Whitcher Letters, Apr. 18, 1847, p. 3.

51. The second Aunt Maguire sketch to appear in the *Lady's Book* (July 1847) is misplaced at the end of the Elmira sketches in *The Widow Bedott Papers.*

52. Whitcher Letters, May 30, 1847, p. 1.

53. Ibid.

54. Ibid.

4. Elmira

1. Halttunen, *Confidence Men,* esp. chap. 3, "Sentimental Culture and the Problem of Fashion," pp. 56–91.

2. Ibid., p. 51f.

3. Whitcher Letters, June 10, 1847, p. 1.

4. Ibid., pp. 1–2.

5. Ibid., pp. 3–4.

6. Ibid., p. 4.

7. Ibid., June 27, 1847, p. 2.

8. Ibid., Sept. 5, 1847, p. 4.

9. Ibid., p. 5.

10. Halttunen, *Confidence Men,* pp. 93–108.

11. Mrs. Frances Trollope, *Domestic Manners of the Americans,* Donald Smalley, ed. (New York: Knopf, 1949), p. 52.

12. Whitcher Letters, July 15, 1847, p. 2.

13. Sarah Josepha Hale, *Mrs. Hale's Receipts for the Million* (Philadephia: Peterson, 1857).

14. Whitcher Letters, Nov. 8, 1847, p. 1.

15. Ibid., p. 3.

16. The series "Letters from Timberville" was reprinted in F. M. Whitcher, *Widow Spriggins.* All page references will be cited in the text.

17. Mrs. Trollope made a similar complaint in her 1832 *Domestic Manners of the Americans,* pronouncing the lack of good domestic servants "the greatest difficulty in organizing a family establishment," p. 52. According to Donald Smalley, a modern editor of Mrs. Trollope's work, her fellow countrywoman, Harriet Martineau, countered Mrs. Trollope in *Society in America* by writing that those who complained about American domestics "were many who, from fault of either judgment or temper, deserved whatever difficulty they met with. This is remarkably the case with English ladies settled in America." *Domestic Manners,* pp. 53–55.

18. Whitcher Letters, Oct. 22, 1847, p. 2.

19. Ibid., Nov. 8, 1847, p. 1.

20. Ibid., Nov. 8, 1847, p. 2.

21. Ibid., Nov. 21, 1847, p. 2.

22. Ibid., p. 2.

23. Ibid., Nov. 29, 1847, p. 5.

24. Ibid., June 27, 1847, p. 4.

25. Thomas F. O'Donnell makes these useful observations, although he mistakenly claims that with a population of 3,600, Elmira was larger than Whitesboro. "Return of the Widow Bedott," p. 28.

26. George A. Mellor, "The Arnots of Elmira," *Chemung Historical Journal* 9, no. 4 (June, 1964): 1261f.

27. Ashburn Towner, *Our County and Its People: A History of the Valley and County of Chemung from the Closing Years of the Eighteenth Century* (Syracuse: D. Mason and Co., 1892), p. 114.

28. Cross, *Burned-Over District,* p. 76.

29. Whitcher Letters, June 10, 1847, p. 2.

30. Trollope, *Domestic Manners,* p. 226.

31. Whitcher Letters, Dec. 19, 1847, pp. 6–7.

32. Towner, *Our County,* p. 96.

33. One person who payed a call on Miriam Whitcher was Olivia L. Langdon, the future mother-in-law of Samuel Clemens. She was not a member of the Episcopal church; Miriam described her as being an abolitionist. Whitcher Letters, Jan. 19, 1848, p. 6.

34. Halttunen locates the Victorian parlor as "the stage upon which the genteel performance was enacted," *Confidence Men,* p. 102. If it denoted a family's arrival

into the middle class, into genteel society, how much more so *two* parlors would signal a family's new wealth and social status.

35. Ibid. p. 193.

36. Whitcher Letters, June 27, 1847, pp. 1–2.

37. Ibid., pp. 5–6.

38. Ibid., Apr. 11, 1847, p. 1.

39. Ibid., Jan. 19, 1848, p. 5.

40. Ibid., Feb. 3, 1848, pp. 4–5.

41. Ibid., Dec. 19, 1847, p. 5.

42. Ibid., Jan. 2, 1848, p. 1.

43. Ibid., p. 2.

44. Ibid. According to Towner, both "Aunty" and "Tommy" Hill were Irish immigrants; Tommy Hill ran the local stable.

45. Ibid., Jan. 19, 1848, p. 3.

46. Ibid., Dec. 19, 1847, p. 5.

47. Ibid., Jan. 19, 1848, p. 6.

48. Ibid., Feb. 25, 1848, p. 4.

49. Towner, *Our County,* p. 150.

50. Whitcher Letters, July 25, 1847, pp. 1–2.

51. Ibid., p. 4.

52. Ibid., Feb.3, 1848, p. 2.

53. Ibid., Nov. 8, 1847, p. 4.

54. Ibid., Nov. 29, 1847, p. 2.

55. Ibid., pp 3–4.

56. Ibid., p. 4.

57. Ibid.

58. Ibid., Aug. 30, 1847, pp. 2–3.

59. Ibid., Jan. 2, 1848, p. 4.

60. Blistering was a common medical practice of the day. A caustic such as a mustard pack was applied to the skin as a counterirritant. It was thought that the blister on the surface would draw out the inflammation from within.

61. Whitcher Letters, July 25, 1847, p. 1.

62. Ibid., Oct. 22, 1847, p. 1.

63. Ibid., Aug. 16, 1847, p. 1.

64. Ibid., Jan. 2, 1848, pp. 1–2.

65. Ibid., Feb. 25, 1848, p. 1–2.

66. Ibid., Jan. 2, 1848, p. 5.

67. Ibid., Jan. 19, 1848, p. 1.

68. According to Ruth F. Finney, a part of Godey's "Americanization" plan included paying his authors: " 'The publisher of this work, with a view to securing *original contributions* for its columns, will give for such articles as he may approve and publish, the highest rate of remuneration offered by any periodical in this country.' " Finney goes on to say that Godey "was not offering much, since in 1836 [when the offer was made] none of the other periodicals in the country were in the habit of paying anything! But Mr. Godey was in earnest. Also he was honest. He promised to

pay liberally, and liberally he paid thereafter to the end." *The Lady of Godey's: Sarah Josepha Hale* (Philadelphia: Lippincott, 1931), p. 45.

5. *Aunt Maguire's Sewing Society*

1. Cornelia Holroyd Richards, *Cousin Alice: A Memoir of Alice B. Haven* (New York: Appleton, 1865), p. 23.

2. Ibid., p. 53.

3. Ibid., p. 57. Alice Neal also published under the name "Clara Cushman" in the *Saturday Gazette,* and later as "Aunt Alice" when she published juvenile fiction.

4. Quoted in Richards, *Memoir,* p. 63.

5. Whitcher Letters, [Mar. 30, 1848,] p. 1.

6. Unlike her friend, whose career she promoted even more vigorously than her husband had, Alice Neal eventually earned between $12,000 and $15,000 annually for her literary publications. Richards, *Memoir,* p. 156.

7. Whitcher Letters, Mar. 7, 1848, p. 1.

8. The inspiration for the character of Mrs. Grimes apparently came in part from a story Miriam's mother told about her former neighbors in Whitesboro, and in part from neighbors of the Whitchers in Elmira. Whitcher Letters, June 19, 1848, p. 7.

9. Followers of William Miller, a New York farmer and religious leader.

10. See, for example, Constance Rourke's "Gamecock of the Wilderness," in *American Humor: A Study of the National Character* (New York: Harcourt Brace Jovanovich, 1959), pp. 33–76.

11. Ibid., p. 3.

12. Simon Suggs used the same technique to work over a camp meeting in Alabama. He confessed he came to the meeting to steal from the crowd, got religion instead, then used his conversion to bilk the "faithful" by collecting money ostensibly to start a new church. "Simon Suggs Attends a Camp-Meeting," in Blair, *Native American Humor,* pp. 316–25.

13. Trollope, *Domestic Manners,* p. 75.

14. Douglas, *The Feminization of American Culture,* p. 97.

15. Whitcher Letters, Mar. 7, 1848, p. 3. The Reverend Mr. Long of Whitesboro also must be considered as an inspiration for this characterization, with his long-winded, tedious sermons, and his evident self-righteousness. At one point Long was so upset over the "defection" of one of the women from his congregation to the Episcopal sewing society that he literally cried over her. Apr. 20, 1847, p. 4.

16. Ibid., Nov. 29, 1847, p. 5.

17. Ibid., Dec. 19, 1847, p. 3.

18. In "Passages," p. 110, Kate Berry claimed that the article had been written before the party took place, a fact that the Whitcher letters corroborate.

19. O'Donnell "Return of the Widow Bedott," p. 29.

20. Whitcher Letters, Mar. 30, 1848, p. 2.

21. Ibid., Apr. 10, 1848, p. 1. Milk fever was the name given to a feverishness that often occurred shortly after childbirth and was associated with the onset of lactation.

22. William's fondness for fresh air had support among a number of physicians of the day. Dr. Potter's *Consumptive's Guide to Health: or, the Invalid's Five Questions, and the Doctor's Five Answers* repeatedly extols the virtue of fresh air as both a prevention and cure for consumption. (New York: Redfield, 1852), pp. 39–41.

23. Whitcher Letters, June 8, 1848, p. 1.

24. Ibid., Nov. 8, 1847, p. 5.

25. For some unknown reason, the publication of this sketch was delayed. Miriam Whitcher submitted the article to Godey in June 1848, but it did not appear in the *Lady's Book* until the November issue. An editor's note in the March issue urged those who submitted articles or poems to the magazine not to "despair" about acceptance or rejection until six months had passed (vol. 36, p. 129). Miriam's work, however, usually received the most prompt attention from Godey himself, and she ordinarily enjoyed a swift turn-around time between submission and publication.

26. Sernett, *Abolition's Axe,* passim.

27. Whitcher Letters, July 27, 1848, p. 1.

28. Ibid., p. 3.

29. Ibid., Nov. 12, 1848, p. 4.

30. Ibid., Oct. 12, 1848, p. 1.

31. Ibid., Oct. 29, 1848, p. 3.

32. Ibid., Nov. 12, 1848, p. 4.

33. Ibid., p. 5.

34. Ibid., p. 1.

35. Ibid., Mar. 7, 1848, p.1.

36. Ibid., Dec. 10, 1848, p. 1.

37. Ibid., pp. 1–2.

38. Ibid., p. 2.

39. Ibid., p. 3.

40. Ibid., Oct. 12, 1848, p. 3.

41. Ibid., Dec. 28, 1848, pp. 1–2.

42. Ibid.

43. Ibid., p. 3.

44. Ibid., Mar. 4, 1849, pp. 1–2.

45. Ibid., Dec. 28, 1848, p. 4.

46. Ibid., p. 3.

47. Blandina D. Miller, "Troubles of the Fiction Writer," Utica *Observer,* Mar. 17, 1906, p. 7.

48. Whitcher Letters, Dec. 28, 1848, p. 6.

49. Ibid., Jan. 1, 1849, p. 1.

50. Mrs. George Archibald Palmer, Elmira *Telegram,* Nov. 4, 1923.

51. Halttunen, *Confidence Men,* p. 117.

52. The former detail is reported in the *Lady's Book* of March 1849, p. 226, and the latter in Mott's *History of American Magazines,* p. 581.

53. Whitcher Letters, Jan. 1, 1849, pp. 1–2.

54. Ibid., Feb. 12, 1849, pp. 1–2.

55. Elmira *Gazette,* Feb. 22, 1849, p. 3.

56. Whitcher Letters, Feb. 12, 1849, p. 1.

57. Ibid.

58. Ibid., pp. 3–5.

59. Ibid., Mar. 4, 1849, p. 2.

60. Ibid., Feb. 12, 1849, pp. 2–3.

61. Ibid., Mar. 14, 1849, p. 2.

6. Return to Whitesboro

1. Whitcher Letters, Apr. 22, 1848, p. 3.

2. Ibid., Apr. 29, 1849, p. 3.

3. Ibid., May 22, 1849, pp. 1–2.

4. Ibid., pp. 2–3.

5. Ibid., Apr. 22, 1849, p. 3.

6. Ibid., May 25, 1849, pp. 1–2.

7. Ibid., May 22, 1849, p. 3.

8. Ibid., May 25, 1849, pp. 1–2.

9. Ibid., Apr. 22, 1849, p. 1.

10. Ibid., Apr. 29, 1849, p. 1.

11. Mrs. L. Thornton, *A Century of Progress: The History of Trinity Church, Elmira, New York* (Elmira: n.p., 1933), p. 13.

12. Whitcher Letters, May 16, 1849, p. 1.

13. Ibid., Dec. 15, 1850, p. 2.

14. This quotation is taken directly from the original *Lady's Book* text rather than *The Widow Bedott Papers* because the story as it appears in the latter is partially abridged. The identity of the abridger is unknown. References especially to the "Captain" figure, the tightfisted storekeeper, are mostly omitted in the book version, as are several long passages about gentility and the one about the revival meeting. It is interesting to hypothesize that references to Capp'n Smalley were omitted because his real-life counterpart was one of the men said to have brought a lawsuit against William, but no ready explanation suggests itself for the other textual deletions. Also, the longer version of the story was originally published in the *Lady's Book* as a single article, not a two-part story as it appears in the book version. All further references to passages found only in *Godey's* will be identified in the text by the initials LB.

15. Finney, *The Lady of Godey's,* pp. 151–52.

16. Halttunen, *Confidence Men,* p. 161.

17. According to Finney in *The Lady of Godey's,* Louis Godey was determined to "Americanize" the literature that appeared in the *Lady's Book,* and his editor, Sarah Hale, was determined to Americanize women's fashions that appeared there as well (pp. 43–44; 152–53).

18. Whitcher Letters, Jan. 24, 1849, p. 3.

19. Quoted in Finney, *The Lady of Godey's*, pp. 165–66; she goes on to observe: "If the subjects' own images frightened them, it is pardonable that their children's children since have wondered why so many of these portraits of their ancestors depict individuals of such fierce and forbidding mien. But with their faces being 'limned in an operating-room' much is explained" (p. 166).

20. All references to this story are to the Appendix at the end of this text (p. 2).

21. See Ryan, *Cradle*, p. 117f.

22. Ibid., p. 121.

23. Ibid.

24. This sketch, published Mar. 16, 1850, is incorrectly placed before "The Rev. Mrs. Sniffles At Home" and "The Rev. Mrs. Sniffles Expresses her Sentiments in Regard to the Parsonage" in the *Widow Bedott Papers*.

25. "Kate Kenype" might well have been the ironic inspiration for Marietta Holley's comic feminist heroine, Josiah Allen's Wife, also known as Samantha Allen. Unmistakably, Holley knew Whitcher's work and was influenced by it, and the name "Samanthy" linked with the subject of "Woman's Rights" suggests a possible prototype for Holley's popular heroine.

26. Whitcher Letters, July 14, 1850, pp. 1–2.

27. Ibid., Aug. 6, 1850, p. 2.

28. Ibid., p. 4.

29. Ibid., Dec. 29, 1850, p. 2.

30. Ibid., Feb. 2, 1851, p. 1.

31. Ibid., May 20, 1850, p. 2.

32. Ibid., Aug. 6, 1850, p. 3.

33. Miriam sent a recipe home from the Springs for flaxseed lemonade that was supposedly good for coughs; she wanted her sister to make some for their mother. As with many of Miriam's own treatments, this one sound thoroughly unpleasant: steep flaxseed in water and let it cool to reduce "the rankness"; then mix it with gum-arabic until the mixture becomes "ropy," then lace it with sugar and lemon to make it palatable, and drink it by the wineglass-full several times a day. Whitcher Letters, May 20, 1850, p. 4.

34. Ibid., Oct. 8, 1850, p. 2.

35. Ibid., Dec. 15, 1850, p. 1–2.

36. Ibid., Dec. 29, 1850, p. 2.

37. Ibid., p. 2.

38. Ibid., July 14, 1850, p. 4.

39. Ibid., Feb. 11, 1851, pp. 2–3.

40. Berry, "Passages," p. 111.

41. According to *Dr. Potter's Consumptive's Guide to Health*, on the average consumption ran its course in approximately eighteen months.

42. Whitcher Letters, July 14, 1850, p. 2.

43. Ibid.

44. Ibid., Oct. 8, 1850, p. 1.

45. For example, Kate Berry had poems or brief articles appearing in the following volumes of the *Lady's Book:* June 1850, Aug. 1850, Sept. 1851, and Dec. 1851.

46. Berry, "Passages." The article was published in two parts; in the second part Kate describes the final months of Miriam's life. *Godey's Lady's Book* 48 (Aug. 1853): 109–115.

47. Whitcher Letters, Feb. 6, 1851, p. 2.

48. Berry, "Passages," p. 111.

49. Ibid., p. 112.

50. Ibid.

51. Ibid., p. 113.

52. Ibid.

53. Ibid., p. 114.

54. Ibid.

Epilogue

1. On the title page of a book William wrote in 1875, he is identified as "Joint author, with his late wife, of the 'Widow Bedott Papers.' " *The Story of a Convert* (New York: O'Shea, 1875). Nowhere in the correspondence or in Kate Berry's memoir is there any reference to William being either an editor, per se, or author of the papers, although as we have seen, he did occasionally try to censor Miriam's submissions to Godey. The official editor of *The Widow Bedott Papers* is Alice Neal, who also wrote the introduction.

2. Blair, *Native American Humor*, p. 49; James D. Hart, *The Popular Book: A History of America's Literary Taste* (Berkeley: Univ. of California Press, 1961), pp. 820–21.

3. F. M. Whitcher, *Widow Spriggins.*

4. The New York Census of 1855 indicates that Martha Whitcher had at that time been in Oneida County only two years; she probably was brought there by William as his new bride. Hence, there is no possibility that she knew Miriam personally, and certainly none that they were friends; Martha would have been no more than twenty years old when Miriam died.

5. F. M. Whitcher, *Widow Spriggins*, p. 24.

6. John M. Harrison, *The Man Who Made Nasby: David Ross Locke* (Chapel Hill: Univ. of North Carolina Press, 1969).

7. George C. Odell, *Annals of the New York Stage*, vol. II (New York: Columbia Univ. Press, 1939), p. 176.

8. Burgess followed the same pattern with Marietta Holley's play "Betsey Bobbet: A Drama," in which he also played the female lead; he made Holley's play a commercial success, then rewrote it under his own name, greatly exaggerating the characteristics of the lead character, and ceasing to pay the author royalties.

9. Odell, *Annals*, vol. 11, p. 170.

10. Ibid., p. 42. See also Morris, "Wolves in Sheep's Clothing," pp. 226–76.

11. Emphasis added. Sanborn, *The Wit of Women*, p. 68.

12. William Whitcher, *Convert.*

13. New York Census of 1855.

14. Alice Miriam Wood, "Sketch of the Life of Frances Miriam Berry Whitcher, Author of 'Widow Bedott Papers.' " *Michigan Pioneer and Historical Society* 35 (1907): 420.

15. Elizabeth Bancroft Schlesinger, "Sara Payson Willis Parton," in *Notable American Women,* ed. Edward T. James, vol. 3 (Cambridge, Mass.: Belknap, 1971), p. 24.

16. The best and most complete work on Marietta Holley is Kate Winter's *Marietta Holley: Life with "Josiah Allen's Wife"* (Syracuse: Syracuse Univ. Press, 1984).

Works Cited

Berry, Kate. "Passages in the Life of the Author of Aunt Maguire's Letters, Bedott Papers, Etc." *Godey's Lady's Book* 47 (July 1853): 49–55; (Aug. 1853): 109–15.

Blair, Walter. *Horse Sense in American Humor, from Benjamin Franklin to Ogden Nash.* New York: Russell and Russell, 1962.

———*Native American Humor.* San Francisco: Chandler, 1960.

Blair, Walter, and Raven I. McDavid, Jr. eds. *The Mirth of a Nation: America's Great Dialect Humor.* Minneapolis: Univ. of Minnesota Press, 1983.

Bruère, Martha Bensley, and Mary Ritter Beard, eds. *Laughing Their Way: Women's Humor in America.* New York: Macmillan, 1934.

Buhle, Mari Jo, and Paul Buhle, eds. *The Concise History of Woman Suffrage: Selections from the Classic Work of Stanton, Anthony, Gage, and Harper.* Urbana: Univ. of Illinois Press, 1978.

Clark, William B., and W. Craig Turner, eds. *Critical Essays in American Humor.* Boston: G. K. Hall, 1984.

Cott, Nancy F. *The Bonds of Womanhood: "Woman's Sphere" in New England, 1790–1835.* New Haven: Yale Univ. Press, 1977.

Cross, Whitney R. *The Burned-Over District: The Social and Intellectual History of Enthusiastic Religion in Western New York, 1800–1850.* Ithaca: Cornell Univ. Press, 1950.

Curry, Jane. "Women as Subjects and Writers of Nineteenth Century American Humor." Ph.D. diss., Univ. of Michigan, 1975.

———ed. *Samantha Rastles the Woman Question.* Urbana: Univ. of Illinois Press, 1983.

Dictionary of American Biography. Vol. 1. New York: Scribners, 1928.

Dictionary of Literary Biography. Vol. 11, pt. 2. Detroit: Gale, 1982.

Douglas, Ann. *The Feminization of American Culture.* New York: Knopf, 1977.

Dublin, Thomas, ed. *Farm to Factory: Women's Letters, 1830–1860*. New York: Columbia Univ. Press, 1981.

Dubos, Rene, and Jean Dubos. *The White Plague: Tuberculosis, Man and Society*. Boston: Little, Brown, 1952.

Edmonds, Walter D. "The Erie Canal." In *40' x 28' x 4': The Erie Canal—150 Years*, edited by Lionel D. Wyld, pp. 5–12. Rome: Oneida County Erie Canal Commemoration Commission, 1967.

Elmira *Gazette*. Feb. 22, 1849, 3.

Elmira *Sunday Telegram*. Nov. 4, 1923; Nov. 27, 1955.

Fetterley, Judith, ed. *Provisions: A Reader from Nineteenth-Century American Women*. Bloomington: Indiana Univ. Press, 1985.

Finney, Charles G. *Memoirs of Rev. Charles G. Finney*. New York: Fleming H. Revell, 1876.

Finney, Ruth E. *The Lady of Godey's: Sarah Josepha Hale*. Philadelphia: Lippincott, 1931.

"First Annual Report of the Female Moral Reform Society of the City of New York." Presented May 1835. N.Y.: W. Newell, 1835. (Papers in the Oneida Historical Society, Utica, N.Y.)

Godey, Louis. *Godey's Lady's Book* 36 (May 1848): 311.

Habegger, Alfred. "Nineteenth-Century Humor: Easygoing Males, Anxious Ladies, and Penelope Lapham." *PMLA* 91 (Oct. 1976): 884–99.

Hale, Sarah Josepha. *Mrs. Hale's Receipts for the Million*. Philadelphia: Peterson, 1857.

Halttunen, Karen. *Confidence Men and Painted Women: A Study of Middle-Class Culture in America, 1830–1870*. New Haven: Yale Univ. Press, 1982.

Harris, Barbara J. *Beyond Her Sphere: Women and the Professions in American History*. Westport: Greenwood Press, 1978.

Harrison, John M. *The Man Who Made Nasby: David Ross Locke*. Chapel Hill: Univ. of North Carolina Press, 1969.

Hart, James D. *The Popular Book: A History of America's Literary Taste*. Berkeley: Univ. of California Press, 1961.

The History of Oneida County: Commemorating the Bicentennial of Our National Independence. Utica: Oneida County, 1977.

Hulbert, Archer Butler. *The Great American Canals: Vol. II, The Erie Canal*. Vol. 14 of *Historic Highways of America*. Cleveland: Arthur H. Clark, 1904.

Johnson, Paul E. *A Shopkeeper's Millenium: Society and Revivals in Rochester, New York, 1815–1837*. New York: Hill and Wang, 1978.

Jones, Pomroy. *Annals and Recollections of Oneida County*. Rome, N.Y.: [Author], 1851.

Kelly, Virginia B. "Utica and the Impact of the Canal." In *40' x 28' x 4': The Erie Canal—150 Years Later,* edited by Lionel D. Wyld, pp. 33–35. Rome, N.Y.: Oneida County Erie Canal Commemoration Commission, 1967.

Lennox, Charlotte. *The Female Quixote: The Adventures of Arabella.* Boston: Pandora, 1986.

Little, Judy. *Comedy and the Woman Writer: Woolf, Spark, and Feminism.* Lincoln: Univ. of Nebraska Press, 1983.

Manzelmann, Richard L. "Revival and Reform." In *The History of Oneida County.* Oneida Co.: N.p., 1977, 53–58.

Matthews, Glenna. *"Just a Housewife": The Rise and Fall of Domesticity in America.* New York: Oxford Univ. Press, 1987.

Mellor, George A. "The Arnots of Elmira." *Chemung Historical Journal* 9, no. 4 (June 1964): 1261–67.

Miller, Blandina D. "Troubles of the Fiction Writer." Utica *Observer,* Mar. 17, 1906, p. 7.

Morris, Linda A. "Frances Miriam Whitcher: Social Satire in the Age of Gentility." In *Last Laughs: Perspectives on Women and Comedy,* edited by Regina Barreca, pp. 99–116. New York: Gordon and Breach, 1988.

———. "Wolves in Sheep's Clothing: Four Male Humorists Who Masqueraded as Women." In *Women Vernacular Humorists in Nineteenth-Century America: Ann Stephens, Frances Whitcher, and Marietta Holley,* edited by Linda A. Morris, pp. 226–76. New York: Garland, 1988.

———, ed. *Women Vernacular Humorists in Nineteenth-Century America: Ann Stephens, Frances Whitcher, and Marietta Holley.* New York: Garland, 1988.

Morrison, Howard A. "The Finney Takeover of the Second Great Awakening During the Oneida Revivals of 1825–1827." *New York History* LVIX, no. 1 (Jan. 1978): 27–53.

Mott, Frank Luther. *The History of American Magazines.* Vol. 1. Cambridge, Mass.: Harvard Univ. Press, 1939.

Neal, Joseph. Neal's *Saturday Gazette* 3, no. 97 (Aug. 15, 1846): 2.

———. Neal's *Saturday Gazette* 3, no. 110 (Nov. 14. 1846): 2.

New York Census, 1850, 1855.

Odell, George C. *Annals of the New York Stage.* Vol 11. New York: Columbia Univ. Press, 1939.

O'Donnell, Thomas F. "The Return of the Widow Bedott: Mrs. F. M. Whitcher of Whitesboro and Elmira." *New York History* 55 (1974): 5–34.

Palmer, Mrs. George Archibald. Elmira *Telegram.* Nov. 4, 1923.

Potter, J. Hamilton. *The Consumptive's Guide to Health; or, The Invalid's Five Questions, and the Doctor's Five Answers.* New York: Redfield, 1852.

"Record of the Organization of St. John's Parish, Whitesboro, from Papers and from the Diocesan Report." St. John's Episcopal Church, Whitesboro, N.Y.

"Record of the Phrenological and Magnetic Society." Paper in the Oneida County Historical Society, Utica, N.Y., 1845.

Richards, Cornelia Holroyd. *Cousin Alice: A Memoir of Alice B. Haven. [Emily Bradley Neal Haven, 1827–1863]* New York: Appleton, 1865.

Rohman, D. Gordon. *Here's Whitesboro: An Informal History.* New York: Stratford House, 1949.

Rourke, Constance. *American Humor: A Study of the National Character.* New York: Harcourt Brace Jovanovich, 1959.

Ryan, Mary P. *Cradle of the Middle Class: The Family in Oneida County, New York, 1790–1865.* Cambridge: Cambridge Univ. Press, 1981.

———. *Womanhood in America: From Colonial Times to the Present.* 2d ed., New York: Watts, 1979.

Sanborn, Kate. *The Wit of Women.* New York: Funk and Wagnalls, 1886.

Schlesinger, Elizabeth Bancroft. "Sara Payson Willis Parton." In *Notable American Women.* Vol. 3, edited by Edward T. James. Cambridge: Belknap, 1971.

Sernett, Milton C. *Abolition's Axe: Beriah Green, Oneida Institute, and the Black Freedom Struggle.* Syracuse: Syracuse Univ. Press, 1986.

Sheppard, Alice. "From Kate Sanborn to Feminist Psychology: The Social Context of Women's Humor, 1885–1985." *Psychology of Women Quarterly* 10 (1986): 155–70.

Sklar, Kathryn Kish. *Catharine Beecher: A Study in American Domesticity.* New Haven: Yale Univ. Press, 1973.

Smith, Henry Nash. *Mark Twain: The Development of a Writer.* Cambridge, Mass.: Harvard Univ. Press, 1961.

Smith-Rosenberg, Carroll. *Disorderly Conduct: Visions of Gender in Victorian America.* New York: Oxford Univ. Press, 1985.

Spacks, Patricia M. *Gossip.* Chicago: Univ. of Chicago Press, 1986.

Spenser, Jane. *The Rise of the Woman Novelist: From Aphra Behn to Jane Austen.* Oxford: Blackwell, 1986.

Stone, Col. William Leete. "Col. Stone's Tour in 1829, from New York to Niagara. Journal of a Tour, in Part by the Erie Canal, in the Year 1829." In *The Holland Land Company.* Vol. 14. Buffalo: Buffalo Historical Society, 1910.

Tandy, Jennette. *Crackerbox Philosophers in American Humor and Satire.* Port Washington, N.Y.: Kennikat, 1964.

Thornton, Mrs. L. *A Century of Progress: The History of Trinity Church, Elmira, New York.* Elmira: N.p. 1933.

Toth, Emily. "A Laughter of Their Own: Women's Humor in the United States." In *Critical Essays in American Humor,* edited by William B. Clark and W. Craig Turner, pp. 199–215. Boston: G. K. Hall, 1984.

Towner, Ashburn. *Our County and Its People: A History of the Valley and County of Chemung from the Closing Years of the Eighteenth Century.* Syracuse, N.Y.: D. Mason and Co., 1892.

Tracy, Charles. "Historical Address" [Whitestown Centennial]. *Transactions of the Oneida Historical Society, at Utica, 1881–1884,* pp. 11–24. Utica: Oneida County Historical Society, 1881.

Trollope, Mrs. Frances. *Domestic Manners of the Americans.* Edited by Donald Smalley. New York: Knopf, 1949.

Utica *Observer,* Mar. 17, 1906, p. 7.

Wager, Daniel E. *Our County and Its People: A Descriptive Work on Oneida County, New York.* Boston: Boston Historical Society, 1896.

———. "Whitesboro's Golden Age." *Transactions of the Oneida County Historical Society of Utica, 1881–1884,* pp. 65–144. Utica: Oneida County Historical Society, 1885.

Walker, Nancy. *The Tradition of Women's Humor in America.* Huntington Beach: American Studies, 1984.

———. *A Very Serious Thing: Women's Humor and American Culture.* Minneapolis: Univ. of Minnesota Press, 1988.

———. "Wit, Sentimentality, and the Image of Women in the Nineteenth Century." *American Studies* 22.2 (1981): 5–22.

Walker, Nancy, and Zita Dresner, eds. *Redressing the Balance: American Women's Literary Humor from Colonial Times to the 1980s.* Jackson, Miss.: Univ. of Mississippi Press, 1988.

Welter, Barbara. "The Cult of True Womanhood: 1820–1860." *American Quarterly* 18 (1966): 151–74.

Whitcher, Benjamin William. *The Story of a Convert, as Told to His Former Parishioners after He Became a Catholic.* New York: O'Shea, 1875.

Whitcher, F. M. Whitcher Letters. Manuscript Collection, New-York Historical Society, New York City.

———. *The Widow Bedott Papers.* New York: D. Mason and Co., 1880.

———. *Widow Spriggins, Mary Elmer, and Other Sketches.* Edited by Mrs. M. L. Ward Whitcher. New York: Carleton, 1867.

Whitcher, M[artha] L. "Berry's House in the Whitestown Country." Manuscript in Dunham Public Library, Whitesboro, N.Y.

"Whitestown Female Charitable Society." Pamphlet, Oneida County Historical Society, Utica, N.Y., 1806.

Winter, Kate H. *Marietta Holley: Life with "Josiah Allen's Wife."* Syracuse: Syracuse Univ. Press, 1984.

Wisbey, Herbert A., Jr. "The Widow Bedott." *New York State Tradition* 26 (Fall 1972): 19.

Wood, Alice Miriam. "Sketch of the Life of Frances Miriam Berry Whitcher, Author of 'Widow Bedott Papers.' " *Michigan Pioneer and Historical Society* 35 (1907): 412–29.

Wyld, Lionel D., ed. *40' x 28' x 4': The Erie Canal—150 Years.* Rome, N.Y.: Oneida County Erie Canal Commemoration Commission, 1967.

Index

Abolition, 2, 36–37, 97
Advice books, 13, 89–90
"Age of the Common Man," 7
Allen, Samantha (Josiah Allen's Wife)
    (fictional character), 14, 212,
    238n. 25
Amanda (fictional character), 39, 40,
    42
Arabella (fictional character), 39–40
Arnot, John, Sr. (Elmira), 95–96, 154,
    180
Arnot, Mrs. John, Sr. (Elmira), 154,
    156, 180. *See also* Savage, Mrs.
    Samson
Arr, E. H. *See* Rollins, Ellen
Arthur, Timothy Shay, 55, 184
Aunt Maguire (fictional character). *See*
    Maguire, Aunt
"Aunt Maguire's Account of the
    Mission to Muffletegawny," 197–
    98
"Aunt Maguire's Visit to Slabtown,"
    171–80

Baily, Polly (fictional character), 93
Barbour, Elizabeth Berry, 23–24, 29,
    52, 143
Barbour, O. L., 23–24, 158
Beard, Mary: *Laughing Their Way,* 9
Bedott, Deacon (fictional character),
    81

Bedott, Kier (fictional character), 78
Bedott, Melissa (fictional character),
    76, 77, 78, 209
Bedott, Priscilla (fictional character), 1,
    3–4, 5, 6, 14, 16, 38, 51, 53–54,
    82; characteristics of, 56, 57–60,
    61–63, 80; courtship of, 46, 74–
    78; in Scrabble Hill, 115, 116–17,
    121–22, 123–24; and Shadrack
    Sniffles, 124–26, 128. *See also*
    Sniffles, Priscilla Bedott
Bedott, Widow. *See* Bedott, Priscilla
Beecher, Lyman, 33
Berry, Cornelia, 23, 36–37, 163, 211
Berry, Elizabeth. *See* Barbour, Eliza-
    beth Berry
Berry, Elizabeth Wells, 20–21, 163,
    196, 211
Berry, Emily, 24
Berry, Eugenia Dorland, 23, 143
Berry, Jane, 22; exhumation of, 164–65
Berry, John, 24, 163–64, 166, 202,
    211
Berry, Katherine (Kate), 24, 28, 29,
    37, 50, 163, 164–65, 211; as
    writer, 201–2
Berry, Lewis, 19–20, 36, 50, 96, 163,
    165
Berry, Lewis T., 23, 24, 50, 164–65
Berry, Mary, 23, 163, 202, 211
Berry, Miriam. *See* Whitcher, Frances
    Miriam Berry

247

Women's Humor in the Age of Gentility
was composed in 10^1/$_2$ on 13 Galliard on a Linotype Linotronic 300
by Partners Composition
with display type in Polonaise Bold by Dix Type, Inc.;
printed by sheet-fed offset 50-pound, acid-free Natural Hi Bulk
and Smyth-sewn and bound over binder's boards in ICG Arrestox B
with dust jackets printed in 2 colors
by Braun-Brumfield, Inc.;
and published by
Syracuse University Press
Syracuse, New York 13244-5160